READER COMMENTS /

Moser
Moser, Nancy
The quest : a novel

$13.86
ocn957557546

"As the facilitator for a Christian B[...]
for selections that our members will [...]
We hit the jackpot with N [...]
couldn't wait until the sec [...]
well worth the wait! The [...]
more depth and substanc [...]
characters who are just as [...]
very clear, but not "preac[...]
particular note. Our club [...]
for #3!" FOLSOM, PENNSYI

"Your books are right up there with Frank Peretti's *Piercing the Darkness, This Present Darkness,* and *The Oath.*" OCALA, FLORIDA

"Moser and Peretti are my favorite fiction authors. What a gift this author has for weaving intricate tales which are jammed pack with biblical truths." EMAIL FROM READER

"My husband has expressed an interest in reading the series too, which is a BIG deal... he's very picky." NEW ZEALAND

"I was going to take the book on vacation but I started reading it the day before and was up until 1:30 finishing it." OLATHE, KANSAS

"I've never read so inspirational and so touching as *The Invitation* and *The Quest*...I pray that your books will touch the hearts of others who are in search of a better life." HOLLYWOOD, FLORIDA

"I wish that this book would be developed into a movie." MULTNOMAHBOOKS.COM

"I just finished *The Quest,* and find I am thoroughly energized in the spirit of Our Lord. I could barely wait to get through the reading of it, but found I was disappointed to let my 'friends' go. I was so sad to finish the last pages..." NEENAH, WISCONSIN

"One thing to remember: just because it's a God book, doesn't mean it isn't good." FROM A 12-YEAR-OLD'S BOOK REPORT ON *THE QUEST* GIVEN TO HER PUBLIC SCHOOL CLASS IN OLATHE, KANSAS

"I don't want *The Quest* to end any more than I wanted to finish *The Invitation*. I will long for each new book you write...I shed more tears in your book than any other. And I'm not an easy crier. "PEACHTREE CITY, GEORGIA

"I have never read books like these that I just couldn't put down. I read *The Invitation* and *The Quest* in six evenings. They are wonderful stories with everyday type people who anyone can relate to. I began to feel as if I knew these characters as friends and hated coming to the end." SUMMERVILLE, SOUTH CAROLINA

"You can relate to the characters, and experience a renewing of the Spirit of God through the constant reminders of Hope throughout the book." ROCKMART, GEORGIA

"This book has opened my eyes in many ways, firstly it helped me understand the Bible verses the way they should be, to overcome the devil and kick his butt!! Praise God for giving us writers like Nancy! She brings out the reality of people with so much ease, not to mention the humour, there were times I actually laughed out a bit too loud and then had to look around to see if someone saw me laugh!! God Bless u Nancy... STILLWATER, OKLAHOMA

"Nancy Moser effectively brings home the reality of evil in the world. The scenes in which the villain, Beau Tenebri, begins to show his true colors are chilling. In my opinion, this book deserves a place right up there on the shelf with the best of Frank Peretti's spiritual warfare classics." ROCKFORD, ILLINOIS

"Read it! Now! The characters are real, the dialogue witty, and the tension between good and evil gripping (if you like Peretti's books, you'll love this one). I look forward to a third book in the Mustard Seed series. May God use this book to reach millions!" MISSOURI

"We all assume we have some purpose in life—some quest. That's what keeps us going. But once we are on that quest, it is inevitable that we face opposition and our own doubt as good and evil vie for control in our lives. *The Quest* takes us along on the life-journey of five characters who try to do the right thing, make mistakes, try again, and in the end, come through triumphantly. It has fantastic characterization, a compelling storyline, and a message that just might change your life. It did mine. Read it!" MISSOURI

The Quest

a novel

Book Two
of the
Mustard Seed Series

Nancy Moser

Overland Park, Kansas

The Quest

ISBN-10: 0986195251
ISBN-13: 978-0-9861952-5-9

Published by:
Mustard Seed Press
PO Box 23002
Overland Park, KS 66283

Copyright © 2016 by Nancy Moser. All rights reserved.

This book, or parts thereof, may not be reproduced, stored in a retrieval system, or transmitted in any form or by any means, electronic, mechanical, photocopying, recording, or otherwise, without the written permission of the publisher.

This story is a work of fiction. Any resemblances to actual people, places, or events are purely coincidental.

All Scripture quotations are taken from The Holy Bible, New International Version.

Front cover design by Mustard Seed Press

Printed and bound in the United States of America
10 9 8 7 6 5 4 3

THE BOOKS of Nancy Moser

CONTEMPORARY BOOKS

- *The Invitation* (Book 1 of Mustard Seed Series)
- *The Quest* (Book 2 of Mustard Seed Series)
- *The Temptation* (Book 3 of Mustard Seed Series)
- *The Seat Beside Me* (Book 1 of Steadfast Series)
- *A Steadfast Surrender* (Book 2 of Steadfast Series)
- *The Ultimatum* (Book 3 of Steadfast Series)
- *The Sister Circle* (Book 1 of Sister Circle Series)
- *Round the Corner* (Book 2 of Sister Circle Series)
- *An Undivided Heart* (Book 3 of Sister Circle Series)
- *A Place to Belong* (Book 4 of Sister Circle Series)
- *Time Lottery* (Book 1 of Time Lottery Series)
- *Second Time Around* (Book 2 of Time Lottery Series)
- *John 3:16*
- *The Good Nearby*
- *Solemnly Swear*
- *Weave of the World*

HISTORICAL NOVELS

- *Mozart's Sister* (biographical novel of Nannerl Mozart)
- *Just Jane* (biographical novel of Jane Austen)
- *Washington's Lady* (biographical novel of Martha Washington)
- *How Do I Love Thee?* (biographical novel of Elizabeth Barrett Browning)
- *Masquerade*
- *An Unlikely Suitor*
- *The Journey of Josephine Cain*
- *Love of the Summerfields* (Book 1 of Manor House Series)
- *Bride of the Summerfields* (Book 2 of Manor Houser Series)
- *A Patchwork Christmas* (novella collection)
- *A Basket Brigade Christmas* (novella collection)

Look for *Rise of the Summerfields* and *The Pattern Artist*
Read excerpts at www.nancymoser.com

DEDICATION

To the grandparents of my life:

George & Ruth
Lester & Lillie
Keith & LaFern
and Moody…

Your lifetimes of strength and integrity
have been my inspiration.

*"May integrity and uprightness protect me,
because my hope, Lord, is in you"*
PSALM 25: 21

ONE

"The kingdom of heaven is like a mustard seed,
which a man took and planted in his field.
Though it is the smallest of all your seeds, yet when it grows,
it is the largest of garden plants and becomes a tree,
so that the birds of the air come and perch in its branches."
MATTHEW 133: 31-32

THE SKY WAS blue. Not a tornado in sight.

Natalie Pasternak drove through central Nebraska on her way to her new life in Lincoln and thought of nothing *but* tornadoes.

Tornadoes had changed her life.

Two years earlier, she had received an anonymous invitation that had sent her on a pilgrimage to a town very close to her present location: Haven, Nebraska. That's where God had shown his power...

The four funnels were close, their teeming tails hidden by the vastness of their upper clouds' greedy inventory of fractured houses, dismembered trees, and mangled cars.

Natalie buried her head in her knees and put a protective hand over the baby growing inside her. "I don't want to die! I don't want to —"

Natalie blinked the memory away and jerked the car onto an exit ramp as if one motion fueled the next. At the bottom of the ramp she stopped the car. The drop in the decibel level had the same effect as a shot. Her senses snapped to attention.

"I've *got* to see Haven," she said aloud, as if in answer to an inner argument. She looked to the right, where an impromptu parking lot sat on the edge of the highway. There was the burl oak tree where she'd first met the others... Julia, Walter, Kathy, Del...they'd each, in one way or another, received invitations with the same, simple message:

You are invited to Haven, Nebraska.
Please arrive August 1.

"If you have faith as small as a mustard seed,
you can say to this mountain, 'Move from here to there'
and it will move. Nothing will be impossible to you."

They had traveled to Haven on faith—some skeptically, some reluctantly, but all hopefully. Circumstances had convinced them that these nondescript invitations were not to be ignored—even if they didn't know who'd sent them. Yet even if they'd known the truth, would they have believed that God had arranged it—believed that God had sent the invitations?

Natalie smiled at the memories of their hesitation. It was natural to question such a thing, but God hadn't given up on them. He had persisted until they were ready to listen. Who'd have thought God would want to use such ordinary people for His important work?

His work. Her work.

But want them He did. And so He'd led them to the small town of Haven, supplied them with special mentors, and given them two event-filled days to get ready for their calling.

Now it was August first. Two years later. And Haven was on Natalie's mind.

She checked for cars coming up behind her on the ramp, then took a moment to close her eyes. "I hope you're not disappointed in me, Lord. I've tried to do what I promised, but I've failed."

It's all Sam's fault skipped through her mind. She hoped God hadn't noticed—but she knew He had. For her own satisfaction, she rephrased her excuse. "I couldn't concentrate on writing my novel back in Colorado with Sam so close. He doesn't understand what I'm trying to do. He doesn't understand You. That's why I'm moving to Lincoln. I have to get away to be by myself."

But first, she had to see Haven again. Maybe just being there would give her the inspiration she seemed to have misplaced amid the day-to-day living of her life.

She turned south onto the highway.

After twenty minutes, she looked at her odometer. She'd traveled a good fifteen miles. She didn't remember Haven being that far off the interstate. She looked around, hoping to recognize some landmark, but the lush fields of corn were interchangeable.

"Haven? Oh, Haven." Natalie sang. "Come out, come out wherever you are." Three more miles went by. Natalie turned onto a tractor pull-off. She shut off the engine and stepped out of the car. Grasshoppers jumped around her ankles, upset by her intrusion. She arched her back and did a three-sixty, scanning the horizon. "Okay Haven. I give up. Where'd you go?"

A blue pickup approached from the north and pulled onto the shoulder. A farmer wearing a John Deere cap got out of the cab. "Problems, little lady?"

"No—" Natalie paused, then changed her mind. "Actually, yes. I seem to have lost a town."

The farmer rubbed his cheek. "That's mighty careless of you. Are we talking a small town or a city?"

"A small town. Haven's the name."

"Haven?" He waved at another pickup as it drove by. "Where'd you last see this Haven?"

Natalie opened her arms. "Out here somewhere. It was just a few miles south of the Platte River. On this highway."

The farmer peered up and down the road. "This highway?"

"This highway. I'm sure of it."

"You sure you're in the right state?" The farmer glanced at Natalie's Colorado license plate.

"Of course I'm in the right state. There *are* other Havens, but the one I'm looking for is in Nebraska. Haven, Nebraska. There's a Pump 'n Eat gas station that was robbed by a kid who kidnapped Julia. There's a school, a cafe, a church, and a bell tower we climbed when the four tornadoes came at us from four different directions. There's a—"

He cocked his head as if he hadn't heard right. "Four tornadoes from four different directions."

"Yes." Natalie fingered the mustard seed pin that had

been her parting gift from Haven. "I know it sounds impossible, but God did it to show us His power."

"God did it?"

Natalie swallowed. She knew how odd it sounded. She wouldn't have believed it herself if she hadn't lived through it.

The farmer took off his cap, ran a hand over his thinning hair, and put the cap back on. "I've lived in this county for sixty-seven years and I've never seen four tornadoes, much less four coming from different directions...at once, you say?"

"At once."

"Mother Nature doesn't work that way."

But God does.

"And you were *up* in a tower during all this?" The farmer squinted at her, as if studying something hinky.

Natalie nodded.

"That's not very smart, little lady. When tornadoes come calling you're supposed to go *below* ground. Going into a tower makes you twister bait."

Natalie raised her chin. "Well, that's what we did and I'm not going to argue with you about it. Now, if you'll tell me where Haven is, I'll be on my—"

He shook his head, cutting her off. "There is no Haven. Never has been. No Haven, Nebraska. Not 'round these parts anyways."

Natalie shooed a fly away from her face. "But there has to be. I was there."

The farmer headed back to his truck, talking over his shoulder. "Sorry. There is no place called Haven, and you and I can't change that fact no matter how many amazing stories you have to tell." He got in and pulled onto the highway, tooting his horn as he passed her heading south.

As the sound of his truck faded, the loneliness of the fields inched closer, covering her arms with goosebumps. The cadence of cicadas pulsed with her heartbeat. She glanced down the highway one way, then the other. No one. She heard herself swallow, felt the sun beating down. She shivered.

She got in the car and locked the doors. She turned the ignition and swung onto the highway, gravel and grass spurting from beneath her tires. She headed north toward the interstate, traveling faster than the speed limit.

Stop me, Mr. Highway Patrol. I dare you! Stop me. Prove to me this is just a dream.

No patrol car pulled her over. She crossed the Platte, ignored the burl oak, and sped onto the interstate.

Haven *had* to be real.

Either that, or she was crazy.

The tower of the Nebraska capital building rose from the prairie, marking Lincoln, a few miles away. Natalie pushed her thoughts of Haven—or no Haven—aside. She let herself be excited. And scared.

She'd never lived on her own. She'd spent her entire twenty years working at her parents' Estes Park resort, Paradise Cabins. As a child she'd changed beds and cleaned toilets, but by sixteen she'd graduated to full-fledged handyman, leaving the maid duties to her younger sister. She was rather proud—while at the same time slightly embarrassed—by the fact she knew how to use a plumber's snake, ground an outlet, and hang a door. As partial payment for her help, her parents had let her live in her own tiny cabin on the resort property. In her spare time she'd worked on her horrible novels. And gotten pregnant.

Such had been her pre-Haven life.

The two years that had been post-Haven were spent somewhat differently—but not differently enough, in Natalie's estimation. She had returned from Haven flying on the wings of inspiration. God had chosen *her* to do His work. Natalie was to write. And have her baby.

If nothing else came from her experience in Haven beyond having her daughter, Natalie was still grateful. She and Sam were best friends. Sleeping together had been an experiment that had spawned a baby, but they had both realized they didn't have the love required to nourish a child — or a marriage. True, Sam had offered to marry her, but she had resisted. Two wrongs didn't make a right. Marriage under those conditions was wrong. So was abortion.

An abortion would have been so easy...just close her eyes and let *it* be gone. Yet, it would have been even harder to open her eyes and realize what she'd done. If it weren't for Kathy, a young mother she'd met in Haven, Natalie would have closed her eyes.

Her parents had been forgiving of her pregnancy. Her mother, immediately, her father, eventually. Natalie had suffered the humiliation of her mistake and had given birth. But adoption? That was a harder decision.

Natalie had been incensed when a guest at one of the cabins had handed her the card for an adoption agency — until she saw the name of the agency: God's Haven, Home for Children. *Haven.* A reminder. A heavenly shove. Such things were not coincidence. Hadn't Haven taught her that?

Sam was not pleased when she told him she'd called the agency.

"But Sam, the name of the agency...it was as if God was telling me to call."

"Oh sure. I suppose it was the *Haven* Agency or something —"

"God's Haven, Home for Children."

"God's Haven?"

She'd nodded. He'd sunk into a chair, convinced. He was a believer in Haven, even if he wasn't completely won over to the God who had invited her there.

That was another reason Natalie was moving away: Sam's unbelief in God. It was hard to stay focused on the Almighty when her best friend was a skeptic. She was too new in her own faith to fan the flame of Sam's belief as well. Recently, one of her oft-repeated prayers was that God would give her a soul mate in Lincoln, someone she could confide in about the struggles of her spiritual life.

Now, Natalie's daughter, Grace, was eighteen months

old. Recently, Natalie had received a photo of her in the mail. The child was beautiful. She shared Natalie's dark hair and hazel eyes, and Sam's strong chin and long fingers. Grace grinned at the camera as she sat in a child-sized chair, her smile framing her baby teeth.

Natalie could see her little girl was happy and thriving with her adoptive parents, Sally and Karl (first names only, please). But that was the past...Sam was the past. Natalie needed to think about the future.

A city limits sign told Natalie she had arrived in Lincoln. She got off the interstate and turned onto "O" Street, a main thoroughfare. She headed east into town, though she had no definite destination. She kept the capital in sight, noticing that the tops of the other downtown buildings hovered near its height but never surpassed it.

Its golden dome stood triumphant in the hot, blue sky. As she got closer, she could see the statue of a man crowning its crest. He held a sack across his shoulders, one arm balancing the weight of the sack on his hip and the other outstretched, sowing the seeds across the plains. A sower. Sowing seeds.

Mustard seeds?

"'Sow the seeds of God's message,'" Natalie said. That had been the farewell direction given by the angelic mentors of Haven. "'Our Lord said, 'Go: I will help you speak and will teach you what to say.'"

So far, Natalie hadn't said a whole lot. For two years, she'd managed to put off spreading God's message. But lately, she'd felt a strange urgency to do...something. And now she was in Lincoln, a town not too far, but far enough, from home.

Actually, it could have been any town—and would have been if Natalie had not met Hayley Spotsman, a woman who'd been a guest at her parents' resort. One day last June, while Natalie had been in Hayley's cabin changing a light bulb, they'd struck up a conversation about antiques. Hayley had revealed that she owned an antique mall in Lincoln. She'd gone on to say that Natalie was welcome to come work for her any time she wanted to get away from caulking guns and trash bags. So when Natalie's restlessness reached its peak, she had called Hayley—and ended up here, in Lincoln.

It was nice how God provided the answers to questions she hadn't even thought to ask yet.

Natalie turned onto a street that bordered the capital. She slowed, leaning forward across the steering wheel so she could look up at the tower. *My life is drawn to towers.*

She slammed on the brakes as a car pulled out of a parking place in front of her. The man waved his apologies and sped away. Natalie swerved into the space.

Her hands fell to her lap. *Natalie Pasternak, what are you doing in a strange town with only a minimum wage job, and no place to stay?*

A white bird fluttered in front of the windshield, landing on the hood of the car. It looked directly at Natalie.

"May I help you?"

The bird pecked at a dried bug. It blinked at her. Then it flew across the capitol grounds to a tree in front of an old house nearby. But no sooner had it landed in the tree than the bird flew back toward her car. It took its place on the hood again and strutted a few steps closer to the windshield.

Natalie shook her head. "If you're a homing pigeon, you're out of luck because at the moment I don't have a home."

The bird took off a second time, retracing its flight to the old house.

Home.

Without thinking about it further, Natalie drove toward the house. It must have been stately once, a jewel in this prime location across from the capitol. Now it had a leaning porch, chipped paint, and crumbling sidewalks. But none of that seemed to bother Natalie's bird, which settled on the roof near a dormer window.

Just then, a woman came out of the house carrying a sign. She placed it in the middle of a yard that struggled between grass and weeds.

Natalie leaned forward, squinting to read what it said.

"Apartment for Rent."

She parked and leaped out of her car. "Ma'am? You have an apartment for rent?"

The woman looked at the sign and scratched her chin. "That has got to be the quickest rent I've ever...fifteen seconds. A new world's record."

Natalie forced herself to feign calmness. She smoothed the line of her shorts. "May I see it, please?"

The woman waved Natalie toward the door. "Your timing is perfect, girl. The tenant in the attic just moved out. Actually, it's been a bad month for me — three vacancies. No offense, but I hate this part of the job. My husband used to do it, but with his bad back...it's such a chore to rent 'em up again. Usually takes a while, but this time it went easy. Must be something going on I don't know about."

They passed one apartment inside the main door and headed up a staircase whose many layers of paint couldn't completely hide a grandiose past.

"The house has been divided into three apartments," the woman said. "Sacrilege to cut up these grand old homes. But money rules and people don't have umpteen kids to fill a house like they used to."

The woman stopped in the second floor hallway and pointed to a door. "Apartment number two is there. And this," she unlocked a slim door, "this leads to number three." Inside was a narrow flight of winding stairs leading up to the attic. The woman glanced back at Natalie and shrugged. "I know. It's strange having the stairs *inside* the apartment, but what can I say? It's eccentric." She led Natalie up the stairs. "It's a cute enough place. Great for artists, nice light." She turned to Natalie. "You an artist?"

"A writer."

"Good enough. An artist of the mind not the hand."

As they reached the top of the stairs, Natalie could barely contain her joy. One large room spanned the length and depth of the house with windows capping each of the four sides. The ceiling was odd, dipping low, forming a cross of sorts. A tiny kitchen was lodged under one dormer, while another held the bed. Tucked within the roofline was also a walk-in closet, and a bathroom with a claw-footed tub and a pull-chain light. An oversized chair hunkered next to a dresser. A small desk and chair sat beneath the west window. A ray of sunlight spotlighted the writing surface.

Natalie walked to the desk and placed a hand on the warm wood. It would be the perfect place to work on her book.

"That desk will do you fine, won't it?" The woman smiled as she opened the window and brushed her hand at a bird. "Pesky dove. Doing its doo-doo on the roof."

Pesky? More like God-sent. Natalie stroked the desktop, feeling as though God's hand were on top of hers.

"Will you be wanting the place? It's $550 a month, all utilities paid. I need a $550 damage deposit up front in case you ruin the carpet or...you don't have a pet, do you?"

"No pet." Natalie turned toward the woman, her heart feeling the warmth of being home. "I'll take it."

TWO

*"A generous man will prosper,
he who refreshes others will himself be refreshed."*
PROVERBS 11: 25

"**YOU'RE GOING TO** what?"

"I'm going to pray." Julia Carson raised one eyebrow. "I assume that is acceptable to you, Benjamin?"

Ben Cranois had to bow to her wish. After all, in just a few minutes Julia would be accepting the nomination for president of the United States. So, for at least this one moment of her life, she had clout. If Ben wanted to rise from campaign manager to a position within her administration, he knew he needed to pick his battles. And this wasn't one of them.

"Ten minutes," she said.

"Maybe, but—"

"I think God deserves ten minutes before I jump into this thing, don't you?"

She didn't wait for his answer. She walked down the hall to find a quiet place in the bowels of the convention center.

"You're impossible," he said.

Julia raised a hand but kept walking. "Glad to know it."

Ben watched her rap on a door, listen, then3 disappear inside. To pray. Absurd. Though he'd helped her become governor of Minnesota, and though he'd helped her gain the presidential nomination, there were things about Julia's character he would never understand.

He heard footsteps and turned around to see Julia's husband coming toward him.

"You look perplexed, Benjamin." Edward Carson smiled. "Is it possible my wife had something to do with it?"

"As always." He sighed. "Why can't she be a peaceful person like you?"

"Me? Peaceful?"

"You never get riled."

Edward raised a finger. "That's not *entirely* true, but I thank you for the compliment." He looked around. "Actually, I remain peaceful to counter Julia's fire. By the way…where is my towering inferno?"

Ben flicked a hand toward the hall. "Down there. Praying." He looked at his watch. "She's making thousands of people wait."

Edward put a hand on Ben's shoulder. "Surely you know that Julia deals with people only after she's conferred with the Boss?"

"Explain that to them." He cocked a thumb in the direction of the raucous cheering and the incessant beat of the music coming from the main hall.

"You worry too much, Benjamin."

"It's my job."

"Actually, your job is to let Julia be Julia. You know the people like her. When the media called her stubborn, the public dubbed her strong. When the press called her opinionated, the public deemed her principled. And when journalists called her close-minded, the people hailed her as the first honest politician since Abe Lincoln grabbed the grass roots of the country and planted them in the White House."

Ben couldn't help but smile. "You sure you don't want to be vice-president?"

Edward brushed off his lapels. "Actually, I'm looking forward to being First Man."

"That sounds so strange."

"Tell me about it."

Ben looked at his watch again. Julia was going to give him an ulcer.

"Now, now, Benjamin," Edward said. "Face the facts. Mr. and Mrs. Citizen think Julia is their best friend, strict grandma, and apple-pie mama rolled into one. They're willing to wait because they know she's on their side."

"Senator Bradley's camp says the same thing about him."

Edward grinned. "He's an apple-pie mama?"

Ben groaned. "You know what I mean."

"Yes I do. But again, stop worrying. Julia offers truth.

Bradley offers pacifiers for the people."

"Can I quote you?"

"Absolutely. I like to share my profundity whenever possible."

At the moment, Ben could do with less profundity and more punctuality.

+++

Julia wondered if it was possible to die of fear.

What was she getting herself into?

In scant minutes she would be called upon to accept the nomination for president of the United States. In doing so, she would fulfill the promise she had made to God in Haven two years before.

Two years ago this very day.

The significance of her nomination occurring on August first was not lost on Julia. She knew God was never random. *Coincidence* was an unbeliever's explanation for God's work.

When she dedicated her leadership abilities to God back in Haven, she hadn't seriously thought of the presidency. She was not a Washington insider. She was the ex-governor of Minnesota, with an emphasis on the *ex*. She had withdrawn from politics when she'd become fed up with its circuitous ways. She had grown weary of having her ideas twisted into a pale reflection of her original intent. Every issue she felt strongly about was ripped from her control as pressure from special interest groups curved her views to fit theirs. The quest for votes and funding bent the issue a little more, until Julia found her idea back at the starting point with nothing accomplished except a circle of hot air. That had been her experience as governor. She vowed that as president things would be different. *She* would be different.

And she was.

Loud voices shouted, unaware that their candidate was sitting alone in an empty office. Praying.

"Carson for president!"

"Jul-i-a! Jul-i-a!"

"Do it! Do it!"

Julia closed her eyes. "Are we going to do it, Lord?" She leaned forward, balancing her elbows on her thighs, and buried her face in her hands. "Father, you've brought me this far and I want to thank you for the ride. These last two years, I've tried to follow Your lead, but I'm not always sure what is Your will and what is my own—or the will of the people on my campaign staff." She rubbed her fingers against her temples. "Can I do it, Lord? Or is this as far as I go?"

It had often occurred to her that perhaps she wasn't meant to become president. Perhaps she was merely supposed to affect change by being part of the process. To be truthful, she didn't care which way the election went. The thought of being president—a woman president of the United States—was exciting, satisfying, and terrifying. So much responsibility. Eyes watching, ears listening. The constant stress of trying to make things better, while others with a different view of the future worked against her.

What was God's view of the future?

Look to the source.

Julia put a hand on the pocket of her jacket. *Of course. The source.* She pulled out her tiny pocket New Testament. She held it to her lips and closed her eyes. "Show me, Lord."

It opened to the book of Ephesians. Her eyes fell upon the words: *"Therefore put on the full armor of God, so that when the day of evil comes, you may be able to stand your ground and after you have done everything, to stand."*

She nodded. The world was a wicked place. Evil was rampant. But the world wasn't defenseless. God was with them. He would help them stand strong.

Julia stood and squared her shoulders. She turned to the door and took a deep breath. "God be with me, it's time to take a stand."

✦✦✦

Julia paused in the middle of her acceptance speech and took a sip of water. She gazed across the masses of people whose hopes hung above her like the balloons that kissed the ceiling of the convention center. If only she could blast a hole in the ceiling of their thoughts, freeing their hopes to rise to infinite heights.

She bowed her head a moment. She had talked, they had listened. Now it was time to give them a final challenge. She glanced at the notes in front of her. Her speechwriter, Paula had done a fine job. But the closing seemed staged, a sound bite, a made-for-the-media slogan with ulterior motives. Now was not the time to win votes.

Now was the time to win hearts.

Julia moved the notes aside and leaned on the podium, feeling like a favorite teacher confiding in her beloved pupils. She scanned the auditorium, trying to take in each corner, each row, each seat. The audience waited in anticipation.

Please, Lord. Give me the words.

She took a deep breath and smiled. "'But as for me, I will always have hope.'" She paused a moment, letting the words sink in. "Those words were written by an anonymous author 3000 years ago. Yet they are true today. They will be true tomorrow. Hope is what I offer you." Many in the audience nodded.

"Life offers no guarantees, and neither do I. We are a diverse party living in a diverse nation in a diverse world. We will not agree — we *should not* agree — because out of our diversity comes wisdom, compassion, and love. It is easy for us to show these traits to someone who is lovable and agrees with us, but it shows true character to extend such gifts to those who are against us."

She pointed across the auditorium. "Some of us believe this — " she held out her right hand, palm up, fingers together — "While others believe this." She made the same movement with her left hand. "When we bring together these different beliefs they may not meld." She pressed palm against palm, rotating her hands against each other. "But..." Julia splayed the fingers of each hand and brought them together until finger wove between finger like puzzle pieces finding their place. "If we open up, we can find ways to come

21

together, to fit. We can be made stronger together, instead of weaker apart." More heads nodded.

"We will not win a victory in this election — or in this life — through force. We will win through hope. Through love. Through understanding. We must complete ourselves. We must stand tall for what we believe is right and good in this life. We must not bend, we must not waiver. We must stand firm with our arms open wide to welcome, not with a fist raised to beat down."

Julia gripped the front of the podium. "We all have hope. Even those who stand against us have hope. But let our hope be different." She repeated the phrase, her voice vibrating with intensity. "Let our hope be different! 'We rejoice in our sufferings because we know that suffering produces perseverance, perseverance character, and character hope.' That will be our power. We will be a nation with character. With integrity and honor, with values that run deep and stem from the Judeo-Christian foundations that are the bedrock of our beginnings."

Julia lowered her head. The audience was hushed, waiting. Finally, she raised her face to them. She thumped a hand on her heart. "I stand here, one person willing to hope. I ask you to stand with me." She held out her hands. The audience rose at her command. "'But as for me, I will always have hope!'"

The crowd roared. Chants of "Jul-i-a! Jul-i-a!" intermixed with "Hope! Hope! Hope!"

Julia turned to her husband, who was seated behind her. Edward came forward, took her hand, and kissed her cheek. Together, they raised their arms in victory. Julia held out her other hand and their daughter Bonnie moved forward, flanked by her husband, Hank, and nine-year-old Carolyn. Five sets of hands raised, standing strong together.

As the band struck up "Happy Days are Here Again", Julia scanned the audience. If only this enthusiasm could last as they spread the message of hope. That's what the nation needed to make it thrive again.

Just then she caught sight of Benjamin, slinking along the

side of the room. She frowned. *Why do I always think of him as slinking?*

She pushed the negative thought away.

It would probably reappear soon enough.

✦✦✦

Ben Cranois was not smiling. Although his candidate had won the nomination—which put him in a powerful position—he was unhappy. He should be the one in charge, the one deciding what was done and when, where they went, and why. He was the one who knew politics far better than any candidate ever could. He knew exactly what to say and to whom, and how to control every aspect of a campaign down to the smallest detail.

His frown and his frustration deepened. Because the one thing he didn't know how to control, was Julia Carson.

THREE

"I am the Lord your God, who teaches you what is best for you,
who directs you in the way you should go."
ISAIAH 48: 17

"I WISH SOMEBODY would tell me what to do!"

Walter Prescott sprawled on the couch. He grabbed a pillow and held it over his face.

His wife, Bette, moved beside him and knocked on the pillow. "May we come in?"

Walter's voice was muffled against the fabric. "Who is it?"

"Laurel and Hardy."

Walter uncovered one eye and glanced at Bette's pregnant midsection. "I know who resembles Hardy."

She lifted the pillow off his face and smacked him with it. "You're lucky I just shaved my mustache." She shoved him upright to make room for herself on the couch. "It's a good opportunity, Walter. It's an honor to have an important TV station in Minneapolis offer you a job."

"But I just got the news department the way I want it here." Walter knew he was whining, but didn't care. "The ratings are good, we're number one in the St. Louis area, and I feel like I've accomplished what Haven sent me to do."

She kissed his ear. "Maybe this is the next step? Maybe God wants you to do the same for someone else."

"I'm not *that* good, Bette. Changing KZTV took a ton of work. It wasn't easy getting them to stop devouring every news item like vultures picking at a corpse."

"But they *did* succumb to your charm and principles." She pinched his ear lobe. "You oozed integrity, making yourself—"

"Sticky?"

"I was going to say irresistible."

"But moving to another state...there's Baby to consider." Walter patted her belly.

"Baby goes where I go. And I go where you go."

"Nice how that works." Walter sighed. "But I was thinking...maybe I've done enough. I've worked hard for two years. I've made a difference. Maybe my part's through."

"I don't think God invited you to Haven to give you a temporary assignment."

Walter wrinkled his nose. "I wonder if He would be open to a long vacation."

"Lazy bum."

"I'm not talking forever. Just twenty or thirty years."

She pushed his head off her lap and stood, using his body as leverage. "That's the thanks God gets after choosing you to go to Haven? After giving you a special assignment? After curing you by taking away that shadow on your lung? You want to do a little work then say, 'Well, God, got to go. I figure things are even now?'"

"Don't get huffy, Bette."

She paced in front of the couch. "God's the one who should be huffy. You're being disrespectful. This lack of enthusiasm isn't good, Walter. In fact, it's downright bad. You need to—" She stopped pacing and strode over to the bookshelf where she pulled out the Bible. She held it up as if it were Exhibit A.

"Uh-oh. What are you up to?"

She leafed through the pages, then drilled a verse with a finger. "Here it is. I just read it this morning. 'Take up the shield of faith with which you can extinguish all the flaming arrows of the evil one.'"

"Did I miss something? I didn't see any flaming arrows."

She shut the Bible with a snap. "Your doubt is a flaming arrow trying to pierce through your faith. You can't let it do that."

He raised his arms in surrender. "Okay, oh mighty warrior. Let's see what we can do to extinguish this doubt-arrow."

"This *flaming* doubt-arrow."

He rolled his eyes. "So let's pretend my work's *not* done. That doesn't mean I'm supposed to move. Maybe I'm supposed to stay here and do more at KZTV. We're settled in St. Louis. Pop's living here, our friends are here. My roots are here."

"Wishy-washy Walter has soggy roots."

"Do not."

"Do too. Rotting, weak, slimy roots."

"Bully Bette is not being nice."

"And you're not being brave." She took his hand. "Where's your 'shield of faith', Walter? We need to pray about it. God sent you this far, He can handle the rest."

"But if I go...if St. Louis was hard to change, Minneapolis may be harder."

"You're not changing an entire city, you're trying to change one station. They must be willing to change if they offered you the job. I'm sure they've heard how you've brought honor to the news on KZTV. They came to you, Walter. Not the other way around."

"I wonder how they got my name."

"Maybe God sent them a letter. Maybe God sent them an invitation." She wrote the words across the air. "'You are invited to hire Walter Prescott to turn your sleazy, degrading network into an organization based on principles and good moral character. Do it or else!'"

"Or else what?"

Bette shrugged. "Or else...Mr. Prescott will work his magic somewhere else."

"Ooh, big threat."

"Don't let the arrow flame to life again, hon. And don't put yourself — or God's intentions — down." She stood to straighten the newspapers on the coffee table. "After all, He did choose *you* to go to Haven where He had enough power to get *you*, Walter the wishy-washy skeptic, to commit to Him. And me. Not too shabby."

"I didn't change easily, Bette. I needed Julia's kidnapper to pull a gun on me, I needed Del to jump in front of a bullet before I'd listen to what God was saying. Haven or no Haven."

"So you weren't an easy sell? God doesn't want weak-minded robots, God wants people with gumption."

"You know this for a fact?" He smiled, challenging her.

She made a face, as if searching her mind. She held up a finger. "'You are my refuge and my *shield*, I have put my hope in your word.'"

"*My* word?"

She gave him a scathing look. Then she leaned down and kissed his forehead. "You're a good man, Walter. Aggravating, annoying, and hardly perfect, but a good man."

"Thanks bunches for that glowing compliment."

"You deserve every bit of it."

He laughed. "Where can I get more like you? It's such a comfort having you on my side."

"I am on your side, Walter. On your side and by your side. God didn't give up on you in Haven and He won't give up on you now. And neither will I."

✦✦✦

Bette tried to get Walter's mind off his decision by tempting him with a Jimmy Stewart marathon. When that didn't lure him, she sweetened the pot with Rita Hayworth. When *that* didn't pull him out of his worries, she surrendered. "I wish I could help you make the decision."

"Sorry, hon." Walter got the Bible off the shelf and patted it affectionately. "Remember you saying, 'I have put my hope in your word?'"

She put a dramatic hand to her chest. "My word?"

"Now who's aggravating, annoying, and hardly perfect?"

Bette waved her arm gallantly. "Although I accept any and all compliments, I defer to a higher power." She switched on the reading lamp by his favorite, ugly, comfortable chair, fluffed a throw pillow, arranged the ottoman, and led him to the seat. "Make us a good one, Walter."

✦✦✦

Walter stared at the slit of light showing under the bedroom door. The muted sounds of canned TV laughter filtered into the living room. What had he done to deserve Bette? And to think he'd nearly lost her.

Before Haven, they'd been dating, but Walter had been reluctant to make a commitment—to Bette or to any woman. He'd been burned too many times. Sometimes the burner, sometimes the burnee.

He'd tried commitment—or a form of it. He'd lived with Donna for two years. They'd had fun partying, taking life for all it was worth. They'd had an agreement. No strings. It was Walter's idea. He didn't want to be tied down by a wife. And kids? No kids. Not ever. So when the novelty of their relationship waned, Walter had dumped her and crushed Donna good. And when she'd taken the pills...she'd lived, but a part of Walter's ego had been forever extinguished. That's when he'd started to analyze his life. Could it be that having fun, spending money, and being carefree wasn't all there was?

Bette had saved him from himself. They'd met at the video store. He'd been dragging himself up and down the aisles, trying to find a movie to yank himself out of himself. They'd met in front of the Nostalgia section. She'd been holding a copy of "All that Heaven Allows," the love story about an older woman, Jane Wyman, and a younger man, Rock Hudson. He'd mentioned how much he liked the movie. She offered it to him. He declined. She insisted. He took it home—along with her phone number.

Bette cooked from scratch, grew African violets, and was not averse to reading books that were written in other centuries. She even went to church—an alien place to Walter back then, one in which he envisioned straight-backed spinsters and broken-down men. It took all her charm and female ingenuity to get him to go with her. Afterward, she graciously accepted his surprised observation that the women were vibrant and the men vigorous, that the atmosphere was joyous and open instead of stifling and closed. Not once did she say, "I told you so", although Walter *could* see a hint of gloating in her eyes.

Bette was blessed with a perceptive view of the world. She had the ability to sense people's needs while weighing their motives. Yet oddly, one didn't mind being scrutinized by Bette Smithton Prescott, because the truth and candor she wrestled from others were already firmly entrenched in her own character.

She was a woman of principle. Bette's standards and rules of life weren't open to negotiation. For example, as their affection began its ascent, she'd made it clear there would be no sex before marriage. The fact she wouldn't back down both impressed and depressed Walter. And though he would have liked to sweep her off her feet and into the bedroom, he had deferred to her integrity and in the process found a bit of his own.

Sacrifice, a foreign concept to the man who *had* been Walter Prescott, became acceptable and even coveted under Bette's tutelage. The compensation was great. Walter was paid in the undivided attention of a loving and lovely woman, an aspect of modern life he had seldom experienced and sorely desired.

When Walter came back from Haven spouting tall tales of tornadoes, gun battles, and heaven-sent revelations, Bette listened attentively. She didn't laugh. She didn't run away. She asked the right questions and celebrated with him in the answers. Soon after Haven, when Walter went to the doctor's for a pre-biopsy appointment to discuss a shadow on his lung and came out with the report that the shadow was gone, Bette accepted the miracle of his healing as God's gift. To both of them. It was a great way to start a life together.

And now the two would become three.

Baby was everything to Walter. He or she was his chance to do something positive. Although he realized at forty-eight he was a mite old to start playing Daddy, he accepted the challenge. If Abraham could be one hundred and father a nation, certainly Walter Prescott could be forty-eight and father a family.

Walter put his hands on the red leather of the Bible,

closed his eyes, and prayed. "Hey, God. You know I'm stubborn and not easily convinced. I need Your help. The truth is, I don't want to move to Minneapolis." He hesitated a moment. "But the other truth is, I'm curious to know what *You* want." He shook his head. "But what if what You want isn't what I want?" Bette said God didn't want weak-minded robots. He hoped she was right.

Walter opened his eyes and held the Bible on end, the spine balanced on his lap. With one hand on either side of the book, he let it go, willing it to flop open to some biblical gem that would tell him what to do.

The Bible seemed to hesitate a moment before leaning to the left, then it fell open to reveal the final few pages of colored maps. Walter set it upright, trying again.

"Come on, you can do better than that."

"What are you doing?"

Walter started and looked up to see Bette in the doorway. He set the Bible flat on his lap.

She pointed to the book. "I've tried that. It didn't work."

"*You've* tried this?"

"Hasn't everybody?"

"And it didn't work?"

"I kept getting the maps in the back."

"Me too!"

They laughed. She took a seat on the ottoman, moving Walter's feet to her lap. She massaged his toes. "You try so hard. I'm sure God is impressed."

"I'm a regular biblical scholar, can't you tell?"

"It might help if *you* opened the pages, not gravity."

He raised a finger. "What a novel idea. I'll have to try it."

There was a moment of silence. Bette looked from Walter to the Bible and back again. "So? What are you waiting for?"

"I'm waiting for you to leave."

"Don't hold back, Walter. Tell me how you truly feel."

"I thought I did."

She wriggled his big toe. "But you were kidding, weren't you? You need me to help with this decision."

"I told you I need to do this alone."

She stuck out her lower lip. "Oh, let me stay. I want to help. Pretty please?"

Walter shook his head. "You are such a pest."

"It takes one to know one." She pushed his feet off her lap. "Move over to the table so I can look at the Bible, too." She took his hand and pulled. He resisted, holding his ground. When she realized he wasn't going to budge, she tossed his hand in his lap. "You are very annoying."

"Probably."

"You won't let me help?"

"I won't let you help." He reached for her hand to make amends, but she pulled it away. "I have to do this alone, Bette."

She whirled around, showing him her back. "Then I'm going to drown myself in a hot fudge sundae."

"Sounds great, can I have—?"

"*One* hot fudge sundae, coming up!" She shook her hair, adding to the drama of her statement. "I have to do *this* alone."

"Touché, madame."

She saluted him and marched to the kitchen where she proceeded to make as much noise as possible while singing a rousing rendition of "I'll Never Fall in Love Again."

"Oh, Lord. Give me strength." Walter leaned back in the chair, his Bible closed. He didn't want to get started only to have Bette—

She swished past him, trailing the sundae under his nose. "What? No decision yet?"

"I'm waiting for the tempest to pass."

She sailed into the bedroom, then paused before closing the door. "I've been called worse." The door shut.

Walter shook his head, looking heavenward. "What would I do without her?"

A muffled answer came from the bedroom. "Suffer unbearably."

Walter laughed and opened the Bible. Although he had no proof, he had the feeling God enjoyed their banter as much as he did.

He looked down at the page he'd turned to. He was in the twelfth chapter of Genesis. "Might as well start at the beginning."

He began to read. "The Lord said to Abram, 'Leave your country, your people and your father's household and go to the land I will show you—'"

Walter stopped abruptly, pulling the Bible to his chest. His heart galloped. He'd kidded Bette about wanting God to show him an answer but he hadn't actually expected it to happen. And so fast.

Walter took a deep breath and lowered the Bible. He read the verse again, then leaned back in his chair. *I'm supposed to move! It says to leave your people and your father's household and go. I'm supposed to leave Pop and my life here and go to Minneapolis. I'm supposed to move!*

Walter swallowed hard. He didn't *want* to move. He noticed the reference next to the verse, leading to similar verses. The first was Hebrews 11:8. Walter turned to the New Testament and found it. "'By faith Abraham, when called to go to a place he would later receive as his inheritance, obeyed and went, even though he did not know where he was going.'"

Walter snapped the Bible shut. "No," he whispered, "I won't do it." He shivered at his own gumption. Bette said God liked gumption. *Even if it causes me to go against Him?*

Walter took the Bible to the bookshelf and put it away. He went back to his chair and turned off the reading lamp.

He sat in the dark a long time.

✦✦✦

"Walter? Honey? Wake up."

Walter's head jerked to the left, making him cringe at the crick in his neck. "I must have fallen asleep." He arched his back.

"It's three in the morning. I woke up. You weren't there." She helped him stand. "Are you all right?"

Walter shuffled into the bedroom. "Fine. I'm fine." He

went into the bathroom and splashed water on his face.

"Did you decide anything?"

Walter caught a glimpse of himself in the mirror, the towel obscuring all but his eyes. His selfish, dishonest eyes. He looked away. "Yes, I did." He unbuttoned his shirt. "We're staying here."

Bette sank onto the foot of the bed. "Staying? I was so sure you were meant to take that job. I had the strongest feeling."

"Well, I'm not taking it!" He stopped, then spoke again in a calmer tone. "We're supposed to stay here."

"How do you know? Did you find a verse to lead you?"

"Yeah...sure. I found a verse."

"Which one?"

Walter flipped off the light so she couldn't see his face. "I forget."

"Will you show it to me tomorrow? I'm curious."

He shoved his feet beneath the blanket and pulled the covers over his shoulder. "I told you, I forgot which verse it was." He raised his head, realizing she was still sitting at the foot of the bed. "You coming?"

Bette hesitated. "I'm going to stay up awhile. You go to sleep."

She left the bedroom, closing the door quietly behind her, leaving him alone in their bed.

Bette sat in the dark of the living room, the moonlight cutting a swath across the carpet. She pulled the afghan around her legs and belly. She was finding it harder and harder to get comfortable as Baby demanded more space. She felt a tiny knee or elbow poking her side and stroked it.

"Sorry, darling, I didn't mean to wake you."

Baby responded to her voice by being still.

Bette rested her head against the back of the cushion, closed her eyes, and prayed. "Father, I was so sure you wanted us to move. I wasn't keen on the idea with Baby coming, but I was willing—I *am* willing—to go wherever you want us to go. Now Walter says we're supposed to stay. He's my husband and he *is* the one you invited to Haven, but..." She wasn't sure she should put her next thought into words. Still, God knew what she was thinking, and so... "Lord, I think Walter's lying."

FOUR

*"All a man's ways seem innocent to him,
but motives are weighed by the Lord."*
PROVERBS 16: 2

FATHER ANTONIO DELATONDO flung himself between two boys who were dueling with sticks. "Yield, Musketeers!"

He got jabbed in the chest.

"Sorry, Father." Both boys took a step back.

Del held out a hand and the sticks were placed in his palm.

"We were just playing, Father."

"Fight with spiritual swords, boys." He tried giving them a stern look, but it wasn't easy. He loved playing with the kids of the parish, and they knew it. "Next time I see you, I want you to be able to tell me which verse talks about the 'sword of the spirit.'"

The taller boy kicked the ground with a toe. "Ah, Father. That's work."

Del put a hand on both their shoulders and drew them close. "Don't let God hear you say that."

The boys' eyes grew wide and they scurried away — most likely to find more sticks.

Del started when he felt a hand on his arm. He turned to see Father Adrian.

"Don't sneak up on me like that. Especially when I'm armed." He brandished one of the boys' sticks like a sword. *"En guarde!"*

Adrian did not smile. He was far too serious for someone so young.

"Sorry to interrupt, Father, but the monsignor is ready to see you."

Del kept a "Finally!" to himself and tossed the sticks over his shoulder. He made a beeline toward the rectory. Father Adrian scrambled after him but kept two steps behind.

Del closed his eyes, praying for strength. "Adrian, get up

here beside me. You know I hate it when you hang back as if you're my lackey."

"But I am."

Del stopped, causing Adrian to bump into him. He put an hand on Adrian's shoulder and spoke softly. "I know you're new, but you've got to stop treating me like I'm God's gift to the parish. I'm a simple man, a flawed, sinful man. If you don't start acting like my equal, I'll begin to believe all this 'chosen' business and I'll wield this lofty power you think I have and short-sheet your bed."

Adrian didn't get the joke. "But you were in Haven. You were invited by God."

"We are *all* invited by God, you fatuous wretch. Every day of our lives. And to be technical about it, I *wasn't* invited to Haven, I stowed away in the back of Walter Prescott's van. Hardly cause for canonization."

"Our Lord rode to Jerusalem on a donkey."

Del groaned. "Which shows us *His* true humility. I, however, would have preferred a car."

Adrian nodded and looked into the distance. "A Lincoln Town Car. Navy blue with leather interior and a great sound syst—" He put a hand to his mouth and blushed.

Del smiled. "Odd you should say *Lincoln.*"

"How so?"

Del shook it off. "Never mind. At any rate, it's clear that neither one of us is as humble as our Lord."

"But you saw *Him.*"

Del took Adrian's arm and peered at his face. "Who told you that?"

Adrian shrugged.

"What else do they say?"

"It's not for me to repeat such things. I'm not worthy—"

"Stop that right now!"

Father Adrian looked at the ground. "I'm sorry, I didn't mean to offend."

Del put a finger under Adrian's chin and raised it. The church needed more young men like him. The temptations of the world wooed too many from a life of devotion to God.

Del didn't want to discourage, but he couldn't let Adrian deify him.

"I am very honored you think so highly of me. But you must consider the truth. Saint Paul, one of Christ's most faithful said, 'Christ Jesus came into the world to save sinners — of whom I am the worst.' So it is with me."

"They say you were led to us."

Del sighed. The mixture of truth and tall tale made for a powerful reputation. And yet, much of the truth was so astounding, so amazing, that Del could understand why it had been elevated the short step to legend.

"I will tell this to you straight, in an effort to separate the falsehoods from the truth. You've heard the story about Mellie?"

Adrian nodded. They'd all heard of how Del, in a blaze of self-righteousness had told a prostitute to get out of the life and go back to her husband. Unfortunately, her husband was her pimp. Her refusal to work the streets got her killed.

"Then you know I left the priesthood. I ran away."

"You took up your penance. You became homeless."

"Don't make it sound better than it was. I blew it. Big time. I couldn't handle the humiliation. I left the priesthood so I could wallow in my sin. It wasn't because I was humble, it was because I was proud. My sacrifice was an icon for all to gaze upon and be impressed with. Oh, how grand a penance I had."

"But you were sorry, weren't you?"

Del lowered his voice. "Of course I was. But when we've sinned, we have to come before God in humility and ask for his forgiveness. I couldn't do that. Not until I'd been to Haven."

"What was it like?"

"It was a small, Midwestern town with a church bell tower, a cafe that could make your mouth water just driving by, and a bunch of people who cared."

"You got shot. You took a bullet for someone else."

Del scratched his toe against the sidewalk. "A fortunate impulse. Not a grand gesture."

"But you saw *Him*."

"I saw the wonder of Him, the power of Him." Del put his arm on Adrian's shoulder as they started to walk. "And my wound was healed by Him."

"Your bullet wound."

Del nodded. "But God didn't heal me because of anything I did, He healed me to show His glory and His power, for all the others to witness."

"You're too humble."

Del kicked a stone. It clattered ahead of them. "I'm not. It's something I struggle with."

"You? Struggle?"

"'When pride comes, then comes disgrace, but with humility comes wisdom.'"

Adrian shook his head. "You always seem so strong and sure of yourself."

"A clever ruse, sir," Del said, clapping him on the back. "An artful, clever ruse."

✦✦✦

Del sat across the desk from Monsignor Albertson, his feet on the floor, his spine erect. Although Del didn't hold the monsignor in the highest regard—the man was much, much too strict with the young prelates—he did respect his position. "Thank you for taking the time to see me, Monsignor."

"I always have time for my brothers."

Del raised an eyebrow, then purposefully lowered it. "Concerning my transfer to Lincoln, Nebraska..."

"I don't want to hear any more of your complaints, Father. The bishop has ordered it, and you must—"

"No, no. That's just it. I *want* to go."

The monsignor looked over the top of his glasses. "May I ask why the sudden change?"

This was the tough part. "Nudges."

"Excuse me?"

Del thought *nudges* was a better way to state it than *signs*.

Less mystical. Perhaps he'd been wrong. "Signs."

It was the monsignor's turn to raise an eyebrow. "Been dipping into the communion wine, Father?"

Del reddened. "I know it sounds like I'm some fanatic, but over the years I've learned to trust coincidences. Actually, there is no such thing."

"Is that so?"

Del took a breath. "Yes, that's so."

Monsignor Albertson readjusted his ample posterior on his chair. "Tell me about these non-coincidences that are strong enough to change your reluctance to acceptance."

It's now or never.

"First there was the book Father Adrian got me from the library. I felt like reading a little history and had asked for a book about a president—I wasn't particular which one. He got me a book on Abraham Lincoln."

"And this made you automatically think of your move to Lincoln."

"No, no. Not that taken alone." Del fingered the crease of his pants. "Then there were the pennies."

"Aha."

"Over the last few weeks I've found twenty-seven pennies in odd places. A penny has Lincoln's—"

"Face on it. I am aware of that, Father. Of what significance is the 24?"

Del hesitated. "I don't know."

"I find that refreshing. Go on."

"Last night there was a documentary of Lincoln on TV."

"And that clinched it?"

Del squirmed. He'd thought that saying it out loud would make it sound convincing. "Then there was Father Adrian, just a few minutes ago."

"A co-noncoincidence-conspirator."

Del ignored him. "He mentioned a *Lincoln* Town Car."

"Ah."

Del rushed ahead. "He could have mentioned a Cadillac or a Mercedes. But he didn't, he mentioned a—"

"Lincoln."

"Exactly."

Del knew he'd blown it. He couldn't blame Monsignor. It was all too bizarre, too contrived. He felt ridiculous. But there was one more thing...

"Then there are the dreams."

"A must in all attitude adjustments."

Del straightened his spine. *It was almost over. Go for it.* "I've been having the same dream for over a week. It happens just before I wake up. Abraham Lincoln is standing alone singing, 'Gloria' over and over, like some piece by Handel."

Monsignor Albertson put a hand to his mouth to cover his smile. "Now that is definitive proof you should go. However, perhaps God wants you to go to a *Gloria* instead of a *Lincoln?* I believe there is a Glorieta in New Mexico..."

Del dropped his head into his hands. The monsignor was laughing at him. Who could blame him? He looked up. "It sounds foolish now. But it seemed to fit. Speaking of fit, there *are* two other names that keep popping up."

The monsignor teetered a pencil between two fingers. "Oh, do tell. Let's add them to the mix and see what develops."

"The names are Stephen and Oscar. St. Stephens is the name of the Lincoln parish—which seems a confirmation. But Oscar? I don't get that one."

Monsignor dropped the pencil. Then he shuffled through the papers on his desk until he found one. He skimmed through it.

"What?" Del asked.

Monsignor raised a hand to wait. Then he set the paper down and clasped his hands on top of it.

Del blinked. "What?"

"A week ago I received this letter from Monsignor Vibrowsky of St. Stephen's, giving me a few more details about your move, who would pick you up at the airport tomorrow, that sort of thing. Although I knew you were being called there to replace a priest who had passed on, I didn't know his name."

Del put a hand to his mouth. "Oscar?"

"Oscar Nelson."

Del looked to the floor. He sighed deeply and raised his chin. "I guess that clinches it. Ever since the bishop requested my transfer, I've been fighting it. I thought he was mistaken. I felt sure I was supposed to stay at the Brothers of Safe Haven. After visiting Haven, and then being sent here, I thought I'd be here forever."

"Forever is a long time."

"I've been praying for peace of mind, Monsignor."

"Have you received it?"

Del stood and shook the monsignor's hand. "Yes. I think I have."

✦✦✦

Father Adrian called Del to the telephone.

"How was your talk with Monsignor?" the caller asked.

It took Del a moment to recognize the voice of his Haven mentor. "John? Is that you?"

"It's been a long time, Del."

"Haven seems like eons ago."

"Two years ago today."

"Today?" Del thought for a moment. "August first. It's today!"

"Absolutely."

Del remembered John's question. "My talk with Monsignor...how did you know?"

"Think about it, Del."

"You? I mean, *Him.* Then He *is* behind all this?"

"God is behind everything. You know that."

"But why Lincoln? What does He have in mind?"

"God does not reveal His plans to me, and I never question His motives."

"I'm not questioning, John. Not exactly. I'm just wondering."

"I'm sure the distinction is duly noted."

Del leaned against the wall of the rectory living room. He

closed his eyes. "Is this some kind of test?"

"Life is a test."

"Uh-oh."

"Your eloquence is overwhelming."

Del sank into a chair. "Suddenly, I'm scared. What if I flunk?"

"'God is faithful, He will not let you be tested or tempted beyond what you can bear.'"

Del felt humbled. "Will you pray with me, John?"

"Anytime, anyplace."

Del bowed his head. "Lord, I know You have a plan for my life if only I will surrender my will to yours. I surrender right here and now. Sorry it took so long."

"Bravo. And a big amen."

"Will I see you in Lincoln, John?"

"I don't know..." There was a pause on the line. "Del? May I speak to Father Adrian, please?"

Del looked around the living room. "Father Adrian's not—"

Father Adrian stepped out of the shadows of the foyer. "You want to talk to me, Father?"

Del handed him the phone. "It's for you."

Adrian took the phone, unsure. "Hello?" He listened, and nodded a few times before hanging up.

It took some doing, but Del didn't laugh at the stunned look on Adrian's face. "What did he say?"

Adrian had difficulty swallowing. "He said, 'Next time don't hide in the foyer, Father Adrian. Peace be with you.'"

Del slapped Adrian on the back. "Good advice."

"But who? How?"

Del pointed heavenward and let his laugh loose, then left Father Adrian to figure it out on his own.

FIVE

"Therefore, my dear brothers, stand firm and let nothing move you.
Always give yourselves fully to the work of the Lord,
because you know that your labor to the Lord is not in vain."
1 CORINTHIANS 15: 58

KATHY FLIPPED ON the light and went downstairs to her
basement studio. Five-year-old Lisa ran behind her.

"I get to change the calendar!"

"Big whoop."

Kathy looked to the top of the stairs and saw six-year-old
Ryan, standing there, his baseball bat and glove in hand.

"It is a big whoop to her, young man. Come on. I'll drop
you off at practice. Lisa and I are bringing some of my
paintings to Sandra's. We'll pick you up on our way home."

He disappeared from the landing. Lisa was waiting for
her mother to remove the stickpin from the calendar on the
bulletin board. "Okay then. Change the month, sweet cakes."

Lisa flipped the page over. "Oooh, looky, Mommy,
kitties!"

"Very cute, now let's—" Kathy noticed the day's date. It
was August first. The memories flooded back...

Two years ago on this day, Kathy and the children were
in Haven—having their lives transformed. Kathy had
received the strangest, most wonderful invitation, and had
taken one of the biggest chances of her life by packing up the
kids and taking a bus to Nebraska without telling her
husband Lenny. She'd never dreamed he would follow them.
It was in Haven that Lenny died because he was an
egotistical, stubborn man who would not, did not, believe
there was a God. He had been offered the chance for
salvation—both eternal and temporal—as the tornadoes
raged outside the bell tower, but he had clung to his own
sense of power and had run into the storm. To disappear.
Forever. So much had happened in the two years since then.

Kathy picked up a painting of a lake and Lisa pointed to
an unfinished canvas of a child being held in a father's arms.

"I like your kid paintings better."

Kathy was surprised she had an opinion. "Why?"

Lisa shrugged. "'Cuz they're people. They're doing something. Trees and grass just sit there."

Kathy studied the hug painting. The father's face wasn't shown, forcing focus to the child cradled in his arms.

As much as she liked her paintings of children, they just weren't practical because they took too much time. And emotion. Her landscapes were easy. Uninvolved. Kathy didn't have to think to paint them. And they sold.

She left the hugging father where it was and gathered two landscapes to take upstairs.

Suddenly a movement outside drew her attention to the basement window well. A man's face flashed from view.

"Hey!" Kathy pointed.

"What, Mommy?"

"I just saw a face in the window!"

Kathy looked close. "Nobody's there now."

"He ran away when I saw him. "

"Who was it, Mommy?"

Kathy shook her head. "Probably just some teenager."

Hopefully just some teenager.

◆◆◆

As it was summer — and the tourist season — Kathy had a hard time finding a place to park on the winding streets of historic Eureka Springs. She finally pulled in back of Sandra Perkins' shop and double-parked behind Sandra's Camaro.

Free of her seatbelt, Lisa ran past Kathy into the back door of the shop, letting the screen door slam. Kathy followed close behind, carrying her two newest landscapes. The store was due to open in ten minutes.

"Morning, Sandra." Kathy set the paintings against the wall, noting that Lisa had already conned two suckers from Sandra — one for herself and one for her stuffed Bunny Bob.

Sandra came to flip through Kathy's canvases. She let them lie, shaking her head.

Kathy frowned. "Don't you like them?"

Sandra helped Lisa pull a box of toys from behind the counter. She set them in the corner for Lisa to play. Then putting a hand on Kathy's shoulder, Sandra led her toward the front of the shop. She pointed to a wall that displayed three of Kathy's paintings.

Kathy looked from the paintings to her friend. "Are you going to talk to me, or not?"

Sandra waved an arm in front of the paintings.

"You haven't sold them? Is that what you're trying to tell me?"

Sandra put a finger to her nose. She walked back to the counter. "Oh, they'll sell," she said, finally breaking her silence. "A public who will buy paintings on velvet will buy your landscapes."

Kathy felt her mouth fall open. "You're comparing my landscapes to velvet paintings?"

"The emotional output is very similar."

"That's rude."

"Rude or not, I have an odd preference for paintings that mean something."

"But you've sold some of them."

Sandra shook her head. "That doesn't make it art."

Kathy stormed over to Lisa, grabbed her hand, and headed for the back door. "I don't have to stay here—" She put the two newest paintings under her arm. "If you don't like my paintings, then I won't burden you with them."

Sandra put her hands on Kathy's cheeks. She shushed her like she would an angry child. "Now, now, Kathy. Calm down. You're not listening to me."

"I *am* listening. Unfortunately, I heard every word you said."

Sandra removed the paintings from Kathy's arms and set them against the wall. She nodded to Lisa, who went back to the toys in the corner. Kathy stood unencumbered in the back hall, her fists clenched, her breathing heavy.

Sandra held out her hand. Kathy looked at it, then at Sandra's eyes. With a sigh, she let herself be led toward the front of the shop a second time. Sandra stopped in front of Kathy's paintings.

"More criticism?"

"More truth."

Kathy saw three tourists peer into the shop, check their watches, and take up residence outside the front door.

"You've got customers. It's time to open."

"You are more important than customers." Sandra raised a finger to the tourists indicating she'd be with them in a minute. She turned to Kathy. "What I've been trying to tell you subtly—"

"Subtly?" Kathy snickered.

"Subtly," Sandra repeated. "Is that your landscapes are old Joe. As you can see, I've got a dozen other artists who can outpaint you when it comes to autumn trees and bubbling brooks."

"Thanks a lot."

Sandra flashed her a look. "What I need—what I want— from Kathy Kraus, are her paintings of children. The ones that capture the euphoria of a child on a swing, the peace of a child at rest, the intensity of a child mastering the alphabet."

"But those take more time." Kathy shook her head. "They don't come as easily as the landscapes. They take something out of me."

Sandra clapped her hands and raised them to the sky. "Alleluia, praise the Lord, she's finally got it!"

"Got what?"

"What your paintings of children take out of you, they give back to the viewer a thousand-fold. I want paintings created with passion, tears and love. Not the ones whipped up out of boredom and the desperation of an empty checkbook."

One of the tourists tapped on the front door, pointing to his watch. Sandra nodded and dug out her keys. She glanced at Kathy. "You get it girl? You understand what I want from you?"

Kathy stared at her paintings knowing that understanding it was far different from actually doing it.

✦✦✦

The desperation of an empty checkbook...

Kathy sat at the kitchen table staring at her bank balance. Thirty-eight dollars and sixty-four cents. That was it. Usually she and the kids did fine if there weren't any emergencies. But there were always emergencies. The washer, the car, the television...

Since Lenny's body had never been recovered, Kathy had not received the benefits from Lenny's meager $10,000 life insurance policy right away. She'd had to wait a year to collect—a tough year. What Lenny *had* left Kathy were car payments, one month behind in the rent, and a debt of $600 on the layaway of a stereo system. Kathy had sold her clunker vehicle to pay off Lenny's better one. She'd told the store to keep the stereo and spent $19.99 to buy the kids a CD player. She'd paid the back rent with a little help from her parents and had hung on until the insurance finally came through.

After Lenny's death, Kathy had needed a job. Through Mrs. Robb, Kathy's high school counselor, Kathy got a part-time job with A Mother's Love, an organization bent on helping pregnant women make a choice for life. She'd also intensified her "hobby" —as Lenny had always called it—her painting.

Although the reality of juggling finances wasn't easy, Kathy found she could deal with that type of decision. Logical, practical situations could be handled with logical, practical answers. It was the *other* situations Lenny left behind that tested her. Women called, asking for him. They refused to leave their names and hung up as soon as Kathy explained Lenny was dead. No word of condolence. Just the swift click on the line. Yet that hurt was an old hurt and had dulled over the years.

Kathy let out a puff of air. "I need a shot of income, Lord. Sandra won't take my landscapes and the other paintings take so long." She tossed the checkbook on the table as if it were to blame. "Painting is my gift. Don't I have the right to use it *my* way?" She put a hand on her blouse where her mustard seed pin was usually attached. She didn't like the empty space. She hadn't been able to find the pin that morning. Maybe Lisa had borrowed it to play dress-up.

With one last glance at her checkbook, she pushed away from the table. Her first priority had to be survival. If that meant cranking out landscapes, that's what she would do. Sandra's store wasn't the only shop in town that took consignments.

Needing distraction, she picked up the woman's magazine she'd looked at during breakfast. The stories listed on the cover blazed their wisdom: "Lose 10 Pounds in 2 Weeks", "Make 30 Meals for $5.00", "Have a Lovely Love-life" and "How to Keep Doing God's Will."

Kathy blinked. She reread the last teaser. "How to Keep Doing..." Where had that come from? It hadn't been there before. She opened to the Table of Contents and turned to the designated page. The article was short, and was centered in a wide border of kid's faces. Kids smiling, kids laughing, kids crying, kids pouting...Kathy began to read.

How To Keep Doing God's Will
Are you feeling guilty for neglecting God's instructions for your life? Put aside your worries and listen to the Lord.

"Stand firm then, with the belt of truth buckled around your waist." Be open to those who speak the truth.

God understands it's easy to get impatient when things aren't happening as fast or as easy as you'd like. Stop deceiving yourself by thinking *you* can handle things. Don't put your work aside. Finish it.

"For you, O God, tested us, you refined us like silver." You cannot shine without polishing. And polishing takes work. Muscle. Effort. And time. God loves you and He will never leave you alone (you wouldn't want Him to, would you?) So, get back to work. Trust in the Lord and He will provide, even when you're down to your last $38.64. "Open your eyes and look at the fields! They are ripe for harvest."

Kathy's eyes flipped back to the mention of $38.64. Why would the writer choose the exact amount she had in her checking account? Speaking of the writer...

She looked to the top of the page and gasped when she saw the writer's name: Anne Newley. Her Haven mentor. Kathy's eyes sped to the end of the article where there was a short blurb about the author: *"Anne Newley is an art lover. She loves paintings of children created from the heart."*

Kathy laughed. "All right, all right. I'll finish the painting."

SIX

*"Such people are not serving our Lord Christ,
but their own appetites.
By smooth talk and flattery they deceive the minds of naive people."*
ROMANS 16: 18

NATALIE HUMMED AS she parked in front of her apartment late the next morning. She had reason to celebrate. She'd talked with Hayley and was starting work this afternoon at Hayley's Antiques.

She jumped across the hopscotch game on the sidewalk, laughing as she did so. No doubt about it, it was a good day. She took the porch steps two at a time.

"Happy, are we?" The voice startled her, and she jerked toward it. A shirtless man wearing jeans sat on the porch swing, his bare feet propped on the railing, his leg muscles working as he pushed himself forward and back. The lazy smile on his handsome face was decidedly disturbing. Clearly, with his jet black hair and saucy smile he was worthy of a stare, but Natalie restrained herself.

"You cheated on the second hop." He inclined his head toward the hopscotch game. "Your toe went over the line."

"It touched the line." Natalie ran a hand through her hair, trying to regain some dignity. "That's within the International Rules of Hopscotch. I checked."

"You always play by the rules?" His smile deepened.

"Always." Natalie made it as firm as she could, though she knew it was a lie. She fingered the top button of her blouse wishing it were prudently closed instead of stylishly open.

"Why are you happy?"

Natalie moved her purse to the other shoulder. "Sorry, I don't discuss my happiness quotient with strangers."

He got out of the swing, making it gyrate wildly at the loss. Natalie had the absurd notion the swing would have gladly given up its aimless freedom to be under the control of this one particular man.

"Well then, let's not be strangers." He held out his hand. He had the torso of an athlete, with sculpted muscles that were impressive without being overdone. Natalie looked away from the man's physique, wishing he were wearing a shirt.

"Beau Tenebri."

Something about the way he said his name, and the way he held her gaze as he said it, left Natalie feeling ... what? Disturbed? Uneasy?

She shook his hand. His long fingers closed around hers gently and, before she could withdraw it, he lifted her hand to his lips. She blushed and hated herself for the rush of unexpected emotion.

Firmly, she pulled her hand away.

"And you are?" The look in his eyes was almost one of humor. Was he laughing at her?

"Natalie Pasternak." She moved to the front door. The sooner she was away from him, the better.

Beau held open the screen door and they went inside. She headed for the stairs, fishing the apartment key from her purse. Beau followed her to the second floor. Natalie glanced back at him. Why was he following her? She considered — but quickly discounted — retreat, as he had a hand on both sides of the railing, blocking her path back down.

She hesitated outside her door. *Don't let him in.* The urging was as clear as it was strong. Beau moved close and leaned a hand against the wall. A masculine fragrance — sweat and aftershave — drifted close. "So, Natalie Pasternak...no, I don't like that name Natalie. Too stodgy. I'll call you Tally." Natalie opened her mouth to object but he continued. "So, Tally Pasternak, it seems we're neighbors."

She looked at the door across the hall, then at Beau. "You live there?"

"Right below you."

He opened his unlocked door, swinging it wide. Natalie caught a glimpse of a couch and a coffee table. It was impeccably clean. Almost too clean. No pictures on the walls. No magazines on the table.

"Looks like a nice place." And one she planned to avoid.

"You expected hellhole number nine?"

Natalie frowned at the odd comment, then glanced past him again. "No, of course not. It's just, well... a lot of men's apartments aren't very...you know..."

"You've seen a lot of men's apartments?"

Natalie's eyes moved between Beau, his apartment, and the floor. "No...I mean not really...I mean, that's really none of your business."

"I didn't mean to embarrass you." He took a step inside. "Come in. Give me the white glove test."

Unconsciously, Natalie took a step back and found her door in the way. "No. No thanks."

Beau laughed, revealing a delicious dimple in his right cheek. "I'm harmless. Trust me."

"Maybe another time." Natalie discovered the key in her palm. "I have to go. I just got a job and they need me to start this afternoon." She turned to unlock her door, but it didn't budge. It seemed stuck. She yanked on it, then jumped when a hand touched her shoulder.

Beau stood beside her again. He was still smiling. "I'm having a party tonight. Consider yourself invited."

She shook her head. Why couldn't she get the stupid door open? "No thanks. I'm not into parties."

He flicked the hoop of her earring, making it sway. "Come on, Tally. Give me a chance. Maybe we're soul mates."

Soul mates? Natalie looked at Beau in surprise. Wasn't that what she'd prayed for? A soul mate?

His face seemed to imply he knew what she wanted—and he wanted it too.

Natalie swallowed hard, pushing words past the sudden lump in her throat. "We'll see." With that, her door swung open and she all but ran inside, closing it behind her as quickly as she could.

◆◆◆

As soon as Natalie entered Hayley's Antiques, she searched for the familiar face of her boss-to-be, Hayley Spotsman. Instead, a thirtyish woman approached. She was so meticulously groomed she reminded Natalie of Carol Brady, the mother of the infamous Brady Bunch. Although the woman's clothes were prim, there was an incongruity about her. The way she moved, the way her eyes flashed, contradicted her proper facade.

"May I help you?" She flashed a perfect set of teeth behind pink-painted lips.

"I work here—" Natalie backtracked. "I mean I'm *going* to work here. This afternoon's my first time. I just moved here from Colorado."

"The resort janitor. I heard you were coming."

Natalie started, not sure of the woman's implications—or if her tone deserved an answer. "I was looking for Hayley?"

"Really." The woman looked Natalie over, and the lift of her eyebrows declared Natalie guilty of breaking some unspoken standard. "Hayley's helping a customer in booth 32." She flipped her hand toward the left.

Natalie walked off in the general direction of booth 32, and the woman called after her, her voice softer and a tiny bit friendlier. "Miss?" Natalie turned to see her fingering a cross necklace, a light of regret in her eyes. "I should have made you feel more welcome." She gave Natalie an apologetic smile and tilted her head to the side. "I'm sorry if I was rude. Hard day. I'm Gloria Wellington. We'll be working together. And you are?"

Natalie accepted the smile but filed the first impression of her coworker for future reference—there was something very *un*glorious about Gloria.

"Natalie!" Hayley approached with her hand extended. "You're early. Two brownie points for you." Hayley led Natalie behind the counter and showed her how to use the cash register. It only took a few minutes.

"You got it, dear." Hayley brushed her hands together. "Next, you start cruising the aisles. If a customer wants to see in a case, come get the keys. Put them back when you're done. If they're lugging around stuff, offer to hold it at the desk for them. Piece of cake?"

"Angel food."

Hayley laughed. "Go for it, Nat."

Natalie did a double take at the nickname. No one had ever called her that except Fran, her mentor from Haven. Come to think of it, Hayley reminded Natalie of the effervescent Fran.

Maybe that's why Natalie liked her so much.

✦✦✦

As Natalie returned a set of keys to the counter, Gloria held the phone toward her. "It's for you."

"Who knows I'm here?"

"How would I know? But Hayley doesn't approve of personal calls on company time." She said it loud enough for the caller to hear.

Natalie took the phone and held it tentatively to her ear. "Hello?"

"Haydeeho, Natty-Jo."

"Fran!"

"Already on the job. I approve of your work ethic, Nat."

"The need to pay bills is very persuasive." Natalie watched Gloria grab her purse and leave, her shift over. "How did you know I was working here?"

"Word gets around, oh dense one. You know that."

"I know that." Natalie noticed a woman coming toward the counter carrying a hand-painted vase. "I've got to go, Fran. Customers."

"I understand. I just wanted to touch base, and considering you don't have a phone in your apartment yet...you really must get a phone. ASAP. Your cell phone number doesn't work either.

"I know. I let it lapse. No money. I'll get a phone. I promise." Natalie smiled at the customer, wedging the phone between her neck and shoulder as she wrote up the sale. "And you called to tell me...?"

"Ah, yes." Fran's tone of voice made Natalie pause. "I called to tell you—to warn you, actually—about Beau."

Natalie felt a chill run up her arms. "What about him?"

"I don't know exactly."

The chills increased. Fran sounded uncertain. And apprehensive.

"I'm not getting *all* the info on him as yet. But I have a feeling...you need to be careful, Nat. 'Watch and pray so that you will not fall into temptation. The spirit is willing, but the body is weak.' He's gorgeous, he's charming, and he's calling you Tally."

Natalie felt her mouth drop open. She would never get used to Fran knowing things she shouldn't.

She went on. "Actually, I like that name...but he could be trouble. Having Sam as a boyfriend hasn't prepared you for Beau's type of man."

Natalie smiled at the customer as she wrapped the vase in tissue. "And that type is?"

"Worldly. It's not just your physical attraction to Beau I'm concerned about. There's something more."

"It'll be all right. I'm a big girl now."

"But—"

"Got to go, Fran. I'll talk to you later."

She hung up.

✦✦✦

After leaving work, Gloria Wellington didn't drive straight home, even though she knew she should. She found herself in front of Riley's Bar. She pulled in and shut off the engine. Her heart raced.

Gloria made herself look at the photo taped to the dashboard. Her family smiled back at her. Stevie, her husband, held nine-month-old, Tasha. He was laughing as their little girl made a funny face.

"Stop me!" Gloria yelled at the picture. Their condemning smiles did not hold the influence she needed.

When she had first taped the picture there, Stevie had

been touched. "How sweet of you, Glory. Now we can be with you wherever you go."

As usual, he had read something good into her intentions. She swallowed painfully. How long would it be until he finalized realized they were usually anything but? Stevie's glorification of her only increased Gloria's awareness of the contemptible vein of her motives. No matter how many times he complimented her, reminding her of his love—and God's—she found herself straying back to her old ways. Her old thoughts.

The truth was, she had taped the photo of her family on the dashboard to remind herself of their existence, to prevent herself from giving in to her urges. However, this evening their visual presence was futile. The guilt they incited was not enough.

Things were getting worse. Now that Stevie was talking about the two of them becoming missionaries, her need to escape screamed incessantly. When she objected to his plans for their life, he didn't listen. "You'll be fine, Glory. It's what we're being called to do."

If there'd been a call, Gloria had missed it. No amount of Stevie's suggestions to pray about it were going to make her look forward to swarms of needy faces, substandard plumbing, and dealing with people who didn't have the brains to know English.

Didn't Stevie understand she was needy too? Didn't she have the right to control her own life? Did she constantly have to be molded into his concept of what a wife should be?

She caught sight of herself in the rearview mirror. What she saw disgusted her. Not a hair out of place. Subdued makeup. Classic, pearl earrings. Lifeless eyes.

"I'm peaches and cream." *Peaches have pits and cream curdles if it sits out too long.* She looked toward the entrance of the bar. Neon signs winked at her, the muffled pulse of music called to her, a wave of laughter teased her with thoughts of male attention. She knew what she'd find in there: liquor, smoke, and testosterone.

It would make her feel alive.

With one last look at her own reflection, Gloria tousled her hair, destroying its perfection. She bit her lips, forcing red to break through the purity of the pink lipstick. She undid two buttons of her blouse, revealing a glimpse of lace.

Do it.

She got out of the car and went inside. Her gut clenched with fear and excitement as she walked over the threshold. It took a moment for her eyes to adjust to the dim light. As it was only 5:15, the place was far from packed. She watched male eyes scanning her body. The lift of their mouths and the flash in their eyes told her they approved.

She slid onto a barstool. "Martini," she told the bartender, though she had no idea what one tasted like. She'd seen them ordered in movies. She liked the shape of the glass and that little olive floating in the bottom, just waiting to be plucked out and enjoyed.

Just like me...waiting to be plucked out and enjoyed.

A man sidled into the seat next to her. "Hey, sweetheart. Can I buy you a drink?"

Although she was seeking male companionship, Mr. Sweetheart was not what she had in mind. Big gut, stale breath, and a wrinkled shirt. She lifted her drink. "I have a drink, thank you."

He raised a finger to the bartender. "Get the lady another one."

She shook her head. "I said no thank you."

He shimmied close, touching shoulder to shoulder. "Aw, come on. We've got to start the evening right."

"*We* don't have to do anything." She moved to the next stool.

He filled her place. "Don't run from me, sweetheart. I'm a good guy. Good for a little fun, a lot of laughs." He reached across and put his thick fingers on her cross necklace. "Or are you a good girl?" He grinned. "But that can't be. Good girls wouldn't be in a bar by themselves, teasing me with a bit of lace." His finger touched the lace of her camisole. She slapped his hand away.

"Leave me alone!"

"Honey? Is this man bothering you?"

Both Gloria and her unwelcome companion turned to look over her shoulder. A man with rich brown eyes leaned forward and gave her a kiss on the cheek. "Sorry I'm late."

Mr. Sweetheart backed away. "Hey, sorry, man. I didn't mean nothing."

Brown Eyes helped Gloria down from the barstool, picked up her drink, and led her to a booth. "That's okay, buddy," he said. "Nothing wrong with having good taste."

Gloria slid onto the bench and watched in awe as her savior sat across from her.

"Thank you." She took her first sip of the martini, and couldn't help but make a face.

The man laughed. "They look better than they taste."

She pushed the drink aside. "Obviously."

He went to the bar and came back with two beers.

"Thanks." She took the drink, fingering the cold glass. "For this and...that."

"You're welcome for this and... that."

They laughed. She held out her hand. "My name's Gloria." She gasped, and he grinned at her.

"You weren't planning on giving your real name tonight, were you?"

She swallowed. "Why do you say that?"

He leaned across the table and took her hands in his. "Because you came here for a little loving."

"I did not."

"You did. But you're married." He pointed to her ring, then sat back and laughed. "Not, unfortunately to me, no matter what the charmer at the bar thinks."

Leave. Leave now! It's not too late.

With a flip of her hair, Gloria pushed the thought aside. "What's your name?"

"Cash."

She raised an eyebrow. "Cash? As in money?"

He traced a figure eight on the back of her hand. "People always say you can't have too much Cash on hand."

Gloria bet they were right.

✦✦✦

Natalie usually read a chapter of the Bible every morning, but today she'd been so consumed with her new job, that she'd forgotten. Now that it was evening, she sat at the desk in her apartment and reread the page of the Bible a second time. The words were a disjointed jumble of letters. She tossed the bookmark on the floor.

"How can I concentrate with that music blaring!"

She closed her eyes. The beat of the bass pulsed from the apartment below her, a repetitive throbbing that synchronized with the throbbing of a growing headache.

"I can't write, I can't read, I can't sleep."

There was a knock on her door.

"Wrong apartment!" she yelled. "Try the door across the hall."

The knocking resumed. She walked down her private stairs to confront her tormentors. "I told you the party's across the—"

"Hall," Beau finished for her. "How rude of you not to RSVP."

"I'm busy working." She did her best not to notice how well his torso filled his T-shirt.

"What are you working on?"

"How to increase my tolerance level."

"Tolerance or abandonment?"

Natalie did a double-take. "What?"

"Abandonment." Beau smiled. "Let yourself go, Tally. You worked all afternoon, now it's time to party." He moved his hips to the music. "You like to dance, don't you?"

"I love to dance." She said it as if reminding herself, then she shook the thought away. "Get back to your guests, Beau. And your music—if you can call it that."

"You don't like it?"

"I prefer music that has a melody, a harmony, and lyrics that incorporate more than one repetitive sentence." She grimaced. "Lyrics that don't mention body parts or their functions."

"What singers do you like?"

"Adele, Shannon LaBrie, Johnny—"

"Johnny Rotten?"

"Mathis."

"'It's Not for Me to Say' but 'Chances Are' you'll be a romantic until 'The Twelfth of Never' and won't that be 'Wonderful, Wonderful?'" Beau laughed.

"Ooh, a quick mind."

"And a patient heart—even with less than neighborly neighbors."

She sighed. *He's right. I've been nothing but prickly since he met me. The least I can do is go to his party. Besides, what harm can it do?*

She ignored the answer to the question and stepped out into the hallway. Surely she deserved to have some fun?

Beau studied her, a small smile on his face. "Well, I'll have to remember this."

"Remember what?"

"Remember that quoting Johnny Mathis is a secret weapon."

"As if there's a war?"

Beau grinned. "There's always a war. Between men and women, good and evil, Coke and Pepsi."

Natalie smiled and pushed her apprehension away. She let Beau lead her into his apartment. He held the door open, bowing as she entered—

She came to a sudden stop, staring.

There was no one else there.

SEVEN

*"Can a man scoop fire into his lap
without his clothes being burned?
Can a man walk on hot coals without his feet being scorched?"*
PROVERBS 6: 27-28

BEFORE NATALIE COULD react, she heard the door close
behind her. Her nerve endings stood at attention as she
slowly turned to Beau. "Where are all the people?"

His wide-eyed look was all innocence. "What people?"

"The people at your party."

"We're it. A party for two."

"But I heard a party. I—"

"You heard music." He shrugged. "I like my music loud."
He went to turn it off.

Natalie eyed the door. "I'd better go."

"Don't you trust me?"

She hesitated, then opted for honesty. "No."

He laughed. "So Tally's not the kind of girl to be alone in
a strange man's apartment?"

"Something like that." Fran's warning echoed in her
mind: *"You need to be careful, Nat."* She turned toward him
and tried to flash her most scathing look. "Listen, I don't
know what you're after—" She shook her head. "No, strike
that, I've got a pretty good idea. But I'm not interested. I'll be
the first to admit I'm no stranger to sin, but I don't want to..."
She realized she was going to reveal too much if she finished
the sentence: *I don't want to tempt myself.*

"Sin?" Beau's gaze was curious. "Who said anything
about sin? And why did you just admit you're a sinner? Most
people wouldn't think of branding themselves like that."

"It's not a brand. It's a fact."

"Who said?"

Natalie hesitated. She barely knew him. How could she
bring up the G-word? But why not? Maybe it would get rid
of him. "Actually, God told me that."

"He *told* you?"

"In the Bible. You know, the Ten Commandments, Christ and the apostles?"

Natalie was amazed at the sudden red that colored Beau's face. He looked down, biting his lip, and when he looked up, there was no trace of the confidence she'd seen earlier. Only regret.

"Tally, I'm sorry. I know I've been coming on kind of strong. I just—" he shrugged—"I just wanted to impress you. To make you notice me."

He'd certainly done that. "It's okay."

He shook his head, clearly troubled. "No, it's not. I shouldn't have acted the way I did. Especially now that I know you're, well, religious and all."

Something about the way he said *religious* made her uneasy. "I wouldn't say I'm religious, exactly..."

He met her eyes. "Exactly?"

She fidgeted, but he went on before she could reply.

"Anyway, I don't know much about that kind of thing."

"You don't?" He looked so dejected, Natalie was starting to feel bad for him. Maybe she had judged him too hastily.

"Hey, you know what? Maybe you could help me learn more about it?"

Natalie blinked. *He wants to learn about God?*

The red in his cheeks deepened. "Yeah, I mean, if you wouldn't mind. I'd really like to know more. You see, I just moved here, too...last Thursday. I was transferred here. My job...I'm a consultant."

"You moved in the day before yesterday? The day before I moved in?"

He smiled. "I pride myself with good timing." He reached toward her shirt and she took a step back. His hand retreated. "What's that?"

He's asking about my mustard seed pin. This is so perfect.

"It's a mustard seed. It represents my faith. You know, a tiny seed growing into something big and meaningful."

"Kind of like the seed of friendship, right?"

Natalie nodded, took a good look at Beau Tenebri, and felt very, very blessed.

"Let's go up on the roof."

"What?"

"Let's go up on the roof."

"The roof?"

Beau pulled her into his bedroom. He opened the window and straddled the sill. "Come on, Tally. What are you afraid of?"

After a moment's hesitation, Natalie crawled through the window with the assistance of Beau's steadying hand. They walked down a short slope to the roof covering the front porch. Beau brushed a cache of leaves from a valley and offered Natalie a seat. He sat beside her.

She glanced around. "You come out here often?"

"I'm like a cat. I like to look down on things. It gives me a feeling of control."

She studied him a moment. Actually, sitting on his haunches, the muscles in his back advertising his strength, he didn't look like a cat. He looked more like...

"A gargoyle." Her hand flew to her mouth when she realized she'd said it out loud.

He squinted at her. "Excuse me?"

She felt wild color flood her cheeks. "You...you look like a gargoyle."

He arched his brows. "Gargoyles were hideous statues created to frighten off evil spirits. They are not made of flesh and blood."

"Sorry, I didn't mean—"

"You're quite the flatterer."

Natalie changed the subject. "If you like to look down on things, why didn't you take the attic apartment when you moved in?"

Beau's face clouded. "It wasn't available."

"Timing *is* everything." Natalie smiled, remembering the landlady displaying the "For Rent" sign just as Natalie pulled up.

Beau snickered. "If you only knew." He blinked, then shrugged. "Besides, that apartment was meant for you."

Natalie shook her head and looked up at her desk

window just a few feet above the window of Beau's bedroom. "If it was truly meant for me, I would've preferred two bedrooms with a balcony, a dishwasher, and cable TV. I'd use the second bedroom as an office. It would have a new computer instead of an old laptop that has a tendency to go wacko on me, a desk, a chair that rocks..."

"Complainer."

"I'm not complaining." But she knew that's exactly what she was doing. "I was just spinning tales, wishing wishes. If things were perfect."

"You want to be happy. You want to grab what you can, experience life to the fullest, give in to what feels good."

Natalie raised her arms and kowtowed in a mock salute. "Oh, mighty guru, what is the meaning of life? What is the meaning of happiness?"

"Satisfaction."

She stopped her homage, frowning. "Sounds self-centered."

"Of course it is. If I'm not happy, how can I make you happy?"

"Being happy is your main concern?"

Beau shrugged. "What else is there?"

Natalie thought a moment. "Accomplishing something, giving something back—"

"I said I'd give my happiness—"

"Only if you had it yourself."

"Hey, I can't give what I don't possess."

"Sure you can."

"I suppose you're talking self-sacrifice. You'll give me happiness even if you aren't happy?"

Natalie hesitated. She knew what she wanted to say, but she couldn't seem to organize her thoughts enough to say it. Why did being near Beau leave her feeling so confused and muddled? She closed her eyes to get her thoughts straightened. "The mark of a true servant is someone who *gives* without considering what they *get* in return."

"Servant? Who wants to be a servant? I want to be served."

64

"We all do." Natalie sighed. "That's the struggle."

"Why does there have to be a struggle?" Beau tossed a twig off the roof. "Life is ours for the taking, Tally. Grab it, seize it—"

"At what cost?"

"At the cost of our happiness if we don't." Beau stood, stretching. "I suppose you're a do-gooder."

"There's nothing wrong with trying to do the right thing."

"Maybe. But what if doing the right thing for someone else is wrong for you?"

"I don't think that's possible. Doing the right thing is always the right thing to do."

Beau sat down, facing her. "Prove it."

"What?"

"I hereby declare that kissing me is the right thing for you to do."

Natalie stared at him, then shook her head. He was unbelievable. "This entire conversation was staged to get a kiss?"

Beau raised his hands. "I assure you, it was totally unpremeditated." Then he grinned. "However, since the natural progression has led to this moment..." He tapped a finger on his lips.

This had to stop. Natalie signaled a time-out with her hands. "Sorry, Beau. I don't kiss men until I've known them at least twelve hours."

"Ah, well." He sighed. "So be it. But when you hear a knock on your door at 11:32 tonight, you'll know it's me."

She fingered her mustard seed pin. He watched her do it.

"You rub the pin and gain the strength to resist me?"

She forced her hand to her lap. "My resolve not to kiss you has nothing to do with a pin. The pin is a symbol of my faith, not some magic talisman. I was instructed to wear it."

Beau sat, turning his body toward hers. "Who told you to wear it?"

Natalie bit her lip. Back in Haven, each of the disciples had been given a pin with the instruction to wear it—and tell about it. *"This pin is a symbol. Wear it as you go about your daily lives as a testament to your faith. And when others ask you about it, tell them. Tell them the power of God's love for the world. Show them how the world can be changed by a single man doing God's work."* But telling Beau about God's love was so personal. It would be a risk. She didn't want to turn him off. Yet if there was any chance he was truly her soul mate...

"I got it in Haven, Nebraska at a...conference. It was a very special place."

"Was? Isn't it still?"

Natalie bit her lip. "I'm not sure."

Beau's arched eyebrows prompted her to push on. Maybe talking about it would help her understand it. "On my way here, to Lincoln, I stopped to visit Haven."

"And?"

She shrugged. "It wasn't there." She met his cynical look. "It was as if it never existed."

"Maybe it never did. Maybe it was all a figment of your imagination."

"It was real. I stayed there. I met the people, I learned important things."

Beau cocked his head. "Like what?"

Natalie took a deep breath. With the life-giving air came confidence. A renewed force. "I learned that God is all-powerful and all-loving. He cares for us and wants us to continue His work. He's on our side. He wants us to take a stand and make a difference."

"Are you sure that's the truth, Tally?"

"Why wouldn't it be?"

"What can one person do?"

"Well...plenty, I think."

Beau shrugged. "Maybe." He gave her one of his mischievous grins. "But I bet if we worked together, we could do more."

Natalie was disconcerted to find she liked the sound of that arrangement. A lot.

◆◆◆

66

Natalie lay in bed, clutching her pillow. She tossed the sheet off her body. She couldn't sleep. She kept thinking about Beau. The way it felt to have him sitting next to her, the way his lips had been so dangerously close when they had said their final words on the roof.

Although she knew she'd done the right thing, she couldn't deny being disappointed that she hadn't kissed him. Maybe Beau was right. What good was doing the right thing when it made her feel so wretched? She touched her lips wondering what his would feel—

The telephone rang.

Natalie sucked in her breath at the foreign sound. Her head whipped toward the extension she'd brought from home... the extension that wasn't due to be hooked up until Monday.

The phone continued to ring. Natalie tiptoed toward it. She gave it a wide berth, picking up the cord. It dangled in her hand, unattached to the phone jack in the wall.

The ringing was insistent. Natalie swallowed, then lifted the receiver.

"Hello?"

"Natalie Jasmine Pasternak! What *are* you doing?"

"Fran?"

"You bet your sweet angel, it's Fran."

Natalie fingered the lifeless phone cord. "But how...? The phone's not hooked up."

"Neither, apparently, are you."

"What?"

"Nat, Nat, Nat. Where are your brains? Did Haven and all God's attention since then mean nothing to you?"

"Of course not! It means everything to—"

"Then why hasn't God heard from you today? You've let the world control every moment. Situations that should have drawn you closer to Him were handled without giving Him a passing thought."

Natalie wiped a hand over her face. Fran was right. Except for a half-hearted attempt to read the Bible, she hadn't opened her mind to God's instruction even once. "I'm sorry,

Fran. With getting a new job, a new apartment, meeting Beau...I was distracted."

Fran made a squawking sound like a game show buzzer. "Wrong answer! You were concentrating *plenty* hard, fantasizing about a man you barely know."

Natalie was glad Fran wasn't there to see her blush. She struggled to sort through her thoughts. "Fran, I prayed for a soul mate."

"And?"

"And God sent me Beau." Why didn't saying it out loud make the uncertainty go away?

There was a moment's hesitation. "How do you know?"

Natalie shook her head, trying to think. "He's the kind of man I like. He's gorgeous, witty, cute—"

"You already mentioned his looks."

"He's handsome, what can I say?"

"What else?"

"He's funny, he's interested in me..." This was sounding terrible. Shallow. Foolish, even. There had to be more. She had to be drawn to more than just Beau's looks. She thought a moment. "And he wants to know more about God. He wants me to teach him. We can learn together, Fran. He's not like Sam, who didn't want to learn. Beau is open to God."

"Maybe."

"He is. He told me so."

"I have a message for you, Nat. Something that is vital as you start your new life in Lincoln."

"An angel message or a Fran message?"

"They are one and the same, Natty-girl. I've been told to remind you that 'It is better to take refuge in the Lord than to trust in man.' Pray to the Father. Worship Him. And don't be drawn into temptation, no matter how good-looking it is."

It was embarrassing to have Fran know about her attraction to Beau. Yet what was wrong with a *little* temptation? She could handle it.

"I love you, Nat," Fran said. "I'm here to help you. 'Are not all angels ministering spirits sent to serve those who will inherit salvation?'"

Natalie pressed a palm to her forehead. "You're confusing me."

"Let me explain it to you again—"

"No, no...not about praying and you being here to help me. I understand I need to be in constant contact with God. I'm confused about Beau. You speak of temptation, yet I still think he might be an answer to my prayer."

"I don't know what to tell you, Nat. Our Lord has not divulged any additional information about your neighbor."

"Can't you ask Him? Can't you find out what I should do?"

"I could, but so could you."

Natalie shook her head, thoroughly ashamed. Why was it so hard for her to accept that only God had the answers—and *she* had access to Him? "I hope He doesn't give up on me."

"Not a chance." Fran's reassurance was immediate and confident. "'The Lord is gracious and righteous, our God is full of compassion.'"

"Good."

"Double good. Say a prayer, Nat. Then get some sleep."

Natalie did as she was told. But even as she prayed—asking God to show her what was right, what was the truth—she couldn't deny the struggle that went on within her.

Or the fact that she wasn't sure she wanted to know what God thought of her relationship with Beau Tenebri.

EIGHT

"Submit to God and be at peace with him,
in this way prosperity will come to you.
Accept instruction from his mouth
and lay up his words in your heart."
JOB 22: 21

WALTER SAT AT his desk, shaving with his electric razor, a mirror propped against his flip calendar. His intercom buzzed.

"You have a visitor, Mr. Prescott."

"I'm a little busy at the moment, Belinda. See if they can come back later."

There was a moment of silence as Belinda relayed the message. The intercom buzzed again. "He says it's important, Mr. Prescott. He says he'll wait."

Walter rolled his eyes. He hated pushy people even though he was one of the worst. "What's his name?"

The door to Walter's office opened and a balding man wearing a cardigan sweater vest presented himself in the doorway. No one wore such a vest in August except...

"Gabe!"

Walter moved to shake Gabe's hand, then impulsively hugged him.

"Does this mean we're engaged?" Gabe smoothed his vest.

Walter offered his Haven mentor a chair. "Don't you want me to be glad to see you?"

Gabe sat down and adjusted his wire glasses. "Of course I do, Walter. But I'm hurt. In two years, you never made a single effort to contact me."

Walter returned to his seat behind the desk and tossed his shaver in a drawer. "I didn't want to bother —"

"Don't give me that blather. Think of who you're talking to. We both know you were encouraged to ask for assistance. 'Take up the shield of faith'"

Walter drummed a pencil on his thigh. "There's that

70

shield again. You been talking to Bette?"

"A better question might be, have you been listening to Bette? She's a smart woman. You can learn from her."

"Come on, Gabe. Don't give me a hard time."

Gabe shook his head. "No deal. Provoking you gives my existence meaning."

"Now I remember why I didn't call on you."

"Chicken."

Walter opened his mouth to respond, but wisely shut it.

Gabe clapped. "Now *that* – " he pointed to Walter's mouth – "was an act of admirable restraint."

"I do my best."

Gabe turned serious. "We know, Walter."

Walter couldn't meet his mentor's eyes. He stood and walked to the window, sitting on the wide ledge, looking out at the street, three stories below. "You're here to make me move to Minneapolis, aren't you?"

"We don't work that way. You know that."

"No, I don't." Walter could barely get the words out past the tightness in his throat.

"You know free will prevails. 'You are free to eat from any tree in the garden.'"

"Except one."

Gabe shrugged. "Adam and Eve blew it. You don't have to."

Walter snorted. "No pressure there."

"Just the pressure to do the right thing."

"Which is?"

Gabe sat forward in his chair. "You asked for God's guidance last night."

"How did you know?"

Gabe stopped his question with a look. "He gave you an answer."

Walter bolted from the windowsill, needing to walk. *"How* do I know that? I'm just a normal Joe-blow, Gabe, no matter how much I may pretend otherwise. How do I know that the verses I found last night were from Him?"

"Because I'm telling you so."

Walter shook his head. "Why am *I* so privileged? Why am I the only one who gets these special tips?"

Gabe's smile was patient. "You're not."

Walter flipped a hand in the air. "Oh, I know, I know. I'm sure the other people who were invited to Haven experience the same sort of thing but—"

"*Many* people experience special guidance like you have experienced. Some even more remarkable. The trouble is, most don't pay attention to it, or they're too busy to notice. You have no idea how many times God tried to reach you before He finally resorted to sending you the invitation to Haven."

Walter stopped pacing. "Really?"

"Really."

"And I didn't notice?"

"You were quite adamant about staying ignorant."

"I can be good at that."

"We know."

Walter returned to his seat, then pointed a pencil at Gabe. "But not everyone has a mentor to guide them. You, an..."

"Angel?" Gabe laughed. "I'll admit, the world goes through phases when we are 'in' and most of the time it cheapens our position, but that doesn't diminish the fact that we do exist."

"But not everyone has an angel sitting in his office."

Gabe shrugged. "More than you know, Walter."

"But most angels aren't bald and decked out in sweater vests." He paused. "Are they?"

"Angels can appear in whatever form is necessary to do God's work."

"But of all the ways you could have looked, why did you choose to be so..."

"Handsome?"

Walter restrained a grin. "That wasn't the adjective I was searching for."

"I did not do the choosing, Walter. Our Lord did. He wants you to be comfortable with me. Balding pates and sweater vests make you comfortable."

"They do?"

"Don't they?"

Walter thought a moment. "I guess they do. You remind me of my father."

"Whom you love very much."

"Yeah."

"Therefore, my appearance is appropriate."

Walter nodded slowly. "You'll do."

"He is so glad you approve."

"Hey," Walter said, glancing upward. "I didn't mean any disrespect. I was just curious, you know?"

"We—"

"—know," Walter said with him.

They laughed.

"So, what's it going to be? Are you going to move to Minneapolis?"

Walter rocked in his chair. "What's going to happen to me there?"

"God's will."

"Oh, *that's* specific."

"It's all you're going to get."

"But if I stay here...no lightning is going to strike me down, is it? God's not going to send a tornado to wipe me out, is He?"

"Our God is an awesome God—and a forgiving God. I hardly think He's as vindictive as your question implies."

Walter fixed him with a grim stare. "I don't know about that. I was in Haven, remember? I saw the four tornadoes—"

"But you survived unscathed."

"Physically."

"Ah, come on, Walter."

He tossed the pencil on the desk. "Oh, all right. Mentally, too."

"You and the others made some important decisions in that tower." Gabe's look was steady.

"Decisions I have fulfilled. I've given the news department at KZTV integrity. Have you seen one sensationalized story since I turned things around? Have you seen one uplifting story passed over to pounce on something juicy?"

"You've done great. We're all proud of you."

"Exactly." He leaned forward. "Now, why can't I do what I want?"

Gabe closed his eyes as if in prayer. Walter didn't like the idea of Gabe and God communicating right there in front of him, but he didn't say anything else until Gabe looked at him.

"Well?" Walter tapped his fingers on the desk. "What did He say?"

Gabe smiled. "Remember your commitment made in the tower?"

"I remember."

Gabe held up a finger and cleared his throat. "This is a quote. From you. From that day two years ago: 'I'm a newsman. I know TV. I dedicate my expertise to God. I have no idea how He wants to use it. I'll leave that up to Him.'"

"I said that?"

"You said that."

Walter thought a moment. "Haven't I done what I said I'd do?"

"I don't recall there being a time limit on your dedication."

Walter swallowed hard. "An oversight on my part."

Gabe slapped his hands on the armrests of his chair. "You are the most arrogant—" He took a deep breath, getting himself under control. He stood and walked to the door of the office, then turned to face Walter. "I have three questions for you. Number one, who gave you your expertise in the first place?" Gabe paused, but held up a hand when Walter started to answer. "Number two, since you are so quick to put a time limit on your work for God, should He put a time limit on his work for you? And number three, you were glad to see me, Walter. But which are you more excited about? Getting to see an angel or hearing the message I bring from the Father? Don't celebrate the messenger and ignore the message."

74

Gabe opened the door, then hesitated, offering one final word. "You missed a spot, Walter." He pointed toward Walter's cheek.

Then he left.

As the door clicked shut, Walter raised a hand to feel the traitorous stubble...and wondered what else he'd missed.

◆◆◆

Since Walter had avoided doing any KZTV work the entire morning after Gabe's visit, he decided to at least appear diligent in the afternoon. He took up residence behind his computer. Before he looked over the news stories for the evening edition, he checked his email.

A message flashed before him. It had no sender's name, and no subject listed. Just two letters:

Go.

Walter looked behind his back, half expecting to see Gabe standing in the doorway, admiring this newest bit of handiwork.

"Real cute, Gabe. You don't give up, do you?" Walter deleted the message and went on to the next one. When it came on the screen, Walter shivered.

Have faith.

It wasn't Gabe who was messing with his computer, it was...

Walter grabbed the computer monitor and leaned his head against it. He clamped his eyes shut. *I want to have faith, Lord. I want to...*

Walter's soul cried out, a jumble of emotions and thoughts. Finally, he whispered a fact he couldn't deny. "But I don't want to go."

Have faith.

"I'm afraid of change."

Have faith.

"What if it doesn't work out?"

Have faith.

"What if I'm not good enough? What if I can't do what

You want me to do?"

Go.

Walter sat up and stared at the words. They seemed to throb with his pulse.

He swallowed, drew a deep breath, and then nodded. "Okay. I'll go."

◆◆◆

Walter burst into his apartment and tossed his briefcase over the back of the couch. "Bette? You'd never believe what hap—"

He turned the corner to the dining room and saw Bette lighting candles above an elegantly set table. "What's going on?"

She shook the match, extinguishing the flame. "A celebration." She kissed his cheek.

Walter put a hand on her protruding tummy. "We're still parents-in-waiting. So what's the party for?" He turned his nose toward the kitchen, then grinned at her. "Do I smell lasagna?"

Bette nodded, straightening a fork on the table. "Lasagna, Caesar salad, garlic bread, and tiramisu for dessert."

His mouth watered "When did you do all this? Did the bank let you go home early?"

"No one can resist the begging of a pregnant woman." She held out a chair for him.

He sat. "And why did you beg?"

She looked at him as though he were crazy. "Because of the emails you sent me."

"Emails?"

"Don't tease me, Walter." She ducked into the kitchen and brought out the salad. She filled their bowls. "Cracked pepper?" She held the pepper mill above his salad.

Walter didn't reply. He stared at the flickering candles.

"Pepper, honey?"

Walter looked up at her. "What did the messages say?"

Bette took a seat. "Walter, the gig is up. I loved them."

He shook his head. "What did the messages say?"

Bette looked confused. "You know very well what they said. The first one said, 'Go', and the second one said, 'Have faith.'" Bette ground some pepper onto her own salad. "I especially liked that last one, Walter. I do have faith. In you—and God."

"I didn't send them, Bette."

She withdrew her hand. "Sure you did. I mean who else...?" She studied his face. "I just assumed they were from you."

"Nope."

"But if you didn't, who did?"

Walter pointed upward.

Bette's eyes widened. She leaned over the table and whispered, "God?"

Walter nodded.

"How do you know?"

"You don't have to whisper, Bette. God has very good ears."

She reddened and stabbed her lettuce. "I know that." She chewed furiously. "So are you going to answer my question or not?"

"In a minute. But first...I saw a friend today."

"Counting or not counting God?"

"You really shouldn't be so sarcastic, dear."

Bette waved her fork in the air. "Please forgive me if I find it hard to believe that God spoke to me with an email. Things like this happen to *you*, Walter, not me. You're the one who went to Haven. You're used to this sort of thing, I'm not. So forgive me if I find it hard to believe that—"

"I saw Gabe Thompson today."

Bette took another bite of salad. "The angel."

"Right."

She considered this a moment. "I think I won, Walter. My message from God outweighs your angel. Now if it were two angels—"

"I got a message from God on my email too."

Bette got up and started toward the kitchen. "You're just

saying that to one-up me."

"No, Bette." He followed her into the kitchen, watching as she took the lasagna out of the oven. "It's true." He told her about Gabe's visit. "In the afternoon I saw the same messages you had on your email, on my email."

Bette stopped cutting the lasagna. "You did?"

Walter raised a hand. "Cross my heart."

She leaned against the counter. "When I saw the messages I thought you were telling me to go to Minneapolis, to have faith..."

"*God* was telling you. Me. Us."

She grabbed a handful of shirt and pulled Walter as close as Baby allowed. "So, are we going?"

Walter nodded.

She kissed him.

✦✦✦

Walter tapped on the doorframe of his father's room at the Hillcrest Retirement Village. He did not receive a reply but entered anyway. His father's back was to him as he watched a baseball game on TV.

"That pitcher hit him on purpose!" Jeb Prescott pointed his cigar at the TV. "What's a batter got to do? Carry a shield?"

There's that word again! Walter almost said something but knew better than to interrupt his father's baseball. He sat down to wait.

"Can you believe that?" Jeb asked Walter after the batter took his base. "Look at him limp. That pitcher's mean."

"Not everyone who plays against the Cardinals is mean, Pop."

"That's your opinion." Jeb chewed on his cigar a moment, took it out and held it toward his son. "Want one?"

"No thanks. I'm surprised they allow you to smoke that stinky thing in here."

"Bet if it was a cigarette you'd be wrestling me for it."

Walter looked away. He still struggled with his desire for

cigarettes, but since God had made the shadow on his lung disappear in the months after Haven, he'd vowed to do his part to stay healthy. So far, so good.

Apparently Jeb took Walter's silence as a yes. "Ha! I'm right about the cigarettes, aren't I?" He shook his head. "Once a smoker always a smoker."

Once a pain in the neck, always a pain – "Pop, I'm here to tell you—"

"Quiet! The bases are loaded. We need a miracle...or at least a new pitcher."

Walter watched the game until the runner batted in two runs. There was a commercial.

"Stupid commercials." Jeb muted the sound. "Breaks the momentum of the game."

"Baseball doesn't *have* momentum. It's the slowest moving, most boring—"

Walter nearly got a cigar in the eye. "Don't you ever talk about baseball that way! It's America. It's the foundation of life. And to think I could have been up there with them. I could have been one of the greats, if only—"

Walter had heard it all before. He had to interrupt or his visit would be swallowed up with detailed accounts of Jeb Prescott's doomed try for baseball fame. "Pop, Bette and I are moving to Minneapolis."

"If it weren't for my shoulder going out—"

"Pop? Did you hear me?"

His father blew a smoke ring into the air. "When you going?"

"Soon." Walter was relieved—and rather surprised—his father had heard.

The game came back on, but Jeb left the sound off. "Does this have something to do with that pin you wear?" He pointed his cigar at Walter's mustard seed pin.

Walter shrugged, then nodded. "I think so."

His father raised his eyebrows. "*Think* so? Thinking is a good trait, boy. You'd better make sure you do plenty of it before moving anywhere."

"I have thought about it, Pop. Both Bette and I think it's

79

the right thing to do."

"Going to have my grandchild up north, are you?"

Walter looked to the floor. "Why don't you come with us? We'll find a nice place for you. Or you could move in with us."

Jeb studied the tip of his cigar. "Never did like the Twins. Or those Vikings neither."

"You can still follow St. Louis. On the TV, just like you do now."

Jeb shook his head. "Wouldn't be the same. I'd be a foreigner up there."

"It's Minnesota, Pop, not Mongolia."

"Same thing. It's not home."

"We could make it home."

"Not for me."

"But, Pop—"

Jeb Prescott turned to face Walter for the first time. He looked him straight in the eye. "Is God telling you to do this? Is this part of that Haven-faith thing?"

"Yes, Pop. I don't know exactly what's expected of me, but I—"

Jeb placed a hand on Walter's knee. "What's expected of you is to follow the feelings in your innards. Whether it's God talking or your own guts, I'm too old to figure. All I know is you've got to listen to the voices in your life. Some come from out here—" he waved his cigar in the air—"and some come from in here." He pointed toward his heart.

Walter felt tears coming, but forced them away. It wouldn't be right to cry in front of his father.

Jeb's voice softened. "Don't worry about me, son. I've listened to my own voices these eighty-one years. Listened to a few I shouldn't have, too, but that's all part of the game. If a man don't listen, it's like making a run by walking the bases. The score may be the same but the satisfaction's missing. Steal a few bases, Walter. Even strike out a few times. But don't just sit there letting the balls whiz by."

Walter nodded, his head down. The sounds of the baseball game returned.

"Gosh darn it! The Cards got two outs while you and me were yapping. We missed it."

Walter stood and kissed his father on the head. "I won't miss it again, Pop. I promise."

Although his face did not turn toward the door, Jeb raised a hand as Walter turned to leave. "You keep me informed about my grandchild, you hear? I've got a lot to teach him or her about baseball."

"I know, Pop," Walter said. "I know." He stood quietly, watching his father, then fumbled with his shirt. He looked at the object in his hand, set it on his father's bed, and left.

Jeb Prescott waited until his son's footsteps had faded away before he looked at the bed. His throat tightened and he sat silent until the tears passed.

Then he picked up Walter's mustard seed pin and proudly pinned it to his shirt.

NINE

*"Therefore, my brothers,
be all the more eager to make your calling and election sure.
For if you do these things, you will never fall."*
2 PETER 1: 10

A FATHER CASPIAN picked up Del at the Lincoln airport. As they cruised down 9th Street, Del noted with satisfaction — and a bit of awe — that he sat in a Lincoln Town Car. Navy blue, with leather interior and a great sound system. The exact car Father Adrian had mentioned a few days earlier.

"God certainly knows how to make me feel welcome." Del smiled at Father Caspian. "I was hoping for a car like this a few days ago. You might say I requested it."

"Requested? As in, God arranged it?"

Del waved the idea away, sorry he'd brought it up. "This is a nice car."

Father Caspian nodded. "The parishioners are generous. The car was donated."

Del ran a hand across the supple leather, enjoying its feel while contemplating the financial inequities of the parishes he'd come to and the one he'd just left.

St. Stephen's, his new parish, was a newer structure on the south side of town. It graced the curve of a boulevard that sported a median populated with neatly trimmed grass, floral plantings, and trees. The homes surrounding the church were old money, their vine-covered walls, leaded windows, and multiple chimneys displaying an elegance that had accompanied a more genteel age.

Father Caspian pulled in front of the one-story rectory. He popped the trunk and retrieved Del's suitcase. "I'll show you to Monsignor Vibrowsky's office. He's anxious to meet you."

Monsignor Vibrowsky was a head taller than Del, and skinnier, making him, in the term of Del's grandfather, a "tall, slim drink of water." His large hand engulfed Del's smaller one. His eyes narrowed as he studied Del—and Del had the absurd image of a vulture sizing up his prey. The Monsignor's eyes seemed to take special note of Del's ponytail.

With a wave of his hand, the monsignor sent Father Caspian away, then motioned for Del to be seated in front of his walnut desk. "So," he finally said, "you're him."

The slight sneer in Monsignor's voice pushed Del to the offensive. "I'm him."

"You don't look like much."

"Don't say that in front of my mother."

"You don't look especially—" the monsignor waved a hand, apparently searching for the right word—"holy."

"Perhaps because I'm not."

"Perhaps your humility proves you *are* holy."

"Perhaps my humility proves I'm realistic." *Lord, what is this man's problem?* Del looked around the room, desperate for some common ground. He pointed to a decorative sword hanging on the wall behind the desk. "A beautiful sword, Monsignor. A mighty 'sword of the Spirit.'"

The monsignor looked at him blankly.

Scratch the flattery.

The monsignor drew in a deep breath behind tented fingers. "I hear you're one of the Haven disciples and a witness to many signs."

Del noted there was no admiration in his voice. "That's me."

"Come to Lincoln to enlighten us."

"Do you need enlightening?"

Monsignor's finger-tent collapsed. "Do I spot a chip on the father's shoulder?"

Del rubbed a hand across his forehead. This meeting was on the wrong track. "Forgive me, Monsignor. People have a tendency to make too much of Haven. As for the signs, it's obvious Monsignor Albertson has filled you in."

"Indeed."

Del leaned forward in his chair. He pushed aside a desk calendar, leaving no obstacles between the two of them. "I don't know why I'm here. I'm not privy to the details of God's plans, but since it feels right, and since the bishop has arranged it, I must leave myself open to do God's—"

The office door burst open. A woman with a blonde pageboy rushed in. She glanced at the monsignor, saw Del, then stopped short.

"I'm so sorry, Monsig—"

"No, no. Mrs. Wellington." The monsignor's voice betrayed a rude weariness. "Come in and meet Father Delatondo."

The woman came closer, and Del had the distinct impression of a subtle mask falling into place. There was no time for analysis, only time for Del to recognize that a change had occurred. She looked at her watch, her movements abrupt, jerky. "I'm so sorry for interrupting your meeting but I really needed to talk to someone and—"

"Having *more* problems?"

She hesitated. "No...no. It's nothing."

Del noticed a deep sadness behind the woman's eyes. He held out a hand. "Father Antonio Delatondo, Mrs. Wellington."

She shook his hand, then fingered her cross necklace. "Nice to meet you, Father. But you can call me Gloria."

Del sucked in a breath as he remembered his dream.

She looked puzzled. "Is there something wrong?"

"No, no," Del said. "Nice to meet you...Gloria."

Once settled into his sleeping quarters, Del sat on the edge of the bed. He stared at the crucifix hanging over the desk.

"I'm here, Lord. I'm here in *Lincoln*, at St. *Stephen's*, replacing *Oscar*, and now I've met a *Gloria.*"

He sat in silence a moment, then started as Monsignor Albertson's mocking voice echoed in his mind: *"Perhaps God wants you to go to a Gloria?"*

Could it be...? He pressed his hands together to stop their trembling.

Was Gloria Wellington the reason he was here?

TEN

*"For it is God who works in you to will
and to act according to his good purpose."*
PHILIPPIANS 2: 13

JULIA TOOK EDWARD'S arm as they entered the tunnel connecting the airplane with the Minneapolis airport. "It's so good to be home."

Edward grinned at her. "You didn't like the glamour of the convention? The tasteful hats, the serene music, the quiet conversation?"

"I'll take my totally tasteless fishing hat, the music of the lake lapping against the boat, and some quiet talk with a Northern Pike."

"You catch him, I'll clean him."

"And eat him."

"It's what I do best."

She squeezed his arm. "No, it isn't."

"Julia! Wait!" The heavy footsteps of her campaign manager thundered in the tunnel behind them.

Edward leaned close to Julia's ear. "He's ba-ack..."

She grimaced. "I'm afraid he never went away."

Ben caught up with them as they entered the terminal, his cell phone at his ear. "Julia, I've scheduled a meeting tomorrow morning to fine-tune the strategy before we leave for our next round of campaign stops."

"The rest of today and tomorrow are booked, Benjamin. After that, I'm yours."

"Booked with what?" He slipped the phone in his shirt pocket.

"With me," Edward said.

As they walked toward the exit, Julia's entourage straggled behind her. Heads turned, fingers pointed and an occasional "Hey, Julia!" sprang from the crowded terminal as people recognized her.

One "Hey, Julia!" sounded familiar. Julia turned her head

toward the gruff voice. She stopped, causing her followers to stumble around her.

"Walter!" Julia dropped Edward's arm and walked toward him. "Walter Prescott!"

✦✦✦

Walter set his suitcase on the floor and held out his arms for Julia. They hugged, neither one caring they were in the middle of the terminal and people were staring.

They pulled apart and looked at each other. Julia put a hand on his arm. "What are you doing here?"

"I'm here to accept a new job and look around."

"Welcome to the Land of Ten Thousand Lakes." Julia shook her head as she studied him. "It's been two years and you're exactly the same as you were back in Haven."

He grinned. "I'm not sure that's a compliment, but I could say the same about you. Trying to run the country just like you ran Haven."

"I did *not* run Haven," Julia said, but Walter could see she was only pretending to be insulted. "If you remember correctly, I was indisposed most of the time."

"Always making excuses. Just because you were kidnapped don't tell me you didn't try to influence —"

"Ahem."

Julia turned toward the distinguished-looking man standing beside them, and Walter recognized him from the campaign. Julia's husband.

"Edward, this is Walter Prescott, one of the Haven disciples."

Walter held out his hand. "I'm the annoying one."

"Ah." Edward nodded. "Your reputation precedes you."

They laughed, and Walter drew Bette into the conversation. "This is my wife Bette. Bette, this is Julia Carson — the next president of the United States — and her husband, Edward."

"The next First Lady," Edward said. He put a hand to his cheek. "I'm absolutely giddy about choosing a new china pattern."

Julia touched his arm. "I'll help you if you'll help me, dear."

Bette shook their hands vigorously. "You've got our votes, Mrs. Carson."

Julia pointed at Bette's ample belly. "Yours and the baby's or yours and Walter's?"

Walter put a tender hand on Bette's midsection. "And you said I hadn't changed? I've gotten married and Baby is due any time now."

"Congratulations. I didn't think you had it in you, Walter." She laughed at her inadvertent joke. "Marriage, I mean. Commitment."

"Yeah, well—" Walter shrugged. "Four tornadoes, a few miracles, and Divine intervention does that to a person."

"*Love* does that to a person," Bette said.

"Here, here, Bette," Julia said.

Bette sucked in her breath. She placed a hand on her stomach.

It took the rest of them a moment to understand the implications of her actions.

Julia touched Bette's shoulder. "The baby?"

Bette took a few breaths then nodded.

Walter stood there, shaking his head. "Uh-uh. No way. We're in Minneapolis. We have everything set in St. Louis. You're pre-registered at the hospital. It was all—"

"Walter!" Julia glared at him. "Quit your yammering and help your wife. Edward, get a wheelchair. Let's get to our car. We'll call the hospital from there." She turned to Bette. "How many contractions have you had?"

"Twelve."

"Twelve?" Walter's face turned white. "When did you have *twelve?*"

"I've been having them all day." Bette rubbed her stomach. "But they weren't bad until this one."

Julia patted her hand. "It's your first baby. It should take hours and hours."

Or not.

ELEVEN

*"But from everlasting to everlasting
the Lord's love is with those who fear him,
and his righteousness with their children's children —
with those who keep his covenant
and remember to obey his precepts."*
PSALM 103: 17-18

"Ahhhhh!"

Bette gripped Walter's hand as hard as she could, hoping the pain would somehow flow out her fingers and be gone. It didn't work.

"Oh, honey, I'm so sorry," he said. "I wish there was something I could do to help."

His words meant little. At this moment, her husband was not a part of her world. He floated somewhere just outside. She was alone — except for the pain. The pain grabbed hold and arched her back, stretching, twisting, fighting against her. She yelled to whoever would listen. "Get the doctor!"

"I'll get him! I'll be right back."

Get who? Be back from where? Bette clamped her eyes shut. Then unexpectedly, she found herself able to take a breath. The pain receded, like a tide going out. *But the waves are building. They'll come again. And again.*

Bette heard the door open, heard the canned music from the hallway drifting into her calm before the storm. When someone held her hand, she didn't care who it was. The tide was out, and she wasn't going to let anyone interrupt this moment of peace.

"'We consider blessed, those who have persevered.'"

Bette opened her eyes and saw a woman wearing a blue nurse's uniform. Her hair was short and curly, her eyes sea-green. Her nametag read "Adelaide".

"It hurts…" Bette moaned. "The baby…"

"'The eyes of the Lord are on the righteous and his ears are attentive to their cry.'"

Bette blinked twice, trying to get the woman into focus.

She was dressed like a nurse...Bette felt the tide shifting. *Oh, no! Not the waves! Can't I have a few more moments of—?*

A contraction slammed into her from the inside out. Tossed her. Pulled her under. She grabbed Adelaide's hand. *Save me! I'm drowning!* Bette felt a hand on her belly. The baby calmed, the pain eased.

Bette looked at her lifesaver. "It's too soon." She gasped for breath. "Four more weeks. Is the baby okay?"

"'The Lord watches over you—the Lord is your shade at your right hand, the sun will not harm you by day, nor the moon by night. The Lord will keep you from all harm—He will watch over your life, the Lord will watch over your coming and going both now and forevermore.'"

"Who...who are you?"

The woman smiled and cradled Bette's cheek in her cool hand. "'Her children will be mighty in the land, the generation of the upright will be blessed.'"

There was the rattle of a cart in the hall. The nurse looked toward the door, then squeezed Bette's hand. "'Give thanks to the Lord, for He is good, His love endures forever.'" She let go and left the room. Bette reached after her.

"But who—?"

A moment later Walter rushed in the door. "The doctor's coming."

Bette didn't have time to tell Walter about her strange visitor, as the tide came in for the final time.

❖❖❖

"Julia? What are you doing at a hospital?" Ben's voice over the phone was less than happy.

Julia poured herself another cup of coffee in the waiting room. "Walter and Bette are having their baby."

"Who are Walter and Bette?"

"The couple I ran into at the airport. Friends. The pregnant lady and her husband? The ones who got a ride in our limo?" Was his attention span *that* short?

"Yes, yes, I get it. It made great press you offering them a ride in an emergency. But why are *you* still at the hospital?"

She took a sip of coffee, not caring if he heard her slurp. "Because Bette went into labor in my presence. Because they don't know anyone in Minneapolis. Because I can't think of any place I'd rather be." Julia sank into a chair and looked at her watch. "It's eleven-thirty at night, Benjamin. Why are you calling me, no matter where I am?"

"We have a problem."

"Can't it wait? Can't I have a night off to witness something good in this world?"

"Paula quit."

Julia sat at attention. Paula was her speech writer. Why would she quit?

"Paula didn't appreciate you leaving out her closing statements during your acceptance speech at the convention. She says she spent long hours on those remarks and to have you wing it like you did—"

"I have a right to wing it. I have a right to scrap every single word she writes." Julia knew she sounded egotistical but at the moment she didn't care. She placed the coffee in a waste basket. "She quit in the middle of the night?"

"She called me at nine-thirty. I've been trying to track you down ever since. Your answering service knew you were at a hospital but they didn't know which one and you didn't leave the name of your friends. Was your cell phone turned on?"

"Thankfully, not—at least for a few blessed minutes." She sighed. "But obviously it is now. You found me. Goody."

"Julia, you have to do something."

She looked up when Walter appeared in the waiting room still wearing his paper slippers and hat from the delivery room.

"Got to go, Benjamin. Tell Paula I'll call her tomorrow. I've got a birth to celebrate." She hung up.

"He's grinning like a banshee," Edward said. "That must be good."

"It's *very* good." Walter took a deep breath. "It's a girl!"

Hugs and handshakes were exchanged. Mother and baby

were doing fine, though Baby was in an incubator for her lungs' sake. She weighed in at 6 pounds, 5 ounces.

Walter motioned toward the hall. "Bette's going to be conking out soon, but she wanted to see you before she did."

He led them to Bette's room. She was resting but perked up when she saw she had company. Julia gave her a hug.

"A girl." Julia shook her head in wonder.

"Adelaide," Bette said.

Walter did a double-take. "I thought we were going to name her Margaret."

Bette extended a hand to him. "Something happened during labor that changed all that. That's why I wanted to see Julia and Edward tonight. I knew they'd understand."

Walter took off his hat and booties. "I'll tell you what happened, you had a baby."

"Before that."

"Where was I?" Walter looked utterly confused.

Bette shook her head. "It happened while you were getting the doctor." She looked at each face and took a deep breath. "I was visited by an angel."

Walter plopped into a chair, clearly exhausted. "Gabe wasn't here, was he?"

"It was a woman."

"Was she in her fifties with unruly black hair?" Julia wouldn't have been surprised to find her Haven mentor, Louise, had stopped in just when she was needed.

"No, no." Bette closed her eyes in exasperation. "Please let me tell you what happened." She waited until they were still. "I was alone and in pain…I was worried about the baby's health since she was coming early." She looked at Walter. "As soon as you left a woman came in. She was dressed like a nurse and wearing a nametag that said *Adelaide*. She had the most comforting touch. At one point she put her hand on my stomach, and the baby calmed."

A shiver ran up Julia's spine. "What did she say?"

"She spoke in Bible verses. Even when I asked her questions, she responded by repeating some wonderful verses about God's love, His comfort, His watching over me and the baby. Because of her words, I knew we would be all right."

"So she was a nurse who knew the Bible," Walter said. "What makes you think she was an angel?"

Bette crossed her arms defiantly. "I just know."

"If you're going to tout that women's intuition stuff," Edward said, "I'll believe you. Julia has proved its existence a hundred times."

Bette shook her head. "It's not that. I feel it here." She put a hand to her heart.

Julia moved toward the door. "I know a way to solve this. I'll go to the nurse's station and ask for Adele."

"Adelaide," Bette said. "Short, curly, brown hair. Pretty green eyes."

"I'll be right back."

◆◆◆

Walter saw Julia standing in the doorway. He rose. "Well?"

Julia straightened her back, looking like a child giving a recitation. "There is no nurse named Adelaide in this hospital."

"Maybe she went home already." That had to be the answer. The alternative was too bizarre.

Julia shook her head. "There has never been a nurse named Adelaide working at this hospital."

"Maybe Bette got the name wrong."

With a groan, Bette raised herself to sitting. "Stop it, Walter! Stop trying to dissect what happened to me. I believed you when you came back from Haven. Now it's your turn to believe me."

"She's got you there," Edward said.

Walter felt terrible. After all Bette had been through tonight, the least he could do was refrain from being such a *nudzh*. Walter helped her lie back down, adjusting her pillows. He kissed her forehead. "I believe you, honey. I apologize for doubting you."

She nodded, stifling a yawn. "Adelaide Margaret

Prescott."

Walter pulled a chair close and sat by her bed. Julia put a finger to her lips and nodded. She nudged Edward. They tiptoed out.

Walter took Bette's hand in his own. "Sleep, hon. Sleep knowing you have an angel watching over you."

She nodded and closed her eyes. "An angel…and you."

✦✦✦

"It's a girl, Pop."

"A grand slam for you, Walter boy!"

Walter ran a hand over his face as he sat at the side of the bed in their hotel room. He wasn't fully awake, but he'd promised himself he'd call his dad first thing in the morning.

"The baby wasn't due yet, was it?"

Walter shook his head before he realized his father couldn't see him. "She's a few weeks early. But she's doing okay, and Bette's fine."

"You certainly got a good start to your new life in Minneapolis."

Walter picked up a pen to doodle with when he saw something sitting by the clock. He stared at the object. Blinked. Stared again.

It was a mustard seed pin.

"Hey, boy? You still there?"

Walter turned the pin over in his hands. "Pop? Did you find the gift I left you?"

"You mean the pin?"

"Yeah."

"That was awful nice of you, son. I know how much it meant to you, coming from Haven and all."

"So you still have it?"

"Course I still have it. You think I'd give it away to someone else?"

"No, no. I didn't mean that."

"What you talking about then? Of course I still have it. It's sitting on my shirt right now. I was just fixing to go down

93

for breakfast when you called."

Walter palmed the pin, feeling stronger. "I'll let you go eat, Pop. Just wanted you to know about Adelaide."

"I'm a mighty proud grandpa."

Walter hung up. He shook the pin in his fist like a gambler hoping for a lucky throw. "Thanks for the pin, God. I'll try not to let You down."

◆◆◆

Julia tapped a finger on the nursery window, knowing it was ridiculous to think that Adelaide, who was less than a day old, would respond.

"She's so beautiful," Julia said to Edward.

"Does she make you think of Bonnie?"

"Hmm." Julia's smile faded.

"And Joey, too?"

Julia nodded, the memory painful even though thirty-five years had passed. "I was so young. So stupid."

"So single. You hadn't met me yet. I wasn't there to sweep you away to marital oblivion."

"If only I knew then what I know now." The familiar pain nudged her again. "I would have had him. I would have kept him or given him up for adoption. Anything but what I did."

Edward put a hand around her shoulders and drew her close. "God forgives you, Julia. One of these days you need to forgive yourself."

Julia's and Edward's heads touched in a moment of shared communion.

Lord, what would I do without this man? Tears pricked her eyes. *What would I do without You?*

◆◆◆

Benjamin Cranois stood in the hospital hall, staring at Julia and Edward. They had no idea he was there...no clue he'd heard their conversation.

So, the righteous Julia had had an abortion. *Now that,* he thought as he turned and silently walked away, *is very interesting.*

✦✦✦

Julia and Edward headed toward Bette's room. Julia stopped short when a middle-aged woman with unruly black hair turned the corner in front of them.

"Louise!" She held out her arms.

Julia's mentor from Haven returned the hug. She held out her hand to Edward. "So this is the lucky man."

"Edward, this is Louise Loy, the mayor of Haven and my mentor."

Edward clicked his heels together and made a little bow. "Charmed, I'm sure."

"Ooh, Julia. Wherever did you find him?"

"He occasionally gets stuck in the nineteenth century."

"I'll take nineteenth-century manners, any day." Louise winked at Edward, then turned to Julia. "I hear congratulations are in order."

Julia nodded. "Her name is Adelaide and she's a real beauty."

"I wasn't talking about the baby, Julia."

Julia laughed. "Can you believe it? I've been so wrapped up in this birth that I forgot about my nomination."

"Don't let Benjamin hear you say that," Edward said.

Louise took Julia's arm and lowered her voice. "I'd like to talk with you about him..."

"Benjamin?"

Louise nodded. "He knows about Joey."

"But how?"

"He overheard your discussion in the hall in front of the nursery."

Edward and Julia looked toward the nursery as if they'd find Benjamin lurking there.

Julia shook her head. "Why didn't he tell us he was there?"

Louise didn't answer.

Julia sighed. "Oh, well. The situation is unfortunate, as Edward *was* the only one who knew. But Benjamin is on my side. He won't use the information against me."

"You can't be sure of that," Louise said.

"Do you know something we don't?"

Louise ran a hand through her terminally unkempt hair. "'Wisdom will save you from the ways of wicked men, from men whose words are perverse.'"

"Are you saying Benjamin is a wicked man?" Edward looked as alarmed as Julia was starting to feel.

Louise held up her hands, tempering her words. "He is a man, therefore he is subject to temptation."

"But do you *know*—?"

Louise shook her head. "Free will prevails, Julia. You know that. I am merely letting you know that he is aware of your secret."

Edward turned to Julia. "Maybe you should fire him."

She shook her head. Now wasn't the time to overreact. "Benjamin's been with me since I was governor. Although he's annoying, he's never given me reason not to trust him."

They looked to Louise for her opinion. "I do not have full knowledge. I only know what the Lord decrees I should know. But..."

"But?"

"I do believe it would be wrong to condemn a man for what he *might* do."

"Then we keep him on." Edward sounded less than certain, but Julia agreed with him.

Louise raised a finger. "But be watchful."

TWELVE

"Endure hardship with us like a good soldier of Christ Jesus."
2 TIMOTHY 2: 3

Kathy stepped to the nurses' station to get Cindy Wallace
some ice chips. One of her responsibilities at A Mother's Love
was to act as coach for unwed mothers. After eight hours, the
labor was progressing nicely. As Kathy headed back to the
room, a doctor looked up from a chart and called after her.

"Miss? Miss?" Kathy turned around and the doctor
walked toward her. He was as handsome as any TV doctor,
with sandy colored hair, bright eyes, and a smile that oozed
charm. "Are you Cindy's coach?"

"Yes. I'm with A Mother's Love."

He stuck a pen in the pocket of his white coat and held
out his hand. "I'm Dr. Bauer. I'll be delivering Cindy's baby."

"They told me. Too bad Cindy's regular doctor is on
vacation. Bad timing."

The doctor tilted his head and grinned. "That depends on
your perspective. I happen to be a first-rate substitution."

Kathy smiled, feeling the red seep into her cheeks. She
hadn't meant to be rude. "You certainly don't lack
confidence."

"I love my job."

"I do, too." She held up the glass of ice. "I better get
back."

"Let me come with you and I'll introduce myself."

"She's not in a very good mood. The intensity of the pain
comes as a shock to these girls."

"Are you speaking from experience?"

"I have two kids, six and five. I'm a widow." Kathy
clamped her teeth together. Why had she felt the need to say
that?

The doctor nodded.

"And you?" Kathy kept talking, hoping to ease her
embarrassment. "How many babies does the baby doctor

have?"

"Alas, none." He shrugged. "You can't have babies without a marriage."

"Actually, you *can* have babies without a marriage." Kathy pointed toward Cindy's room.

He studied Kathy thoughtfully. "What's going to happen to Cindy's baby?"

"The adoptive parents are on their way."

"Adoption? She made a good choice."

Kathy warmed to the doctor even more.

Kathy loved this part of her job. Within seconds of entering the waiting room, the adoptive parents stood. They clutched each other's hands.

Kathy didn't keep them in suspense. "It's a boy. A healthy boy."

The new mother squealed and threw her arms around her husband, who immediately began to cry. They rocked and clung to each other, turning in a circle. Kathy cried with them.

The woman was the first to let go. "Can I see him? And Cindy? Is Cindy doing all right?"

Kathy nodded. "They are both doing fine. They are—" She stopped when Dr. Bauer walked in the room.

He extended his hand to the couple. "The proud parents?"

They introduced themselves, and he filled them in on the vital statistics of their baby's weight and length. He laughed at their excitement. "You want to see him, don't you?" The mother nodded vigorously. He pointed down the hall. "The nurses are getting him settled in the nursery. Go have a look."

The couple ran down the hall to see their child.

"Wow." Kathy looked after them.

"Double wow," Dr. Bauer added.

"Aren't we the eloquent ones?" Kathy poured two cups of

coffee. She gave him a cup and sat.

Dr. Bauer sank down beside her. "Some events in life are too wondrous to say more than *wow*."

"So much for the professionally restrained doctor." Kathy liked the way his excitement brought a tinge of color to his cheeks.

"Being restrained is not in the job description."

"Could have fooled me. Most doctors I deal with are lacking in the bedside manner and overabundant with their own sense of superiority."

He gave her a cockeyed grin. "Don't hold back."

"I won't." Kathy blew across the top of the coffee. "Most doctors are competent but not compassionate. And when they find out their patient is an unwed mother, they are quick to condemn and slow to sympathize."

"'He will judge the world in righteousness, He will govern the peoples with justice.'"

Kathy stared at him. "Are you trying to impress me?"

The good doctor held up a finger and squinted. "Let's see… that was Psalm 9: 8. Want another one?"

"I wouldn't want to test your repertoire."

"No problem." He cleared his throat. "Also from the book of Psalms, the twenty-second chapter 'Future generations will be told about the Lord. They will proclaim His righteousness to a people yet unborn— for He has done it.'"

Kathy applauded. "A two-liner. I *am* in awe."

Dr. Bauer spread his hands in a mock bow.

A bubble of laughter escaped. Oh, but it felt good to laugh. "You seem to like verses about righteousness." She smiled. "Are you claiming at attribute?"

"Only a goal."

"And a worthy one at that. But I'm confused. A doctor who believes in God? I thought most of you only believed in science and the power of your own talents."

"*Now* who's being judgmental? Faith and science don't need to be mutually exclusive. Science, God, and our talents, can work together with great results."

"You are the proof?" She didn't even try to hold back a

grin.

He shrugged. "So I have to work on my humility. I can't be perfect."

You're pretty close. She started at the thought. This man was entirely too engaging.

Before she had the chance to dissect her feelings, he downed the rest of his coffee. "Got to go. There are babies to catch, mothers to comfort, and dads to congratulate." He stood and faced her, and she was surprised to see him looking suddenly awkward. "Would...uh, that is, would you like to go with me to the hospital picnic Monday evening? I'd like to hear more about your work at A Mother's Love...and learn about you, of course."

Her heartbeat beat double-time, and she bit her lip. *Was he actually asking her out?* "I don't know. The kids..."

"The kids. Yes. A picnic isn't a picnic...of course, bring your kids."

He actually sounded excited about the prospect. "Okay," Kathy said, surprising herself. "We'd love to."

"By the way—" he held out his hand ceremoniously— "the name is Roy. Doctor Roy Bauer, at your service."

She took his hand, noting how it completely engulfed her own. It wasn't a bad thing. Not at all.

◆◆◆

Kathy was exhausted. Not only had she been with Cindy during the birth, but in the hours after, when Cindy had dealt with mixed feelings about the adoption. It was totally normal, but Kathy was drained. Going home became both a destination and a state of mind.

She got in the elevator to leave. Roy slipped in beside her. "Your duty is done?"

"My counselor duty. My mom duty awaits."

"Walk you to your car?"

"That would be nice." Kathy covered the pleasure she took in his offer by giving her attention to the numbers lighting up as the elevator descended.

"We look forward to the picnic," Kathy said, finding her key. "The kids love pic—" She stopped short and stared at her car. "What?" She pointed.

The tires were slashed. The car balanced on its rims. Kathy ran to its side as though she could save it. "Who did this?"

Roy circled the car. He scanned the dark parking lot as though looking for someone suspicious. Seeing no one, he took out his phone. "I'll call the police and get a repair truck."

Kathy didn't even nod. She was too stunned.

Lord, who would do such a thing? For an instant, she remembered the face she'd seen at her basement window. Was someone after her? Why?

A sense of dread enveloped her.

◆◆◆

Roy insisted on taking Kathy home while her car was being fixed. He was glad it didn't take much to convince her.

He watched her closely on the drive, making sure she was all right. He wasn't quite sure how it had happened, but this lovely woman had gotten to him. And he was downright furious that someone had done something as malicious as slit her tires. He just hoped it was a random act of idiocy. But why her tires? Only her tires?

"I can't believe it," Kathy said for the tenth time. She had bounced from ranting to contemplative silence the entire trip.

"Everything will be all right." Roy repeated the assurance for *his* tenth time. He knew it was a trite response, but he couldn't think of anything more profound. A truth was a truth. Tires could be fixed. Everything *would* be all right.

Kathy's kids greeted them at the door—a boy and a girl, cute as could be, dressed in their pajamas, waiting to say good night. Kathy invited Roy in for a minute.

The boy pinned Roy with a stare. "Who's he?"

Roy extended his hand. "I'm Doctor Roy from the hospital."

Kathy plopped on the couch, a hand covering her eyes. "Kids, Dr. Roy, my savior. Roy, this is Ryan and Lisa."

"Nice to meet—"

"I still can't believe this happened."

"What happened, Mommy?"

Kathy told her kids the story—in more detail than Roy would have offered such youngsters. But maybe that's what happened when you were a single parent. With no spouse to talk to, you spilled your guts to your kids.

"A bad man hurt your tires?" Lisa asked.

Kathy snapped out of her pity-mode to comfort them. "They did, but Dr. Roy helped me take care of getting them fixed and gave me a ride home to you." She drew in a deep breath and leaned her head back on the couch. "I'm beat."

Roy got an idea. "Where's the bathroom?"

Ryan looked puzzled and eyed his mother as if wondering if he should answer.

"At the end of the hall."

"Come on kids," he said—which he immediately realized sounded odd.

"What are you up to?" Kathy asked.

"Never you mind." He headed down the hall to the bathroom with the kids pattering after him. He turned on the water in the bathtub, his hand under the spout, waiting for the hot water.

Ryan peeked in the bathroom door, eyes wide. "What are you doing?"

"Your mom's going to take a long, hot bath. He saw some bath salts by the sink, and added a liberal dose .

Kathy appeared in the doorway. "Okay, you three. What's going on?"

Roy handed her a towel. "The doctor's prescription for a bad day is pruning in a hot bath before bed. I'll be waiting for you in the living room with the kids to make sure you get tucked in for the night. All right?"

Kathy looked back at him, the nightgown clutched to her chest. "You're a good man, Dr. Bauer." She bit her lip.

"Roy," he reminded her. "And I'm a gem."

When Kathy emerged three-quarters of an hour later, her skin was glowing and her eyes showed signs of life. She came into the living room wearing a chenille robe. She was combing out her wet hair.

"Well, well." Roy smiled. "She lives."

Kathy smiled back. "It seems my children hooked you and reeled you in." She pointed to the couch where Roy was sandwiched between the dozing Ryan and Lisa. A pile of Dr. Suess books lay on his lap. He took the remote and turned the volume down on the opera that was on the TV.

"I'm an easy catch."

She took a seat in the rocking chair across from them. "I feel better." Her eyes met his, and their genuine gratitude warmed him. "Thanks."

"No problem. I like rescuing damsels from their long, hard days." He pointed to the TV. "I'm drawn to damsels."

They watched the woman belt out an aria, and Kathy shook her head. "Hmph. I must have left my breastplate at the cleaners."

Roy smiled. "The 'breastplate of righteousness.'"

She gave him an odd look. "There's that righteousness again."

He shrugged and stood. What could he say? The struggle to be righteous and good never left his mind. He had so much to make up for.

"It's been a long day for you too," she said.

He stood, letting the kids snuggle into the warm spot he'd left behind.

Kathy rose to see him to the door. "I don't know what I would have done without your help."

He held up a hand. "Everything *will* be all right, Kathy. I've made arrangements to have your car delivered here tomorrow morning."

"*This* morning. It's Sunday already."

"Like we said, it's been a *long* day." He dug his keys out of his pocket. "I want you to know that whoever did this to you will be caught. I'm not going to let anyone hurt you, do you understand?" He meant it.

She nodded, but he saw tears in her eyes.

He squeezed her hand. "I'll say a prayer for you."

And he did. An impassioned one, because in the last hour it had suddenly become very important to Roy that Kathy and her children were safe.

Finally back in his apartment, Roy glanced in the mirror to see if he looked as worn-out as he felt. His eyelids were heavy, his face drawn. It *had* been a long, hard day.

He took a deep cleansing breath. "Come on, Lord, stay with me — with us. Give us a liberal shot of strength. Kathy and her kids need you, and I could use a dose of your care myself."

Roy noticed the pin sitting on his dresser. He was so forgetful. Half the time he forgot to wear it. God would not be pleased with his oversight. "I'll wear it tomorrow. I promise."

THIRTEEN

"A righteous man is cautious in friendship,
but the way of the wicked leads them astray."
PROVERBS 12: 26

NATALIE THOUGHT ABOUT asking Beau to go to church with
her, but decided against it. She didn't want to push. Besides,
after Fran's admonition, maybe it was best she stay away
from him.

She ended up walking alone to a church just up the street.
It was an old building, built before air conditioning was a
requisite. The stained glass windows were flung open to let
in the morning breezes.

Taking a seat halfway up while the organist played the
prelude, Natalie took a moment to appreciate the carved
wood that adorned the altar. *You don't see craftsmanship like
that any –*

A man slid in beside her and surprised her by leaning
close. "You don't see craftsmanship like that anymore, do
you?"

She looked at him, amazed. "I was just thinking that exact
thing."

"Two great minds…"

"With but a single thought," she finished. She took a
moment to study him. He was far from handsome, someone
she would skim over in a crowd. Still … his eyes were full of
a rare joy.

"Jack Cummings," he said, extending a hand.

"Natalie Pasternak."

"Glad to meet you."

The pastor began the service. When the first hymn was
sung, Jack offered to share a hymnal with her. His voice was
nothing special, but what he lacked in quality, he made up
for in volume. Jack Cummings knew how to praise the Lord
with fervor.

Natalie smiled at the thought of God listening with
earplugs, like a father patiently enduring a tone deaf child

practicing an instrument. During the last verse, Jack noticed her smile and threw his head back, closed his eyes, and sang the final refrain with everything he had. "'Faith of our fathers, holy faith! We will be true to thee till death.'"

They sat down. Natalie looked at him, shaking her head.

He leaned close. "What can I say? I love the Lord."

"I can *hear* that."

When they stood at the end of the service, Natalie found herself asking Jack to go out for Sunday brunch.

"Love to, but can't," he said, as they eased down the aisle toward the narthex. "I'm moving into a new apartment today. I was supposed to move in last weekend, but an unbelievable series of events stopped me, so I have to do it today. In fact, I've borrowed a friend's van and have it parked out front, stuffed with all my worldly possessions, such as they are. My new apartment's just down the street."

"Where?" Natalie asked after shaking the pastor's hand at the door.

When Jack said the address, Natalie stopped on the steps, causing the man behind her to pull up short.

"That's where I live!" She stared at him.

"No."

"I just moved in Friday. Which apartment is yours?"

"Apartment one, on the first floor."

"I'm in three, in the attic." She saw a van packed with belongings nearby. "Give me a ride home, and I'll help you move in."

"Are you sure that's how you want to spend the rest of your Sunday?"

She hesitated, then nodded. "I have to work at an antique store at two, but until then, I'm sure."

"I'll owe you one."

"Two." She grinned "You forgot your singing."

✦✦✦

Natalie joined Jack on the front step. She handed him an iced tea, and he held the glass to his forehead.

"It's an oven out here."

Natalie repeatedly pulled her T-shirt away from her skin, trying to make a breeze. "At least we're done."

"The advantage of not having many possessions is that moving doesn't take long. As you can see, I live simply."

"Nothing wrong with that."

"A simple life for a simple man."

Natalie squinted at him, not sure if he was searching for a compliment. His face showed he was sincere.

Besides, he *was* a simple man. Ordinary. A nose too big for his face. Dishwater hair combed in a traditional man-cut. Even his clothes ... jeans shorts, a red T-shirt, and tennis shoes with an obscure logo. But he had a great smile. And soft eyes that seemed to observe and understand, not merely see.

He held his glass in a toast. "To Natalie and Jack. May the Lord bless our friendship."

She nodded and clinked her glass against his.

Natalie realized they'd been so busy with moving in that she hadn't asked him about himself. "So, Jack. What do you do?"

"In general, or for a living?"

"Ooh, choices ... let's start with in general."

"I try to do the right thing."

Natalie thought about her conversation with Beau the night before. She remembered his request for a kiss and felt herself blush.

She saw Jack studying her. Then, as though sensing her discomfort, he said, "But it's not always easy to do that right thing." He stretched his legs in front of him. "Actually, I don't think life's supposed to be easy. God said, 'My grace is sufficient for you, for my power is made perfect in weakness.'" He shrugged. "So when I'm weak and struggle, I figure I'm giving God a chance to show His power. It's the least I can do."

"Good answer." She put her thoughts of Beau aside. "Now for the other half of the question, what do you do for a living?"

"I'm a teacher."

"You look like a teacher."

He laughed. "I'm not sure what that means, but you're probably right."

"You look...wise."

"Boy, do I have you fooled." He ran a hand over his face as if applying a mask. "Actually, it's a clever disguise."

"What do you teach?"

"English. I love to read."

Natalie's stomach jumped. "I'm a writer—or I'm trying to be. I work at an antique store to make money, but writing is in my heart."

Jack nodded, obviously impressed. "It's a good heart to have. Have you gotten anything published?"

Natalie threw a pebble into the yard. "Nothing. I wrote a couple novels a few years ago but they turned out to be practice. I was on the wrong track."

"And now you're on the right one?"

"I hope so. That's one reason I moved to Lincoln. I was having trouble concentrating at home."

"People problems?" He raised a hand, stopping her answer. "Sorry. I shouldn't pry."

"No, go ahead." She surprised herself by meaning it.

"Pry?"

"Pry."

He took a new breath. "People problems?"

She smiled. "Mostly Sam. He's my best friend, but he wants to be more. The trouble is he isn't...he doesn't...he doesn't care about the same things I care about."

"Such as?"

Natalie felt no hesitation in being honest with him. "He doesn't care about God, or growing closer to Him. He doesn't understand why I try so hard to do what I promised to do." She bit her lip, realizing she was getting into deep history. "Anyway, I needed a change. A chance to start over."

"What did you promise to do?"

She squinted at him. "You don't miss much, do you?"

"I'm a good listener."

She gave him a level look. "Yes, you are."

"So?"

She told him about the invitation to Haven and her experiences there. "After the tornadoes, we were asked to make a decision. Each of us chose to dedicate our lives to God, each using his or her own special gifts in whatever way *He* wanted."

"And your gift is writing."

"I think so."

He put a hand on her shoulder. "Don't get discouraged. As long as you're trying to do your best, God will arrange the results he wants."

"Which so far is zilch."

"God is never late and never early. He measures time differently."

She considered this. "That's a nice way to tell me to be patient."

The screen door opened behind them. "If you ask me, patience is *not* a virtue."

Beau came onto the porch wearing only gym shorts. He ran a hand through his sleep-tousled hair.

"Hi." Jack rose and extended his hand. "Jack Cummings. I just moved into apartment one."

Beau shook his hand. "Beau Tenebri. Two."

Beau reached down to tug a lock of Natalie's hair. "Want to go grab a late lunch?"

She looked at Jack, hoping Beau would include him. When he didn't, she stood up and said, "Actually, I have to get to work."

Beau shrugged. "Suit yourself." He turned to go inside.

"Nice meeting you, Beau," Jack said.

Beau gave him a back-handed wave. "You too, Mack."

Jack stretched. "You make a nice-looking couple."

"We do?"

"You're both very attractive."

"That's nice of you to say."

He shrugged, then gave her a quick hug. "Thanks for the help and the talk, Natalie. And later, I'd love to read some of your writing."

"Maybe…that depends."

"On what?"

"On whether Jack the English teacher would be grading it, or Jack the friend, would be reading it."

He made a face. "Unfortunately, I think the two are joined at the hip."

"You're telling me you'd be brutally honest?"

"You want dishonest?"

"Maybe."

Jack laughed and they went inside, each to their own apartment.

After work that afternoon and a stop at the grocery store, Natalie tried to use her key in the door to her apartment.

It was already unlocked.

I'm sure I locked it. I'm real careful about that sort of thing.

She peered up the tiny staircase, unsure if she should go up alone. She listened but didn't hear anything. She looked across the hall at Beau's door. *Maybe I should get him to come up with me.*

She set the groceries on the floor and tiptoed to his apartment. She tapped a knuckle on his door. "Beau?"

She jumped when his voice answered from her apartment. "I'm up here."

She grabbed her groceries and stormed up the stairs. "How did you get in?"

She found him sitting at her desk, her laptop open. She dropped the sack on the floor and saw he was reading her manuscript. She flipped the laptop shut. "What are you doing?"

He looked at her calmly. "Reading."

"It's my book! Nobody said you could read it."

"Aren't books meant to be read?" He actually looked hurt.

"Not until they're done. And not without the author's

110

permission."

He nodded as if considering this detail. "May I read it?"

"No." She couldn't believe his gumption. To open her laptop at all was an assault on her privacy. Not to mention his uninvited presence. "How did you get in here?"

He shrugged. "It was unlocked."

"No, it wasn't."

"Are you accusing me of breaking and entering? What would be my motive?"

She ran a hand through her hair, trying to sort it out. She waved the confusion away and picked up the groceries. "I was going to make you and Jack a pan of brownies, but now I'm not so sure."

"Don't you want to hear what I think of your book?"

She feigned indifference as she put the groceries away. "Not really."

"Liar."

She turned to look at him, leaning on the counter. "Fine. Tell me."

He straddled the chair. "Do you consider yourself a good writer?"

"Of course I...I don't know. I hope so. I do know those pages were created with a lot of hard work, a lot of passion...and I really don't want other people read—"

"Passion, Tally? Surely you jest. Those are the most passionless pages I have ever read. The subject matter is way beyond real life. Where's the sex? Where's the violence?"

She stared at him, then felt the color drain from her face and rush back again with a vengeance. Who did he think he was? "Sex and violence don't epitomize real life."

"Where did you say you were from, Dorothy? The Emerald City? Or was that Kansas?"

"I think you'd better leave." She pointed toward the door.

"Can't take the truth?"

She glared at him. She'd lived through plenty of truths. Hard truths that in the long run had made her stronger.

When he didn't leave she turned her back on him, and got a bowl and a pan from the cupboard. "If you're implying

111

I'm naive, you're wrong. I may not be as worldly as you, Mr. Tenebri, but I have sown some oats in my short life. Not all wild, but certainly not oatmeal either."

"Tell me more."

She opened the box of brownie mix.

"Who do you hope to reach with your kind of writing, Tally? You're whitewashing the world, you're not being honest." He moved to her side as she poured in the water and began stirring the batter with a vengeance. His voice softened. "I can see you've got talent. I just don't want you to waste it. You can change people's lives, but first you need to prove that you understand where they're coming from — which means you should write about the stuff of real life, like sex and violence. And you need to use the language real people use — cuss words and all."

She pointed the spoon at him. "Two years ago a friend told me my writing contained too *much* sex, violence, and cussing. So, I changed it. Now you're telling me to put it back in?"

"I know I'm right."

"I don't think so. Fran said a pyramid gets smaller as it reaches the top. She told me to rise above the rest. She said there will always be masses of the mediocre. She said I'm supposed to aim high." *Lord, Fran was right, wasn't she? I haven't been wasting my time, have I?*

"There's nothing wrong with aiming high, but..." Beau looked away.

"But what?"

"But what good has her advice done you? People want to read about the struggles of the flesh. It's a fact."

"But Fran has my best interests at heart." *And she implements the will of God.* "She wouldn't steer me wrong."

"Maybe not on purpose." Beau shook his head. "Don't you see? If she was concerned with your best interests she wouldn't encourage you to write watered down stories no one's going to read. She'd encourage you to write what reaches people. Stories involving scandal and thrills, stories with meat on them."

"My stories can have meat on them without dripping with blood."

"But you need a little blood and guts to get people interested."

"People are interested in more than blood and guts."

"True. They're interested in sex and scandal."

"You have a shallow view of humankind."

He looked wounded. "No, Tally, I have a *realistic* view of humankind. I know what people are looking for, what they hunger for. Look at what sells in books, on TV, and in the movies. You're not being honest with yourself or your work when you insist on writing stories that give simple answers when there are none. Life is hard. Like it or not, it's full of violence and hurt and sorrow. And those are the people who need you, who need your stories to distract them from their own problems." He waved a dismissive hand at her laptop. "Who's your audience? Pollyanna? Donna Reed? Little Red Riding Hood?"

Each word struck deep, cutting and wounding. Was he right?

Lord, it can't be true…

She kept stirring the ingredients way past the fifty strokes required. She was afraid if she stopped, Beau would see how her hands were shaking. "My readers are people who are desperate for decent stories. People who are tired of the sex, violence, and scandal you support. They want a good story about good people who struggle with life but rise above and get answers that change their lives. They want a story that recognizes God, instead of one that ignores or berates Him."

"Do you know how clueless and naïve you sound, Tally? Do you really see yourself as someone who has all the answers?"

That's not what she was saying. "*I* don't have the answers, but the One I'm writing for does."

He shook his head. "God?"

"Well…yes."

He laughed. "I don't think God reads many books."

"He reads mine."

He cocked his head and studied her, a troubled frown on his face. "Maybe I'm misreading the whole situation. Maybe you're not innocent so much as arrogant."

"I don't mean He actually *reads* it." She spooned the batter into a pan. "What I mean is that He knows all about me, He helps me."

"So with His help you've written a couple hundred pages in...how many years?"

"He works through me, but sometimes I'm a slow learner."

Beau held up a hand like a priest giving a blessing. "Oh, holy Tally. I hereby bless your pages in the name of the Father, the Son—"

"That's it!" She slid the pan into the oven with a clatter. "I'm not going to listen to you mock me—or God."

Beau moved close and tried to calm her. She fended off his touch. He didn't give up until he got hold of her upper arms.

"Get away!"

"You don't mean that."

"I do!"

"Look at me, Tally."

She shook her head.

He took hold of her face so she had to look at him. "I'm sorry if I've hurt your feelings. I certainly don't want to upset you. But you've got to listen to yourself. You're in nowhere land. You're talking fantasy island. God is not a literary agent, making deals for your book, figuring out who's going to read it. Next you'll be claiming He gives you the words and you merely transcribe them."

Natalie pushed away from him. "No. *I* write the words. *My* words. But He *is* the one who gave me the talent in the first place. He gives me the inspiration. He has a plan. I've wasted far too much time. I have to get going. I need to fulfill my promise before it fades away."

"God's given you a deadline?"

She began to pace in front of her desk. "I wish He had. I wish He would. He's far too patient with me. He has all the time in the world. But do I?"

"'With the Lord a day is like a thousand years, and a thousand years are like a day.'"

"Who said that?"

Beau shrugged. "You're not the only one who can quote the Bible."

"I'm impressed."

"Don't be. It's not what you think."

"And what exactly do I think?"

"You think I quoted the Bible because I believe it. That's not necessarily true."

"It's a start."

"It's finished."

Natalie was struck by the finality of his voice. She looked toward the laptop, trying to get the connection. "What do you mean, 'it's finished'? My book isn't finished."

"Maybe it should be."

Natalie hesitated.

Beau's gaze was steady. "You know I'm right. You need to stop writing."

"Well, maybe, but not exactly." Natalie walked away from him. "I have had the notion to stop writing my novel and write about Haven instead. In fact, I've even started."

"Writing about a town that doesn't exist?"

"It *did* exist!" He was making her head spin, confusing her. She wanted to scream. "I was thinking I should write about what really happened, rather than some story created from my imagination. Surely, that would come easier."

There was a moment of silence. She frowned at the uncharacteristic look of confusion on his face. Then it was gone, and he simply said, "Stick with the fiction."

Natalie cocked her head. "A moment ago you acted like it was junk. Now, you want me to work on my novel?"

He hesitated. "Better that than fantasies about an invisible town. Nobody would believe you. They'd think you were crazy, especially if you made the story out to be fact."

Natalie hesitated, a profound weariness taking over. "Maybe you're right. Who'd believe what happened in

Haven?"

"Exactly." Beau sounded relieved. He began to wander through her apartment, running a hand along the dresser, fluffing a pillow, even peeking in her closet.

Natalie drew a steadying breath, grateful for the change in his focus. Yet his interest in her things was disconcerting. "Why do I feel as if I'm being subject to enemy reconnaissance?"

"Because you are." His grin was like an after-thought. His eyes found two photos stuck in the frame of the mirror, and he took one down. "Who's this?"

Natalie moved to take the picture away from him. She drew it to her chest. "This is my daughter, Grace."

Beau's eyebrows lifted. "Why, Tally...it appears I've misjudged you."

Natalie returned Grace's picture to its place. "Hopefully you haven't judged me at all."

He nodded. "You're right. I don't judge you. Everyone has done things they regret. I don't hold anything in your past against you. I'm no angel myself."

"I appreciate that. As for regrets, I regret the situation I put myself in, but I have no regrets over the outcome."

"Where is your daughter now?"

"With a good family. Adopted."

Beau removed the other picture, a photo of Sam on the trail to Mills Lake. "Is this the father?"

"Yes."

"You love him?"

"Of course."

He raised an eyebrow. "Then where is he?"

"Back in Estes. But I'll always love him. He's my best friend."

"Ah."

His reactions were driving her batty. "What do you mean by that?" He sidled close and traced a hand up her arm. "What are you doing?" She pulled away, oddly chilled at the contact.

"*I* want to be more than your friend, Tally. I want to be

your boyfriend." He nuzzled the back of her neck.

The intensity of her body's reaction scared her. More than anything in the world, she wanted to turn around and let Beau devour her. *But you've just met. You know nothing about him.*

She broke away, taking refuge in the desk chair. Beau pressed behind her, putting his hands on her shoulders. He ran a finger up her spine. She arched her back. *Speaking of struggles of the flesh... what am I supposed to do now?*

"It's good you're a woman of experience, Tally. I like—"

She reached back and put a hand on his, stopping his caress. "But I'm not a woman of experience. There's only been the one time."

"Once is enough. The floodgates have been opened."

"Don't be ridiculous."

"I could love you better than Sam."

Natalie snapped to attention. She turned in her chair to face him. "Sam? You said Sam. I never told you his name."

Beau didn't reply, he just traced the line of her cheek. "I know everything there is to know about you, Tally. I'm your soul mate, remember?"

She jumped out of the chair, sweeping her arms to ward off his touch. "Once again, I think you'd better go."

He took a step toward her. She took a step back. Natalie scanned the room, eyeing the stairs leading to the door. Even if she ran, Beau could overtake her, overpower her if he really wanted to. She had to call on her wits and intellect, she had to call on...

God! Please get me out of this.

The timer on the oven buzzed.

Natalie ran to it, knowing there was no way the brownies were done. *Thanks for the diversion, Lord.* Beau came up behind her and put his hands on her waist. Her resolve renewed, she turned and shoved him away. "That's enough!"

"Now, Tally..."

She went to the top of the stairs, stood to the side, and pointed. "Out!"

"Hey, I didn't mean any—"

"Out!"

Beau walked down the stairs, smiling back at her as if this were only the first round and he could afford such an insignificant defeat. She ran after him, slammed the door, and locked it. She leaned against it, out of breath.

Then she heard him whisper through the door. "I won't be alone for long, Tally. You can either choose me or lose me."

Natalie sank onto the tiny stairs, put her face in her hands and begged God to still the shaking that consumed her.

FOURTEEN

"He will bring to light what is hidden in darkness
and will expose the motives of men's hearts."
1 CORINTHIANS 4: 5

IT WAS HARD to leave Bette and Addy at the hospital, but
Walter forced himself to remember why they had traveled to
Minneapolis in the first place. He had been scheduled to meet
his new boss at KMPS. And now he was late — two days late.

Mr. Wingow came toward him, hand extended. "Glad to
finally meet you, Mr. Prescott." He offered a seat and settled
in his chair. "I must say it's odd to have someone accept a
position without ever meeting face to face." He raised a
hand, as though forestalling Walter's response. "It's nice,
mind you, but usually we have to go through the whole
rigmarole of flying a prospect in to see the station and
wining, dining, and otherwise coaxing them to join our little
family."

Walter felt himself redden. He had never considered how
his quick decision to take the job could appear. Perhaps he
should have played the game a little longer, taken advantage
of the perks of being wooed. Yet, his direction from God had
been very insistent.

"Speaking of family...congratulations on your daughter's
birth. I hope mother and daughter are doing fine?"

"They're great." Walter pulled out a "It's a girl" cigar and
handed it to his new boss.

Wingow pulled it beneath his nose. "I do appreciate you
coming in. I realize your mind is probably elsewhere."

Walter shrugged off the understatement. "Bette gets out
of the hospital this afternoon, though Addy has to stay a few
more days. I've got a five o'clock flight to St. Louis where I'll
arrange the move. Bette's better at this sort of organizing stuff
than I am, but I guess she has a good excuse."

"The best," Rolf said. "And you've got full day in front of
you because I arranged an appointment with a realtor later

this morning. So…what do you say we get down to business?"

"Absolutely."

"First off, let's dispense with the *Misters*. Rolf and Walter, okay?"

"Sure."

"Next, I've got to be honest with you, Walter. Our station manager was not keen on the idea of hiring you, especially in a position that was created especially *for* you. He thought the whole idea was a bit odd. And risky."

Walter straightened in his chair and cleared his throat. "I don't understand. Created for me? He thought what idea was risky?"

Rolf leaned forward. "You know. The Honor Roll thing."

Walter shook his head, totally confused. He'd thought he earned the job because of his work with the news department at KZTV. The only ones who knew about the Honor Roll were Walter himself and Gabe. It was a Haven idea, which meant … "How do you know about Haven?"

Rolf's eyebrows dipped. "How do we know about what?"

"Haven. I certainly haven't advertised my experience. Although maybe I *should* have told people about it."

Rolf shook his head. "I don't know a thing about Haven. I was given your name because of your Honor Roll idea."

"*My* Honor Roll idea?"

Rolf removed his glasses and rubbed his eyes. "I hope this wasn't a mistake. The entire affair has been odd from the beginning, but I felt so positive this was the right thing to do."

Walter scratched behind his ear. "Perhaps you should start from the beginning, Mr. Win—Rolf. Give me some background. We seem to be moving forward from different starting points."

Rolf stood and paced in front of the window. "I know it's not proper to ask this question, but I feel it's necessary...are you a religious man, Walter?"

"Yes, I feel strongly about God."

"That's good to hear." Rolf was obviously relieved. "It

will make my story easier to tell."

Walter leaned forward in his chair. "This doesn't have to do with an invitation, does it? An invitation with the mustard seed verse on it?"

Rolf shook his head. "Not that I know of. What's this invitation for?"

Walter shook his head. "Never mind. Go on."

Rolf paced up and back twice as though gathering his thoughts. "I feel strongly about God myself. In fact, just this June, I was going through some times when I questioned how I could best use my abilities to do something for Him."

"I've been through that, too."

Rolf spread his arms to take in his office. "You know how it is in the TV business. Ninety percent of the shows we get are mediocre, and a great majority of those are trash I wouldn't want my kids to watch. Television is the most powerful medium in the world and yet so much of it is wasted." He flipped a hand. "Yet this has been my career for thirty-two years. I began to wonder if there was a way I could help God through my work."

"Work and God. A tough combination."

"Absolutely. Anyway, I'd been praying about it for about a month when one day I was sitting in this office, the day after my daughter graduated from college. I was looking at the graduation program, feeling mighty proud of her—she'd gotten on the honor roll. I was thinking how nice it was to commend those students who did the right thing by doing their best. The thought came to me: *Too bad there isn't an Honor Roll for other aspects of life.* That very moment, an advertiser came into this very office, sat in that very chair, and asked to be placed on the Honor Roll. I was floored. I had no idea what he was talking about. He had to explain it to *me.*"

Walter fidgeted. Gabe had shown him the concept of the Honor Roll in Haven. It was a list of advertisers who supported wholesome television shows. These advertisers were placed on a public Honor Roll so people could take note and support them as they supported honorable shows. It was

121

a no-lose situation. Good television got the financial backing it needed, and the advertisers got good press and an increase in sales. Walter had never heard of it anywhere outside of Haven. So how did Rolf...? "What was this man's name?"

Rolf stopped pacing. "I am so awful with names." He sat at his desk and leafed through some papers. "I've got it around here somewhere. He was not a typical marketing type. He was older, in his sixties, practically bald, and he was wearing a cardigan vest. One of those sweater vests. I remember that because I thought it was an odd choice considering it was June."

Walter's throat was dry. "Did he wear old-fashioned spectacles and have a habit of looking over the top of them?"

Rolf stopped shuffling and pointed a finger at Walter. "Of course! What am I thinking? You would know him."

"Why?"

"Because he knew you. He was the one who gave me your name."

"What?"

Rolf shoved the papers aside. "When I told him I didn't know anything about the Honor Roll, he told me how it works and said that KMPS could be a pioneer in the industry. We could start something good, contribute something to the betterment of man. Make the industry respectable again. It's what I'd been praying for."

"How did my name come up?"

"He implied the list could be a success if we used someone well-versed in its particulars. He gave me your name. I went to the station manager with the idea. It was not an easy sell. He didn't care about the good-will aspects of the Honor Roll, but the financial advantages finally won him over. He said to try and get you, so I did."

"I was the only prospect?"

"It was you or nothing."

It was Walter's turn to stand and pace. "Then why didn't you mention the Honor Roll to me when you called about a job?"

"That was your friend's idea. He said it was important

you take the position based on other factors — he didn't specify what, exactly. He said he would do his part in getting you to accept, but the Honor Roll was not to be mentioned until you were here, in this office."

Walter held the back of his chair and shook his head. "To think I came all this way..."

"You don't regret your decision, do you?"

Walter laughed. "No. I'm just amazed how God arranged things so it *could* be my decision."

Rolf's face asked a silent question. Walter brushed his concern away. "You wanted God to use you? You got your wish. God has us exactly where He wants us. Both of us."

"That's good, isn't it?"

Walter laughed again. "I'm sure it will be." He took a deep breath and looked around the office. "Where do we begin?"

"Your friend said you would know where to start."

Thanks a lot, Gabe.

Walter rubbed his chin, caught off guard. "Okay... the way I figure it, setting up an Honor Roll is a Catch-22 situation. The list doesn't exist until an advertiser's name is on it, and few will want to be the first one on the list. But once it gets started, and an advertiser takes a stand...the Honor Roll list gets publicity as being representative of advertisers who promote good programming. Eventually, everybody will see monetary benefits."

"We need a brave guinea pig."

"The bravest."

"What about your friend?"

"Gabe?"

"Right. I tried getting a hold of him, but I'm afraid he forgot to leave his number."

No problem. Just dial 1-800-HEAVEN.

Rolf looked up with a new thought in his eyes. "But you would have his number, wouldn't you?"

Walter hesitated. "Not exactly."

"But you two are friends."

Walter needed a diversion. An earthquake or a fire would

do nicely. "It's hard to explain. It's kind of a 'don't call me, I'll call you' relationship."

"Sounds a bit mysterious..."

"You have no idea."

"Care to explain?"

"Not really. Let's just say it's...God stuff."

Rolf raised an eyebrow. "Someday, I'd love to hear about it."

Walter shrugged. "Maybe. Someday."

Rolf tapped his lips, thinking. "Let's back up a step. The purpose of the Honor Roll is to reward and encourage wholesome programming. So the first thing we need to do is to pick the television shows that will earn an advertiser a place on the list."

"You do have some decent, wholesome programs in your line-up don't you?"

Rolf smiled. "A few." His face turned serious. "But I want more. That's why I want the Honor Roll. Not to get more advertising revenue — although success will bring its monetary rewards — but to encourage the creation of more wholesome programming."

"We'll be making waves. Not everyone will appreciate that," Walter said. "People don't like change, even if it's change for the better."

"We'll make them an offer they can't refuse. A positive offer."

Walter sighed. "We're just one television station in Minnesota. That's a long way from Hollywood. Do you really think the producers in La-La land are going to listen? Or care?"

Rolf traced a finger around his coffee mug. "I hope they will. I pray they will." He broke the somber mood with a slap on his desk. "So, let's do it. Let's make some waves."

Walter shook his head, the weight of their task heavy. "I hope I remember how to swim."

✦✦✦

Walter looked at the list of television shows that would be the basis for the Honor Roll. "Twenty-two shows out of seventy-five." He shook his head in disappointment. "I didn't realize it was this bad."

"It's a third," Rolf said.

"Or to look at it in my typical Walter fashion, it means that two-thirds of our shows are objectionable in one way or another."

"*Our* shows?" Rolf arched his brows.

"They're mine now. Once I take a job, I get very possessive."

"Admirable."

Walter shrugged and got back to the subject. "I thought there would be more shows with larger advertisers. The big accounts seem to back the sleazy shows."

"Might doesn't make right."

But it packs a powerful punch.

"I'm just hoping right wins in the long run."

Rolf looked to the ceiling as if catching a memory. "'In Your light we see light.'"

"Sounds good."

Rolf studied his hands. "Do you think God approves of what we're doing?"

I hope so. "Sure, He does. What's not to approve?"

Rolf didn't answer immediately. "Are our motives virtuous? We're creating the Honor Roll to clean up the rubbish that's on TV, to reward the good hoping the bad will change its ways. But we're also doing it to make money and to make a name for ourselves."

Walter tapped a pencil on his pad of paper. "Be honest, Rolf, most of what people do is full of mixed motives. Even the most sincere act of kindness tends to have a hint of pride in it—before, during or after. A 'Look at me, I'm so good.'"

"So it's no use trying to have pure motives?"

"Try all you want. I'm merely being realistic."

"Pessimistic."

Walter turned to a clean sheet on his yellow legal pad. "Now, for the press release."

Rolf shook his head, clearly unsure. "I admire your enthusiasm, but reality keeps nipping at my good intentions. Can we do this?"

"We can." Walter nodded firmly. "We will."

"Good will conquer evil?"

"You bet."

Rolf ran a hand across his forehead, as if trying to rub away his doubts. "I hope you're right. Otherwise...I guess it wouldn't be the first time the good guys got creamed."

◆◆◆

"The realtor is here, Mr. Wingow."

The woman didn't enter a room, she conquered it.

"I am never merely *here*, dearie." She dismissed the secretary with a backward hand. "I have *arrived.*"

Walter and Rolf looked up from their work and gawked. Walter knew Minnesota was a long way from Hollywood, but with this woman's presence, Hollywood had found them. Ready or not.

Her hair was big, her nails were long, her clothes were loud, and her gardenia perfume was as overpowering as her will.

"Which one of you lucky gentlemen gets to spend the afternoon with me?"

Walter raised a timid hand, not sure he wanted to accept the honor.

She captured his hand on its way down and shook it. Then she pulled him to standing. "Hello there, Mr. Prescott, I'm Emma Emerson, and I have the perfect house for you and the missus."

"My wife is Bette," Walter said. "She gave birth to a daughter Saturday—"

"Fandango-tastic!" Emma slapped him on the back. "They said you had a kid, but a brand, spanking, new one? That's special." She took a step toward the door. "Shall we go?"

Walter looked to Rolf for permission. Or to be rescued.

He wasn't sure which.

"Go ahead, Walter. I'll send out the press release. And have a good trip to St. Louis. We'll see you back here in a few days." Rolf waved a hand toward the door, failing to hold back his grin. "Take him, Ms. Emerson. He's all yours."

As they left the office, Rolf's laugh followed them down the hall.

✦✦✦

Emma Emerson drove a 1968 Mustang convertible with the top down. Walter was glad he had never succumbed to the urge to cover his balding pate with a hairpiece because it surely would have been airborne within the first block. On the other hand, the mass that was Emma's hair barely moved in the draft of the speeding car.

She whipped a sheet of listings from her purse. "You've seen these?" she asked as she changed lanes.

Walter risked easing his grip on the seat to take it from her. He hoped she'd put both hands on the steering wheel. She didn't. Unencumbered, her right hand waved with her words.

"Those are nice houses, don't get me wrong, but they have no style." She took a sidelong glance at Walter. "You, Wally-boy, look like a man with style—masked under a befuddled veneer, I admit—but style nonetheless."

"These houses are just fine." He grimaced as she sped through a yellow light. "Bette and I aren't flashy people. We don't need anything fancy."

She snatched the page away from him, lifted her arm in the air and let it go.

"Hey!" Walter watched the flyer sail away behind them.

"Trust me, Wally. You don't want those houses. You want a house that speaks to you, not one that puts you to sleep."

"But we have a budget."

"Budget-*smudget*. I know where you stand and I'm not going to make you spend a penny more than your pocket allows. But don't settle for cookie-cutter houses with particleboard cupboards and a concrete patio where you and wifey can cram two lawn chairs. You can do better."

Having found the bold rhythm of Emma's driving, Walter found himself relaxing. "What do you have in mind?"

"Now you're talking." She turned left without signaling. "I've got the perfect house for you."

She had the perfect house for him.

As soon as Emma turned into the neighborhood, Walter felt at home. The streets were narrow and veined with tar. The trees created a canopy with flickers of sunlight breaking through to dance on the front lawns. The houses were smaller than those on the listing sheet, but Emma was right. They had style.

She pulled in front of a brick, two-story with red geraniums in window boxes. A one-car garage was pushed behind the house marking a time when automobiles were not a priority but a luxury. Ivy framed the door and curled around an upper window as if it were holding it in place with green fingers.

Emma studied Walter as he stood on the cracked sidewalk, taking it in. "I was right, wasn't I?"

He nodded, not trusting words to make their way through his tightened throat.

She put a gentle hand on his shoulder, surprising him. But he was grateful for the adjustment in her brusque ways. "Let's go in."

Walter followed her, his eyes taking in every detail of his new home. The shutters needed painting. *Red would be perfect.* And the lawn needed mowing. *I can buy my own lawn mower.*

On impulse, he rang the doorbell as he passed. *Ding-dong.* Welcome. Come on in.

Don't mind if I do.

The rest of the house confirmed what Walter had already decided. Oak floors and walnut woodwork. A nook for the telephone in the hall. Plaster walls. A brass chandelier that wasn't hollow and shiny but heavy and burnished with age. Two bedrooms and an unfinished attic that reminded him of his grandma's treasure trove.

Emma followed behind his wanderings, not saying a word. Watching. She seemed to know that silence was needed for house and man to bond.

After they'd toured every room, Walter's eyes were as clear as his mind. "I'll take it."

Emma beamed. "Do I know how to match 'em, or what?"

"You know how to match 'em."

"Your wife will love it?"

Walter's eyes continued to scan the room. "My wife will love it."

Emma pulled the necessary papers and a cell phone out of her briefcase. "Have a seat on the stairs while I call the owners. Let's buy you a house."

◆◆◆

Walter had never paid full price for anything in his life. Not clothes, not groceries, and certainly not his much-used Chevy van. Yet he bought the house without one moment of quibbling. Without one moment of regret. He was home.

"Sign here and we're done." Emma pointed to the last of many pages. She tapped the pile on the kitchen counter. "Nice doing business with you, Wally. You certainly know how to be at the right place at the right time. This house had a contract pending until this morning. In fact, I heard the news right before I picked you up. Real strange. Thought it was a done deal, then *poof!* It's available. I guess we've got a miracle to celebrate." She held up one finger. "Speaking of celebrate...you wait right here, I've got something for you."

She went out to the Mustang, only to return with a bottle of sparkling cider and two glasses.

"You are either overly prepared or overly confident," Walter said as she turned the cap.

"Take your pick." She leaned forward confidentially.

"Actually, I always keep a bottle on ice in my cooler." She poured and held up her glass. "To Wally, Bette, and Baby. May their lives in their new home be happy and blessed."

Walter fingered the mustard seed pin. *Blessed... I hope this is the right thing to do.*

"I've been meaning to ask you about that pin you wear," Emma said after they'd clinked glasses.

Walter dropped his hand, suddenly panicked. His old explanation surfaced. "It's my grandmother's." He stopped, ashamed. He'd been given a replacement pin. He'd promised to do better with this one.

And he'd just been given the perfect house.

"No." He looked at his glass. "That's a lie. The truth is it's a mustard seed pin. It represents my faith in God."

"Really." She took a sip of cider. "You surprise me. You don't look like the religious type."

Walter felt himself redden. "And what does a religious type look like?"

Emma's right hand began waving again. "You know, buttoned-up collar, slicked-down hair, skinny black tie."

"You don't look the realtor type."

Emma poured herself another glass. "And that is?"

"Business suit, sensible pumps, a tailored hairdo."

She fluffed the hair-sprayed sculpture that was her hair. "Don't you like my hair?"

"That's not the point."

She pouted. "No, it isn't." She leaned forward to see the pin better. "Can I see it close?" Walter took it off for her. She turned it over in her hands, making the tiny mustard seed move inside its glass globe. "How does this little thing represent God?"

"Not God exactly, but faith in God." *I can't believe I'm actually doing this.* "There's a verse in the Bible." He repeated it for her.

Emma leaned against the wall. "Too cool. Is that true?"

"Sure it's true. Not that I've tried to move any mountains lately, but I've seen God do some pretty amazing stuff."

"Like what?"

Like assigning me Gabe as my own personal angel. Like inviting me to Haven where I learned I'm not king of the world. Like making the shadow on my lung disappear. Like giving me Bette and Addy.

Without willing it to, his mind condensed his thoughts into a single sentence. "My God is an awesome God."

Emma smiled. "Maybe I can meet Him sometime."

Walter blinked. *Now, what am I supposed to do?* "Oh...wow...I mean you could pray right now..."

With one last look, Emma gave him back the pin. "Not now, Wally. But someday. I'll let you know."

Walter felt very relieved — and very guilty for feeling that way.

FIFTEEN

*"Then those who feared the Lord talked with each other,
and the Lord listened and heard."*
MALACHI 3: 16

NATALIE BARELY HAD the energy to get out of her car after work. It had turned into a really bad day. She couldn't concentrate at work because of her argument with Beau over her book, so the cash register had come up short and she was positive it was her fault.

She trudged up the front walk, ignoring the hopscotch game.

"Hard day?"

She looked up to see Jack on the front steps. "The pits."

He moved over and patted the step beside him. She slumped on it like a rag doll.

"Want to talk about it?" She shook her head. Then with an exaggerated sigh, she sat up straight and attempted to clear her mind of her mood. "What did you do today?"

"Nothing."

"Didn't you have to work?"

"I'm a teacher, remember? Summer school's over. I have two weeks to do nothing until the regular school year starts."

"What I wouldn't give for two weeks. I could write—"
She thought of something. "You're an English teacher. Doesn't every English teacher want to write a book?"

"Nah. I'll just read yours."

"Hmm."

"What's wrong?"

Natalie turned sideways on the step, leaning her back against a column. "I've been wondering if I'm writing the right book."

He mimicked her position, leaning on the opposite post. "Do you want to write a different novel?"

"Actually, I thought I wanted to write about Haven, but now I don't know."

He considered this. "Fiction to nonfiction. Interesting."

Natalie shook her head adamantly, Beau's comments ringing in her mind. "The Haven idea is dumb. Even if I wrote it, no one would believe it really happened."

"I believe it."

She pinched the toe of his shoe. "You're different. You're special."

He tipped an imaginary hat. "Why, thank ya, ma'am. I 'preciate the compliment."

Natalie studied him a moment. He *was* special. If only he weren't so...so...

Jack looked away, and she had the uncomfortable feeling he knew what she was thinking.

Plain. She rubbed her forehead, ashamed for completing the thought. *Don't be so shallow, Natalie. Looks aren't everything. Jack has a good heart.*

"You have a good heart, Natalie. You need to follow it."

Natalie's jaw dropped. She couldn't believe that once again his thoughts had mirrored hers.

"What'd I say?"

She laughed, making an excuse. "I need to follow my heart, huh? Sounds like Jack should write romance novels."

He blushed. "Not *that* part of the heart, the part that belongs to God."

She nodded. She understood.

"Would you let me read your writing now?"

She shook her head, still too raw from the confrontation with Beau to risk it. "The novel's not done and I don't—"

"Not the novel. The book about Haven."

That stopped her. "I only have a few pages."

"Then it won't take me long, will it?"

The idea of sharing Haven with someone who cared was irresistible. Before she could talk herself out of it, she stood. "I accept your offer." She held out her hand and pulled him beside her. Face to face, eye to eye, she felt a distinct connection.

"I'm glad you moved here, Jack Cummings."

"I'm glad you moved here, Jack Cummings"

The words echoed in Beau's mind, taunting him.

Neither Natalie nor Jack had noticed him listening to their conversation from the open window of his apartment. More's the pity. He would have loved to show Mr. "Glad-you-moved-here" what *he* thought of him. Would have loved to see the look on his face when he saw Beau's power.

But soon enough Cummings wouldn't matter. Beau clenched his fists. Soon he himself would be the only one in the whole world who mattered to sweet little Tally.

And dear old Jack would be nothing more than a dim and feeble memory.

Natalie cut two brownies while Jack read her Haven pages on the laptop. She couldn't help but notice how different he looked, sitting in the same chair that Beau had occupied the night before. Other than the obvious differences in their appearance, there was another distinction that she couldn't quite pinpoint, something less tangible but more significant...

Then she understood. Where Beau had possessed the chair—straddling it as if he claimed some power over it— Jack sat upon it gingerly, as if he didn't want to offend. He filled Natalie's apartment with the respect of a visitor, while Beau had captured it like a conqueror.

He looked up from the computer.

"Well?"

"It's good."

"It is?"

He nodded and was silent a moment. "There's a spirit of encouragement here. You portray yourself as just an ordinary person who was given an extraordinary experience. You aren't cocky about it."

"I don't want people to think I was chosen, even though I was, in a way. What God did in Haven to a few of us, He wants to do for all of us."

"And that is?"

"He wants us to open our hearts so He can show us our unique purpose."

Jack shook his head in amazement. "Who wouldn't want to read a message like that?"

Natalie put a hand to her mouth, more excited than she'd been in months. "You think so?"

He left the chair to touch her shoulder. "I know so."

Natalie flung her arms around him, sending him off-balance. "This is what I've been wanting to hear for two years!" She broke away and looked at him. "I've had a gut feeling that this is the way I'm supposed to go, but no one ever gave me any encouragement. Thank you."

"You're welcome."

She handed him a brownie.

"Boy, a hug *and* a brownie? I'm overpaid."

"Never!" She took a bite of her own brownie, then stopped in mid-chew. "You're not just being polite, are you? You are telling me the truth?"

He raised a hand, as though taking an oath. "Know this, Natalie Pasternak. I, Jack Cummings hereby promise that I will always tell you the truth."

She knew, as surely as she'd ever known anything, it was a promise he would keep. Whether she liked it or not.

No one was in Jack's apartment. The light from the house foyer shown under the door, a slice of light that pulsed with shadows as someone stood outside.

A piece of paper was slid under the door, then removed. Left behind were a dozen spiders. They were small and shiny black, with red markings on their backs—markings that resembled an hourglass. They scurried across the floor toward Jack's bed as if they had a united purpose.

✦✦✦

Jack stared at himself in the mirror. He tried combing his hair differently. It didn't work. "What you see is what you get."

In spite of this fact, he got into bed feeling happy. "Natalie…" He grinned at the very sound of her name. Such happiness deserved a proper response. He slid onto the floor to kneel, and bowed his head.

"Lord, thank you for sending Natalie into my life — or me into hers. I'm not sure who's helping who, but it doesn't matter. She's wonderful for me, and I hope I'm wonderful for her." He hesitated, leaning his head on his hands. "You haven't made me a handsome man, Lord, and I'm not complaining." He smiled. "Well, maybe a little. But I know you have your reasons. Yet if it fits into your plans that this plain man can love this beautiful woman — and vice versa — then let it be so. I trust you to — "

Jack heard a tap at his window. He was surprised to see a dove sitting on the sill, tapping its beak on the glass. Moving deliberately so as not to frighten it, he grabbed the crust of his dinner sandwich, went to the window, and opened it. He pulled off a tiny piece of bread.

"Here, birdie. Want some dinner?"

He scrambled backward when the bird flew into the room. What in the world?

The bird landed on his bed, and Jack went to shoo him away, then stopped short.

There was a cluster of black dots on his sheet. He turned on the light. Spiders ran for cover. He grabbed a newspaper to swat them, then noticed that the dove was eating them, one after the other.

He stood aside and watched, shaking his head. When the dove was finished, it flew out the window. "Come back anytime," Jack called after it.

Just to be sure the spiders were gone, Jack shook out his sheets. Then he slept and dreamt of a future with Natalie.

SIXTEEN

"Let those who love the Lord hate evil, for he guards the lives of his faithful ones and delivers them from the hand of the wicked."
PSALM 97: 10

LISA RAN OUT of her bedroom, her shoes on the wrong feet, wearing her Barbie visor. "Picnic! Picnic!" She zoomed past Kathy to the kitchen.

Kathy felt the same excitement. All day she'd looked forward to spending time with Roy. He was such a caring guy, kind, compassionate, wise, patient, and handsome—yes, even righteous. If she tried hard, maybe she could keep those wonderful thoughts close and let the memory of the slit tires fade into the background of her day.

"Take the visor off, Lisa." Ryan smoothed a piece of paper on the table next to his bowl of cereal. "I'm trying to memorize my verse for Sunday school and you look so dumb I can't concentrate."

Kathy flipped a finger at Lisa's visor and smiled. "It looks cute. But fix your shoes. They're on the wrong feet." She pointed to Ryan's paper. "Say it out loud, sweetie. Let's hear what you know."

Ryan handed her the paper, then at the ceiling. "Stand firm then, with the belt of..."

"Truth."

*"Truth...*buckled..." he hesitated.

"Around your waist."

"Yeah, yeah, I know the rest." He sucked in a breath. "'Buckled around your waist, with the breastplate of righteousness in place.'" He beamed. "How's that?"

Breastplate of righteousness? Kathy would have to share the verse with Roy. "That was—" She stopped when Ryan ran past her. "Ryan? Where are you going?"

In a matter of seconds, he ran back into the kitchen with a belt in his hand. "I'm going to do what it says." He snaked the belt through the loops of his shorts. "I'm buckling the belt

137

of truth around my waist."

She had to laugh. Her literal child. "That's one way to remember it."

The doorbell rang. Lisa ran to get it with Kathy and Ryan close behind.

"Alo-ha!" Roy was wearing a Hawaiian shirt, a baseball hat turned backwards, and pink sunglasses with sparkles on them.

Lisa giggled. "You look silly."

Roy put an incredulous hand to his chest. "I do? Then maybe you should have these glasses, and Ryan can have the hat."

"What do you say, kids?"

"Thank you."

Kathy gave Roy the once over. "Who gets the shirt?" He began unbuttoning it but she stopped him. "That's okay. It's all yours. Come in a minute while I get my salad."

"You didn't have to make anything."

"Of course I did. My mother taught me well."

Roy followed her to the kitchen. He pointed to a red blinking light.

"You have a phone message."

Kathy shook her head. It wasn't the first time she'd forgotten to check. "I was so busy cooking and getting ready..." She pushed the play button.

"I'm here."

Kathy whipped her head toward the words. The voice was deep, menacing. She moved closer, wanting—but not wanting—to hear more. *"I see you... I can get—"*

Kathy lunged toward the stop button, not wanting the kids to hear. "Ryan, take Lisa out to Roy's car."

Ryan gave his mother a worried look. "Who was that?"

"I don't know...now go. We'll be out in a minute."

Ryan led Lisa outside, looking back at his mother with worry on his face. Kathy rewound the answering machine tape and played it again. *"I'm here...I see you. I can get you anytime I want. Remember that."*

Kathy grabbed her arms to stop their shaking. "Who's

doing this to me?"

"Have you had any other messages like this?"

"Not messages. Unless you count the symbolic messages from a man who peeked in my window and slashed my tires."

"Hold on there...who peeked in your window?"

"I have no idea." Kathy stared at the answering machine. "My life is not usually this high-maintenance."

He picked up the phone. "We're calling the police."

"I don't know if that's necessary."

"Believe me, it is."

"But what can they do?"

"They can be aware."

"A lot of good that will do."

He squeezed her hand. "And as soon as we're done calling, we pray."

She felt a spark of relief curb her panic. "I have only one objection."

"What's that?"

"Let's reverse the order. Let's get the prayers done first."

Roy hung up the phone. "Your point is well taken."

There were five grills set along the perimeter of the picnic area. Hand-lettered cards were taped to each one, announcing the delicacies cooking inside: barbecue ribs, chicken, beef, hot dogs, and hamburgers. The people at the picnic tables were in a flurry, arranging bowls of food.

"Looks good, doesn't it?"

Kathy didn't reply. She surveyed the area, feeling tension in every muscle.

"Earth to Kathy."

She stopped looking around and put a hand on Roy's arm, trying to draw some sense of security from him. "I feel something."

"I hope you feel hungry."

"No." Kathy fought a wave of panic. "He's here."

"The man who's been harassing you?" Roy began to look with her. "How do you know?"

"I *feel* him." Kathy knew she sounded crazy, but what she said was true. "I feel eyes looking at me."

Roy put a hand on her shoulder. "There are always eyes looking at you, Kathy. You're a beautiful woman."

She shook his compliment away. The tingling in her spine retained its intensity. She scanned the park, suddenly frantic. "Where are the kids?"

"I introduced them to Doctor Jeffries' kids. They're playing."

Roy's reassurance wasn't enough. *Lord, something isn't right. Keep us safe.*

Kathy didn't relax until she spotted Ryan and Lisa running through the picnic tables. She slid a hand through her hair, hating the foreign feeling of dread. She'd never felt afraid before. Not in Eureka Springs. Why did her pursuer have to ruin the one thing she'd been able to count on — her peace of mind?

It wasn't fair.

◆◆◆

It wasn't fair.

The man moved, hiding further behind a stand of fir trees. All around him people were laughing and having fun, acting as though they didn't have a care. Didn't they realize there was serious stuff happening? Battles were being fought, lives were being changed.

Choices were being made.

Choices. It would be nice to have a choice again. It had been a long time since he'd followed his own scenario. Not that he couldn't refuse to do what his superior told him. He could. If he were a stupid idiot. You didn't say no to his boss's kind. Not if you wanted to live. No, he'd made his choice two years ago and he'd had to live with it ever since.

The man turned toward Kathy's laugh. It wasn't fair that she was happy, having a good time with some hotshot doctor who wanted to play kiss-the-cook. It was enough to make a guy puke up his breakfast.

He ducked when Kathy looked in his direction. It was tough moving around a town where people might recognize him. And strange that no one had. It was as if his experiences had changed him—on the inside *and* the outside. He didn't feel like the same man. Maybe he didn't look like him, either. A part of him wanted to step out in front of everyone, give a little wave and ask, "Hey, people, remember me?"

Of course, if he did any such thing, his boss would be furious. That was not a pleasant option. So he hid and waited for a moment to make a move. But how, with all these people around? If only he had a plan. Should he slash some more tires? Leave some more messages?

No. Each time had to be different. He had to make Kathy feel like he was everywhere and could do anything.

He saw Lisa run to the sandbox.

He got an idea.

Kathy perked her ears, suddenly alert. She saw Dr. Jeffries' children staking out the desserts, but no Lisa or Ryan. She started walking. Jogging. Roy rushed to keep up with her.

"What's wrong?"

She didn't answer, but accelerated, her eyes sweeping the area like a searchlight. *I should never have let them out of my sight! If anything happens to them —*

When Kathy spotted Lisa sitting in the sandbox, her fears were flooded with relief—until a man stood up beside her. Lisa raised Bunny Bob, as if showing it to him. The man put a hand on her head.

Why is a strange man talking with my daughter? Why is he touching — ?

Kathy was too far away to see the man's features, and as soon as she started running toward the sandbox, he turned and fled.

"Hey!" Kathy yelled, hurrying faster. "You! What are you

doing talking to my little girl?"

Lisa climbed out of the sandbox and ran toward her. "Mommy, Mommy!"

Kathy stooped and wrapped her arms around her daughter. "Are you all right, sweet cakes? Where's Ryan?"

Lisa pointed to a slide nearby. Ryan was fine. The man was gone.

"Did the man hurt you, honey? Did he scare you?"

Lisa shook her head, brushing the sand out of Bunny Bob's fur. "No, Mommy. I'm not afraid of him."

Kathy shivered as she realized that a child molester's first line might be, "Don't be afraid."

"What did the man say to you?"

"Don't call him 'the man', Mommy."

"Why not?"

"It wasn't a man. It was Daddy."

She stared at Lisa for one second—then everything went black.

✦✦✦

Since it was a hospital picnic, there were plenty of people to take care of Kathy's physical needs. Though few could understand her emotional upheaval.

Her husband was alive.

Roy drove them home, but Kathy refused to lie down. "I'm fine."

"No, you're not. You fainted. You're upset."

"I am not upset!"

Roy herded the kids toward the back door. "Go outside and play, guys. Give your mother a little quiet."

"No!" Kathy pushed past him to bar the door. "They can't go outside. *He's* out there!"

Ryan looked between Roy and his mother. He bit his lip. "Who's out there, Mom?"

Lisa tugged on his shirt. "Daddy's out there, that's who."

Ryan's eyes widened. He shook his head. "But he's dead."

Kathy knelt to his level. "We *thought* he was dead, Ryan.

When the tornadoes came, and when your father chose to go out into them...when we never found a...when he never came home, we just assumed he was dead."

Ryan waved a hand toward his sister. "Lisa saw him?"

Lisa nodded. "He played with me in the sandbox."

Ryan considered this a moment. "He didn't come see *me*." He looked at his mother. "Why didn't Daddy come play with me?"

Kathy was dumfounded. *That's* what Ryan was worried about?

"It's because he doesn't love me, isn't it?" Ryan's eyes filled. "Daddy never loved me!" He ran into his room, slamming the door.

Lisa rocked back and forth. "Daddy loves *me*."

"Lisa!"

She pouted, dragging Bunny Bob away.

Kathy put a hand to her head. "What do I do now? My husband is presumed dead, stays away for two years, then appears out of nowhere, approaches Lisa, but not Ryan—"

"Why hasn't he approached *you*?" Roy thought a moment. "But maybe he has. Maybe he's the one who's been harassing you."

Kathy looked at him. "You think Lenny's the *man*?"

"I have no idea. I don't know him. Is it something he'd do?"

"I don't think so. Although he wasn't the best husband, although he was unfaithful, I don't think he'd be this vindictive. This mean. He'd have no reason—"

"Where's he been for two years?"

Kathy rubbed the place above her eyebrows. "Probably sleeping around. Living the high life of a bachelor."

"Why has he come back now?"

Kathy bit her lip. "I hope he hasn't come back for the kids." Her voice rose. "I won't give him any custody of the kids!"

Roy put a hand on her arm, calming her. "Why don't you talk to Ryan. He needs you."

She shook her head. "I have no idea what to say."

Roy touched her cheek. "Tell him *you* love him."

Kathy smiled wistfully. "Will that be enough?"

It was enough. For the moment. A few minutes later Ryan came out of his room holding his mother's hand. He went up to Roy and asked, "Can we have hot dogs now? I'm hungry."

They had hot dogs.

◆◆◆

After their picnic—with hot dogs made in the microwave and eaten in the safety of the kitchen—Kathy and Roy got the kids settled in their room playing Candy Land. They went willingly, especially Lisa who complained of a tummy ache. Too many hot dogs. Too much excitement.

Kathy felt a need to look at photo albums. She stood near the shelf, leafing through the pages. She found a picture of Lenny. She ran a finger across his face.

Roy looked over her shoulder. "Memories?"

She sighed. "Mostly questions. What happened to the man I loved? The sweet high-school boy with the contagious smile?"

They studied the photo. Lenny was slim, a bit wily looking—a testament to the mischief in his heart. His hair was badly cut and the twinkle in his eye told of self-satisfaction rather than joy.

"You're prettier now than you were then." Roy smiled at her. "More serene."

"What did I have to be serene about back then? I was a teenager who got married because I had to. Not the most serene start to my adult life." She sighed deeply. "I'm smarter now. Not that I planned it that way. I didn't seek wisdom... it found me, jumped me, and tied me down until I listened. If only I didn't have to learn everything the hard way."

She set the album aside and moved to the couch. She held out her hand to Roy, and he joined her.

"Suddenly, I'm married again."

He nodded.

"That matters, doesn't it?"

He nodded again.

She cringed in defeat. "Why did Lenny have to come back? We were doing fine without him. He doesn't want to be a family again. Otherwise he would have contacted us ages ago."

"Perhaps he's had a change of heart."

Kathy snickered. "If he has one." She shook her head, ashamed at the bitterness in her words—and her own heart. *Father, forgive me.* "Lenny wasn't all bad. I loved him once. But he was never easy to live with."

"Is anybody?"

Kathy shrugged. "I'm not giving him all the blame." She tried to smile. "Just most of it."

Roy put his arm around her and they sat quietly. Kathy noted the way they fit together, how they synchronized their breathing without meaning to.

"I don't want to see him," Kathy finally said. "I don't want to talk with him."

"You're going to have to. He's the father of your children."

She sat upright. "I'm not going to let him near the kids."

"He's their father, Kathy."

She shook her head fiercely. "He never *wanted* to be their father. He only wanted to have fun. The children were a by-product of that fun, not the intent."

Roy's voice softened. "You didn't plan to have the children and yet *you* love them."

"I'm different. I saw beyond the 'now.' I understood how important those kids are to me—and to God." She turned to face him. "God has a plan for Ryan and Lisa. The circumstances that brought them into this world were not ideal. Their parents are not ideal. But for whatever reason, God wanted them to be born. And they were. Now it's my responsibility to make sure they are loved and cared for. They need to know about their *heavenly* Father. But as for their earthly one..."

She pushed herself away from the coziness of his arm.

"I'm no good for you, Roy. I've got so much baggage I need two porters."

He pulled her back. "We've all got baggage. Some is simply a little more worn and ragged than the rest."

"And some is missing a handle and has broken locks—"

"And some is fancy and some is basic—"

"Can yours fit into the overhead bin, Roy? Is your baggage small enough to do that?"

"If I rearrange things and give it a good shove."

Kathy sighed. "I'm not sure mine can ever be small enough to fit into a regular life. I have the feeling I'm always going to be paying for the extra weight of my past."

"I'm willing to pay the cost, Kathy."

She looked at his eyes and knew he meant it. "I'm married," she said again.

He took her hands in his. "Then maybe we should pray about it."

"About us?"

"About us and Lenny and the kids..."

"I'm not used to praying with a man—especially twice in one day."

He flicked the tip of her nose. "Then you have never experienced true intimacy."

"Sounds exciting," she said.

He bowed his head. "You have no idea."

✦✦✦

"What in the devil's name are you doing?"

Lenny flinched, holding the phone away from his ear. "I'm doing what you said. I'm breaking her."

"That's not what I've heard."

"Heard? Who's been telling you what's going on down here? You got somebody else on the job? I don't like the idea of someone checking up on me."

"We don't care what you like or dislike. What we care about it getting some results. You showed yourself. She knows it's you!"

Lenny shook his head. "Nah. She may know I'm back but she doesn't know I'm the one messing with her life. I didn't show myself to her. I simply went up to my daughter and talked a bit. I don't think Lisa even recognized me. She was only three when the tornado took me."

"We didn't enlist you to *spook* her. The deal was you *break* her. Get her to stop her work at that baby factory. Stop her before she starts talking about Haven. Break her until she turns away from Him."

"Him?"

"Are you a complete moron?"

There was a pause on the line. "Oh. I get it. *Him.*"

"You need to do more. Now we've got two of *them* working together."

"Them?"

"Haven disciples. The doctor's one, too."

"I didn't figure on two of them. What am I supposed to do?"

"We want you to break them up. Everything you've done has backfired. It's pushed them together. The doctor's comforting her. He's stronger than we imagined. You need to discredit him."

"How? From what I've seen he's a pretty up-and-up guy."

"Maybe now. But it wasn't always so."

Lenny smiled. "You got something on him?"

"Indeed we do."

"This should be fun. I love bringing a good man down."

SEVENTEEN

*"But thanks be to God, who always leads us
in triumphant procession in Christ and through us
spreads everywhere the fragrance of the knowledge of him."*
2 CORINTHIANS 2: 14

THE RALLY IN Kansas City was scheduled as one of those
routine campaign stops that blended with the next.
Interchangeable meeting halls, music, and the ever-present
red, white, and blue Carson/Marrow signs held by exuberant
supporters. A rousing speech with just enough time for a few
questions.

Too much time.

♦♦♦

Julia raised her hands and smiled at the inevitable applause
that followed her speech. She reveled in the chants of "Ju-li-a!
Ju-li-a!" As she lowered her hands, the crowd quieted. "I
have time for a few questions," she said.

The reporter was unpretentious. Average height, weight,
and degree of good looks. An everyman. An everyman who
wanted to know the answer to something...

Governor Carson, can you please explain that pin you
wear? I've noticed you always have it on. What is it and what
does it represent?"

On reflex, Julia touched the mustard seed pin. Her mind
filled with the pat answer she'd prepared for such a moment.
It's a symbol of my faith...next question please.

Julia glanced at Edward. He shrugged slightly. She saw
Benjamin standing off to the right. His arms were crossed
defensively. They—and her audience—were waiting for her
answer. Julia felt an inner stirring.

You have to do more, Julia. Take a stand. Take a chance.

She took a deep breath and removed the pin, holding it
out for everyone to see. The red lights of the video cameras

were a warning that whatever she said would be on the evening news.

"Inside the glass globe of this pin is a mustard seed, one of the smallest seeds on earth. And yet if planted, this seed grows into a large plant. I wear it as evidence of my faith in God. For he said, 'If you have faith as small as a mustard seed, you can say to this mountain, "Move from here to there" and it will move. Nothing will be impossible for you.'"

"You planning to move some mountains?"

Julia smiled. "Not the rock and soil kind. But I hope to give the heart and soul kind a mighty shove."

"If you're talking religion, what about the separation of church and state?"

"Daniel Webster once said, 'Whatever makes men good Christians makes them good citizens.' I believe that to be true. The morals and ethics of a believing person effect *every* aspect of their lives."

"So you're wanting everyone to become a Christian?"

Julia sighed. "This nation was founded under God. My beliefs are my own. They stem from *my* relationship with God and with his Son, Jesus Christ. His plan for me is not His plan for you. But there is a common ground. God loves all of us and has a purpose for all of us. There are many, many opportunities to work toward His will."

"Is it God's will you become president?"

Julia paused. "I hope so. I plan to continue doing what I'm doing until God tells me different."

"So you're hearing voices?"

Julia shook her head. "Only in here." She pointed to her heart. "Although I believe in God, I also believe that He doesn't have a political agenda. There are godly people on both sides. Did you know that more people attend church on any given Sunday than attend all the American sports events put together?" She leaned forward on the podium. "If so many of us believe, then why do we act as if *God* and *Jesus* are dirty words? My faith is as much a part of me as the fact that I am a woman or a mother or a wife. It permeates every facet of my life. It is vital toward defining who I am."

"So what are you? A Presbyterian? A Catholic?"

"It doesn't matter. We need to stop worrying about denominations and ceremonies. Sit down? Stand up? Kneel? Silent prayer? Shouted prayer? Those are manmade rules that feed the differences in our personalities, not our souls. Each person needs to concentrate on his or her individual faith. If we get our own hearts in order, the rest will come. Just as God changes us one person at a time, so we can conquer the problems of our nation and the world one person at a time. I touch one person, they touch another and another. Each one, reach one...pass it on."

"An individual can't change the world," said her original questioner.

Julia hesitated, trying to find the right words. *God, help me.* "Not alone. 'Let the nations know they are but men.'"

"Is that from the Bible?"

"Yes, it is. The Old Testament."

"So if you're elected president, are you going to be spouting the Bible in cabinet meetings? The State of the Union address will come from Matthew, Mark, Luke, and John?"

"Would you rather I quoted the *National Enquirer?*"

A titter.

"So you're going to make everybody believe in God and Jesus?"

"I'm not going to *make* anybody believe anything. Freedom is the American way. But it is also God's way. He doesn't *make* us do anything. He doesn't want mindless machines that bow down and say, 'Yes, oh master.' He wants to hear those words said out of love, not duty. He's given us free will to make choices, good and bad. It's the same with our government. We have the freedom to make choices, good and bad. I'm concerned about the basis of those choices. We need to start listening with our hearts to all the possibilities, not closing our eyes as if we had no choice."

She looked at the crowd before her. "As far as people believing in God and Jesus, the majority of us already do, though too many tend to forget it or shove it into the background of their lives as they try to handle things themselves." She pinned her mustard seed back on. "Through this nation's belief in God, we can become changed from the inside out. He will rearrange our attitudes, our desires, and our motives. Being born physically put us in our parents' family, being born spiritually, puts us in God's family. And only in His family can individuals make a difference. The mustard seed is in all of us, waiting patiently to grow."

There was murmuring in the crowd. Julia held out her hands, quieting them. "Don't follow me. I'm human, I'm fallible. Follow God. Now. Because now is all you can change. Once that happens, God will take care of the rest."

She left the podium. The applause began tentatively, then grew as if mustard seeds had been planted in all of them and had sparked to life and had begun to grow. The reporters frantically scribbled down the evening's sound bites.

Julia was news and she knew it. She had done something foreign to politicians: she had taken a stand. A firm, irrevocable stand. The question was, would it win her the election? Or lose it?

✦✦✦

Julia had just put her feet up when Benjamin burst through the door of the hotel suite that served as their KC office.

"How could you be so stupid?" He slammed a file folder on a chair.

Edward started at the outburst. His muscles tensed, and Julia moved between them.

"Edward, you sit down," she ordered. "And you, Benjamin..." She walked toward him, staring at his face. To his credit, Benjamin did not back up, although he did find it hard to accept her gaze. When Julia was close enough for him to feel her breath, she whispered in his face. "Never, *ever* again."

Then she went back to her chair as if nothing had happened. "Well, hello, Benjamin. What's up?" She dared

151

him to deny his *faux pas*.

Instead, he retrieved the file folder and held it like a shield. "I'd like to know what you were thinking? Talking about God and faith like that. And *Jesus*? It's simply not done."

"It should be done." Julia poured a glass of ice water.

"Maybe during a Sunday service, but not during a presidential campaign and *certainly* not in front of reporters."

Julia cocked her head. "So we're only supposed to speak of God in hushed tones, behind closed doors?"

Benjamin squirmed. "If you want to win the election badly enough...yes."

"Maybe I don't want to win the election."

Both men exclaimed: "Julia!"

She held up a hand, calming them. "You men. Your competitive nature gets the best of you. Don't you realize there are times when winning isn't the final goal? Times when the race may be as important as the finish line?"

Benjamin threw up his hands. "If this is the attitude you have then we might as well give up. Right now. It's stupid—"

Edward stood. "That will be enough." He took his wife's hand.

Benjamin stood alone. He let the file drop to his side and shook his head. "So this is how it's going to be? You're going to continue with this mustard seed fiasco?"

"I am."

"Don't you realize what the press will do to you?" He ran an invisible headline across the air. "Reverend Julia says, 'Praise the Lord or else.'"

"That's not what I said."

"Believe me, that's what they heard."

"Then I will pray for them." Julia went to Benjamin's side. "We've been together a long time, you and I. I've been remiss in not taking a stand for my faith before now. I've played your game. I've said the easy words and taken the easy stands. I got elected governor that way. But when I got back from Haven, when I was given a second chance to do things the right way..."

She put a hand on his shoulder, willing him to understand. "I can't remain silent any longer. It's time. I didn't plan it this way. I had no intention of declaring myself this afternoon. But don't you see? God had other plans. And I have found—and I continue to find—that His plans are far better than my own. He has the big picture in mind, while my view tends to be limited and self-serving. If He wants me to become president, it will happen. If He wants me to stir things up so someone else can win, so be it. I've stood up. I can't sit down."

"But maybe if you softened it a bit—"

"No," Julia said. "The votes I lose are better lost and those gained will be true votes of support—for me and all that I stand for."

He stared at her eyes. "I'm sorry, Julia. If that's the way it is, I can't be here."

She'd was shocked and saddened. But maybe this was part of God's plan too. She gave his shoulders a squeeze. "I understand. You need to take your stand, and I need to take mine." He turned to leave. "Benjamin?" He paused, but did not look back. "God loves you, son. He's waiting for you to notice."

He left the room.

◆◆◆

Julia and Edward were having a quiet dinner in their room when there was a knock on the door.

"No one's here," Edward said. Another knock. "Oh, well, it was worth a shot." He got up to answer it.

Thad Kelley, the newly appointed replacement for Benjamin, entered carrying a six-inch stack of pink messages.

Julia shook her head. "If you think I'm going to return all those people's calls tonight, you're—"

Thad threw the pile in the air like a lottery winner with his first million.

"Thaddeus! What are you—?"

"You did it, Governor!"

She shook her head. "I just promoted a crazy man?"

"You *reached* people! These are messages from all over the country. They're from people wanting to get a mustard seed pin."

Julia and Edward left their chairs and retrieved some of the messages.

"Vermont, Florida, Oregon..." Edward read aloud.

"Look at this one," Julia said, "It says, 'Your heartfelt words renewed my faith in God and the system. How do I get a pin?'"

"The messages are still coming in," Thad said, picking up his mess. "Who do I call to order some of those pins?"

Julia stopped reading.

"I wonder how many we should order." Edward shuffled through the pile. "A thousand? Ten thousand?"

Her thoughts sped to one answer: "None."

Thad and Edward looked at her. "What do you mean *none?*"

"They're not ours to give." She blinked, bringing her thoughts into focus. "My mustard seed pin didn't come from a store, it was given to me by God."

"Do you think He'd be willing to whip up a few thousand more?" Thad asked.

Julia gave him a look.

Edward leafed through his pile of messages. "It is a terrific opportunity, Julia. Would it be so wrong to encourage people by passing around a few pins?"

Julia moved to the window, looking out over the evening skyline of Kansas City. "Isn't it just like Americans to jump into the newest fad?" She shook her head. "I don't want this to be a fad. I cherish my pin and I take its meaning too seriously to cheapen it by making it a campaign button."

"So what do I tell all these people?" Thad looked at her, clearly confused. "And what do we tell the press when they get wind of it?"

Julia's eyes returned to the sunset. "We repeat what I said in my speech. Tell them to follow God's will instead of their own. Now. Because now is all they can change. Once that happens, God will take care of the rest." She faced them. "It's up to us to do the same. We follow God."

Thad stared at her, then shrugged. "Yeah, well, I just hope He knows what He's doing."

EIGHTEEN

*"When times are good, be happy, but when times are bad consider:
God has made the one as well as the other."*
ECCLESIASTES 7:14

By the time Walter transferred Bette from the hospital to
Julia's and Edward's empty house, flew to St. Louis, drove to
their apartment, and negotiated with a moving company, it
was late evening. He fell onto the couch and closed his eyes.
It would be so easy to call it a day in spite of the fact the sun
hadn't set. He resisted the urge to turn on his side and
snuggle into the cushions. He had one more thing to do. He
called Bette.

They spoke of the logistics of packing, and Bette made
Walter promise to personally take her grandmother's crystal
punch bowl in their car.

"How's your dad?" she asked.

Walter's jaw fell.

"You didn't call him, did you?"

"I forgot."

"Walter, you *promised* to keep him posted. You need to go
see him."

"Ah, Bette, I'm tired. I'll do it tomorrow."

She was silent.

"Did you hear me? I said I'll go see Pop tomor—"

"No, Walter." Her voice was quiet. Intense. "You need to
go see him tonight."

"Why?"

"I don't know."

"That's a concrete reason."

"I can't describe...it's just a feeling."

"So you want me to believe in women's intuition?"

A pause. "I don't care if you believe in it or not. It exists.
It's God's special gift to females. So just do it. For me. For
your father. For Addy."

"No fair taking out the big guns—the baby guns."

"So you're going?"

He punched a pillow. "What choice do I have?"

✦✦✦

Walter knocked on the doorframe of his father's room. Jeb Prescott was watching the evening news.

"Hey, Pop."

Jeb turned toward the voice. His eyes widened. He struggled out of his chair. "There's my boy! There's my proud papa!"

Walter was overwhelmed with his father's greeting.

"Hi ya, Pop. How you doing?"

Jeb eased himself into the chair. "Fair to partly cloudy. Can't complain." He chuckled. "I'd like to complain, but I can't."

"Sure you can. I've heard you."

Jeb shook his head. "You'd better have brought me a picture of my new granddaughter."

Walter was glad he'd remembered. He pulled out a photo of Bette holding Addy just hours after the birth. Jeb's face softened. "She's a prize, boy. A mighty prize." He set the picture on his knee and kept a hand on it. "But how's she doing? And Bette?"

"They're doing fine."

Jeb pulled a cigar from his pocket and stroked it. "They move into your new house already?"

"No, Pop, that's why I'm here, to arrange for the moving company. Bette's staying at our friend Julia's house —"

Striking a match, his dad lit the cigar. "Julia Carson? That lady president?"

"She's not president yet."

"Will be. Should be, if all were fair. Seems nice enough. Real sincere, though I've never seen a candidate win by being nice. Usually they need to get down and get dirty —" He pointed to the television — "why, eggs and bacon! There she is."

Walter looked at the screen. Sure enough, Julia stood at a

podium with a huge Carson/Marrow banner behind her. She was leaning forward as if she wanted to draw her listeners close. "If so many of us believe, then why do we act as if God and Jesus are dirty words? My faith is as much a part of me as the fact that I am a woman or a mother or a wife. It permeates every facet of my life. It is vital in defining who I am."

"Uh, oh," Walter said.

"Shh!"

A reporter came on the screen. "Julia Carson laid it all on the line this afternoon by challenging individuals to nurture their own relationship with God. And Jesus. To quote former governor Carson, 'Through this nation's belief in God, we can be changed from the inside out. He will rearrange our attitudes, our desires, and our motives. Being born physically put us in our parents' family, being born spiritually puts us in God's family. And only in His family can individuals make a difference. The mustard seed is in all of us, waiting patiently to grow.'"

"She's got one of those mustard seed pins just like you gave me, boy." Jeb's grin was proud as he pulled at the pin attached to his shirt.

Walter shook his head. "I can't believe she's actually doing it. She's actually coming out and telling about it."

"The pin?"

"Yeah. And faith. And Jesus. She's taking a huge risk."

Jeb pointed his cigar at the television. "More people need to take risks like that. She's got guts, I'll give her —" Jeb stopped in mid-sentence and sucked in a breath. He ended with a fit of coughing.

"Pop!" Walter took the cigar away from his father and got him a drink of water. When Jeb had calmed down, Walter shook his head. "I told you to give up the cigars. They're not good for you."

"Neither is sitting here pining for one." He held out his hand.

"No way. I'm not giving it back."

"I just want to hold it. I won't light it."

"You are such a liar."

His father shrugged. "You can either give it to me, or I'll call in my secret cigar connections and use your inheritance to get another one."

"You're incorrigible." Walter chuckled and handed his father the unlit cigar.

"Ha. You should talk." Jeb put the cigar in his mouth and moved it back and forth. "Don't look disgusted. At my age a fellow's only got so many pleasures and if one of them happens to make him cough a bit, I figure it's worth the price." He leaned back in his chair and looked to the ceiling. "If I knew then what I knew now I'd do things different."

"Like what?"

Jeb blinked as if he'd forgotten his son was in the room. "They say a man never comes to the end of his life saying, 'I wish I would have worked more.'"

An uneasy sense of dread washed over Walter. End of his life? "What are you talking about, Pop?"

Jeb waved his cigar. "Just a figure of speech, boy. Point is, I worked too much and lived too little. I'm not talking about acting as if nothing matters but feeling good and having fun, but there were things I could have enjoyed more. Cherished more." He gave his cigar a good chew. "Like you, boy. I could have cherished you."

Walter stared at his father, a bit stunned. Cherish was not a word Walter had ever heard from his mouth.

Jeb nodded as if agreeing with himself. "You cherish your little Addy, boy. You cherish her with your time, your love, and your good intentions. You make her grow up smart, feisty, and full of pepper. Just like you."

"Me?"

"You bet. You're smarter than most, more feisty than what's good for you, and so full of pepper you make me sneeze." He laughed at his own joke.

Walter laughed with him. As the closing credits ended the news, Walter watched the way his father fingered his mustard seed pin.

His dad looked at him. "You help that woman become

president, boy. You help her win. She's right about this here mustard seed being in all of us, waiting to grow. If I'd only known, mine could have grown a little sooner. But better late than never."

"You talking about faith, Pop?"

Jeb nodded. "I believe, boy. I believe in God and Jesus and heaven and hell. When a fellow gets older, you start thinking past the here and now and start hoping there's a hereafter. And I know there is. I know there is."

Walter could hardly speak past the lump in his throat. "How do you know, Pop?"

"Ever since you gave me this pin...people around here started asking me about it. At first I felt pretty dumb, not even knowing the right Bible verse and all, but then I looked it up. I have your grandma's Bible, right over there by my bed. Funny thing, once I started reading, I couldn't stop. Why, there's all sorts of neat stuff in that book. Tells a person about life, death, marriage, kids, work, fun...the whole shebang. And stories? Why, it's better than any soap opera."

Walter grinned. He'd never seen his father so impassioned.

"Why, I've even got a favorite verse." Jeb pushed himself straighter in his chair. "You wanna hear it?"

Walter was shocked—and shamed. In two years he hadn't taken the time to memorize a single verse and yet his father, in the span of a few days..."You memorized one?"

"I may be old, but I still got a few brain cells working." Jeb's grin offset his sarcasm. He cleared his throat. "This is from those Psalms. Psalm 121, verses 7 and 8. 'The Lord will keep you from all harm—He will watch over your life, the Lord will watch over your coming and going both now and forevermore.' Isn't that grand?"

Walter hoped his dad couldn't see the way his mouth was trembling. "That's grand, Pop. I'm proud of you."

"T'weren't nothing. Just a few minutes of my time." He picked up the photo of Addy and Bette. "Should have made time for more of those minutes."

"Mr. Prescott!"

Both Jeb and Walter turned toward the voice. A nurse stood in the doorway, her arms akimbo.

"I smell cigars in here."

"That's just my aftershave," Jeb said. "Eau de Cuba."

"You know smoking's not good for you anymore, Mr. Prescott."

"Never *was* good for me. But that didn't stop me doing it."

Walter stood to leave. "I'd better be going, Pop. Seems like you have your hands full."

Jeb snorted. "Oh, I can handle her."

"But can I handle you?" the nurse said.

Jeb leaned toward Walter and whispered, "The battle's half the fun."

Chuckling, Walter started to walk toward the door, but his father took his hand and held him where he was. Walter watched in stunned wonder as his father pushed himself to standing and reached out to give him a hug.

"You remember what I said, boy. You be taking care of that wife and daughter of yours. You be cherishing them, you hear?"

"I hear you, Pop." Walter moved to the door. "I'll come back tomorrow and we'll play some Pinochle. Does that sound good?"

Jeb nodded. "I'll whip you bad, boy."

"Bye, Pop." As Walter walked down the hall, he heard his father call after him, "I'm proud of you, Son."

Walter stopped walking. He turned back toward the door and hesitated. He was tempted to run into his father's room, sit at his feet, and gush, *"Really, Pop? Really? Tell me more. How are you proud of me?"*

The playful bickering between Pop and the nurse filtered into the hall. The mood had changed. The time for serious sentiment had passed. Walter acknowledged the fact with a nod. Then he turned to leave, accepting the blessing he'd already received from his father as more than he deserved.

◆◆◆

161

The phone woke Walter. He squinted at the clock at the same time he fumbled for the receiver. 6:15. *In the morning? Who the heck?*

"Yeah?"

"Mr. Prescott?"

"Yeah?"

"This is Jerome Nelson, from the Hillcrest Retirement Village."

Walter sat up on an elbow, trying to clear his brain. "Yeah?"

"I'm so sorry, but your father had a stroke during the night."

Walter blinked, trying to take it in. "A stroke?"

"I'm afraid he passed away."

Walter felt the earth fall away. He dropped the receiver to the bed and rubbed at his eyes. *God, please no.*

"Mr. Prescott?"

He put the receiver back to his ear. "When?"

"At 5:30 this morning. We tried to revive him, but we were unsuccessful. If you'd like to come over, we could assist you in making arrange—"

Walter hung up.

✦✦✦

The doorbell rang. It rang again. There was a knock. A pounding. Voices outside. A few minutes later Walter saw a coverall-clad man cup his hands on the sliding glass door. It was the moving company. It was moving day.

He stumbled to the door and slid it aside.

"Hey, sorry man. We rang the bell and knocked but nobody—"

Walter turned his back on the worker. "Go ahead. Do what you have to do. Just give me a few minutes to get dressed."

Walter went in the bedroom and shut the door. He heard workmen moving around—probably starting to pack boxes.

He sat on the edge of the bed and called Bette to tell her the news. She had no words that numbed the pain.

Nothing would help. His father was gone.

✦✦✦

Father Delatondo was assigned to pick up Mrs. Bronson and Mrs. Kinney for evening mass. The two women were devout, but housebound. Although both of them could have easily afforded a cab, they seemed to enjoy the personal attention of their priestly chauffeurs. Del had been told they were especially excited to be picked up this evening, because they had never met the new Father.

Del offered his arm to Mrs. Bronson as they walked from her door to the parish car. "I like your hat." Del indicated the woman's veiled hat. "It reminds me of the ones my grandmother used to wear to church."

"Your grandmother had good taste," Mrs. Bronson said. "My Walter loved my hats. He said a lady wasn't a lady without a hat."

"Your Walter had good taste, too." Del started to help her into the front seat of the Town Car, but she protested. "No, no. Put me in the back. Mrs. Kinney detests the back seat. Her Walter used to make her sit back there to mind the kids. And oh, did those kids need minding. Why, I would have — "

"That's unusual," Del said with a smile. "Both of you ladies had husbands named Walter."

She gave him a puzzled look. "Our husbands weren't named Walter. My husband was Martin and Martha's was George." She eased herself into the seat. "Where did you get the idea our husbands were named Walter?"

Where indeed?

After depositing the women in the sanctuary, Del made a quick phone call to the only Walter he knew.

"Walter? It's Del."

"Del." Walter's voice was flat.

"Is everything all right? I had the strangest thing happen as I was picking up two ladies for mass. I'm in my new parish in Lincoln, Nebraska — I bet you didn't know that, did you? That I'm in Lincoln? Anyway, this morning I thought I heard these two ladies say your name. Twice. But then I was mistaken. Anyway, it got me thinking about you... and I couldn't shake this feeling... so how are you?"

"My dad's dead, Del. He died early this morning."

"Oh, Walter, I'm so sorry."

"And I really need to get back to Bette and Addy."

"Who's Addy?"

"She's my daughter."

"Walter! Congratulations! But you said, 'back to Addy.' Where are they?"

"Minneapolis. We've moved. I'm just here to finish up...Del, he's dead. Pop's dead."

Monsignor Vibrowsky motioned for Del to hurry up. The mass was about to start. "Would you like me to come to the funeral?"

"No. I'll be okay. But the call...thanks. It helped."

"I'll pray for you, Walter."

"I'd appreciate it."

NINETEEN

"And lead us not into temptation,
but deliver us from the evil one."
MATTHEW 6: 13

GLORIA NEEDED HELP. She sat outside St. Stephen's, her cell
phone in hand. If only Monsignor had taken the time to talk
to her the other day. But he'd been busy with that new priest.

Yet maybe it was for the best. Lately, the monsignor had
not been very open to hear her emotional outpourings. She'd
seen the glint of judgment in his eyes. And who could blame
him? She was a bad woman who thought bad thoughts and
felt bad feelings. No wonder he didn't want to hear it.

But the new priest...maybe Father Delatondo could help.
She ran a hand through her hair, trying to organize what she
would tell him.

Gloria didn't like herself. Oh, she was plenty satisfied
with her physical body but inside she felt empty, as though
something vital — something she couldn't live without — was
missing. And that lack touched everything... her family life,
her working life, her spiritual life.

There was an inner unrest that tormented her like the
growl of an empty stomach. It would go away, only to
return, gnawing with new teeth. In a moment of weakness,
she had tried to describe the hunger to Stevie. He had been
very solicitous, putting down the newspaper and leaning
toward her with interest. But the more she told him about her
weaknesses, the weaker she felt. He was so strong, so
together. He had taken her hand and prayed for her, and she
had felt unworthy, as if the prayers of this good man were
not to be wasted on the likes of this wretched woman.

All her life Gloria had wanted to be married and have
children. When she met Steve Wellington at a party after her
high school graduation, she'd jumped on him like a groupie
on a rock star. He had all the ingredients she'd been looking
for: looks, humor, a good job, and most importantly, the
desire to be married. A perfect match. The fact he was a

religious man was a nice touch, comparable to the bonus that he liked to dance.

For the first year Gloria had been content to play house in their two-bedroom apartment. She'd made bread, sewed curtains, and had been there with an eager ear when Stevie came home from work. Yet there was only so much cleaning and cooking she could do in an 800-square foot apartment. She needed more to occupy her time.

At her insistence, they had purchased their present house, which sat on a side street near St. Stephen's. It wasn't a stately mansion like those on the boulevard, but it had character — a bit worn and threadbare — but character nonetheless. Gloria had attacked her new project with gusto.

Then she got pregnant. Having her dream baby was a nightmare. Being pregnant had been terrible. She couldn't work on the house because she felt queasy, and paint fumes only made it worse. When the morning sickness finally wore off, Stevie wouldn't let her climb ladders to wallpaper the dining room ceiling or hang a light fixture she'd found at a garage sale for $10. And in the last two months of the pregnancy, she found that her bigger midriff and the downward pressure of the baby got in the way of most everything. Her days were consumed with the desire to have the birth done with. *Now.*

Tasha's birth was unlike anything Gloria had ever experienced. She'd never suffered a pain hungry enough to devour her. The fact a baby was the result of the pain was secondary. The fact the pain was gone was enough.

Gloria expected to be happy. Surely, the cooing, wriggling baby would bring about a sense of wonder and goodwill? Instead, Gloria cried. And cried.

As usual, Stevie was wonderful. Too wonderful. He got up for the two o'clock feedings, rocked Tasha when she was fussy, made spaghetti, and even did the dishes. At night, he pulled Gloria close, finding a place for her in the crook of his arm.

But the nicer he was, the lower Gloria sank. Not that she didn't occasionally feel joy. When Tasha smiled for the first time or when she raised her hands to be held, Gloria thought her heart would break with love. During those moments she felt as if she understood the God Stevie talked about. She would grab onto that feeling in a desperate attempt to claim it forever. But like trying to grab your breath as it hung in the air on a cold day, the feeling of communion with God faded.

It was she who had brought up the idea of her going back to work. She had claimed financial considerations, yet with the cost of day-care, her take-home pay made a negligible dent in the bills. Even so, if Stevie realized her true reason for wanting to get away from the house — that she was unhappy — he didn't acknowledge it. Perhaps it was too painful to admit that his wife and the mother of his daughter didn't like being either one.

At least Gloria's venture back to work had been successful in one way. Since returning to the world, she had begun to feel hope — though not necessarily in the way she had first anticipated. By dealing with the public, she'd discovered new possibilities. She found she could be quite charming when she wanted to be, and she had seen more than one man give her a second look. This renewed sensation of physical confidence made her feel exciting. Sexy. But not toward Stevie...

Toward Cash.

Gloria blinked at the revelation. Cash was the problem. Or was he the answer? She dialed St. Stephen's.

✦✦✦

Del started. He'd just been thinking about Gloria Wellington, and now she was calling him. He smiled. *OK, Lord, show me what you want from me.*

"I'd like to talk with you, too, Mrs. Wellington."

Monsignor Vibrowsky passed by, giving Del a questioning look.

"What time would be convenient for — ?"

"Now!" Gloria's voice was almost desperate. "I need to talk to you now."

What's going on, Lord? "Come right over."

Del hung up and turned to find the monsignor, arching his eyebrows. "Is there something wrong, Father?"

"I have a meeting with Mrs. Wellington."

The monsignor dismissed her with a wave. "You don't need the distraction of Mrs. Wellington. Your time is spoken for. In a few weeks you're going to be taking over Father Oscar's history classes."

"But Mrs. Wellington sounded desperate."

Monsignor shook his head. "Meeting with a priest won't change that."

Del moved toward him. "Is there something I should know?"

Monsignor Vibrowsky put a finger to his lips, then shook his head. "Let's just say that Gloria has talked with each of us here at St. Stephen's."

"She has a lot of problems?"

"She has a lot of...concerns."

"Trivial things?"

"Nothing is trivial in the eyes of the Lord."

Del recognized the response for what it was: hollow words said for effect. He hesitated. "Should I take what she says seriously?"

"By all means." The monsignor smiled. "But also take her troubles with the proverbial grain of salt."

Del nodded, thinking. "'Let your conversation be always full of grace, seasoned with salt, so that you may know how to answer everyone.'"

Monsignor laughed. "Gloria will fill you in on the current spices in her life and you, in return, can fill her with the salt of God's Word."

Del felt a twinge of guilt. "We shouldn't be making fun of her problems."

The monsignor once again waved away his concern. "Listen to the woman. That's all she really wants. Someone to listen to the reasons she doesn't want to follow the mission trail with her husband...or why she's sad because it's raining. It doesn't take much. Pray with her, then send her on her way." With that, he turned and walked down the hall.

Del felt very sorry for the monsignor, for Gloria Wellington—and for the parish of St. Stephen's. Where did compassion fit in? Patience? Love? Surely Gloria deserved to have her worries met with the utmost dignity and—

He looked up to see her in the doorway. "Mrs. Wellington, how nice to see you."

"Where can we talk, Father?"

Okay, no time for chitchat. He led her to an empty office. By the time he closed the door, she was settled in the guest chair, shredding a tissue in her lap. He sat down. "So, Mrs. Wellington, what can I do for you?"

"I'm on the verge, Father. The verge of something wicked." She put a hand to her forehead. "I feel it welling up inside. After work I met...the temptation...I don't know if I can stay away."

Del held up a hand. "Mrs. Wellington. You have to slow down. I can't follow—"

She made two fists and held them on either side of her head, squeezing her eyes shut. "I'm about to burst."

Del reached across the desk and touched her arm. "Calm. Calm."

She opened her eyes and stared at him. Her voice was weary. "I'm not sure I know what calm is, Father."

Del was amazed at the torment in her eyes. They were constantly shifting, as if every thought that flew through her mind was furiously studied.

Lord, how do I help her? "Is there a beginning? A place to start?"

"Cash."

He blinked. "You need money?"

She shook her head. "No, no. Cash is a name." She met his gaze. "A man's name."

"Is he your husband?"

"No! Stevie's my husband." Gloria looked at her lap. "Stevie and my daughter are so good, they are just what I wanted." She looked up. "Then why am I so unhappy?"

Inwardly, Del cringed. So it was the "I'm not happy"

169

complaint. Why everyone in the world thought they had the right to be gloriously happy was beyond him. Of course, it was an ancient grievance. King Solomon had expressed it perfectly with, "What has been will be again, what has been done will be done again, there is nothing new under the sun."

Del sighed. "Perhaps you need to redefine your notion of happiness. Perhaps you need to reassess your life and appreciate —"

Gloria slammed a hand on the desk. "I *know* I should be content with what I have. But I'm not! I *can't* be. There's something going on inside of me that makes it impossible."

"Perhaps prayer —"

"Father! Listen to me!"

Del raised his hands in surrender.

She put a hand to her breast and took a breath. "I'm sorry. I know the monsignor and the other priests think I'm nuts with all my complaints this last year. And my troubles may not seem serious to them, but they're —"

"I assure you, Mrs. Wellington, we take your concerns very seriously."

Liar.

He pushed the taunt away. *Surely, Lord, it wouldn't help to tell her she's right? She doesn't need that kind of hurtful truth.*

She ran a hand over her eyes, and when she spoke, her voice was soft. "I hope so, Father." She peered at him with a deep intensity. "Because I have the feeling that something more than my happiness is at stake."

The monsignor was right about one thing: Gloria Wellington liked to be dramatic. "Such as?"

She swallowed. "Such as my soul."

Her *soul?* Del hesitated…how was he supposed to respond to this? The stakes had just been raised. "Why do you feel your soul is in jeopardy?"

"Because of Cash."

"And who exactly *is* Cash?"

"He's the man I want to sleep with."

It was Del's turn for a deep breath.

"There's something so compelling about him. It's as if he draws me like...like..."

"Like a moth to a flame?"

"Exactly." Gloria shuddered. "And I know, deep down, if I don't fly away real fast I'm going to get burned."

Del sat back in his chair. So it was nothing more than an issue of infidelity. That, he could handle. For a moment he had feared the discussion was going to move beyond his abilities into something—

Profound?

Abstract, he substituted. But the solution for this was easy. "You have to stay away from him, Mrs. Wellington. Stay away so you won't be tempted. It's like keeping chocolate out of your kitchen if you're on a diet. You can't be tempted if the house is empty."

Gloria stared at him, then shook her head wearily. "You don't understand. I've only seen him the one time, but he has a hold on me. Just the thought of him makes me think things, want to do things that I normally wouldn't."

The old "the devil made me do it," eh? Well, Del wasn't falling for it. "It is in *your* control, Mrs. Wellington. Your behavior, your response, it's in your control. God doesn't allow any temptation to come into our lives that we can't conquer with His help."

"But I can't—"

"You *can.* You can go home, make your husband and child a nice dinner, and snuggle beside them on the couch while you watch television. Have a normal life. Wallow in its normality. These other feelings you have—" he waved a hand as though they were written in the air between them—"this lust. This is not real life. It's fantasy. A bit of excitement and thrill. But just like waking up from a dream, you can wake up from these fantasies and move on."

Gloria's shoulders slumped. Her eyes were dull.

Del felt bad. He'd taken the zing out of her life, but sometimes it was best to lay the truth straight out. Even if it hurt. He stood, holding out his hand. "I hope I've been of some help."

She nodded but Del saw her eyes change from hopeful to hopeless.

Suddenly, three words invaded his thoughts: *Feed my sheep.* With the directive still echoing in his consciousness, he watched Gloria lean down to retrieve her purse as if the simple movement pained her. *Feed her? Help her?* Hadn't he just done that? What more could he possibly do? He'd listened, just as the monsignor had instructed. Besides, the monsignor had warned him not to get too involved.

Del moved around his desk to open the door for her. She slid past him into the hallway, lifting her gaze once more to meet his—and the tragic expression he saw there touched his soul.

"I'll...I'll pray for you," he called after her. She did not look back to acknowledge his charity. Closing the door, he stood there, wondering why his offer had sounded—and felt—like an empty promise.

Del strolled back to the desk, pausing at the window. He watched as Gloria approached a black sports car. A dark-haired man got out. The man put a hand on her shoulder.

Her ride must have come. That must be her husband.

But no...Gloria's face was a mask of panic. She shook her head and ran to her car, leaving the man standing alone. With a screech of the tires, she pulled onto the boulevard and sped away.

Why was she so upset?

The man turned and looked in Del's direction. He flashed a cocky smile before he got in his car and drove away.

Del shuddered, and had the oddest feeling ... as if a dark cloud had descended.

An urgent need to pray swept over him. He fell to his knees.

I felt such evil, Lord. Who was that man with Gloria? Is this why you've brought me to Lincoln? To feel afraid? To feel inept?

He looked up at the cross hanging on the wall and knew the answer would be given to him—eventually.

✦✦✦

Gloria sped away, her eyes on the rearview mirror. *Good...there's no one behind me.* Suddenly, a black car came into view.

Cash!

Gloria's heart beat in her throat. She knew what he wanted. He'd made it very clear in the parking lot. She had to get away and she had three choices: church, work, or home. She'd tried church. He'd found her at church...home was closest.

She turned down her street, glad that Cash had been stopped at a red light. She squealed into her driveway, cursing the slowness of the garage door. She pulled inside, barely clearing the door. She pushed the button to close it. *Faster! Faster! Hide me!* She got out and fumbled for her keys. Checking the window in the garage she saw the coast was clear. She ran for the kitchen door. She slammed it behind her, locked it, and leaned against it, trying to breathe.

"Hello, gorgeous."

She gasped. Cash stood in the doorway to the living room. "How did you get in here?"

"You invited me."

"I did not. I told you to leave me alone."

Cash sidled up beside her. "But you didn't mean it." He slipped a hand between her arm and waist and Gloria felt her heart skip. She couldn't let this man...it was like Father Del had said...she needed to keep the temptation away. What she really should do is shove him out the door and lock it. Double-lock it.

"Go...please go."

He pulled her close and she could smell his aftershave. "You don't mean that. You want me, you *need* me, because unlike your dear husband, I'm willing to give you the attention you deserve."

Gloria tried to push away. "Let me go! I have to pick up my daughter at the sitter's."

Her declaration had no effect on him. He leaned forward to nuzzle her hair, finding her ear. "You deserve the best, Gloria, and I am the best."

She managed to get some space between them. She fingered her cross necklace. "I can't. I'm married."

"So you are." He glanced around. "But where is he? *I'm* here, Gloria. Stevie's not."

"He will be." She looked past him to the street. *Come on, Stevie. Come home!*

Cash ran a hand up her back, and her nerve endings sprang to life. "No, he won't. Stevie has to work late. He told you that. You and I have all the time we need."

Her unease made a quick shift into dread. He was right. How could she have forgotten? She was alone with no chance—or hope—of interruption. "I—"

He covered her mouth with his. She gasped at the force and the domination of the kiss. It stirred something deep within her, something that seemed to have its own shape, as though it were a separate entity... it grew until it enveloped her. Her mind clouded.

Then, like the heroine in a romantic tale, Gloria was swept off her feet and carried up the stairs to her bedroom.

Her mind screamed for help. But the only answer to her inner plea was Cash's deep chuckle, and the pounding of her panicked, tantalized, utterly mesmerized heart.

Gloria lay on her side, staring at the wall. The intertwining ivy in the wallpaper had given her such pleasure to pick out and hang, now looked like sinuous, creeping vines...vines that would wrap themselves around her and hold her down with the strength of chains, making her powerless. Powerless to escape. To break free. To say no.

She felt Cash get up from the bed, but didn't turn her head to watch him. She'd seen enough. Felt enough. The kisses that had inflamed her at first had grown overwhelming, even foul. His eyes, which at first had dazzled with desire, had turned black and lifeless at her conquest. As lifeless as she felt.

Her old life was gone.

She heard Cash getting dressed. She wanted him gone. She wanted to forget. She felt him standing over her and shivered. *Would she ever feel warm again?* A tear fell onto the pillow.

"What's this, my dear Gloria? You are so moved by our lovemaking that you're crying?"

Gloria forced herself to look at him. "We did not make love."

"No, indeed, we did not."

He walked toward the bedroom door, then stopped abruptly, raising a finger. He turned toward her. "I'd like something from you, Gloria."

She closed her eyes again. "Please leave."

"Not so fast." She heard him take a step closer. "I said I wanted something."

She was going to be sick. "Haven't you taken enough?"

His reply was smug. "Never."

She opened her eyes to look at him, and he trailed a finger down her arm. His touch was like ice. She scrambled to the far corner of the bed, grabbing the sheets around her. "Get out!"

He scanned the room. "Not until I get my token. Something I can remember you by."

"Take anything. Just go. Go!"

His eyes fell on her chest. "Ah..." He leaned closer. "No!"

He laughed and reached for the chain of her necklace. "I don't want *you*. At least not right now. What I want is *this*—"

With a harsh yank, the necklace broke in his hands. He held the chain and dangled the cross in the air. "How very appropriate." He smiled. "Yes, this will do quite nicely."

Gloria lunged for the cross. "Give it back! Stevie gave that to me for our first anniversary."

He jerked it out of her grasp and shoved it in his pocket. "Give it up, Gloria." He glanced around the room. "For that matter, give everything up. Your life is worthless. Over. You don't deserve to have anniversaries."

His eyes held hers until she had to look away. Shame

washed over her, hot and bitter. He was right. Oh, God, he was right...

"You've committed adultery. You have *sinned!*" He laughed. "Obviously, I don't mind, but I'm sure your God does. And Stevie will."

Gloria clapped her hands over her ears. "Stop it. Just go!"

Cash headed toward the door. "Suit yourself. But you'd better not think your God is going to forgive you this time, Gloria. Because you know He won't. You've gone too far. *I've* got you now and He can't reach you—even if He wanted to."

Gloria swallowed. "God can reach me."

His laughter chilled her from the inside out.

"You people...your own Bible says, 'The night is nearly over, the day is almost here. So let us put aside the deeds of darkness and put on the armor of light. Let us behave decently, as in the daytime, not in orgies and drunkenness, not in sexual immorality and debauchery, not in dissension and jealousy. Rather, clothe yourselves with the Lord Jesus Christ, and do not think about how to gratify the desires of the sinful nature.'"

He shook his head and laughed again. "Was there ever a bigger bunch of drivel? I have a better version: The night is *never* over. So let us revel in the deeds of darkness and put on the armor of power. Let us behave in orgies and drunkenness, in sexual immorality and debauchery, in dissension and jealousy." He extended his arms, inviting her in. "Clothe yourselves with the lord of darkness, and think of how to gratify the desires of the sinful nature."

Gloria stared at him, transfixed. Appalled. "You're the devil."

He shrugged. "Close enough."

She bolted from the bed, dragging the bedclothes with her. But there was no place to hide.

He grabbed her arm. "Where are you going?"

She shook her head over and over, trying to convince herself this wasn't happening. "I've got to go—"

Cash yanked her close, pinning her arm behind her back. He whispered in her ear. "Do you actually think I'm going to let you leave to stir up trouble for me?"

"Leave me alone!"

"That's what I should have done. Leave you alone. I'm not here for you. You were an afterthought—a bonus—such as you are." He shoved her away as if she disgusted him. "You are nothing. Less than nothing. Worthless."

Gloria leaned against the wall, then sank to the floor, his words echoing over and over, taunting her: *Nothing...less than nothing...worthless...*

"Get it over with, Gloria."

She jerked her head to stare at him, but he only smiled.

"There's only one way to stop the pain, and you know it."

With that he sauntered from the room. She heard his laugh as he left the house.

✦✦✦

Gloria was numb. She wished she could cry herself to sleep. But sleep would bring dreams, and dreams would bring memories. Of him.

Gloria reached for the cross necklace.

It was gone. *He* had it.

She remembered when Stevie had given it to her. He'd taken her out to dinner and had made her close her eyes while he went around behind her and placed the cross around her neck. "This represents our commitment to each other and to Christ," he'd said. She put a hand on the spot where it usually touched her skin, trying to conjure up the feel of it. The comfort. But the memories were dead.

As you should be.

The suddenness of the thought made her blink, as if the words had been spoken. "No, I won't. No, I don't want—"

What you want doesn't matter anymore. You have sinned. You don't deserve a husband like Stevie, you don't deserve a daughter like Tasha. You don't deserve to live.

"I don't deserve..."

It was true. She knew it was true.

Gloria knew what she had to do.

177

✦✦✦

Del was restless, uneasy… he had a nervous stomach when there was nothing to be nervous about. At dinner, the nerves gave way to a heavy cloak of lethargy. *Why am I suddenly so tired?* He felt as if he could sleep for a week. He headed to bed early.

Why did he feel as if something had drained the life out of him?

Yet he couldn't sleep. The unease that plagued him broke through the lethargy, gnawing at him, making his muscles refuse to relax. Finally, he sank to his knees beside his bed. "Lord, please give me peace."

God's answer came, loud and clear.

He said no.

✦✦✦

Gloria stared at her reflection in the bathroom mirror. *My eyes are already dead. I might as well finish the job.* She opened the medicine cabinet. A row of prescriptions stood at attention. She knew the one she wanted. She held it close to her heart. As she closed the cabinet, a lipstick fell into the sink. She opened the tube. The color was red. Blood red.

It was appropriate. She wrote on the mirror her confession, her legacy: *Evil won.*

Gloria nodded. It would have to do. Her pitiful life had been swirling in a whirlpool that funneled into this one event, this essence of her unworthiness. She didn't have space to ask for Stevie's forgiveness. She didn't want his forgiveness. She didn't deserve it.

Moving to the bedroom, she remade the bed with extraordinary precision. *There should be a certain dignity in a deathbed.* She put on the white, silk nightgown she'd worn on her honeymoon. It pleased her that even after having a baby it still hung gracefully on her curves. She brushed her hair and applied a spritz of perfume.

She sat at the edge of the bed and emptied the bottle of pills into her hand. It would be so easy. There would be no more pain. No more worries. No more shame.

Death...the image of a minister standing over a gravesite came to her. She'd seen the scene in a dozen movies. Heard the words... "Even though I walk through the valley of the shadow of death, I will fear no evil, for you are with me, your rod and your staff, they comfort me."

Comfort? Maybe there was still a way out. As the last remnant of hope fought for strength, Gloria telephoned St. Stephens.

"Father Delatondo, please." She had to repeat her request twice to be heard.

"Father has asked not to be disturbed. May I take a message?"

The irony struck her like a slap. It was just her luck to call for help and have no one there. It must be fate.

Gloria swallowed the pills, stretched out on the bed, and waited to die.

Del adjusted his position on the floor, on his knees, next to his bed. He buried his face deeper into his hands. He'd prayed for peace of mind and had found none. A continuing litany of images and verses snaked their way through his mind like a tickertape.

'He despairs of escaping the darkness, he is marked for the sword...the sword of the Spirit, which is the word of God...the Word of God is living and active. Sharper than any double-edged sword, it penetrates even to dividing soul and spirit, joints and marrow, it judges the thoughts and attitudes of the heart'...Gloria, gloria, gloria...

Del lifted his head and with an utter certainty knew what he had to do. He ran to the telephone.

The spinning lights of the ambulance and police cars lit the night sky. Gloria Wellington's sheet-draped form was removed from the house.

A crowd had gathered. Del glanced at them sadly. Neighbors wrenched from their homes by the sounds of the sirens stood in small groups of two or three, their arms waving in illustration. Del turned back to Stevie Wellington, who stood beside him in stunned silence, his face buried in his baby's soft hair.

Del put a hand on Stevie's arm. "Maybe we'd better go inside and—" He broke off as a shiver ran up his neck. His skin pricked and his heart raced. He felt something. A presence. Something dim and foul from the depths of darkness.

"Father?"

Del started, then focused on Stevie. "Yes, yes, I'm coming." He followed the man toward his home, but couldn't help glancing around again. *Lord, what is it? What am I feeling?*

Del noticed a man standing alone in the background. His expression as he stared at Gloria's shrouded form was not that of grief, but of utter delight. Del felt his mouth go dry, and his palms grow moist.

Dear Jesus, it looks like the man in the black car. Cash...is it him?

The man looked as though he was wallowing in the chaos around him. The lights and the fear had the neighbors clinging to friends and family. But this man stood there, an odd, half-smile on his face. Amid the tears, the furrowed brows, and the shaking heads, his reaction stood out. Foreign, alien, appalling.

He looked up, his gaze meeting Del's. It was all Del could do to not turn and run into the house. The man merely smiled and nodded in satisfaction. And then he mouthed something.

Del frowned, horror washing over him—then almost jumped out of his skin when someone touched his arm. He jerked around to face Stevie again.

"Father Delatondo, are you all right?"

Del cleared his throat, nodding quickly. "Yes, yes, of course. Let's go inside."

A quick glance behind him told him the man was gone. But the word he'd mouthed rang in Del's mind as clearly as if it had been shouted.

"One."

✦✦✦

Del's mentor, John, spoke to the assembly of angels. "We need to speak of the other force. He is active in the lives of many of our charges."

"His evil is powerful," Fran said. "I fear for them all."

"He won't give up easily."

"He has taken Gloria." Gabe shook his head. "May God have mercy on her soul."

"Amen."

"It is too late for her." John studied those gathered. "She did not pray. She did not call out for help. Our hands were tied. If only..."

"Now he has enlisted the help of Kathy's husband," Anne said. "Lenny is a demon in disguise."

John shook his head. "He is a man. He has a soul that can be saved."

"Or lost forever like..." Anne didn't have to finish. They all knew the ending: *"Like Gloria's."*

"Who wants to volunteer to save him?" Louise looked around. "I've searched for his mentor, but I can't find him."

"I'm sure Lenny's mentor is sorely discouraged." John said. "Lenny rejected God two years ago. He has been living with evil ever since. 'The good man brings good things out of the good stored up in him, and the evil man brings evil things out of the evil stored up in him.' Yet no matter how many prayers we bring before our Lord, everything still rests on the free will of our charges. We can give them opportunities for change, we can give them the knowledge of salvation, but it is still up to them to do or die."

Anne sighed. "I fear he will die. Lenny is too far gone."

181

"Don't say that!" Fran touched her arm. "If you concede, Satan wins Lenny, and then my Natalie is a goner too."

"No, she isn't," Louise said. "She still speaks to God. She yearns to reach out to Him. With that tie to our Lord there is hope."

"Hope." Gabe's voice rang with certainty. "Hope is something Walter needs."

"His father is happy in heaven," Anne said. "I saw him. I spoke to him. But he is concerned about his son."

"Rightly so," Gabe said. "Walter suffers. He doubts."

"Through doubt they become strong," John said. "If they did not doubt, they would never grow."

Louise nodded. "Julia will be of help to him."

"But Julia will soon have other things to think about."

"I know, John, but she will persevere. And they will help each other."

He inclined his head. "I did get Del to contact Walter."

"What about Stevie Wellington? His prayers have been heard. We must add ours to those of his family."

"We should pray that God will reveal the glory in these circumstances," Gabe said.

The mentors formed a circle and raised their voices. "Lord, help our charges open their hearts to You, amid all their ordeals. Help them remember the words of Your disciple, James: 'Consider it pure joy, my brothers, whenever you face trials of many kinds, because you know that the testing of your faith develops perseverance. Perseverance must finish its work so that you may be mature and complete, not lacking anything. If any of you lacks wisdom, he should ask God, who gives generously to all without finding fault, and it will be given to him. But when he asks, he must believe and not doubt, because he who doubts is like a wave of the sea, blown and tossed by the wind.'"

Their voices were heard.

TWENTY

"For in him we live and move and have our being."
As some of your own poets have said, "We are his offspring."
ACTS 17: 28

THE SUN RISING on a new day usually filled Kathy with
hope. No matter what troubles or stresses were present in her
life, she could be rejuvenated by the daily opportunity to
start over.

But not today. The morning after the picnic, after
discovering her husband was alive, Kathy found no comfort
in the sunrise. It was an intrusion into her shroud of gloom
and dread. Was Lenny back in her life for good? Would he
want to act as her husband again? The children's father? *No.*
Please no.

He was still alive...and she wished he were dead. The
revelation shocked and shamed her.

When she went outside to get the morning paper, she
scanned the neighborhood, remembering how she might
have two men to worry about: Lenny and the man harassing
her. Roy had mentioned that maybe they were one and the
same, but she couldn't believe that. It wouldn't make sense
for Lenny to torment her if he had come back to town to be a
part of their lives.

A neighbor drove by, and tooted a horn in greeting.
Kathy waved and with the reminder that life was going on as
usual, she chastised herself. Things were a bit confusing at
the moment, but they'd all be all right if she took things one
step at a —

Kathy saw a note taped to the outside of the door. Her
stomach tightened. She ripped it off, not letting her eyes read
its contents. She hurried inside and bolted the door. She
leaned against it. Her heart pounded. Her fist crushed the
note into a ball. She let it fall to the floor.

Ryan came out from the kitchen. "Mom, can I make Lisa
instant oatmeal? She says her tummy still hurts and she

doesn't want Lucky Charms." He picked up the balled-up note and turned it over in his hands. "What's this?"

Kathy grabbed it away from him. "Go on! Go eat."

Ryan retreated to the kitchen, looking hurt and worried.

Kathy stared at the rumpled paper in her hand. The weight of its contents made it feel heavy, a stone...a rock waiting to be heaved into the thin pane of glass that kept her family safe. Yet surely reading the note couldn't hurt her any more than she'd already been hurt?

I don't know, Lord. I just don't understand what's going on. Help me get through all of this.

Feeling a dose of heaven-provided strength, she took a deep breath and opened her eyes. Then she read the note.

◆◆◆

"Good morning, Kathy. At least I hope it's a good morning," Roy said on the phone. "Anything would be better than going through what you did last night. Are you calling from work?"

She ignored his question and pounced. "I just want to know...is it true?"

"Huh?" Roy fumbled for words. "Well—I mean—I guess that depends. If you're asking if I'm a handsome hunk who is the greatest thing since Band-Aids, then yes, it's—"

"Are you an abortionist?"

Silence.

"Roy? Are you an abortionist?"

"I'll be right over."

Kathy hung up and cried. It was true.

◆◆◆

Roy stood in the doorway of A Mother's Love, still in his lab coat. "Do I dare enter?"

Kathy's crossed arms and blazing eyes made him consider retreat. "That depends on whether or not it's true."

He looked around the office and was relieved they were alone. Whether by coincidence or design, Kathy was by herself. He moved to stand by her desk, letting it be a buffer between them. "It *was* true. It isn't any more." He sat down. "How did you find out?"

Kathy handed him a wrinkled note.

He opened it and read. "So maybe our friendly neighborhood stalker is after me too?"

"Tell me everything, Mr. Righteous. The entire truth."

Roy nodded. "I was just out of my residency. I was superior to all men. I was a doctor. I was God. I had the power over life and death. I was in control."

"A bit cocky?"

"No 'bit' about it. I was steaming hot." He rose to pace, stuffing his hands into his pockets. "A colleague asked me to come in with him. He had this clinic in California. He said it was great money and I would be helping women get their lives in order."

Kathy shook her head at the lie.

"I know, I know—now," Roy said. "But I didn't know then. It was legal. I didn't think of the ethics or morality of it. I wasn't into God much back then. I was too consumed with my own deity."

"Somehow 'Roy, Wonderful Counselor, Prince of Peace' doesn't have the right ring to it."

"You couldn't tell *me* that. It was something I had to learn the hard way." He raised an eyebrow. "You're not the only one who's had to travel that road." He ran a hand through his hair. "I performed abortions for ten months. I tried to overlook the fact there was no satisfaction in it. The women came in scared and worried and left scared and worried."

"And bruised for life."

He nodded. "And bruised for life."

"What got you out of it?"

"I didn't suddenly wake up one morning and decide, 'This is wrong.' It was slower than that. At the beginning, I didn't pay much attention to the patients as individuals. But slowly I became aware of their stories, their roads to the clinic. With each woman, a part of my conscience was awakened. Once awakened, it wouldn't sleep. It just kept gnawing at me..." He sat, leaning his arms on his legs, wringing his hands, looking anywhere but at Kathy's eyes. He hated telling her this. But he knew it was right.

"The clincher was a girl named Jerri. She didn't have any horror story to tell. No rape, incest, or abusive husband. Maybe her ordinariness moved me. She was a college freshman. She was cute and bright, with her life promising years and years of possibilities. She met a boy during her first semester. They thought 'What the heck? Everyone's doing it,' and had sex. She became pregnant. It's an old story." He paused to take a cleansing breath. "She was brought in by her father *and* the father of the baby. The baby's father was against the abortion. Up until she walked into the operating room, he tried to talk her out of it, pleading, cajoling, promising. But Jerri's father was for it. He acted as if the abortion would erase his daughter's shame. He was angry with her, annoyed. Unfortunately, he was the stronger influence."

"What about Jerri?" Kathy's eyes were moist. "What did she want?"

"Jerri wanted to have the whole thing disappear. She was young, weak, and desperate."

"Her father won." Roy felt the sorrow all over again. "That's the point. Nobody won. That's what hit me. Changed me. When the men came back to see Jerri after the procedure, the father bawled. Because of his lost little girl? Because of his lost grandchild? And the father of the baby bawled. For *his* loss of innocence? For the death of his child? Jerri didn't cry. She lay there with the men of her life falling apart around her, and stared past them. Her face was as dead as her baby."

Kathy cried new tears, and gave Roy a tissue for his own.

"That's when I realized how much died when a baby was aborted. Innocence, hope, love, family. All that child could have been, would have been. Their joys and sorrows are over before they've begun. Their children and grandchildren are extinguished with them. A life God had planned, known, and

186

loved is gone before a breath of life. It didn't matter that it was legal. It didn't matter whether people were prochoice or prolife. The reality of that baby's death affected everyone without mercy. There was no right in such a wrong."

"So you stopped."

Roy hesitated. "Let's just say a few more things happened that made me understand how much God wanted me to stop." He looked at her. This was the hardest part of all. What would she think...? *No, don't second-guess. Just tell it.* "I was invited to a place where everything was made exquisitely clear. And after that experience, I changed my specialty from killing babies to delivering them. I joined Physicians for Life, an organization of doctors who are visibly and audibly prolife." He shook his head. "So often our mistakes determine the direction of our lives as much — if not more — than our successes."

Kathy nodded. The look on her face said she understood. "I'm sorry."

"So am —"

The telephone rang. Kathy answered it, but the other person did most of the talking. She hung up and grabbed her purse in the same movement.

"What's wrong?" "Lisa's sick. The babysitter thinks she should go to the hospital."

◆◆◆

Kathy was in a daze. She let herself be led from one checkpoint to another. *Name, address, insurance? Sign here. Go to the third floor waiting room. Check in. Wait. The doctor will be in to see you soon...*

Kathy called her parents and Lenny's mother to tell them of Lisa's surgery for appendicitis. Lisa looked so tiny on the hospital bed. Her cotton gown was dotted with bunnies. They counted them while they waited, and Lisa named them in between spasms of pain. The one on her right sleeve was Elmo, the one on her left, Bert, which led to Ernie and a strange bunny named Big Bird.

187

Finally it was time. The nurses came to take Lisa into the operating room.

Kathy kissed her baby girl, hoping to comfort her.

"Don't be scared, Mommy." Lisa turned Bunny Bob over and began fumbling with something on his back.

"What do you have there, sweet cakes?"

Lisa held the stuffed animal so Kathy could see. Kathy's mustard seed pin was fastened to the back of its head. "Here, Mommy. Take the God pin."

"When did you take...?" Kathy let the question go. It didn't matter. She took the pin and fastened it to her blouse.

Lisa nodded as if she approved. "Pray, okay?"

Kathy bit the inside of her mouth to hold back her tears.

"We have to go now, little one," a nurse said.

Kathy nodded and held Lisa's hand as the nurses wheeled her out into the hall. She prayed harder than she ever had in her life. It was nearly unbearable to have Lisa go through the operating room doors without her.

Kathy wasn't sure how, but she found her way to the waiting room. She sank into a chair. The inane chatter of a television threatened to break into her prayers, but she wouldn't let it. "Please..." Kathy closed her eyes. "Please, Father, make her all right." She felt a hand on her shoulder.

"She will be." Roy took a seat. "She will—"

Kathy saw his eyes fall onto the mustard seed pin on her chest. Then he put a hand on his own chest, covering something. When he moved his hand away, she saw...

It was a mustard seed pin!

She sat up, barely daring to breathe. "Where ...where did you get that?"

"Where did you get *that*?"

"Haven," she said.

"Haven," he said.

✦✦✦

Roy knelt in front of Kathy, knowing but not caring that he was drawing attention. He took her hands. "Don't you see,

Kathy? God brought us together for a reason."

Kathy hugged herself, shivering. "You're one of us?"

Roy nodded in shock. "We're the same."

Kathy put a hand over her mouth and started to cry. "I always felt...there was this bond...we're the same."

Roy shook his head, still trying to take it all in. "We heard there were other Havens, but I've never met anyone...I visited the one in California. Two years ago—"

"August first."

He nodded. "And you?"

"Haven, Nebraska. That's when Lenny disappeared in a tornado."

"*He* was invited, too?" Roy felt the quick blush that followed his incredulous response. Who was *he* to question who was invited to Haven?

Kathy's smile was understanding. "No. He came after me, to find me, to take me home. God welcomed him there, but Lenny rejected him. He ran out in the storm and we never saw him again...until yesterday."

Roy nodded. *Amazing, Lord...you're amazing.* He took a seat beside her. "What did you dedicate to God? How did He change you?"

"I dedicated my paintings, and I promised to do everything in my power to promote the sanctity of children."

"You've certainly done that last part. But what's this about paintings?"

"I used to paint children, but then I got sidetracked doing landscapes—paintings that could be whipped up and sold quick."

She was an artist. Someone who put beauty on canvas so others could share it. The image seemed so right. "I'd like to see them—the paintings of children."

"Sometime." She put a hand on his knee. "Was Haven the reason you stopped performing abortions?"

He nodded. "God is very persuasive, but being a Haven disciple...it hasn't been easy living up to it. Sometimes I feel so guilty for having been chosen to go to Haven. I feel so unworthy. I mean, who am I? This huge sinner. How can

189

God use me, someone who has wronged Him so deeply?"

"And how can God use me? A housewife with two small kids, a high school diploma, and a bad marriage?"

"Two ordinary people."

"From whom he expects the extraordinary?" Kathy smiled slightly.

Roy shrugged.

"Don't you feel like you've blown it sometimes?" Kathy's eyes begged him to understand. "It's been two years and I don't think I've accomplished much. Sure, I've started to work at A Mother's Love and I've dabbled with my paintings, but nothing tremendous has happened—either by my hand, or His."

"You met me." Roy grinned.

She laughed, and the sound of it was music. "God certainly didn't choose you because of your humility."

He shrugged. "I can't be *entirely* perfect. I'd scare people off."

"I can imagine."

"So..." Roy looked at her, drinking in the sight of her face, the way her eyes— "What do we do now?"

Kathy put her fingers through his. "I guess we carry on. We wait to see what God does with us."

"We have faith?"

She nodded. "We have faith."

✦✦✦

Lenny opened the door of the men's room and peered out. He could hear his mother and Kathy's parents talking in the waiting room. What was left of his heart melted at the sound.

Maybe I made the wrong choice back in Haven? Maybe when they talked of Christ and God and heaven I should have listened. Maybe I wouldn't have had to live the last two years in the shadows if I would've listened to their talk about the Light. Maybe if I'd made a choice for God instead of against Him, I would've been strong enough to say no when I was offered —

Lenny frowned. What exactly *had* he been offered? Once

it had seemed so clear. What *was* he getting for his trouble? For his risk? For this alienation from his family?

Something about power. Wealth. Good times. Odd, Lenny didn't feel very powerful, and the only money he had was in his pockets. As for the good times? Sex. Booze. A bit of dope now and then. The memories were dim and hardly good.

Now little Lisa was hurting. His daughter. He couldn't even go to the room and comfort her. He had to stay away. Stay back. Stay in those shadows.

Lenny heard his mother laugh. She had a ridiculous laugh. High and grating. But it sang to him, flooding his mind with memories of home.

It's not fair, it's not fair, it's not —

Lenny was seized by an impulse. He didn't need to stay in the shadows any more. No one was forcing him to stay there. His boss was hundreds of miles away.

He backtracked to the restroom mirror. How did he look? He grimaced. He looked awful. Why hadn't he noticed it before?

His clothes were filthy. A pair of torn jeans and a scrubby T-shirt sporting a faded silk-screen ad for vodka. He tucked the shirt into his jeans and ran a hand through his hair. How'd it get so long? And greasy. When was the last time he'd taken a shower? He combed his fingers through his beard. His family had never seen him with a beard. If only he'd had time to plan, he could have shaved it off or at least trimmed it proper. He rubbed a finger over the front of his teeth trying to wipe away the film.

There. That was as good as it could get on such short—

Lenny paused. He leaned forward and studied his reflection. Something was missing ... His face was gaunt, his skin pulled tight against his skull. His eyes were shadowed sockets punctuated by pale eyes that looked as if the color of life had been washed out of them. He looked old. Very, very old.

What had happened to him?

He knew the answer to that. His life had been poisoned.

After the tornado, he'd found himself in a soggy ditch in the middle of a Nebraska nowhere. He'd staggered to his feet, soaked, bruised, and bleeding. Farm fields surrounded him on all sides. Stands of far-off trees broke the horizon. But no houses. No buildings. No people to help him or care whether he lived or —

"*Lenny.*"

He had turned toward his name and seen a man standing above him on the road. A handsome man with dark eyes, who had held out a hand. Lenny took it and the man pulled him out of the ditch...

Since then, Lenny often rethought that moment. He questioned how his boss had happened to be on that particular deserted road at that particular time. He wondered how he'd known Lenny was in the ditch... how he'd known Lenny's name.

One by one, Lenny discounted these questions. A few unanswered queries were a small price to pay for his boss's attention. He'd cleaned Lenny up, fed him, bandaged him, and seemed genuinely interested when Lenny had detailed his gripes about Kathy and Haven. Most people didn't care about other people's problems. But his boss had. He'd listened. He'd agreed when Lenny decided to have fun and toss the inane responsibilities of his family aside.

"Serve yourself," his boss had said. Only later had he added, "Serve me."

The bits of mischief Lenny had been told to carry out hadn't seemed so bad. A little thievery. A few lies. Just setting things square with the world. Taking what was due. Doing it to strangers made it easy. But when the boss had brought up doing such things to Kathy...

"I should've said no." Lenny started at the sound of his voice in the empty restroom. "I should've turned and run." He looked away from his reflection. Running from his boss was next to impossible, but maybe...

Lenny put a hand to his mouth, shaking with hope. "Maybe?" he repeated to the mirror. His eyes sparked with new life. He nodded with his decision. Squaring his

shoulders, he pushed open the restroom door. He stepped
into the hall and walked toward the voices.

✦✦✦

The conversation among Lenny's family continued as the
strange man stopped and stood at the edge of the room.
Gladys Kraus was the first to notice him, and looked
confused, as if she was wondering why a man was just
standing there as though he had something to say. She gave
him the once-over and looked a bit disgusted. He WAS filthy.
He knew he probably looked like a transient who'd crawled
out from under a bridge. His eyes met hers...

"Lenny!" Then she screamed, and nurses and doctors
came running.

✦✦✦

Recognizing her mother-in-law's voice, Kathy ran out of
Lisa's room to find Gladys sitting in a chair, Kathy's parents
hovering close. A nurse brought Gladys a glass of water.

Kathy frowned. "What's going on?"

Her mother took her hand, leading her to a chair. "Sit
down, Kathy."

She shook off her mother's hand. "I don't want to sit
down. I have to get back to Lisa. Just tell me what hap—"

A man walked into Kathy's view. She backed away. "You
get away from us! We don't want you here."

Gladys Kraus suddenly came to life. "Don't you *dare* say
that to my son! He's alive! He's here. He's back!"

Kathy couldn't listen to another word. She spun and
hurried down the hall to Lisa's room, yelling at the group
behind her. "He may be back, but he's *not* welcome. And he's
not going to see my daughter!"

She ran into Lisa's room and slammed the door.

✦✦✦

Lenny felt better after a shower, a shave, and a good meal at his mother's house. She'd made him a steak and mashed potatoes, just like she used to. And strawberry shortcake with Cool Whip. He washed it down with a beer.

This was the life.

Gladys Kraus sat next to him, eating nothing herself. She leaned her head on one hand, staring at him. "You're looking almost human now with that awful beard gone. It is so good to have you back. I knew you weren't dead. I *knew* it. Your wife gave up on you years ago. She didn't believe like I did."

"That's nice, Ma." Lenny squirmed. He wasn't used to such scrutiny. He was used to being by himself. He finished the shortcake and stood, still chewing. "Got to make a phone call, Ma."

"There's the phone, right over there where it's always—"

He pulled out his cellphone. "I'm going in the bedroom. I need some privacy."

She looked hurt.

"And no listening. Okay, Ma?"

It was obvious by her blush that she'd considered it. She nodded, and Lenny went to her bedroom. He locked the door and sat on the bed. His eyes were drawn to a family picture on the bedside table. His father.

Although Lenny had never thought about it before, it was odd that his mother still had the photo by her bedside. What had it been? Twelve years? Did she still wait for her husband's return, just as she had waited for his?

He picked up the photo. His father looked back at him, his curly black hair in a constant tousled state, his five o'clock shadow evident at noon. A ten-year-old Lenny stood in front of his dad, grinning as if he enjoyed having his father's arm skimming his ear, draped over his shoulder and chest. He *had* enjoyed it. But little else. Lenny's memories of his father were limited to this photo and the man's love of Juicy Fruit gum. That was all his father had ever given him, a token when he was in a good mood.

"Want a piece of gum, son?"

Lenny had always taken a piece, even if he had three

pieces in his pocket. It was a way to connect, to share with his dad. A few short years and a few sticks of gum. That was it.

Lenny set the photo aside. He'd abandoned his family just like his dad had done. No, it wasn't just like his dad. Lenny was back. He would right the wrongs he'd caused. But first, he had to get away from...

He dialed the number. His stomach yanked with every ring. *Maybe he won't be home. Maybe he's forgotten about me.*

"What do you want, Lenny?"

He shivered, hating how his boss had known he was calling before he'd even said a word.

"Just checking in."

"No you're not. You're trying to check out. You're trying to *get* out."

"Why...why would you say such a thing?"

"How dumb do you think we are? I know you showed yourself to your family *and* Kathy. I know you had a steak and a baked potato at your—"

"Mashed potatoes."

"Whatever. The point is, I *know*. We know what you're doing before you do, Einstein. And I'm telling you right now, there is no way you're backing out now. No way in hell."

Lenny gulped. "My daughter needed surgery. I was worried about her. I wanted to see her. Is there anything wrong with that?"

"She's not your daughter anymore, you idiot. When you came in with us you relinquished your rights to everything you had in this world. You gave them up for a few cheap thrills and no bills."

Lenny wanted to cry. "Maybe we could strike another deal? Change a few of the conditions?"

"I'm sure you'd like that. Everyone would like that. But that's not the way it works. Once you make a deal, that's it. There's no way out. No way—"

"What if I ask God to forgive me?"

There was silence on the line. Lenny's eyes widened. If he didn't know better, he'd think his boss was surprised. Even scared. He decided to risk asking the question again. "What if I ask God to forgive—"

"Don't do a thing! I'm coming down. You've screwed things up so...I have a few things to tie up here and then I'm coming. Don't do anything stupid."

Lenny hung up the phone, confused. Was asking God for forgiveness stupid?

Or would the truly stupid thing be to wait to see his boss face to face?

TWENTY-ONE

"I am he who will sustain you.
I have made you and I will carry you,
I will sustain you and I will rescue you."
ISAIAH 46: 4

WALTER SAT ON the bed in his father's room at the Hillcrest Retirement Village. Boxes of Jeb Prescott's possessions surrounded him. Odd how a baseball glove, a box of old photos, and some military bars and medals represented a life.

And a mustard seed pin.

Walter had found the pin on the table next to his father's bed. Under it was a note scribbled in his father's abysmal handwriting.

My dear son,

My time is coming. Don't know when exactly, but it's like a switch is ready to burn out. Sooner than I'd like, but later than I deserve. It's made me realize there's business that needs to be taken care of. Father-Son business. You're a good boy, Walter. A good man. But to be honest, Bette's made you better. She's a jewel, boy. And now you have a little jewel in Addy. Sure wish I could see her in person, but if it isn't to be...give her a hug for me and tell her Grandpa was only half bad.

I'm all right about dying, boy. Like I told you this afternoon, I believe. I believe in all of it. I used to think believing was for the womenfolk. That's why I left such things to your mother. But then she let it slide and you got half of nothing. Forgive us, son. We didn't know — or if we did, we weren't strong enough to own up to it.

Before I go to bed, I'm taking off this mustard seed pin and setting it aside for you. Don't know why. Just a feeling. If nothing comes of it, I'll pin it on in the morning like I always do. But if something

197

happens...

I sure do appreciate getting it from you, boy. It made me feel special, it made me feel closer to you—and to God.

I'm all right, Walter. Don't worry about me. Thanks to you and this little pin, I know where I'm going.

But wait...Son? I was looking at the Bible tonight and I came across this one verse and a strange kind of feeling came over me, like it was meant for you. So, whatever it's worth, here it is: "Take up the shield of faith, with which you can extinguish all the flaming arrows of the evil one." That's Ephesians 6:16. Don't know what it means, but I feel better for having passed it on...

Love you, boy,
Pop

Walter's shoulders shook with sobs. "I hate him! I hate—"
He stopped himself before he said "God". The hate was selfish. Pop was gone. But Pop had said what needed to be said. If only Walter had done the same.

Yet, the part of Walter that thought beyond himself was grateful to God. For somehow, God had touched his pop, and made him see what Walter had come to see, that having faith was the *only* way to live. And die.

Pop's life may not have been a grand slam, but it was still a mark in the win column, and it deserved a mighty shout.

The funeral was over. It was just like Pop had been: short, simple, and even sarcastic, as some of Pop's friends shared stories revealing Jeb Prescott's witty, wily ways.

Walter drove through the night toward Minneapolis. Although his body was aching for sleep, he didn't allow himself the option. He didn't want to dream. And he didn't want to wake up and realize all over again that Pop was gone. He chose to keep the pain quietly beside him, rather than have it pounce on him new and fresh.

He dreaded the nine-hour drive. Too much time to think. Yet oddly, his thoughts didn't dwell on his father's death. They seemed to follow the van, toward Minneapolis, toward Bette and Addy. As the sun set at the closing of the day, it also set on what was left of Walter's old life.

He had a new family now. He had become two things he'd never thought he would be: a husband and a father. He'd grown into being a husband and while he knew he wasn't the best, he figured he was better than many. But a father...how could he be a father when he had no experience with children? How should he hold his daughter? When would Addy sit up, walk, and talk? What should he say to her? Would she listen?

In the endless dark of the night, his mind swam with all that could go wrong. All the mistakes he could make.

The interstate stretched before him, a slice of illumination leading from one life to another, the elements beyond the road, shaded and unknown. He longed for the daylight so he could see what lay on either side of his path. In the dark he was fearful, but in the light—

An overpass loomed ahead. His headlights lit graffiti on the concrete pillar of the bridge. Walter read it...and gasped.

TRUST JESUS.

He nearly went off the road trying to keep the words in sight as he passed under the bridge. The feeling of relief was so great he made an illegal U-turn in an emergency turnoff and backtracked.

Did I really see it? Was it really there?

He passed under the overpass heading in the opposite direction. He looked over his shoulder trying to see the message, but without his headlights to illuminate the words, he couldn't see a thing. He found another turnoff and headed back north.

Be there. Be there.

He saw the dark on dark silhouette of the overpass looming ahead of him. His heart pounded with the excitement of seeing the message.

Closer. Closer. He turned his lights on high-beam. They lit the overpass. He searched for the words.

They weren't there.

"I *saw* them!" Walter hit the steering wheel. "I saw them. I know it!"

Panic rose in Walter's throat—but only for a moment. Then he shook his head and laughed. "OK, God, I saw it. I saw your message. And once should be enough, shouldn't it?"

There was no visible or audible answer, but Walter felt it clearly, in his heart:

Once is enough, Walter. Trust Jesus.

The sun was just coming up when Walter pulled in front of Julia's house. He tiptoed into the foyer, not wanting to wake up Bette.

There was a light on in the living room. He moved to turn it off and found Bette in the shadows, curled on the love seat. Cradled near her chest was a pink blanket.

The blanket moved, and Walter's heart skipped. He lifted the corner of the fuzzy material and peered in. The precious face of his daughter looked back at him and blinked.

"Hi ya, Addy," he whispered.

Bette opened her eyes. She smiled and held out her hand. Walter kissed it, then knelt on the floor beside them. His arms were big enough to hold them both.

It felt good to be back to work. Although the people at KMPS didn't know him very well, Walter felt their sympathy for his father's passing and saw their joy in his daughter's birth. It felt good to belong, to be welcomed.

Yet Walter felt odd going into his new office... as though

he'd neglected his job before he'd even started. He and Rolf had no sooner made the list of the television shows that would earn advertising sponsors a spot of the Honor Roll when Walter's world had rushed into fast forward. There was a knock on his opened door. It was Rolf.

"How you doing, Walter?"

"Fair to partly cloudy," Walter said, using Pop's line. "Can't complain. Actually, I'd like to complain but..."

Rolf raised a hand. "I understand completely." He came into the room and sat down. "I'd love to tell you to take all the time you need but I'm afraid that won't be possible."

Walter was embarrassed by his own relief. A part of him would have liked to wallow in his situation, and yet...he needed to get on with things. He needed to set circumstances aside and follow the instructions he'd received. He needed to trust Jesus.

He studied his boss's face. "Did something go wrong with the implementation of the Honor Roll?"

"Just the opposite." Rolf grinned. "Ever since the press release we've been getting calls from sponsors who are interested in the *idea* of being on the list, but none have actually signed up. We've also had some coverage against it, some reports saying it's a stupid idea, just a marketing ploy. The normal skeptics."

"We don't have *anyone* signed up yet?"

"On the verge, Walter. On the verge. That's why we need you back on track." He handed Walter a list of advertisers. "Here are the sponsors who have shown interest. I have the account department working up a special contract as we speak. And our legal department is looking at a way to shield us from—"

Walter blinked at the word. "Shield?"

"Yes. They think we need a good, strong shield against lawsuits prejudiced against the honor roll. Protection. Something between us and the opposition."

Walter remembered Pop's letter. "A shield of faith against flaming arrows of evil."

Rolf raised an eyebrow. "Well...that's a little dramatic,

but the basics are there. Dare I ask where those words came from? They don't sound like your usual vocabulary."

Walter was glad it was Rolf he was talking to. "The Bible. Ephesians. Actually, Pop quoted the verse in a letter, and Bette quoted it before we moved up here."

"A double-hitter." Rolf lifted a finger in recognition. "I know those verses... God's armor."

"Really?"

"Sure. Heady stuff. Good versus evil. Utilizing God's power."

"Wow. You think we need that kind of power for the Honor Roll?"

Rolf made a face. "Well...I never thought of it...but we *did* jump into this project without working out the specifics, hoping they'd fall into place. Perhaps we should have waited, but I felt so sure—"

Walter shook his head. I'm sure too. Sometimes you have to go for it and worry about the details later. Go on faith. You know? Sorry I got us off the track. What you said just reminded me of Pop and..." He shrugged.

"It will take some time, Walter. Grief is a process."

"But work is good. Keep me busy."

Rolf nodded. "We can do that. Those details, remember? Unfortunately, getting signed contracts is no detail. A deal's not a deal until they sign. Get them to sign, Walter."

Walter looked over the list of advertisers who had called about the Honor Roll. Some hefty accounts were intermixed with some lesser ones. A good cross section.

Walter's intercom buzzed. "There's a call for you, Mr. Wingow. Ted Brighton from Brighton's Fried Chicken. He wants to talk with you about the Honor Roll and...he said something about a pin?"

"We'll take it in here, Ms. Kane." Rolf turned to Walter. "Brighton Chicken is one of our bigger accounts for evening prime time. Ted Brighton is a great guy and runs a quality business. He serves up meals to the poor and gives part of his profits to various charities. He has a reputation as a good man, someone who gives more than he takes. If we get him, others will follow."

Walter leaned back in his chair. "What's this about a pin?"

"I have no idea. Let's ask him."

They put the call on speakerphone. "Nice to hear from you, Mr. Brighton," Rolf said. "I'm here with Walter Prescott, the coordinator of the Honor Roll. What can we do for you?"

"I got a pin in the mail, Wingow. A mustard seed pin like Julia Carson talked about on television the other day. I just wanted to thank you for it."

Rolf looked at Walter, eyebrows raised. Walter shook his head. He hadn't sent the pin. And clearly Rolf hadn't. So where had it come from?

Rolf went on. "That's great, Mr. Brighton, but I'm afraid we didn't have anything to do with it."

"Hmm, strange. There wasn't a note saying who'd sent it. Just a note with a verse on it. Let me see if I can find it...yes, here it is, 'Good will come to him who is generous and lends freely, who conducts his affairs with justice. He has scattered abroad his gifts to the poor, his righteousness endures forever, his horn will be lifted high in honor.' Honor. It talked about honor. That's why I thought it came from you and your Honor Roll."

Walter shook his head. *I wish it had.* "Maybe Carson's campaign is sending them out?"

"I thought of that. But wouldn't you think there'd be a campaign card inside? If they were doing it, I'm sure they'd want to get the credit."

There was a moment of silence as each man tried to think of an explanation. Walter came up with one first, but was unsure how to say it. "Now this is a long-shot—" he tapped a pencil on his desk—"but maybe the pin came from someone...well, higher up. You know, the source."

Rolf started and stared at Walter. *God? he mouthed.*

Walter nodded.

"You don't mean God, do you?" Brighton asked.

Walter was relieved that Brighton had been the one to say the *G*-word. "It's a possibility, isn't it?"

Silence. Then, "You know, I like the idea of that. I've tried to be a God-fearing man. I've had great financial success and I've always felt it was my duty to pass it on—"

"Pass it on," Rolf said. "Didn't Governor Carson say that in her speech?"

Walter wasn't listening. He had sudden visions of Brighton Fried Chicken using their receipt of the mustard seed pin as a means of selling more mashed potatoes and chicken wings. "But maybe we're getting caught up in something. We shouldn't jump to any—"

"Oh, let me jump," Brighton said. "Whether it's true or not, I'm honored and I plan on wearing the pin proudly. And when anyone asks about it, I'll say what Carson said on TV."

Rolf frowned. "What did she say?"

"She said she wore her pin as a testament to her faith in God and Jesus. We're supposed to pass it on, to encourage the good things in each other."

Rolf gave a firm nod. "Good things like the Honor Roll."

"Exactly. That's one reason I called. I want to sign up. Am I too late?"

Walter smiled. *Your timing is perfect, Lord. Why do I ever doubt it?* "You're just in time. In fact, because of your enthusiasm, we'll put your name at the top of the list."

There was a moment's hesitation. "I'm not the *only* sponsor on the list, am I?"

Rolf wagged his hand in the air at Walter. Walter hedged. "You're the first sponsor to receive a mustard seed pin. You should feel very honored."

"I'm also the first on the list, aren't I?"

Rolf shrugged and grinned. "You have that distinct honor, too."

Brighton laughed. "Sign me up."

◆◆◆

Although signing Brighton Fried Chicken was a great start to the day, God wasn't through. Walter fielded seven phone calls from interested sponsors. All of them had received a mustard seed pin in the mail, each with a different verse regarding honor that spoke to their own situation. At noon, Walter put a call into Julia's headquarters, hoping to track her down. He left a message. As he was getting ready to leave for the day, she returned his call.

"How's that baby, Walter?" Walter smiled at her cheerful tones. "Addy and Bette are doing fine, thanks to your hospitality."

"And a heavy dose of fatherly attention, I hope."

"I'm giving it a good shot." He decided not to tell her about his father. He had a more positive reason for his call. "Julia, Has your office been sending out mustard seed pins?"

She hesitated. "Why do you ask?"

Walter explained about the Honor Roll sponsors.

"I'd love to claim responsibility, but I can't," she said. "Actually, we thought about cashing in on the idea because we've fielded hundreds — make that thousands — of phone calls from people wanting a pin."

"But you didn't send them?"

"It was tempting, but I didn't think it was my place."

"So you think God's sending them out?"

"God or the pin fairy."

"It's wonderful, *whoever* is responsible." Walter sighed and leaned back in his chair. "The Honor Roll already has eight sponsors. We're on a roll."

Julia laughed. "You'd better amend that, Walter. *God's* the One on a roll."

TWENTY-TWO

"For when I called, no one answered, when I spoke, no one listened. They did evil in my sight and chose what displeases me."
ISAIAH 66: 4

NATALIE'S FINGERS FLEW across her laptop, filling page after page with her experiences in Haven. Ever since Jack had encouraged her, she'd been consumed with the need to work on it. If only she never had to sleep.

For two mornings, she'd started writing at 5:30, hoping to get a few pages written before going to work. On the second day, there was a knock on her door at seven, and she ran down the stairs, anxious to tell Jack about her progress.

It was Beau. "Long time no see."

She put a hand to her hair, suddenly aware that it was uncombed, that she wore no makeup, and that she was wearing an extra-large T-shirt that said, "Don't mess with me, I'm sleeping."

Beau took in every detail, then grinned. "So this is how you look in the morning."

"No, not really...I mean, I usually look better, but I—" She gave up. "Why are you knocking on my door so early?"

He lifted a hand toward the top of the stairs. "May I?"

She put a hand on either side of the narrow stairs, blocking his way. "I don't know. Are you going to behave yourself?"

He raised his hand in a pledge. "On my honor—such as it is."

"No comment." She led him upstairs. "Want some coffee?" She detoured to the sleeping area and slipped on a pair of shorts under her T-shirt.

"No thanks." He brazenly watched her. "I don't believe I need any further stimulation this morning."

"Should I feel relieved or wary?"

"That depends..." He picked up a stack of printed pages and read a few lines. He frowned. "What's this? What happened to your novel?"

Natalie thought of grabbing the pages away from him, but decided to try the subtle approach. She took a sip of her coffee, pretending it wasn't cold. She leaned against the counter. "The novel is still around. But I was talking to Jack and he suggested I work on the Haven—"

"Jack suggested?"

"He *is* an English teacher." She knew that was not the reason she'd taken his advice.

"But I'm a consultant. My job is telling people what's best for them. And I told you to work on your novel."

"After tearing it apart."

"It has potential."

"Since when?"

He tossed the pages on the desk and sank into the cushions of the over-sized chair. "I came up here with great news, but now... I don't know if I should even tell you."

"What great news?"

He crossed his arms and pouted, and though she knew he was teasing her with the reluctance game, her curiosity was too strong not to play along.

"Tell me!"

He looked up at her and grinned. "I have a publisher who's interested in seeing your manuscript—your novel."

She was shocked to silence. Then, "Who? Why? When?"

He laughed. "I'll worry about the who, the why is because I asked them to look at it, and the when is Friday. In person. A meeting."

She ran a hand through her hair, trying to think. "Friday? That's two days away." She bit a fingernail. "They do know the manuscript isn't complete, don't they?"

"They'll look at what you've got."

Natalie began to pace. "I'll have to get off work Friday...."

"You'll have to get off work for more than just Friday."

She stopped pacing. "Why?"

"Because the publisher is meeting us in Eureka Springs, Arkansas."

Natalie wasn't sure which piece of information to digest

first. The fact the meeting was in Arkansas, or the fact Beau had said, *we*. She picked the one that seemed the most urgent.

"We?"

"I arranged the meeting. I go, or it's no go." He gave her a look. "Is that a problem?"

She said, "No, no," even though her instinct said, "Yes, yes." She moved on to her next concern. "Eureka Springs? I've never heard of a publisher from Eureka Springs."

"He's out of New York but he's going to be on vacation in Eureka Springs. As a favor to me, he's agreed to see us Friday. He's even picking up the tab."

She went to her desk and collected the pages from her novel. "I wish I had time to edit this more...I know how important presentation is."

"This publisher won't care."

"But I will." She sat at her desk, opened her laptop and the folder containing her novel. "There isn't enough time. I just started a new job. I can't ask for more time off."

Beau shrugged. "If you can't deal with the time-frame, I suppose I'll tell him you're not interested."

Natalie pulled at her lower lip, completely torn.

Beau got up and strolled across the room. "Plus, there would be the added bonus of seeing your friend Kathy Kraus from Haven."

"Kathy!"

"She lives in Eureka—"

"How did you know that?"

"You told me." Beau shoved his hands in his pockets and looked out the window above her desk. "You told me when you talked about Haven."

Natalie couldn't remember saying such a thing, but let it pass. Everything seemed to be fitting together. Perhaps it was meant to be.

The telephone rang.

"Hey, Nat, it's Hayley. Oh, dear. I don't know how to say this gently...Gloria is dead."

Natalie sank onto the unmade bed. "Dead?"

"Suicide. Last night."

Natalie shook her head. Although she hadn't known Gloria well, the woman had not seemed the type to give up on anything, much less life. She noticed Beau watching her. His face asked a silent question. She put a hand over the receiver. "A lady from work killed herself."

"Hmm. Too bad."

Hayley continued. "The funeral's tomorrow morning. We're going to close for the day so we can all go."

Natalie felt guilty for being relieved that she wouldn't have to ask for Thursday off to go to Arkansas. But Friday, she still needed to get off Friday... Natalie walked to a far corner of her apartment, turning her back on Beau and lowering her voice.

"Hayley, I know now may not be the ideal time to ask for some time off, but..." She told her about the meeting with a publisher, ending with, "It's the chance I've been waiting for my whole life."

"Oh, Nat. Your timing is atrocious, but who am I to stand in the way of your destiny? Life's too short—Gloria proved that. Work late for me tonight and you're off till Monday."

"You are a lifesaver." She hung up. *Everything's set to go. I guess it's meant to —*

When she turned around, she found Beau right behind her. He put a hand on her arm. "You okay?"

She was appalled that it took her a moment to understand that he was talking about Gloria. Her mind was swimming with thoughts about Eureka Springs and publishers. She'd forgotten all about poor Gloria.

She covered her guilt by putting on a sorrowful face. She slid past him to the comfort of her desk chair. "I feel so bad about Gloria. I know she was married and I think she had a little girl." She looked to Beau, hoping her delayed compassion played true. Then she asked two questions that genuinely bothered her. "Why would she kill herself? What could have been so bad?"

Beau leaned on the edge of the desk. "You'd be surprised."

"Why do you say that?"

He shrugged. He looked to the floor, then back to her. "So are you going?"

She nodded. "Would you like to go to the funeral with me?"

"Not the funeral. Are you going to Eureka Springs with me?"

Natalie was pleased that she *had* forgotten about herself—at least for a few moments. "Yes. I would love to go with you. I appreciate your support and your help in setting up the meeting with—"

"Good. Tomorrow we'll leave early."

She blinked with a thought. "But wait. The funeral."

"Skip it."

"I'd feel better if I went. It's the right thing to do." Beau shook his head. She moved to touch his arm. "Could we leave after the funeral? I'd skip the graveside service and just go to the church..."

Beau crossed his arms. "Somehow, I thought I'd get a stronger reaction when I gave you the news. I went to a lot of trouble to set this thing up."

She leaned toward him and gave him a hug. "And I thank you. I thank you." His arms wrapped around her back and he pulled her close. She laughed nervously and pushed herself away. "See? I'm enthusiastic. I'm grateful." His hand reached for her, but she intercepted it and held it in hers. "So? Can we leave after the funeral?"

He let out an exaggerated sigh. "I suppose. If we must." She squeezed his hand, then got behind him to push him toward the door. "What's this? This is the thanks I get?"

She shooed him down the stairs. "Sorry, mister. But if we're leaving tomorrow, I have a ton of work to do. Alone."

He walked down the narrow stairs toward her door. "You're no fun."

"That remains to be seen. For all I know, my destiny awaits me in Eureka Springs."

He stopped on the bottom step and looked up at her. "Thanks to me."

Oddly, Natalie shivered.

✦✦✦

Natalie trudged up the porch steps Wednesday night, completely out of steam. Jack was on his way out to empty the trash.

"Hey, stranger."

She grunted and fell onto the steps like a sack of potatoes.

He set the trash aside and sat with her. "I didn't know the antique business was so strenuous."

"I worked a double shift so I can go out of town."

"Where are you going?"

She looked toward the door, wishing she hadn't run into him. Now, she was going to have to tell him. He would not be pleased.

"I'm going to Eureka Springs with Beau to—"

"Oh."

She put a hand on his knee. "It's not like that." *No, but you're not exactly making sure it doesn't turn into something like that.* She pushed the troubling thought away. "He's arranged for a publisher to look at my...my novel."

Jack's eyes reflected his hurt. "I thought you were working on the Haven book. That's why I've left you alone these past two days. You seemed so excited the other night, I assumed you'd be writing every spare minute."

"I was. I did." She fingered the strap of her purse. "After you left, I was so pumped I wrote until two in the morning. I've been getting up at 5:30 to write more."

"Then what happened?"

Beau happened. "Beau told me about this opportunity. I couldn't pass it up."

"No, I suppose not..."

She closed her eyes and leaned her head on the post. "Don't give me a hard time, Jack. Not you. Working double shifts, getting ready to go out of town, and with Gloria killing herself—"

"Who's Gloria?"

"A woman I worked with. She committed suicide."

"That's awful."

Yes, it was. *So why don't I feel anything?* "The funeral's tomorrow. Beau's going to pick me up at the church and we'll head for Arkansas."

"He's not going with you to the funeral?"

She shook her head. "I asked him to—" She looked up, afraid she had hurt him again. "Would you go with me?"

He looked at the ground a moment and she watched a series of expressions move over his face. When he spoke, it was in a soft, regretful voice. "I'm not a leftover, Natalie. My friendship is not a consolation prize."

She put an arm around his shoulders and leaned her head against his. He smelled like soap and bologna sandwiches.

"You're right, Jack. Your friendship is a prize. First prize."

He pulled back to look at her. "I care about you, Natalie. I don't want anything bad to happen to you."

She laughed but she was very touched. "Nothing bad is going to happen. In, fact, I'm hoping the opposite will take place. Down in Arkansas, my dreams may come true."

"With Beau along."

"Well, yes....with Beau. He's the one who arranged it. It's all very innocent. We're having separate motel rooms, if that's what you're worried about."

Are you? Are you sure? Again, Natalie ignored the uncertainty.

Jack sighed. "Your love life is woefully none of my business. You don't have to defend yourself to me."

Natalie slipped her hand through his arm. "I want to defend myself to you. You're my friend, Jack—and a bit of my conscience." Why did she feel like putting her head against his shoulder and crying? Instead, she kissed him on the cheek and stood. "Don't worry about me. Before you know it, I'll be back, ready to start a new life as the great author, Natalie Pasternak."

"Just protect the old Natalie, okay?"

She tousled his hair, but he caught her hand and held it. "What?"

"I'd feel better if we prayed about your trip."

Natalie looked down at him. No one had ever asked to pray with her. "Sure." She took a seat beside him. He kept hold of her hand and smiled at her. His cheeks were flushed. "You do this often, Mr. Cummings?"

He shrugged. "My mom used to tell me, "'Pray in the Spirit, Jack. Keep on praying for all the saints.'" He shrugged again. "So I do."

"I'm no saint."

"You're a believer. That makes you a saint. Little s."

"Then do me a little s kind of prayer."

"You got it. He bowed his head. "Lord, be with Natalie on her trip. Keep her safe and wise. Help her feel your presence and know that our struggles are not always against flesh and blood. Give her Your strength. And help her dreams come true because she is a very special lady with a heart for you. Amen."

Natalie opened her eyes and leaned her shoulder against Jack's. "That was nice."

"I meant it."

She squeezed his hand. "I know you did."

◆◆◆

Del stood at the door of St. Stephen's offering comfort to those leaving Gloria's service.

Each sad face and handshake only added to his guilt. His mind tried not to make parallels between Gloria and the situation with Mellie he'd faced years before…the woman who'd come to him for help…the woman whose life had ended because of him.

Just like Gloria

He'd sent both women on their way, back into the turmoil of their lives until they had died. Mellie had come to him, pleading with him to help her leave her husband, to give her hope. Instead, he'd given her platitudes. And sent her home.

A cold voice mocked him from within. *Sound familiar?*

He closed his eyes for a moment, praying for strength. This wasn't the same. Mellie had been beaten to death by her pimp of a husband...Gloria had killed herself in total despair.

Different means to the same end?

The answer hit him between the eyes...Lost souls.

"Del?"

The voice was familiar. Del turned to the next mourner filing out of the church and felt his heart leap with unexpected pleasure.

"Natalie!"

They hugged and laughed, then both put a hand to their smiles as they realized how inappropriate their joy was at such an occasion. Del pulled Natalie to his side. "Wait with me a few minutes until the line ends. I want to talk to you."

He finished his reception duty under the steady gaze of Monsignor Vibrowsky, who eyed he and Natalie like a chaperone at a high school dance.

Once the last mourners had gone by, he turned to Natalie. "I'm so glad to see you. What are you doing in Lincoln, and here, at Gloria's funeral?"

"I moved here a week ago. I met Gloria at work. And you?"

"I was called here a week ago. What a coincidence." Del noticed a man standing close by. The man had the gentle eyes of someone who felt things very deeply. "And this is...?"

Natalie blushed and motioned the man forward. "This is Jack Cummings. He lives in the same apartment house as I do. He's a dear...friend."

Del noticed the emphasis on the final word. It made sense. At first glance, they were a mis-matched couple, the plain man and the striking young woman. Jack held out his hand and Del shook it.

Just then, Del heard someone snap their fingers. He turned to see Monsignor's stormy face. The cars were queuing for the funeral procession to the cemetery. Del turned back to Natalie. "I wish I had more time to talk, but I have to get to the graveside."

Natalie looked at her watch. "Unfortunately, I'm not going to make it to the cemetery. I'm on my way out of town."

Del looked at the two of them. "You two going on a trip?"

Natalie looked away and Jack blushed. "Not us two. I'm going with another man, well, not really *with* him, I mean I have a meeting in Eureka Springs with a publisher."

"Your writing?"

"Maybe." She sounded so hopeful...so full of longing. "Plus, since it's Eureka Springs, it's a bonus because—"

"Kathy lives there!" Del clapped his hands. "How wonderful. I talked to Walter a few days ago. His father..." He decided not to go into it. "How I wish I could see everyone again."

Suddenly, Natalie tensed. Del frowned as he watched her look over his shoulder toward the parking lot. "Oh, dear...I have to go. I'll call you once I get back, okay?"

Del took her hand in his, unable to shake the strong sense that something wasn't quite right. "You do that." He squeezed her hand. Then he watched as Natalie kissed Jack on the cheek and ran toward the parking lot.

Del smiled at Jack. "She's quite a girl, isn't she? Full of ideas and—"

The back of Del's head suddenly felt uncomfortably hot, as if the August sun were beating down on it. He glanced around, hoping that by taking a step to the right or left, he could find a patch of shade and ease the heat. The awful, burning...

Odd. He was already standing in the shade. With a hand to the back of his head, Del turned, looking for the heat's source. A black sports car was pulling out of the parking lot. It looked familiar.

Just then the passenger window rolled down, and Natalie leaned out to wave at Del and Jack. Shivers went up Del's spine, and he quickly bent down to see the driver's face.

He blinked, not believing what he saw. He pointed at the car. "It's Cash!"

"What?" Jack looked from Del to the car, clearly confused.

Del took a few steps toward the car, but it pulled away, tires squealing. He turned back to Jack. "What is Natalie doing with Cash, the man who made Gloria so miserable?"

"That Gloria?" Jack pointed to the hearse in front of the church.

Del nodded, pinching his lower lip. "I don't like this. Gloria came to me extremely troubled about..." He stopped before he disclosed a confidence. "I think I saw him outside the Wellington house the night Gloria died. He gave me the creeps. I had the strangest feeling of—" Del shivered.

"Evil?"

Del leaned toward Jack in shock. "You know him?"

"You're talking about the man with Natalie?"

"Yes. Cash. I don't know his last name."

Jack shook his head. "I don't know anyone named Cash. The man with Natalie is Beau Tenebri. He lives in the same house we do. He's the one who arranged a meeting with a publisher for Natalie."

Del felt a chill. "Tenebri...tenebrae..." His eyes widened as the familiar word fell into place. "Tenebrae. The Latin word for 'darkness.'"

Jack ran a hand through his hair. "What's going on, Father? If this Beau is really Cash, and Cash was involved with a woman who was so distraught she killed herself..." Jack's face whitened and he looked after the car. "Then what does he have in mind for Natalie?"

Del looked down the street where Beau and Natalie had driven, then at the monsignor who was tapping his watch. He looked at the funeral procession pulling away for the cemetery.

He had no choice. "I have to go after her."

"To Eureka Springs?"

Del nodded.

"Don't you have a graveside service to officiate?"

Del didn't answer. He rushed toward Monsignor Vibrowsky and told him he had to leave. He'd expected an argument and got one. But soon he rushed back to Jack. "Can you drive?"

"Aren't you going to get in trouble?"

"I *am* in trouble, Jack, but I have the distinct feeling if we don't get to Natalie, she'll experience a trouble beyond our worst imaginings."

Jack displayed his car keys. "Let's go."

✦✦✦

"What's wrong, Beau?" Natalie asked. "You keep looking over your shoulder like someone's following us."

Beau gripped the steering wheel, his jaw set, his eyes darting.

Natalie carefully folded the jacket to her dress and placed it in the backseat of Beau's car. "I probably should have called Kathy and told her we were coming. You'll just love Kathy and her kids. Ryan must be about six now and Lisa, she was only three when I knew her in Haven. She was the cutest little thing with curly blonde hair and those rubber-toed sneakers that make kids look—"

"Shut up!" Beau spit the words.

Natalie shrank against the passenger door. She forced herself to begin breathing again. "I'm sorry. I didn't mean to ramble."

"Then don't! I'll handle it!"

"Handle what?"

She watched Beau take a deep breath. Then he turned to her and offered a smile. "Sorry. I didn't mean to snap. It's just that I'm a little preoccupied."

"With what?"

He shrugged. And though she wasn't satisfied with his half-answer, she settled into her seat normally and vowed to take it down a notch. Just because she was excited about their trip to meet a publisher, didn't mean he was. He was doing her a favor, and sometimes she *could* talk too much. She turned to make this confession her last words for miles and miles, when she noticed Beau check the road behind them— again. Who was he looking for?

He readjusted his grip on the steering wheel and she saw that his knuckles were white. The muscles in his jaw tightened.

Natalie closed her mouth and remained silent, because it was obvious that whoever he was looking for made Beau very, very afraid.

◆◆◆

Del gripped the steering wheel of Jack's car. His body tensed as if he could will the vehicle to move faster. He pushed the speed limit just a bit, hoping God and the state patrol would overlook his breach and understand that his speeding was for a good cause: to save a friend.

It was strange to be chasing after Natalie and a man he had never met, had barely even seen. It was stranger still to feel such deep emotions about such a man: distrust, apprehension, anger. But most of all, fear.

Del was terrified.

He had no idea what he and Jack would do once they found Natalie. Of course, she'd be shocked to see them. There would be no way to explain away their presence. They'd have to admit they were there to save her — when she didn't even know she needed saving.

How would he account for his feelings? Would she listen to his story about Gloria's death and his assumption that the evil Gloria wrote about in her suicide note was Cash. Or Beau.

"Lord, please watch over Natalie and keep her —"

"Safe." Jack finished the prayer.

Del looked at his passenger. "You care about her a lot, don't you?"

"More than I should."

"I don't think that's possible. We're supposed to love our neighbors as ourselves."

Jack laughed sarcastically. "Well, this man certainly does love his neighbor. At least one of them."

Well, well. "You love her as more than a neighbor?"

Jack shook his head. "I know it's dumb. We've just met, and, of course, she's vibrant and gorgeous, and I'm quiet and plain."

"Don't worry about it so much. The prophet Isaiah said the Messiah: 'had no beauty or majesty to attract us to Him, nothing in His appearance that we should desire Him.' Perhaps God has made you a plain man so your gentle spirit can shine through."

Jack turned to look out the car window. "But women like Natalie see flash, not a gentle spirit."

"She *sees* flash, and her body may even respond to it, but her heart—" Del smiled—"ah, that part of a woman's soul, the part that is the treasure, that part responds to gentleness."

"'Let your gentleness be evident to all. The Lord is near.'"

"Absolutely." Del took his eyes off the road to glance at his wise companion. "I like you, Jack. And I can see why Natalie calls you her friend."

"But what if I want more?"

"Pray that—"

The car began to vibrate. The steering wheel quaked in Del's hands as if the vehicle were warring between right and left, forward and reverse.

"What's going on?"

Del was sure he heard three words, faint and far away: *"I'll handle it!"*

A moment later, the car was fine. If only he could get his pulse to calm down as quickly. "Hmm, I'm glad that's over." He gave Jack an uncertain smile, hoping his nervousness didn't show...

And wondering why he was so very sure that "it" — whatever it was— was far from over.

TWENTY-THREE

"Therefore this generation will be held responsible for the blood of all the prophets that has been shed since the beginning of the world ...Yes, I tell you, this generation will be held responsible for it all."
LUKE 11: 50-51

BENJAMIN CRANOIS SAT on a recliner in his apartment in Minneapolis, switching channels, and drinking beer. He knew he was acting like the stereotypical couch potato, but he didn't care. Ever since quitting Julia's campaign, he'd let his lesser instincts prevail. He'd eaten badly, dressed worse, and spent his time stewing over the slights against him—as well as his own stupidity for quitting the best job he'd ever had.

And now the latest...

He gritted his teeth. KMPS was reporting on some advertising ploy combining Julia's ridiculous mustard seed pins with a list of sponsors who wanted to promote "wholesome, family" shows on their station. In spite of his disdain, he turned up the sound to hear more.

"We asked Ted Brighton, CEO and founder of the national food chain of Brighton Fried Chicken, why he chose to put his name on the Honor Roll at KMPS."

The man stood there, looking all pleased with himself. *Jerk.*

"I felt it was an opportunity to take a stand for better programming," Brighton said, looking sincere for the camera. "Sometimes the only way to instigate change is to pinpoint our wallets. If more sponsors attach themselves to positive programming and withhold their support of programs that are of lesser taste, then the powers that be in the television industry will be forced to change. They will be forced to create the kind of programs that promote positive values."

"Some might view this as a form of censorship," said the reporter.

Ben curled his lip. *Only if they have brains.*

"Not at all. As every parent or employer knows, you get

220

better response by praising good behavior than punishing bad. We are not looking to hurt the questionable programming as much as we hope to reinforce positive behavior by supporting the programs that portray the beneficial aspects of life."

"How does Julia Carson's mustard seed pin fit into the Honor Roll promotion?"

Ted Brighton tugged at the pin on his lapel. "I'm not sure it has anything to do with the Honor Roll, at least not directly. But it is a fact that many of the initial sponsors listed on the Honor Roll received mustard seed pins in the mail. Anonymously."

Ben's disgust raised a notch. *Nice touch, Julia. You get all the glory while still spouting off about not capitalizing on "God's work." I didn't think you had it in you.*

"No note or return address?"

"None," the chicken man said. He looked at the ground for a moment, then raised his eyes to meet the camera. "Actually, a verse pertaining to honor was enclosed with my pin."

"A verse?"

Oh, please! Spare us the sermon!

The reporter looked confused. "As in a poem?"

I'm warning you...let it go, man!

He didn't. Neither did Mr. Chicken. "As in Bible verse."

The reporter raised an eyebrow, but let the subject drop. *Finally!*

Instead, he took a different take. "Are you going to pull your support from programming that will not earn you a place on the Honor Roll?"

"Actually, there are only two shows on KMPS where we had previously purchased spots that are not connected to the Honor Roll. And yes, we will withdraw our support of those programs."

"What do you hope to gain by this?"

"Respect. Good will." Brighton smiled. "And of course, increased sales as the consumer supports us because we support the programs they want on the air."

"You're assuming viewers will prefer your programming? Isn't that naive?"

Ooooo, good hit.

But Brighton wasn't fazed. "Not at all. We know we're in for a battle. Should we give up before we've tried? We hope that once we raise the standards of television, viewers will become accustomed to a higher criterion. We are sure that once they get used to the sparkle of true diamonds, they'll never want to go back to scratched glass."

Ben rolled his eyes. This was getting positively revolting.

"One last question," said the reporter. "Do you hope the other television stations will implement a similar Honor Roll policy?"

Ted Brighton smiled even broader. "Of course. Furthermore, I think it's inevitable—a matter of self-preservation on their part."

With a snarl, Benjamin turned the channel—just in time to catch Julia being interviewed on national news.

"Governor Carson, do you have an explanation for the rash of mustard seed pins that have reportedly been delivered to various people across the country?"

"Not one you'd like to hear."

Oh, no. Not again. Ben pointed the remote to change the channel, but something held his finger.

"Are you or members of your campaign staff responsible?"

"Certainly not."

Here it comes...the righteous Julia strikes again.

She went on. "I'd love to take credit, but I cannot. Ever since my speech in Kansas City, when I explained the symbolism of my mustard seed pin, our offices have been inundated with thousands of phone calls and messages from people wanting to receive one."

"So you *are* behind the pins?"

"Not at all. They are not mine to give."

"Whose are they?"

Julia looked straight at the camera. "God's."

Ben shook his head as the reporter continued. "Do you

realize many of the sponsors of the Minneapolis-based Honor Roll program have been sent a pin?"

"Indeed. A friend of mine who implemented the Honor Roll called and informed me of the phenomenon."

"So you personally endorse the Honor Roll?"

Ben leaned forward, his eyes narrowing. How would she respond to that?

"*Endorse* is not the right word. I have nothing to do with the Honor Roll, but I do applaud its purpose, and I hope it catches on. As far as the sponsors who have received a mustard seed pin...perhaps they are being rewarded."

"Are you saying the recipients of the pin are being rewarded for good behavior?"

Julia smiled. "It's a nice thought, isn't it?"

"So the mustard seed pin has to be earned?"

"'The faithless will be fully repaid for their ways, and the good man rewarded for his.'"

"So the pin is earned by faith and good works?"

"The first inspires the second. After all, 'Faith without deeds is dead.' But as I've said, the pins are not mine to—"

Benjamin had heard enough. With a muttered oath, he shut it off. Without the glow of the television as a light source, he found himself steeped in darkness. The shadows matched his mood.

The nation was going crazy. He couldn't remember the last time the Bible had been mentioned on the news unless it was a case of someone disputing its authenticity. And all the good press Julia was getting, added to the fact it was done without his help—or in spite of his help—infuriated him.

It wasn't fair.

He threw a beer at the screen. The can fell on the carpet, and Ben listened to the soft *glug-glug* as the liquid poured itself onto the floor.

A bump sounded from the bedroom. Benjamin started, holding his breath.

"Who's there?"

A rustle.

His heart pounded. He reached for something to use as a

weapon, but only found a bag of chips, empty beer cans, and a magazine. He fumbled to turn the floor lamp on, straining to touch the switch. *Just a little further...got it!*

Nothing happened. No light filled the room.

Benjamin's skin crawled. *The television...turn on the television for light.* In his haste, he knocked the remote on the floor. He felt around on the carpet but couldn't find it. In a panic he slipped off the chair and groped on his hands and knees.

A scratching sound.

Benjamin looked to the bedroom, but could only see black on black. Where was the moon? Usually some moonlight cut through the blinds. But there was none...only darkness. Seized with a consuming dread, Benjamin whimpered as he patted the floor, searching for the remote.

Light! I want light!

Seconds passed before he realized he could move to the television and turn it on at the source. He scrambled across the floor. He bumped into something but kept going until he felt the screen and slid his hand down to the control panel. He pushed the button. The television came to life, flooding the room with *light*, motion, and sound. He sagged against it, feeling the puddle of beer soaking into his sweat pants. He didn't care. *It* was real. *It* made sense.

Scanning the room he saw that the remote sat at the base of the table, exactly where he'd felt for it. He frowned. There was nothing between him and the chair.

What did I bump into?

Benjamin looked toward the bedroom where he'd heard the thump. The rustle. The scratching. The bedroom lay in darkness, the space between him and the room undulating with the flashes of the moving television picture.

Drawing a steadying breath, he spoke again. "Who's there?"

Blessedly, there was no response. His breathing slowed. His heart found its regular rhythm. His muscles relaxed. He lifted his T-shirt to wipe the sweat off his face, only to find the material soaked with perspiration. He forced his mind to leave the land of bogeymen and drift into the reality of now.

The words of the television became clear. It was the news again. But the news wasn't about Julia.

Or was it?

"Abortion protesters stood vigil outside an Ohio abortion clinic today, waving placards as they tried to urge prospective clients to..."

Benjamin smiled. Oh my, it was too sweet to bear. He could make things even. All he had to do was make one phone call and Julia Carson would get what was coming to her. All he had to do was utter one single word.

His smile broadened. Sometimes he was so brilliant he even surprised himself.

The jangle of the telephone jarred Edward awake. Without opening his eyes, he reached for it.

"Mr. Carson, it's Thad."

Edward squinted at the clock. Six in the morning. "You doing the wake-up calls, Thaddeus? If so, you're off by thirty minutes."

"We've got problems. The morning headlines."

Edward sat up and turned on the bedside light. Julia rolled toward him, blinking at the intrusion. He motioned her to relax. No sense alarming her until he knew what was going on. "What do they say?"

Thad cleared his throat, as though something was sticking in it, then began reading aloud. "'Pro-lifer Julia Carson had an Abortion.'" Thad gave an angry snort. "I can't believe they'd print such lies. We ought to—"

Edward put a hand to his forehead. "Oh, no. He did it."

Thad paused. "Who did it? What it?"

"Who did what?" Julia sat up.

Edward put a hand over the receiver. *God, help us. Please. How do I tell her this?* He took one of her hands. Best to say it straight out. "Benjamin got his revenge, Julia. There's a headline in this morning's paper about your abortion."

She drew her pillow to her chest. Edward turned his attention to the telephone. "Bring us the paper, Thaddeus." He hung up. When he turned back to his wife, she was biting the tip of her pillow, staring straight ahead.

"Julia, are you all right?" Without breaking her gaze she shook her head. He put an arm around her. She let herself be pulled close. Edward began to rock her.

But with a burst, she broke free. "I will *not* let them destroy everything we've worked for because of a mistake I made thirty-five years ago!"

"We can't deny it, Julia."

She swung her legs to the floor. "I'm not going to deny it. It's the truth." She yanked her nightgown over her head and began to get dressed. "I've been touting the truth. I can't apply the principle selectively. They found the truth, so we will have to deal with the truth. But by heaven, I will not let them do it without me!"

✦✦✦

Julia had insisted Thad call a press conference. The hotel conference room was packed.

Julia knew that whenever she entered a room, she commanded attention. It was generally a pleasing sensation.

Not this time.

She'd spoken before antagonistic audiences before, of course, but she had never felt such an atmosphere of malice and spitefulness. *Well, Lord, looks as though they're out to get me.*

She took the podium. She had no notes, but she didn't need any. She was defending a subject she knew intimately: Her life.

"Thank you for coming this morning." She tugged her suit jacket taut over her hips. "I am very disturbed by the headlines that appeared in the morning paper." There was a group snicker. "But not for the reason you think."

She made a point of looking into the faces of her accusers. Their bluster dimmed.

She drew a steadying breath. "The headline is true." The room exploded with murmurs, but Julia didn't let that distract her. "Thirty-five years ago, I had an abortion. It was an illegal, dangerous, and terrifying procedure." She closed her eyes, wracked by an involuntary shiver. "I was single, young, and stupid—a state many of us can remember." A few titters of recognition sounded. "I made the biggest mistake a person can make. I chose convenience over conscience. I chose my life over the life of my child." She opened her eyes and met their stares. "I killed him."

She didn't even try to stop the tears. "There is not one day that goes by where I don't think of my son. How I long to have him standing by my side right now. What would he have accomplished with his life? And what lives would he have touched? Made better? What about the children he might have had? Or my grandchildren?"

She took a moment to dry her eyes and blow her nose, then shook her head. "What I did was illegal and immoral, and I was punished..." With a trembling hand, she touched her heart. "In here. I do not wish this ache and longing on anyone. Today, abortion is legal, and this raises a host of questions. If abortion broke a moral law thirty-five years ago, has that changed? Isn't it still a moral crime? Does making something legal make it right? Civil laws are made by men and women who are flawed and have motives that put self before community, ego before the common good."

She leaned on the podium, wanting them to hear her, to truly understand. "I am responsible for my sin. And I have confessed to my God and have been forgiven. But I have another confession to make. I am responsible for other sins that plague our nation: apathy, crime, racism... for the lowering of our moral, educational, ethical, and spiritual standards. It's too easy to assign guilt to that catch-all entity called *society*. But society is made of individuals. Individuals like you and me." She shook her head. "Don't you see? Apathy is a disease that eats away at the foundation of our lives. Our disinterest—our insistence that 'it doesn't matter because it doesn't affect me' —attaches itself to all that is good in this country. It overpowers the good with a sticky decay until nothing is left but a hideous, festering wound. If this wound is not tended to, it will kill us. It will kill us all. That is my responsibility. And yours."

She clasped her hands together. "Make me an example. I beg you. Hold me up before the entire country as a direct witness to the devastating effects of abortion. If my pain, which cuts deep even after thirty-five years, can stop one child from being killed, then use me. Pray for me." *Father, Father, forgive me…*

"But please, let's go beyond this one issue. Stop passing the buck. Stop blaming our parents, our boss, our spouse, our lack of this or overabundance of that, for our mistakes. Take responsibility for your own actions—and the actions of your nation. Pray. For ourselves and for our country."

She smiled at them through the tears that were still falling. "As amazing as it may seem, God loves us enough to hold us accountable. If we are unwilling to accept the blame, how can we accept the glory? Let's be accountable to ourselves, our God, and to each other. Let our battle cry change from 'Not me!' to 'I am accountable!'" She stood taller, straighter, and repeated the words. And though her voice was choked with emotion, the conviction rang clear.

"I am accountable."

She left the room.

Bonnie Carson Pearson called her mother.

"I had a big brother?"

"Joey."

"I always wanted a brother or sister."

"I know, honey."

"How could you do it, Mother? How could you?"

Julia didn't have an answer.

TWENTY-FOUR

"Some people are like seed along the path, where the word is sown.
As soon as they hear it,
Satan comes and takes away the word that was sown in them."
MARK 4: 15

BEN SAT AT a park bench and stared at the ground. Nothing was working out. He'd leaked the abortion story and the world had proceeded to forgive Julia. The morning headlines had been divided into two camps: For Julia and Against Julia. He'd written them down. He reread the page. The Against Julia column read:

Is Carson a Hypocrite?
Carson Admits Wrongdoing
Senator Bradley Condemns Carson
The Aftermath of the Carson Confession

He especially liked that last one: the Carson Confession. It had a judgmental ring to it. A finality. He wished he'd thought of it.

Unfortunately, the For Julia column was just as impressive:

The Buck Stops Here
Carson says, "Make Me an Example"
Is the Law Wrong?
Are We Accountable?

Actually, Ben had to admit the tag lines created in favor of Julia were stronger than those against her. He stuffed the page into his pocket. He'd been so certain that leaking the news about her abortion would be a death knell to Julia's campaign. It *should* have been. It could have been. If only—

Let it go.

Ben started and looked around. *Who said that?*

Kids played on the swings as their parents chatted close by. A jogger passed, veered around an old man on the path. Ben watched the old guy. He wore a plaid shirt and walked slowly toward the bench, leaning heavily on a cane.

Ben shook his head. "I'm hearing things."

The man looked up as though he'd heard Ben's words. He sought Ben's eyes and tipped his hat. Ben looked to the ground. He didn't need some old geezer striking up a conversation about the weather. He had things to figure out. Important things. Life thing.

The old man eased himself onto Ben's bench. He placed the cane between his feet and rested both hands upon it. "The park's a good place."

Great. Ben tried to ignore him.

"The park's a good place to figure out life."

"I wouldn't know."

The man nodded. "You could."

Ben scooted toward the end of the bench. "I don't know what you're talking about, gramps. Furthermore, I don't want to know."

The man brushed a fly from his sleeve. "That's a shame."

"What's that supposed to mean?"

"There are always choices to make. Things to do and other things to leave behind."

Let it go.

The man reminded Ben of his Uncle Marlon. Uncle Marlon always wore plaid shirts. He used to take Ben to the zoo. They'd get cotton candy and hot dogs and talk...

"I've messed things up." Ben could have bit his tongue. Why on earth had he said that?

"Ah."

"I don't like the way I feel." *Stop with the confession, you fool!*

"Feelings stem from actions."

"Then...I don't like the way I've acted." Ben felt heat in his face. It was absurd, but the truth was making him blush.

"Ah."

"*Ah* isn't much help."

"So you're asking for help?"

This is stupid. He's a stranger. How can he – ?

"I'm asking for help." Ben's couldn't believe what he'd said.

"'God is our refuge and strength, an ever-present help in

trouble.'"

Ben stared at the man, who met his gaze and smiled. *Just like Uncle Marlon used to smile.*

"You're one of them. You're like Julia. You believe in all that God stuff."

"I do." He paused. "And you do."

Ben shook his head violently. "No, I don't! I don't believe in any of it."

"Maybe not in here," the man pointed to Ben's head, "but you do believe in here." He pointed to Ben's heart.

Ben looked down at his chest. Suddenly, he couldn't breathe. He looked up at the man again, desperate, though he wasn't sure why. "Who *are* you?"

The man put a hand on Ben's shoulder. "Someone to tell you there is a better way. You don't have to continue on the same road. Turn, Benny. Turn."

Benny. His childhood name. "You know my name?"

The man stood, groaning as he put his weight on the cane. "'He heals the brokenhearted and binds up their wounds. He determines the number of the stars and calls them each by name.'" With that, he walked away.

Ben stood. "But wait..."

The man turned and smiled, raising a hand. He looked like a rabbi offering a benediction... "'Stand at the crossroads and look, ask for the ancient paths, ask where the good way is, and walk in it and you will find rest for your soul.'"

Ben dropped back onto the bench, his strength spent. He sat for a long time, watching the man make his way down the path. His mind swam with ideas. *Choices.* His heart swelled with a foreign longing. A need.

I need...I need...

Maybe he could start fresh. Maybe there was a God who cared about him. Maybe he could put aside his bitterness and work with Julia again. Maybe he'd learn something from her. Maybe she was right. Maybe the old man was right. Maybe he could have a second—

A football hit him in the torso. Ben clutched his chest, blinking at the pain. The point of the football had nailed him

231

right over the heart. The ball fell to his feet, innocently rocking on its axis. He scanned the park. "Who threw that?"

No answer. The park was suddenly empty.

Ben rose from the bench, rubbing his chest and shaking his head. What had he been thinking? He wasn't a weakling who needed anybody or anything. He must have gone soft in the head for a minute, been swayed by some old man who reminded him of his uncle...and by some obscure yearning for an even more obscure God. But that was wrong. Life was real. Life was full of power and pain, not paralyzing peace.

Ben walked down the path, then hesitated. He looked back toward the football. It was gone.

Was it ever there?

He put a hand to his chest. The pain had dulled. Perhaps he had only imagined it. Perhaps the old man had never sat beside him, either. Perhaps Ben had never doubted. Or needed. Or yearned.

None of this happened. Everything is as it was. There is no second chance.

With that, Ben walked on, determined to keep his focus where it belonged.

On himself.

TWENTY-FIVE

"And pray that we may be delivered from wicked and evil men,
for not everyone has faith. But the Lord is faithful,
and he will strengthen and protect you from the evil one."
2 THESSALONIANS 3: 2-3

"HEL-LO-O? BEAU? ARE you ever going to talk to me?"

He didn't answer. He kept his eyes straight ahead and his hands clamped on the steering wheel as though Natalie didn't exist.

She raised her hands then let them drop into her lap. "We're having some fun now...odd how I envisioned a seven-hour drive as containing conversation? Silly me."

Beau turned his head and Natalie was encouraged. Maybe the freeze was beginning to thaw? Then she realized he was once again monitoring the road behind them.

"Why do I feel like you're a jockey gauging your placement in a race?

No reaction.

She noticed the speedometer. "Oh, I get it. You're watching for the law. I'm sure the state of Missouri will love filling their coffers with your money."

Still nothing.

"Actually, I'd welcome a patrol man. At least *he'd* talk to me." Natalie looked at her watch. They'd been on the road two hours. "Do you want me to drive for a while? I can speed with the best of them."

Beau pushed on the accelerator. Their speed increased.

"Fine, fine, Mr. Macho Man. You win. I hereby crown you King of the Road, though if the king ever feels like letting his captive subject use a restroom and get some lunch, she would be eternally grate—"

Beau swerved onto an exit ramp. It took all the car's braking power to stop before they ran out of ramp. With a jerk, Beau turned the vehicle toward a gas station and pulled in for fueling. Natalie got out of the car. "Want anything, your majesty?"

He took off the gas cap and shook his head.

"Wow! A shake of the head. I do wish you'd quit blathering on." She rolled her eyes, but he didn't seem to notice. She stormed off to use the facilities, muttering to herself. The monologue continued as she washed her hands. "Exasperating, rude...I should never have agreed to go with—"

"Trouble, little lady?" Natalie turned to see a grandmotherly woman applying lipstick nearby.

Natalie put a hand to her mouth. "I was talking to myself, wasn't I?"

"The question is, were you listening?"

Natalie laughed. "Apparently not." She wiped her hands. "I guess if he won't talk and listen, I have to do it for both of us."

"Ah." The woman nodded as if she understood. "A moody man?"

"You got it. Moody and..." Natalie looked to the ceiling. "Intense. Extremely intense."

"Be watchful."

Natalie hesitated. "Watchful?"

The woman put her lipstick in her purse and zipped it shut, then faced Natalie.

She has such wise eyes...

"A good rule when traveling with moody, intense men is to be watchful. 'Watch out that you are not deceived.'"

That's a Bible verse. What were the odds of meeting a Bible-quoting woman in a rural restroom? Unless...

The woman moved to the door, and Natalie hurried after her. She put a hand on the woman's arm. "Ma'am?" When the woman turned around, Natalie looked at her closely, hoping to see her mentor's face. But it wasn't Fran. It was just an old woman—and old, godly woman. Natalie fought back the disappointment. "What do you mean, *deceived?*"

The woman smiled. "Be watchful. Be wary. And be prayerful." She patted Natalie's hand. "God bless."

Natalie stood in the restroom doorway and watched her go.

✦✦✦

Back on the road after eating her hot dog and chips, Natalie slept and dreamed of palace guards, kings of the road, and women with wise eyes.

She was jolted awake by the car stopping. She opened her eyes and saw they were at an intersection, surrounded by lush trees.

"Are we here?"

"Where does your friend live?"

Natalie pushed herself upright. "He speaks. I don't believe it."

"Answer my question."

Natalie rubbed the sleep from her eyes. "I don't know, Beau. I've never been to Eureka Springs. I'm sure Kathy's in the phone book. I'll give her a call."

He looked at his watch and nodded. "We made good time. Five hours."

"You drove over four hundred miles in five hours?"

Beau smiled for the first time since they'd left. "When I get something into my head, nothing can stop me."

"Obviously.

"Call Kathy. Tell her we're here. See if she knows of a place we can stay."

Natalie dug out her phone. "I never asked, but I assume the publisher will pay for two rooms? Correct?"

Beau grinned. "If two rooms will make you feel safe, sure. But remember, when I get something into my head, nothing can stop me."

Natalie paused. "I don't like you this way, Beau."

"What way?"

"Arrogant, bossy, and disgustingly rude."

"Hey, I'm—"

She held up a hand. "Let me finish. I know I owe you for setting up this meeting with a publisher, and I'm grateful."

"No problem—"

She raised a finger to stop his words for the second time. "But that doesn't mean I'm going to tolerate being treated like scum off a pond. One reason I agreed to come on this trip with you is that I thought it might be nice to *be* with you. Get to know you." She took a deep breath. "Enjoy your company, not endure it."

"Are you through?"

"For the moment."

So what if he wasn't thrilled with what he'd heard. Tough. She felt better for saying it.

He startled her by taking her hand and drawing it to his lips. "Sorry for being so moody. So intense."

Natalie raised an eyebrow at his choice of words.

"What?"

She shook her head. "Nothing. I'll call Kathy."

Kathy squealed when she heard Natalie's voice. Natalie asked her for the name of a nice motel, actually a bed and breakfast.

There was a pause, then, "You're not sleeping with him, are you, Natalie?"

"Blunt, as ever. Of *course* I'm not. Remember what I told you? I'm here on business? To meet a publisher?"

"I stand utterly chastised. I've been working with teenagers too long. I don't jump to conclusions, I hurdle them."

"I'm not a teenager any more, Kath. I'm twenty."

"And, as such, a very old woman. Old *and* wise, I hope?"

"Is young and wary good enough?"

"Time will tell. Just don't let yourself be deceived—"

"Deceived?"

"Fooled, burned, lied to—"

"I know the definition. It's just that this is the second time today someone has told me that."

"Me and who else?"

"A stranger in a gas station restroom."

"Ah. The perfect place to receive gems of wisdom."

"It's so strange..." Beau honked the horn. "Got to go."

"Come over for dinner tonight."

"I don't know. Beau might have other plans."

"I won't take no. You come. Six o'clock."

"I hope you don't mind that I accepted Kathy's invitation."

Beau hesitated just a moment. "No. It's fine. I'm anxious to meet Kathy—and all her family."

Natalie studied his profile as he pulled the car onto the street. "The way you say that...it's like you know something I don't."

Beau patted her thigh. "Face it, Tally. That's a given."

Kathy opened the door before Natalie could ring the bell. "Natalie! I can't believe you're really here!"

When Natalie hugged her, Kathy felt an odd relief. Although they'd only known each other those few days in Haven, their experience forever bonded them. Natalie must have felt it too, because she held on a moment longer than necessary.

A dark-haired man walked in, and Kathy had two reactions in quick succession. First, she was stunned by his incredible good looks. His dark eyes made promises—

Yet before Kathy completed the romantic thought, the man's eyes seemed to flicker, his gaze seemed to harden—and suddenly, she felt as if a cloud had entered the room.

This is ridiculous. He's Natalie's friend.

Natalie did the introductions. "Beau, this is Kathy Kraus. Kathy, Beau Tenebri."

Beau captured Kathy's hand and pulled it to his lips. "Mrs. Kraus."

Kathy laughed at her momentary unease, but then Beau took her other hand and kissed it too.

Roy came into the entry. "Looks like I'm missing lessons

in Hand-Kissing 101." He extended his hand to Beau, who took it and started to bring it to his lips. Roy pulled it away, laughing. "A handshake will do just fine. The name's Bauer. Roy Bauer."

Beau looked confused. "You're not Mr. Kraus?"

Kathy looked at Roy, then back to Beau. "I'm afraid there is no Mister....well, not exactly—"

"If you're not Kathy's husband, then—"

Natalie took Beau's arm. "Kathy's husband died in the tornado. I should have told you."

"I'm sorry, I assumed..."

Kathy felt the heat in her face. "Actually, my husband isn't dead."

Natalie touched Kathy's arm. "Lenny's alive?"

She couldn't bear to go into it right now, so she waved the subject away. "We'll talk about it later. Right now, I have dinner to make. Natalie, care to assist me? Maybe Beau can help Roy burn the steaks on the grill."

"Love to." Beau's smile was positively smug. "Hot coals are my specialty."

♦♦♦

Beau accepted an iced tea as Roy tended the meat.

"It's not burned yet. There is hope."

Beau cocked his head. "Less often than you think."

"With all the hand-kissing going on, I don't think I caught your name."

"It wasn't thrown." Beau ran a finger down the condensation on the glass, then licked it. "The name's Beau Tenebri."

"And you're Natalie's...?"

"Lover."

Roy blinked.

"That shouldn't shock you. Not when you're hot to trot for *Mrs. Kraus*."

"Excuse me?"

Beau shrugged.

"I am not hot to trot for —"

"Semantics."

Roy took a cleansing breath, determined to be a good host. "How long have you known Natalie?"

"Long enough."

"You're here on business?"

Beau grinned. "Life is business."

"But you're here to help Natalie get her book published?"

"It will never be published."

"What?"

"She has no talent." He strolled across the deck, and Roy had the distinct impression of a caged animal pacing, waiting for an opportunity to escape. Or attack. "At least, not for writing."

"If you feel that way, why are you here helping her?"

"There are other parts of Natalie's life that interest me."

"Such as...?"

Roy saw Ryan standing by the sliding glass door. The little boy raised a finger, pointing at Beau. "Who are *you?*"

Beau's expression was less than pleased. "Don't point at me, boy. I hate it when people point at me."

Ryan held his pointed finger a moment longer before letting it drop to his side. He repeated the question. "Who are you?"

Beau didn't move. He didn't lean forward. He didn't lighten his voice as adults usually do when talking with a child.

"I'm Beau. And you are Ryan."

Ryan didn't answer, but took a deep breath. Then he turned to Roy and said, "Lisa wants to see you."

Roy sprang at the chance to leave Beau's presence. He shepherded Ryan down the hall to the bedrooms, leaving Beau alone.

◆◆◆

"He seems ...nice, Natalie." Kathy took the tub of margarine out of the refrigerator. "He certainly is gorgeous."

Natalie looked out the window to the men on the deck. "He is, isn't he?"

Kathy couldn't help but smile. "Looks stoke the fire, but it takes character to keep it burning."

"Do you have that cross-stitched somewhere?"

"I'm working on it." She handed Natalie a butter knife and pointed to the slices of French bread. "What does he do? Tell me about him."

"He's a consultant."

"Now there's a catch-all title."

"He helps people make decisions."

"What kind of decisions?"

Natalie looked up from the bread. "I don't know."

"A man arranges a meeting with a publisher, drives you 400 miles, and you don't know the details of his work?"

"We've only known each other a week."

Kathy threw her hands in the air. "What"

"It's not as bad as it sounds."

"Where's he from?"

Natalie didn't look up. "I don't know."

"How old is he?"

"Twenty-something."

"Good guess."

"How many brothers and sisters does he have?"

"I don't know."

"What church does he go to?"

"I was thinking about asking him to go to church with me last Sunday—"

"But you didn't, did you?"

Natalie pointed the knife at her. "The first day I knew him Beau said he wanted to learn more about God."

"Now *that's* a unique pick-up line."

"It wasn't a pick—"

"Has he asked you about God since?"

Natalie hesitated, and felt a sinking sensation in her stomach when she realized the truth. "We've had other things to talk about."

"What's his favorite kind of salad dressing?"

"What?"

"He hasn't taken you to a nice place to eat, has he?" Kathy raised her fingers, counting off a list. "Let's get this straight. You don't know what the man does for a living, where he's from, if he has siblings, what he believes, or what kind of salad dressing he likes."

"Do you know all that about Roy?"

Kathy thought a moment. "Yes, I do."

"But you've known him a long—"

"One week."

Natalie blinked. "You've only known him a week?"

Kathy put a hand on the back of her friend's neck. "I'm not saying anything against your new beau, Natalie."

"He's not my beau. Not really."

"Glad to hear it. Because it seems significant to me that the typical subjects covered on a first date haven't even been mentioned. What *have* you guys talked about?"

Natalie tried to think. "He knows about Grace and Sam. And my writing."

"He has asked the right questions and smiled the right smile to get *you* to reveal your past and your hopes for the future."

"I'm not that easily won."

"Be careful, Natalie. Sometimes the gorgeous ones are used to getting their own way."

Natalie sighed. There is was again. *Be careful. Be watchful.* Once again, the restroom lady's wisdom had been repeated. She was getting the distinct impression this was not a coincidence.

Roy came into the kitchen, shaking his head.

"What's wrong?" Kathy asked.

"Natalie, I know I have no right, but your boyfriend is the rudest, most egotistical—"

"What are you talking about?"

"What's more, Ryan says he's evil."

Kathy turned to Natalie. "Oh dear. I'm so sorry. You know kids..." She turned back to Roy. "When did Ryan meet him?"

"Just now. He came to tell me Lisa wanted to see me. When I went back to check on her — by the way, she wants a Popsicle — Ryan stood by the door to her room like he was standing guard. When I asked what he was doing he said, 'I don't like that man. I don't want him near Lisa. He's evil.'"

Kathy stared at Roy, clearly dumbfounded. "My little boy said that?"

Natalie buttered a piece of bread with extra care. "That's not very nice of Ryan. Kathy, you should talk to him. He shouldn't say such things."

Roy moved close, with a backward glance to the deck. "Look, I know Beau is your friend, but kids *know* these kinds of things, Natalie. They often sense things the rest of us don't. I can't explain it, but I've got a strong feeling that we should take Ryan seriously."

Natalie swung toward him. *"Now* who's being rude?" She lowered her voice, afraid Beau would hear their disagreement and come inside. That last thing she needed was for him to overhear what her friends were saying about him, especially her *Haven* friends. "Beau is my friend and you shouldn't be so —"

Roy gave her a firm look. "Beau said he was your lover." Natalie gawked. *"What?"*

"That's what he told me on the deck. It was one of the first things he said, as if he wanted me to know the extent of his hold on you."

This couldn't be happening. "I don't believe you. He would have no reason to say such a thing."

Just then, Beau sauntered into the kitchen, stopping all further discussion. "Kathy, can I help with anything?" He was the epitome of politeness.

The three friends looked at each other, and Natalie saw Roy and Kathy were as confused as she was.

Beau took the initiative and carried the salad bowl to the table. "Got any thousand island? That's my favorite."

Kathy gave Natalie a look. "I'll get some." Turning to the oven, Kathy shoved the pan of garlic bread under the broiler, flipping knobs as if a bomb were going to explode if she

242

didn't diffuse it in time. "Roy, are the steaks ready?"

"Pretty much."

"*Get* them." When she glanced at Natalie, Natalie could tell Kathy's smile was little more than pasted on. "Sit, everyone. It's time to eat."

Natalie went to the table with the disquieting feeling that her time of having a normal life was ticking by.

✦✦✦

When Ryan refused to sit at the table, Kathy filled a plate and carried it into Lisa's bedroom for him. She brought Lisa a cherry Popsicle. As she was going back to her guests, she noticed Ryan strapping on a belt. "What are you doing?"

"Buckling on the belt of truth."

"Again? It's good you memorized your verse, sweetie, but don't you think you're getting a little carried away?" Ryan shook his head adamantly. She put a hand on his head. "Are you okay? Is something bothering you?"

Ryan bit his lip. "How come you're letting us eat in our rooms? Aren't you going to tell us not to spill?"

Was that all? "Fine. Don't spill." She turned to leave.

"Mom?"

"What?"

"Is everything okay with *you*?"

Kathy attempted a smile. "It will be."

"I remember that Natty-girl from Haven. She was nice."

"She *is* nice."

"I don't like her boyfriend. He's icky."

Icky was a word she could handle. She had no idea where Roy got the idea Ryan had said Beau was evil. It was ridiculous. Her little boy didn't even know what evil was. But as she walked back to the kitchen she had to admit that she agreed with Ryan's assessment—whichever word he had used.

The garlic bread was only slightly burned, and Kathy was relieved that no one seemed to notice. The steaks and salad were eaten with effusive compliments inappropriate for so simple a meal. Thankfully, the conversation eddied around such inconsequential subjects as politics, the economy, and world peace. Personal relationships and other *faux pas* were not mentioned.

Until dessert.

Beau fired the first volley.

"You said your husband wasn't dead, Mrs. Kraus?"

"That's right." Natalie perked up for the news. "Lenny's alive?"

Kathy didn't want to get into it, but she had no choice. "He showed up a few days ago."

Natalie's eyes were wide. "Where's he been for two years?"

Kathy played with the whipped topping on her apple crisp. "I don't know. I haven't talked to him."

"You haven't talked to your own husband?" Beau dabbed a napkin at his mouth.

"We weren't close."

"But you thought he was dead. Now, he's alive...I would think you'd be thrilled."

Kathy looked at Roy.

Beau nodded slowly. "Oh, I get it. You and Roy...the husband's back..."

Heat rushed to Kathy's face. "That has nothing to do with it."

"Beau," Natalie put a hand on his, "it's none of our business."

Beau leaned his arms on the table. "I'm just curious." He nodded to Kathy. "And if I'm out of bounds, please tell me and I'll keep to myself."

Keep to yourself! Kathy remained silent.

"I simply find it interesting. With your husband back and...Tally's mentioned this Haven place you went to. In Nebraska?"

Kathy spoke up. "Roy went to a Haven in California."

Natalie turned to him. "I meant to ask you about your pin. I thought you were one of those people who had it sent to you, the ones who've popped up since Julia's speech. But you were in Haven too?"

He nodded.

"That's marvelous. I can't believe you and Kathy met and—"

"*Any*way," Beau lifted a hand, interrupting, "if Haven was a special place, a place you were invited to by God, then—"

Natalie's mouth fell open and she stared at Beau. "I never told you that."

Beau dismissed her with a wave of a hand. "Sure you did. On the roof."

Natalie shook her head. "No, I didn't. I know I didn't."

"How *else* would I know?"

Kathy jumped at the sharp tone of Beau's voice. When Natalie didn't have an answer, unfortunately, he turned his attention to Kathy.

"If God invited you to Haven, and Lenny was there, how come Lenny was thrown into the tornado? Doesn't God take better care of his people than that?"

Kathy stabbed her fork into her dessert. "Lenny wasn't thrown into the tornado. He chose to go outside."

Beau's forehead creased. "Why would he do that? Wasn't he one of the chosen ones?"

"No, he wasn't, I mean..." Kathy put a hand on her forehead, feeling a headache coming on. "God *did* choose Lenny. God wants *all* of us to come to Him. And though Lenny wasn't officially invited to Haven, he was welcomed there. God gave him the chance to choose the right way."

Beau's shrug was eloquent. "Sounds like he went the wrong way to me."

"Yes, he did. God offered Lenny the chance to be saved, but he rejected—"

"He rejected a chance to be saved from the tornado?" Beau sat back in his chair, disbelief painted across his features.

Natalie chimed in. "Not just the tornado. He was offered the chance to be *spiritually* saved, to gain eternal life by believing in Jesus Christ."

Beau seemed to consider this. "I agree with Lenny."

"What?"

"I would have gone outside too."

Natalie stared at him, a dull red creeping into her cheeks. "You don't mean that."

"Sure I do. Any God who shows favoritism by inviting only certain righteous people to a town—"

"Many towns—" Roy said.

"A *few* towns...doesn't sound like the kind of God I would want to follow. Or, more appropriately, kowtow to."

Natalie leaned toward him. "But you said you wanted to know about God. You wanted me to teach you."

Kathy felt bad for her friend. She wished she could stop this entire disturbing conversation. Maybe she should go borrow Ryan's belt of truth. *Lord, what's going on here?*

Beau shook his head. "Hey, maybe I'm wrong. I'm just trying to learn."

Roy was watching Beau, a distrusting look on his face. "You're just trying to tear apart."

"Roy..." Kathy raised her hands, trying to keep the peace.

"No." Roy tossed his napkin on the table. "I've had enough of this man. Within minutes of meeting him he insults me, then indiscreetly—and untruthfully—informs me that he is Natalie's lover. Now he tries to twist things, accusing God of being unfair."

"You take things too literally." Beau's tone was patronizing.

"Did you or did you not say you were Natalie's lover?"

"I did *not* say that."

Roy stared at him. "You did so. Right out there on the deck. You accused me of being hot to trot for Kathy while informing me that you two were lovers. Then you said that Natalie had no talent for writing."

Beau shook his head, as if dealing with a petulant child. "Why would I have brought Natalie all the way down here

246

for a meeting with a publisher if I didn't think she had talent?"

Roy's eyes narrowed. "Why indeed?"

Natalie stood, close to tears. "Kathy, I'm sorry, but I think we better leave."

Beau stood too and immediately steered her toward the door. Kathy ran after them. "Natalie, don't go! There's been a misunderstanding...don't leave. Not with him!"

Beau walked out the door, but Natalie hung back one last moment.

Please, please let her see the truth!

Natalie's teary eyes came to rest on Roy. "I don't know why you chose to tell such hurtful lies about Beau, but you know what? Right now, I'm ashamed of being a Haven disciple." She bit her lip and turned away. "I think God chose wrong."

◆◆◆

Kathy and Roy stood in stunned silence as Natalie and Beau drove away. Kathy felt Ryan slip under her arm.

"Is he gone, Mommy?"

"Yes, sweetie, he's gone."

Ryan nodded. "Good. He's evil."

Kathy flung her hands in the air. "That's it! I'm going after her."

Roy grabbed her arm. "She went of her own free will. What are you going to do, drag her away from him?"

"Why not? Ryan's right. The creep is evil. And conniving. And manipulative."

Strong arms circled her, and Roy held her close. "I think we've done enough for one evening. We can't confront him. Not yet." Roy shook his head. "I get the feeling we're out of our league."

Kathy shivered. "I agree, but I don't know why."

Roy rubbed his forehead. "Beau...confused me. I've been proud of my mustard seed pin—especially lately, since it's been getting all that publicity. Yet when three of us were together tonight, what did we do? We let ourselves be intimidated by a rude, egotistical man." He sighed. "We went on the defensive. We're a pitiful lot. It seems we haven't done God or ourselves any good whatsoever. Before we act any further we need to think things through."

Kathy took his hand. "And pray."

It was a good plan.

◆◆◆

"It's a good plan." Kathy's mentor, Anne, smiled at the others.

"None better." John motioned her close. "Let's gather round and pray for all our charges."

The angels gathered, but one was missing.

John looked around. "Where's Fran?"

"She's worshiping at the feet of the Father," Louise answered, "for Natalie's sake."

"Indeed." Gabe nodded. "Let us all follow the instructions of King David: 'Praise the Lord, you His angels, you mighty ones who do His bidding, who obey His word. Praise the Lord, all His heavenly hosts, you His servants who do His will.'"

The angels worshiped the Lord and accepted His instruction.

TWENTY-SIX

"For in my inner being I delight in God's law,
but I see another law at work in the members of my body,
waging war against the law of my mind and making me
a prisoner of the law of sin at work within my members."
ROMANS 7: 22-23

BEAU PULLED ONTO a side street a few blocks from Kathy's
house. He parked and turned toward Natalie—but not before
he'd pasted on the wimpy countenance of a sensitive man.
"Why the tears, Tally? I'm the one who should be crying."

Natalie blew her nose. "I hate leaving that way."

"But they were rude to me. They made up lies about me."

"Maybe, but—"

"No buts." He tried to look stricken. "You Haven people
seem to think you belong to this chosen clan. You act as if it
gives you special privileges. Well, it doesn't. You're no
different than anyone else."

She looked at him over her tissue. "Why do you say it
that way? *You Haven people,* like it's something terrible? It was
a good thing. Wonderful."

Beau hesitated. *Watch it. Slow and steady. Don't alarm her.*
"Haven is the one thing that the three of you have in
common, isn't it?"

"We have more in common than that. We have our faith
and—"

Don't let her get distracted. "But you all experienced
Haven."

"Well, yes."

He moved a stray hair behind her ear. "It just seems as if
you—or at least Kathy and Roy—have the attitude that you
are better than the rest of us." *Zero in for the kill.* He shook his
head and looked down. "It makes me feel...worthless."

She put a hand on his shoulder. "Oh, Beau. We don't
mean to sound like that. We're just trying to figure out where
we're supposed to be, what we're supposed to do."

"According to whom?"

She hesitated.

Perfect. He hid a smile behind a hand as he watched her blush, clear evidence of her reluctance — maybe even embarrassment — at saying God's name, at giving Him credit. Beau barely held back a chuckle. Her need for his approval was pathetic. And exactly what he wanted. *Don't say it. Don't say —*

"According to God."

Fortunately, the oath that flew to his mind didn't pass his lips. Instead, he put a hand to her cheek, wishing he could slap her silly. "Oh, Tally, Tally. When are you going to wake up? Where has your precious Haven gotten you these past two years? Are you better off now than you were then?"

"I don't know —"

"You'd better know. Open your eyes. You're living alone in an attic apartment decorated with second-hand furniture. Your job pays minimum wage. You drive a nominal car, wear clothes à la thrift shop, and have an empty refrigerator."

"It's true, I don't spend a lot of money but —"

"You don't spend it, because you don't have it. And you never will." *Come on...you know you're dissatisfied. Start wanting what you don't have...*

"Maybe money isn't important to me."

Beau wanted to scream, but he quickly adapted to the moment. If he couldn't get to her through greed, maybe ambition was the key. He ran a hand along the steering wheel as if contemplating if he should actually say...he looked at her, showing his concern. "I don't want to sound mean, but in the two years since Haven, have you sold anything you've written?"

"I've been working on my novel." She made a face. "You didn't tell Roy I was a bad writer, did you?"

You are so naïve! He gave her a wide-eyed look. "Why would I say that? It's those so-called friends of yours. You may have Haven in common, but that's all you have. They're mean. Selfish. Obviously, you don't really know what kind of people they are."

"They're good people."

Beau *loved* that ambiguous phrase: *good people*. It was such a catch-all. "Good people who lied in order to hurt you."

She looked more confused than ever. "But why would they do that?"

Why...?

Beau was momentarily stumped. He tried distraction. Skin-to-skin contact was always good, so he took her hand, weaving his fingers through hers. "Don't you see, Tally? You have nothing. No money, no career, no real friends, no future." Yeah, that was good.

"But the meeting tomorrow with the publisher..."

He shrugged. "It's a chance, not a guarantee."

"But my friends. Kathy...I'm sure there's a good reason Roy said what he did."

Beau stifled a laugh. *Yeah. He was telling the truth! The cretin.* "Come on, Tally. Give it up. They're losers. Running after impossible dreams that only drop them deeper into mediocrity. It's pretty clear that Haven hasn't gotten them very far either."

"They have each other."

"No, they don't. Your friend, Kathy, is married. Her husband's back."

"Oh. That's right." She shook her head. "What a mess."

Natalie stared into her lap, and Beau traced the line of her cheekbone. "I know it's hard to face the truth." *My brand of the truth.* "But better now than when it's too late and you've wasted another two years chasing after Haven rainbows."

She rubbed her eyes. "I'm so tired."

Good, good. Fatigue affects judgment.

"I just don't know what to think."

Beau took her hand. "Let me do the thinking for you. I'll expose you to all sorts of new opportunities. I'll make you happy and take care of you. We're a good team. Together we can blow the rest of them out of the water." He kissed her cheek. "How does that sound?"

Natalie gave a nod—just a small affirmation. But that was enough.

He had her.

Lenny was at his mother's when the telephone rang. He answered it.

"Get ready."

A jolt of fear shot through him. "Beau?"

"Tomorrow's the showdown. Be ready for me."

"But how—?"

The line went dead.

Del and Jack cruised the streets of Eureka Springs. They were exhausted and hungry. The only food they'd had in seven hours was from gas stations and rest-stop vending machines. Now that they were at their destination, they had no idea where to find Natalie. They knew Beau was driving a black car, but that was it. And with all the curving streets of the town, Beau and Natalie could be a block ahead and they'd miss them.

Del bit his lip, feeling it was hopeless. But then an idea whispered through his mind. *Call Kathy. Maybe she'll be able to help.*

Del didn't have a cellphone, but borrowed Jack's. He looked up Kathy's number. Forcing his fingers to stop trembling, he dialed. "Kathy, it's Del—from Haven."

"I don't believe this." Kathy sounded stunned.

"What?"

"You're not in town, are you?"

"How did you know?"

"Del, you *have* to come over. Something strange is going on. Julia's coming to town tomorrow with her campaign, Natalie's here, and now you're—"

His pulse jumped. "You've seen Natalie?"

"She's in trouble, Del. Come over and we'll fill you in."

✦✦✦

"Ryan says Beau is evil." Kathy watched for Del's reaction. She'd detailed the evening's events, saving this tidbit for last. Del didn't hesitate. "He is."

Kathy stopped her coffee cup halfway to her mouth. "What?"

Del and Jack nodded. Kathy and Roy exchanged worried glances. Kathy's worry only increased as Del told the story of Gloria Wellington.

"Do you think Gloria killed herself because of Beau?" Roy's tone was somber.

"Yes."

Kathy shredded a napkin. "And now he's got Natalie."

"I've witnessed his smooth talk." Jack sighed. "Natalie and I would be having a nice conversation, and then Beau would appear and I'd lose her. Mentally at first, but then physically. She's drawn to him."

"We have to save her." Del put his hands on the table. "Maybe this is why we've been gathered together. To save Natalie. To save ourselves."

"Ourselves?" Kathy frowned. "What do you mean by that?"

Del ran a hand across his face. "I've been having a struggle lately—internal and external. It's not the normal, day-to-day crises." He put a fist to his chest. "It's rooted deeper. As if there's some concept, some…I don't know, some *quest* I'm supposed to grab onto, but I keep missing it."

Kathy nodded. "It has to do with Haven."

"And what we learned there." Roy's words were sure.

Del nodded. "I think it's time."

Kathy was so relieved to know she wasn't alone. "It's time to pay up."

Roy reached for her hand. "It's time to spread the word about Haven. What were the last words Jesus left his disciples? 'Go and make disciples of all nations.' And what did the mentors instruct us to do before we left Haven? Sow the seeds? Spread the word? In the two years since Haven, we haven't done that." He looked down at the table. "At least I haven't."

"Neither have I." Sadness swept over Kathy. "I've been so busy—" She stopped, shaking her head. Now was not the time for excuses. "I never got around to it. I didn't make it a priority. I let the promises I made in Haven fade. Until a few weeks ago, I rarely thought about what I was supposed to be doing."

Del leaned forward. "You've felt this new push to do something too?"

Kathy nodded.

"God measures time differently," Del said.

Jack waved a hand. "That's exactly what I told Natalie about her writing! She was writing the most awesome book about your Haven experiences, and I—"

"But Beau's pushing to get her novel published." Kathy raised a brow. "Isn't that odd?"

They were silent a moment. Then Del spoke. "He's gotten her off track. Away from what God wants her to do."

"That's for sure." Kathy remembered the look on Natalie's face as she watched Beau through the kitchen window earlier. "She's completely bowled over. He has her conned. She is blind to what we see."

Del bit a fingernail, deep in thought. "It seems that God has gone out of His way to get our attention. He's done whatever it takes and used whatever means He could to spur us to action. He's engineered our circumstances to make it possible for all of us to meet—for His purposes."

"And what are those purposes?" Roy asked.

"I don't know."

"Julia's on her way to Eureka Springs for her campaign," Kathy said. "But Walter's not here."

"We can fix that." Del looked around for a phone. "I talked to Walter a few days ago."

Kathy pointed to the counter. "St. Louis isn't that far away. He could be here in a few—"

Del shook his head. "He lives in Minneapolis now. But the miles won't matter. He'll come. I'll call him, and he'll come."

So. That's settled. Kathy looked at those gathered around

her table, in awe at how God had brought them together. But one question remained. "Once we get together, what are we supposed to do?"

Del shook his head. "We'll have to let God handle it."

Del and Jack refused the offer of Kathy's couch, as well as a bed at Roy's. They both felt the need to be closer to Natalie. They checked in at the Treetop Bed and Breakfast—the place Kathy had suggested to Natalie and Beau. They were relieved when they asked at the desk and found that Natalie and Beau had separate rooms. But when they knocked on Natalie's door, there was no answer. She was out. With *him*.

They retreated to their room to wait. And pray.

TWENTY-SEVEN

"But the plans of the Lord stand firm forever,
the purposes of his heart through all generations."
PSALM 33: 11

WALTER STORMED INTO Rolf Wingow's office and slammed the newspaper on the desk. "It's not fair!"

Rolf didn't stop what he was doing to glance at the paper. Apparently he'd seen it.

Walter started pacing. "We've got to stage a counterattack. Execute an offensive."

Rolf looked up. "I will not be offensive."

"I didn't say we should *be* offensive. I said we should *execute* an offensive."

Rolf clasped his hands across his midsection. "Sometimes they are one and the same, Walter."

Walter's bluster deflated. He dropped into a chair and pointed to the newspaper. "'The Honor Roll Marks the Drum Roll to Free Speech.' This isn't the truth. They're overreacting."

Rolf raised one eyebrow. Walter got his point.

"Okay, okay. But we can't let reports like this go unanswered. They're missing our objective. They're not seeing the good we're trying to accomplish. They're acting like we're trying to change the world."

"Aren't we?"

Walter stopped fidgeting.

Rolf sat forward. "Some people are going to object to what we're doing, Walter. There will always be someone objecting to change. If we tried to paint the hallways a different shade of beige, someone would complain."

"Yeah, but—"

Rolf raised a hand. "Yeah but this is important?"

Walter nodded.

"And we're only trying to change things for the better?"

Walter nodded again.

"Who can object to such good intentions that create such positive results?"

"Exactly."

Rolf held out his fingers, ready to count. "Who will object? Number one, the sponsors who don't get on the Honor Roll. Number two, the other television stations who don't like the publicity we're getting."

"They can have publicity like this."

Rolf ignored him. "Three, the so-called freedom people who make a living objecting to anything and everything that doesn't allow anything and everything."

"Liberal fascists."

"They can't be both, Walter." He continued. "Four, the producers, writers, actors, costumers, make-up people, and best boys who will be out of a job if their show ends up canceled for lack of sponsor dollars. That's a lot of people, Walter."

"That last bunch can get new jobs on the good shows that will be produced because of the Honor Roll."

"That takes time. People need to eat now."

Walter crossed his arms. "You make it sound like we're doing something bad."

"We're doing something good. Very, very good. We're changing things. But in doing so, some people are going to suffer."

"They deserve it."

"Walter."

Quick shame washed over Walter and he let out a huff. "Why do you have to be so fair?"

"Somebody has to." Rolf picked up the paper he'd been working on. "Look at the bright side. Have you seen the messages left by viewers?"

"A few."

"You need to read them all. People like the Honor Roll. They approve."

Walter shrugged.

"Don't shrug it off. If you key in on the negative response and flip away the positive, you're as bad as the worst. There will always be people against us. What we do with the Honor Roll will not remove every act of violence, crudity, or bad taste from television. As long as there is free will, there will be people who choose the low road because it's easy, flat, and goes absolutely nowhere. But there are others, and those are the people we hope to serve. We're a success, Walter. We have fourteen sponsors on the Honor Roll. And it's growing every—"

Rolf's secretary burst into the room. "Sorry to disturb you gentlemen, but I thought you'd like to see this." She spread a newspaper in front of them. The caption was clear and bold: "Honor Roll Makes the Grade." She stood back, clearly as proud as if she'd written it herself.

Rolf read from the editorial. "'KMPS should be commended for taking a stand against the dearth of virtue on television. Not just for what they're doing, but for how they're doing it. They aren't griping about the bad, they are commending and encouraging the good. The way to Hollywood's heart is through their wallet. Only when the shows that pander to our lesser side start getting the lesser sponsors and hence the lesser bucks, will the powers-that-be open their eyes and see there is a better way. Come on producers, you've had your fun testing the limits. It's time to find the middle again and maybe even take a few steps onto the other side. Television, heal thyself!'"

"That's great!" Walter grinned. "Where'd it come from?"

"It came from AP."

"Yee-*ha!*" Walter pounded the desk. "We've gone national!"

There was a knock on the doorjamb. "Excuse me?"

They turned to see a uniformed deliveryman in the doorway. "Sorry, but no one was at the desk." He read the package in his hand. "I have a special delivery for a Rolf Wingow."

"I'm Rolf Wingow."

The man pulled a pen from above his ear. "I need your signature, sir."

Rolf signed, and the man grinned as if he knew a secret.

"Have a nice day—and congratulations."

"Congratulations?" Walter stared at Rolf. "What'd you do?"

"I have no—"

Rolf's secretary started to leave.

"Stay, Ms. Kane." Rolf turned the padded envelope over in his hands. "There's no return address."

"Just open it," Walter said.

"I bet you're a pain on Christmas, aren't you?"

"First up and first to open."

Rolf opened the package and pulled out a letter.

"Is that it?" Walter craned his neck for a better view.

Rolf looked in the envelope—and froze.

Walter frowned. "What's wrong?"

Slowly, his boss turned the envelope over above his hand. A mustard seed pin dropped into it.

Ms. Kane gasped. "Oh, my...you got one!"

"Way to go, Rolf!" Walter clapped, so proud he thought he'd split. *Thanks, Lord. Thanks!* "What's the note say?"

Rolf cleared his throat. "'What good is it, my brother, if a man claims to have faith but has no deeds? Faith by itself, if it is not accompanied by action, is dead.'"

"And out of your faith you created the Honor Roll." Ms. Kane had tears in her eyes.

Rolf looked at her, his eyes widening a bit. "Why, Ms. Kane, I didn't know you believed."

She blushed. "I'm a misplaced Southern Baptist up here with you Minnesota Lutherans. But God's the same whether we're eating grits or lefse."

"A-a-men," Rolf said with flourish.

They laughed, and Rolf turned to Walter, holding out the pin. "Will you do the honors, Walter? It's only because of you that I got one of these."

It took Walter a minute to be able to respond around the lump in his throat. He got up and took the pin. "That's not true, Rolf." He attached the pin to Rolf's shirt. "You earned this pin all by yourself."

Ms. Kane looked at Walter's pin. "How did you earn *your*

pin, Walter?"

"By being a stubborn fool."

"What?"

Walter waved his last answer away and began to lead her out of Rolf's office. "Actually, it all happened two years ago when I got a strange invitation..."

✦✦✦

When Walter pulled up to his new home, he had to park a half block away as the moving van was front and center. He found Bette and Addy in the kitchen.

Bette pulled out a chair so he could sit. "How was your day?"

"Interesting." Walter ran a finger along Addy's cheek. "Rolf got a mustard seed pin in the mail."

"What for?" Bette immediately added. "I mean, why him?"

"For the Honor Roll. At least I assume that's what it's for, though Rolf's a good guy. Faithful. He's probably done tons of stuff that would make God proud." He smiled. "More than me, and I've had a pin for ages."

Bette put a hand on his shoulder. "I'm sure God judges each person's faith on an individual basis." Her voice softened. "At least I hope He does."

There was something in the tone of her voice that perked Walter's ears. He looked up at her. "What's wrong?"

Bette shook her head, but took a seat, apparently readying herself to talk. "It's silly, really. But I was wondering how I can get one of those pins."

Walter felt like a selfish fool. He'd never once thought of how Bette must feel with him getting all the glory and her working just as hard. She'd been wrenched from St. Louis, given birth to Addy, and put up with the likes of him.

Then Walter remembered. "Here, take Addy. I'll be back in a minute." He went out to their car. When he returned to the kitchen, he was holding a mustard seed pin. "This is for you."

She stared at it. "Where did you get that?"

"It's my original pin. I gave it to Pop. I'm sure he'd like you to have—"

"I don't want it."

"But you said—"

"I don't want *you* to give me a pin. I want God to give me one."

"But God wouldn't mind. When I gave this to Pop, God gave me another one, which seems to prove—"

She shook her head adamantly. "I don't want it. I want my own." She snuggled her face against Addy's hair, but she couldn't hide her tears so easily.

Walter felt like a louse—and he wasn't quite sure why. "Ah, Bette. I don't know how to get you that. That's beyond my control."

She raised her face to him, and he watched as a tear fell on Addy's arm. "I know." She sniffed. "I'll have to earn it myself. I *want* to earn it myself." She sniffed loudly as more tears fell. "But how do I do that, Walter? How do I show God I'm faithful?"

Walter's heart broke. Bette, above all people deserved—

He stopped himself. *Sorry, Lord. I know, I know, it's not up to me. If it were, I'd give her a thousand pins, just for being herself. For being Bette...*

He paused. Maybe that was the answer.

He touched her cheek. "Just be yourself, hon. Give God yourself. That's all He can ask."

Walter had never been so content. Although his heart still ached for his father, when he was lying with Bette under his arm, with Addy in a crib nearby, in their very own house...

He looked toward the ceiling and smiled. *Thanks, God. I'm sorry I got mad at You for wanting me to move and for taking Pop. You know I'm not patient. Yet, You still give me so much.* He sighed deeply, causing Bette to snuggle into his shoulder.

Life was peaceful. Life was calm. Life was—

The telephone rang.
Life was about to change. In a big way.
It was Del.

TWENTY-EIGHT

"Do not withhold your mercy from me, O Lord,
may your love and your truth always protect me.
For troubles without number surround me,
my sins have overtaken me, and I cannot see."
PSALM 40: 11-12

HUMANS ARE SO *weak. They have absolutely no stamina at all.*

After the dinner at Kathy's, Beau hadn't wanted to go back to the bed and breakfast. He wasn't sure why, but he felt it was best to keep Natalie away as long as possible. And even so, he'd had the distinct feeling they were being followed. But finally, she had insisted and he'd had no choice but to give in to her limitations and need for sleep.

Beau put a finger to his lips as they climbed the stairs of the Treetop Bed and Breakfast. It was after two in the morning. Hopefully, late enough for whoever was following them to give up.

As they turned down the hall, Beau hesitated. *What is that? What am I feeling?* He backtracked to the door of one of the bedrooms, then cocked his ear toward it. Nothing. He heard nothing.

He put a hand on the wood and immediately jerked it away as odd vibrations sped through him.

"What?" Natalie sounded tired and cranky. Beau was about to use another dose of sweet talk when a certainty struck him dead center as though he'd been plowed into by a semi. But as he focused, he knew it was true.

They're here.

Beau grabbed Natalie's arm and hurried her down the hall—away from Del and Jack's room.

✦✦✦

Natalie took an extra-long shower, luxuriating in the facilities: a massaging showerhead, extra-large towels, mirrored walls, and delightfully scented toiletries. It was a lot better than her claw-footed tub with a stopper that didn't work. Finally starting to prune, she got out. The bathroom was a cloud of steam, but she didn't turn on the fan. The mist matched her mental state.

She started to wipe the mirror over the sink so she could comb her hair, then stopped when she saw a word written on the mirror, its presence come to life amid the steam: *live*.

"Live?" Had the past customer left some love note to his or her mate? If so, it didn't make much—

Natalie froze when she saw the reflection of the word in the mirrored wall behind her. The mirror-image word had a far different meaning: evil.

She sucked in a breath, ran into the bedroom and slammed the door, hoping the word – and the uneasy feeling it elicited – would dissipate with the steam.

Be watchful. Be wary. And be prayerful.

Natalie climbed into bed, pulled the covers up to her neck – and prayed.

Natalie's eyes shot open. It took her a moment to remember where she was. She held her breath and listened. There was a soft click. A stirring of air.

Across the room, she saw the faint square of the window, against a darker void, dark on dark. Where was the moon? When she'd gotten into bed, she'd noticed how the moonlight fell across the window seat. Now all was dark.

There was no moon.

Close your eyes. Find the contentment that comes with not knowing. Not seeing. Not hear—

She heard a whisper of movement near the foot of her bed. A brush. A hush.

Her throat tightened. If only her arm were under the protective shield of the cover. If only she could take a moment to snuggle deep within the blankets, the way she'd done as a child against the monsters of the night. But Natalie

264

didn't dare move. To move would declare her existence. She did not want to exist right now. If only she could fade away to some safe haven—

A dark form slid in front of the window, undulating toward her and away. She squeezed her eyes shut, not wanting to see. A fetid stench invaded the room.

A muted thump sounded as something dropped on the carpet.

Natalie was certain the beating of her heart moved the bed as its pulse drummed in her ears. Her muscles tensed as she felt the slightest weight skim over her thigh. There, but not there. The hair on her arm came to attention. She opened her eyes, positive she would see the silhouette of a man standing over her, ready to attack—

She saw nothing but darkness... felt nothing but the certainty that she was not alone.

Another rustle of air against air. Another click as soft as the first.

The smell faded and was replaced with the odor of her own sweat. She risked a breath. Her muscles screamed, aching to move from their self-imposed prison. Natalie looked toward the window. The outline appeared stronger, more distinct. The moon was finally free.

She allowed the seconds to pass into minutes before she let herself relax. Then, in a burst of bravado, she lurched toward the bedside lamp and turned it on. The light told the simple facts: the door of her room was closed, the clothes she'd been wearing were strewn on the floor, her suitcase sat on the rack by the bathroom, its lid open.

Everything was just as she'd left it. Normal. *But I didn't dream it. It really happened. I know it did.*

She traced a hand up her thigh where she'd felt a touch, cringing at the memory.

Suddenly, the lid of the suitcase fell closed. Natalie threw off the covers and ran into the hall, toward safety.

Toward Beau.

✦✦✦

265

Beau opened the door before her knuckle knocked twice. She sprang into his arms.

"Someone was in my room!"

He opened his arms and she went into them gratefully. He rubbed her back and pulled her head to his bare chest. "You must have been dreaming."

"I wasn't. I *know* I wasn't."

He ran a finger along the curve of her spine. "Do you want me to check out your room?"

She nodded and he helped her across the hall. She hesitated outside the opened door. He went in first and looked around, then stood in the middle of the room and crooked a finger at her. "Come back in, Tally. All's clear. No monsters in residence."

She took a tentative step toward the door. Then another. Beau met her halfway and drew her inside. He shut the door with a soft click.

Natalie's eyes scanned the room. "But there *was* someone here. I know it."

"Now why would anyone come into your room at four o'clock in the morning?"

Natalie sought her purse. It was safely on the dresser, zipped up tight. She laughed nervously. "Not that I have much to steal..."

Beau put his hands on her shoulders and propelled her toward the bed. He smoothed the covers and fluffed the pillow. "Get in."

For the first time, Natalie noticed that Beau was only wearing a pair of gym shorts. No shirt. And she in her cotton nightshirt. "I don't want to go back to bed. I—"

"Get in." His voice had an edge to it. "You need some sleep. Tomorrow's a busy day."

Natalie acquiesced and climbed in the bed. As she started to pull up the covers, Beau held them open. "Move over."

"What?"

"Move over." He started to push his way in beside her, but she jerked the covers loose, pulling them around her, creating a cocoon.

She scooted to the other side of the bed. He shook his head. He wasn't smiling. She looked away, embarrassed at her instinctive reaction. *He thinks I'm acting like a child.*

Was she?

If only she could backtrack... The entire scenario had happened so fast. She'd been afraid. She'd wanted comfort and had gone running for help. Now she had traded one fear for another.

God, I'm sorry for getting myself into this. I wasn't thinking...

But maybe she was overreacting. Beau was an okay guy, and she'd handled men before. Then she remembered the glint in Beau's eyes when they'd first gotten to Eureka Springs. She remembered his hard words: *"When I get something into my head, nothing can stop me."* Looking at him now, his words held more than a surface threat.

Unease pressed in on her, making her feel as though there was something heavy sitting on her chest. *Go away. I don't want to deal with this.* If only he wouldn't just stand there, staring at her. "Beau, having you here...it doesn't seem right. You'd better —"

"Who came to whose door, Tally?"

"But I was scared."

"And I'm here to make you feel safe. He tucked the covers around her forcefully. Then he shook his head with a snicker. "Do you think you're protected from me now?"

She found it hard to swallow.

He turned off the light and sat on the bed. She saw the silhouette of his face against the window. "I'm not going to ravish you, Tally." He moved beside her, wrapped an arm around her torso and pulled her close, blankets and all. He snuggled against her like a puzzle piece finding its match. "I'm merely going to comfort and protect you from the intruder who had the audacity to sneak into your room and stroke your thigh. Now be quiet and go to sleep."

Natalie closed her eyes and felt a rush of relief. Maybe it *would* be all —

Her eyes shot open. She hadn't told him about her thigh.

Natalie finally slept with Beau's arms holding her fast. But she didn't feel protected ...didn't feel safe...

She felt imprisoned.

And as she slept, she dreamed.

She and Beau were in her room at the bed and breakfast. She was on the edge of sleep when Beau yanked off the covers. She turned toward him to ask what he was doing, when he covered her with his body. He smothered her with his presence. He overpowered her. Dark eyes. Strong arms. Groping hands. Fetid, foul breath—

She opened her eyes. Early daylight shone through the window, lighting the dresser, the door, and the suitcase. She turned to the other side of the bed. Beau was gone.

She pulled the covers around herself and went back to sleep.

Everything was all right. It was only a dream.

✦✦✦

Beau stood by the window of his room and held Natalie's mustard seed pin up to the light. Humans were so misguided to think this little seed was significant. It was nothing. It was inconsequential. Its symbolism was weak and pitiful.

He was very relieved he'd gotten it away from Natalie.

TWENTY-NINE

"Where can I go from your Spirit?
Where can I flee from your presence? If I go up to the heavens,
you are there, if I make my bed in the depths, you are there.
If I rise on the wings of the dawn, if I settle on the far side of the sea,
even there your hand will guide me,
your right hand will hold me fast."
PSALM 139: 7-10

DEL KNOCKED ON Natalie's door.

No answer.

Jack knocked, a little louder.

Nothing.

"Natalie?" Jack whispered against the door. He checked his watch. Eleven. Although Del had set the clock radio to wake them at six so they could catch Natalie early, it hadn't gone off. And though neither man had ever slept past eight, this morning they'd awakened at 10:45 in a panic.

She was gone.

They moved to Beau's door, and Jack could see Del was as unsure what to do as he was. Jack felt ill prepared to meet Beau. Especially without talking with Natalie first.

Jack watched Del put an ear to the door, then shake his head. Apparently all was quiet.

They went downstairs to find the owner of the bed and breakfast. They found her in the kitchen, making cake batter.

"Father Delatondo and Mr. Cummings," she said. "I'm sorry you missed breakfast. Give me a minute and I'll whip up some Belgian waffles. I have blackberry syrup — or cherry if you'd like. And there's coffee."

"No, thank you, Mrs. Ransom. Actually we're looking for two of your other guests. Natalie Pasternak and — "

"Her beau, Beau?" She laughed at her joke. "They left, for the morning." She wiped a drip off the side of the bowl.

"Did they say what time they'd be back?"

"No, in fact Mr. Tenebri said if anyone asked after them I was to say they were out and..." She seemed hesitant to add

269

this last bit. "And it was none of anyone else's business."

"Did you tell them we were here?"

"No, no. You told me not to and I didn't." She set the batter aside. "But if you are friends of Ms. Pasternak's, I'd think you'd want her to know."

"We are *not* friends of Beau's."

"Oh." She glanced at Del's priest-collar.

"We're worried about her."

"Mr. Tenebri seems like a nice enough fellow. They had separate rooms. You don't see that these days. Single people stay together whether I like it or not. I've threatened to make some house rules but if I didn't rent rooms to single couples, I'd go out of business." She blushed. "You know how it is, Father. I'm not in a position to—"

"Take a stand?"

Jack knew it was harsh, but he had to agree. Mrs. Ransom looked away, wiping her hands on her apron. "Would you like to leave them a message?"

"No...yes." Jack looked at Del. "Tell Natalie we're here and we need to talk to her. It's an emergency."

✦✦✦

Natalie swirled a French fry in her chocolate malt.

"Eat," Beau said.

"I can't. I'm nervous about the meeting with the publisher and sick about my pin."

"We looked all over for your pin. So what if it's gone? It's just a pin."

She shook her head. "You don't understand."

"Give it up, Tally. You're acting like it was the holy grail."

She swallowed the sudden tears that sprang to her eyes. "It was holy to me."

He snickered. "Are you saying *you're* holy because you had it?"

"Of course not."

"Because you didn't look very holy at four o'clock this morning in your nightgown. You looked tempting. Very tempting."

"Beau..."

He shrugged. "Don't pretend you don't like my opinion. Wouldn't you rather I thought of you as Tempting Tally rather than Holy Tally?"

"That's not a fair question."

"Being holy will get you a seat in a pew. Being tempting will get you a seat in life. Choose to live life, not agonize over it. Let the pin go."

Natalie watched as an elderly woman came into the cafe and moved from table to table handing out cards.

"But that pin was *given* to me." Natalie couldn't let it go.

Beau flipped a hand in the air. "God gives and God takes away. Takes away more than gives, from what I've seen. *C'est la vie.*"

Natalie wished Beau would stop saying things like that. He was making her head hurt. "For someone who wanted to learn about God, you sure have a lot of strong opinions."

"I speak my mind."

"Obviously. But God didn't take my pin away. I simply lost it."

"Are you sure?"

"Why do you say that?"

"Maybe God changed His mind? Maybe He thought you weren't worthy of wearing the pin anymore."

His words struck deep, and a sickening sensation filled her. "What? No."

"Maybe you don't deserve to wear it." Beau leaned his arms on the table. "Or maybe you're too good to wear it. From what I hear, God doesn't like independent people who make their own decisions. He wants to control the whole ball game. As long as you wore that pin, you were under His thumb."

Natalie stared across the table. "I... don't deserve it?"

"You've been brainwashed into being a weakling for so long, you don't know how to be strong."

She closed her eyes. Why couldn't he just leave her alone? "I haven't been a weakling."

"You certainly haven't been strong. You haven't taken hold of your life and whipped it into what *you* want. You've sat back waiting for God to get around to you. Let me assure you, He's busy. Always will be. Don't you think He has more important things to do than fiddle around with your meager life?"

"I suppose. But He loves me. He cares—"

"From what I've seen, He loves to keep you on a string, like a disjointed puppet. You've been hanging there waiting for two years. For your entire life, for that matter. Every once in a while He pulls a string and allows you to move an arm or a leg, but you never get anywhere. You're still hanging limp and lifeless." Beau put a hand on hers, and it took all her willpower not to jump. She wanted the touch to be warm, encouraging…but it wasn't. It was cold. "That's where our life together will be different. We're not going to wait around for your God to yank our strings. We're going to get moving, get living. It's time to stop being a coward."

Our life? *Natalie didn't like the sounds of that. She wanted Beau's help, his friendship, even his attention, but* our life? *No way. Especially not now. Since coming to Eureka Springs, Beau had changed. He was more aggressive, less patient, and more demanding. And to think she had wondered if he was her soul mate…*

Natalie prayed, feeling sick, confused, as if everything black was white, and everything wrong was right. If it weren't for the meeting about her book, she'd leave and catch a bus back to Lincoln. But this was her big chance. She couldn't just walk away from it.

"When are we meeting the publisher?" she asked Beau.

"Soon."

She looked at the seat of the booth beside her and realized it was empty. "Oh, no, I didn't bring my manuscript! We have to go back."

Beau put a hand on her arm. "No, we don't."

"Of course, we do. He'll want to see—"

"No, he won't."

She stopped fidgeting. "What?"

He squinted at her, offering the mischievous smile she used to find endearing. "There is no publisher, Tally."

She felt her jaw go slack. He was joking. He had to be.

He read her eyes. "There is no publisher, never was a publisher. I wanted to get you to Eureka Springs so I made it up."

She felt as if she'd been punched. She forced herself to stand and sucked in a breath. "You liar! You sleaze!" She grabbed her glass of water and threw it in his face.

The other diners looked up from their burger platters. The elderly woman stopped handing out her cards.

Beau dabbed his face with a napkin, then pointed to the booth. "Sit!"

She shook her head.

He grabbed her hand and jerked her down beside him, wrapping an arm around her shoulders, pulling her close. He whispered in her ear. "I only did it because I love you."

Love me? She shook her head. "Love has nothing to do with this. You want me."

He traced a finger up her arm. "That too." He loosened his grip, and she slipped out of his side of the booth and took refuge on the opposite seat.

Beau watched her, looking bored. "Nevertheless, my dear Tally, the true reason I lied was to knock some sense into you. You're heading nowhere. Writing nothing for nobody."

She couldn't believe there was no publisher. How could he lead her on like that? What kind of man was he? "You know nothing about my writing. Nothing."

He reached for her hand, but she pulled it away.

"I know plenty. I read it."

It's all been a lie. A complete lie.

"It's my job to evaluate prospective...material." He snickered as if he'd just said something funny. "I'm a consultant, remember?"

Natalie remembered Kathy's questions. "Who do you work for?"

Beau smiled. "He'd love to meet you. In fact he's planning to meet you real soon."

They both looked up as the elderly woman reached their table. She smiled down at them, letting her gaze hold Natalie's eyes. "Is everything all right?"

Beau flipped a hand at the woman. "Go on, grandma, we're busy."

Natalie smiled an apology. "Thanks, ma'am. I'm okay."

The woman nodded and handed Natalie one of the cards she had been handing out.

Beau reached for it. "We don't want one of your stupid cards."

Natalie pulled it to her chest. "I want it. It's mine." She looked at it, then at the woman. "It's a Bible verse."

"Indeed it is."

"It's from Ephesians." She read the verse aloud. "'Be strong in the Lord and in his mighty power. Put on the full armor of God so that you can take your stand against the devil's schemes. For our struggle is not against flesh and blood but against the spiritual forces of evil in the heavenly realms.'"

"Give me that!"

Natalie pulled the card out of Beau's reach a second time. What was all this about the devil? And spiritual forces? It sounded like science fiction.

The woman lingered. "I picked it especially for you, dear."

"But, I don't understand."

The woman turned her attention to Beau and gave him a level stare. Yet her expression remained passive and patient. "I have one for you too, son. Especially for you."

"I'll pass."

She laid it on the table in front of him. Beau shoved it aside without looking at it.

"Take it back, lady. I don't want it. I don't need it."

The woman did not smile or cajole or tease. "You need what you cannot have."

Natalie saw the muscles in Beau's neck tighten. "What's that supposed to mean?" The woman turned and walked away.

Natalie looked at the card on the table. *What does it say?* She had the feeling if she reached for it, Beau would grab it and then she'd never know. Her nerves began to dance. She tried to act casual. "Aren't you going to read it?"

He shoved it across the table—toward her. Natalie picked it up as if it had as little consequence as the saying in a fortune cookie. But when she read it, a chill traveled from head to toe. She looked at her companion. She looked to the door where the woman was just leaving. The woman turned, met Natalie's look, and nodded, a slight smile on her face. Natalie frowned... the elderly woman looked familiar—

No, wait! She wasn't elderly anymore. She was slightly overweight and had flaming red hair...Fran! Natalie let the card fall to the table. She slid out of the booth. At Beau's exclamation, she glanced at him, then heart pounding, she looked to the door.

Her mentor was gone.

Beau lunged at her, grabbing her arm. "Where do you think you're going?"

"I've got to see...I've got to go—"

"Sit *down!*" He yanked her toward him.

"Hey!" A man sitting at the counter started to stand. "I've had just about enough of you, buddy. You let go of her."

Beau swung to face the man, his eyes blazing. The man fell into a bout of coughing.

Natalie took advantage of the moment and pulled away. With a moan, she staggered out the door.

✦✦✦

Beau tossed some money onto the table. He stood at his place and glared at the other diners.

"It's none of your business. Stay out of it."

The people looked away and went back to their food— accompanied by the hacking cough of the man who'd tried to help Natalie. Beau smiled, then sauntered toward the door.

It was so easy to make people do what he wanted. So pathetically easy.

275

✦✦✦

The waitress moved to the table Prince Charming had just left, shaking her head. How had a nice, little girl like that one ended up with such a creep? She retrieved the money and raised an eyebrow at the amount. At least the jerk tipped decent. As she stacked the dishes, she noticed a small card in a puddle of catsup. She wiped it on her apron and read it aloud, "Away from me, Satan! For it is written: 'Worship the Lord your God, and serve Him only.'" She nodded. "Amen to that."

✦✦✦

The messages had been from Fran! Natalie's stomach churned at the meaning of the verses on the cards ... on Beau's card. What was Fran saying? That Beau was...Beau was ... the devil? A spiritual force of evil? Satan?

She needed to talk to her mentor. Fran would know what to do. If only Natalie had listened to her earlier warnings. And to the warning from the woman at the gas station. And to Kathy's warning...and all the warnings within her own conscience.

Holy Spirit, You've been trying to tell me, but I wouldn't listen. I drowned You out. I liked Beau's attention. I wanted —

Natalie staggered down the sidewalk in front of the diner, her eyes searching. Fran was nowhere in sight. There were souvenir shops, a craft mall, and a store whose windows were plastered with signs promising "3 T-shirts for $10". She felt exposed and alone. She needed to find Fran and lose Beau. Find good and ditch evil.

Desperate, she did a three-sixty. Then drawing from her diaphragm, she yelled, "Fran!"

Beau appeared on the street near the diner. "That's right, Tally. Call for your angel. I'd love to meet her head-on."

Natalie stumbled further away from him, gripped with terror. Beau knew Fran was an angel! So it was true. He wasn't a man at all!

This wasn't happening. It was a bad, bad dream. If only she could close her eyes and wake up in her attic apartment in Lincoln—or better yet, in her childhood home in Estes Park. If only she could start again, she would do things so differently.

Beau strolled across the parking lot, his hands in his pockets, his eyes on her. He acted as if he were in no hurry to chase after her. Well, why should he? Despair rocked her. She couldn't think. She needed time...a place to hide. But she had nowhere to go.

Natalie lurched across the highway, dodging a motor home and a pickup, her skin prickling at the blare of their horns. She ran along the shoulder, putting as much space between herself and Beau as she could. When a glance showed him opening his car door, she began to cry. He had a car. He could follow her anywhere. He could get her. But...maybe he didn't need a car at all! She was lost. All was lost.

Oh, Lord! Oh God! Help!

A vehicle zoomed past then skidded to a stop, half on the shoulder, half in the highway. The door opened. A man put a leg out and turned toward her.

"Natalie?"

Natalie blinked twice, not sure whom she was seeing. "W-Walter?"

"Natalie? What are you doing?"

She ran to his car and yanked open the passenger door. "Drive! Get in and drive!"

Walter did as he was told.

After they had driven a few miles, and after Natalie had directed Walter to turn onto three side streets in a seemingly aimless maze, he stopped the car.

"Care to tell me what's going on?"

Natalie dropped her face into her hands and sobbed.

"Hey...hey, Natalie. It's all right. Everything's going to be all right."

She raised her head. "No it isn't. Don't you see? He's after me."

"Who's after you?"

"Beau. My fr—" *Friend? Hardly. What exactly was he?*

"Is he hurting you?" Walter's face hardened. "Has he hit you?"

Natalie laughed. "I wish he had. *That* I could handle."

"Then what—?"

She grabbed chunks of her hair and pulled, wishing the pain would give her strength. "You wouldn't believe how he talks. He turns everything around. He makes me question everything."

"A smooth talker?"

"Not like that, not about that." She took a deep breath and wiped the tears with the back of her hand. "It's other things, Walter. Spiritual things. He knows Fran is an angel."

Walter looked confused. "I don't get it. How could he know that?"

She couldn't bring herself to say it. It was too farfetched. Too terrifyingly possible. "He makes me doubt God."

"Everybody doubts God at one time or another. When my father died I—"

"But God leads you back. He understands and leads you back to Him. Beau wants to lead me away." She stared past Walter. "Looking back, I see that Beau's been doing that since the first day we met."

"Then say no."

She felt like laughing. *Just say no? Please.* "It's not that easy. Beau has a power...he wants to lead me into places, into ideas, where God can't find me."

"God can find you anywhere, Natalie."

She hugged herself, her mind in a whirl, her emotions jumbled and roiling. "Beau's evil. I'm not sure of anything when he's around."

"Evil's a strong word."

"Beau's a strong..." She couldn't finish the sentence.

"Then you need to stay away from him."

"That's what I'm trying to do." She looked up and down the street. "I need to go back to the bed and breakfast and get my things."

"Then what?"

"I don't know."

"I've got reservations at The Woodside. I'm sure they'd have an extra room."

"I can't afford it. The publisher—" She stopped when she remembered there was no publisher. *Do not be deceived.* The phrase had come to life by the ultimate deceiver. "Beau paid for everything. He drove me here, he paid—" Her eyes shot open as she thought of every devil-movie she had ever seen. *Have I sold my soul to the devil for a few nights in a bed and breakfast and the possibility of literary success?*

"Don't worry about money," Walter said. "Come with me, and I'll pay—"

"No. I can't be around you." The thought sprang into her mind with utter certainty.

"Excuse me?"

She shook her head as it all became clear. "Not just you. Any of my friends from Haven. Beau hates all of you. I have to put some distance between myself and you." For their sakes. For their safety. If she went near them, they would die. She was as sure of it.

"But we're your friends, Natalie. Del called me down here because of you."

She looked at him, stunned. Then she began to cry. Her simple trip to Eureka Springs had taken on massive implications. Her friends were gathering because of her? She didn't deserve such attention, she didn't *want* such attention—or such responsibility. "No...I don't want to be the cause of all this."

"We're here to help you, Natalie." He put the car in gear. "Let's get your things. Then I'll take you—"

Natalie agreed--to the first part. She needed her things.

But the rest? She would not involve the others. Wherever she went, she would leave--alone.

Natalie made Walter check the area near the Treetop Bed and Breakfast for Beau's car. It wasn't there. While Walter waited out front, she hurried inside and ran up the stairs. She tiptoed past Beau's room and unlocked her door, cringing when the hinge creaked. The fact that Mrs. Ransom had cleaned her room seemed odd. How could ordinary, day-to-day chores continue when her life was in crisis?

She grabbed her suitcase and stuffed her clothes inside. After a cursory glance at the room, she left. If only she'd found her mustard seed pin…but she didn't have time to look any further.

Natalie ran down the stairs, fear nipping at her heels. She glanced once toward the front door, toward Walter's car, then detoured toward the back of the house. She sped through the kitchen, nearly knocking Mr. Ransom over as he put a coat of paint on the back door.

"Hey, Ms. Pasternak? Where you going?"

"I'm checking out." Natalie tossed the explanation over her shoulder. "My friend…Mr. Tenebri will pay for everything."

"Does he know you're leaving?"

"No! And don't tell him. Please don't tell him!"

"Oh. Okay then. No problem."

She squeezed through a break in the back hedge and heard him call after her. "Hey, Ms. Pasternak. Why are you running like the devil's after you?"

✦✦✦

"Anybody home?" Walter entered the front door of the bed and breakfast.

"Back here. In the kitchen."

Walter followed the voice and stuck his head in the room. "Hi. I'm looking for one of your guests? Natalie Pasternak?"

The man eyed Walter like he was something that'd just

crawled out from under a rock. "Who are you?"

Walter arched a brow. "A friend. I gave Natalie a ride so she could pick up her things. She's having some trouble with her companion, and I—"

"She left." The man pointed toward the backyard. "Real upset. Told me not to tell the boyfriend." He ran his eyes over Walter a second time. "Only reason I told you was you ain't him."

Oh, no. Lord, no. Walter swallowed. "Where did she go?"

"Dunno."

"Is she coming back?"

"Dunno."

He sighed. The man was no help whatsoever. "If she does comes back will you tell her Walter is looking for her?"

"Walter. Sure thing." The man raised his brush in a thought. "Say, do you know the boyfriend? Because if you do...could *you* could be the one to tell him she's gone? He's not the type I like to annoy."

Walter left without answering. From what he'd heard about Beau Tenebri, he agreed completely.

THIRTY

"In God I trust, I will not be afraid.
What can mortal man do to me?
All day long they twist my words,
they are always plotting to harm me."
PSALM 56: 4-5

JULIA SAT AT the front of the campaign bus, her chair reclined, her eyes closed. Edward rested in the seat across the aisle.

Julia felt uneasy and had no idea why. The polls showed her neck-and-neck with her opponent, Nathan Bradley. Even the negative aspects of her campaign were leveling out. The press was evenly divided three ways on her abortion. There were those who wanted to lynch her, those who wanted to crown her empress of all women (though she didn't know if it was for having the abortion or for regretting it), and those who'd rather get a tooth pulled than think about it at all.

Yet despite the way things had worked out, the pit of her stomach grabbed, let go, and grabbed again.

Something wasn't right.

She opened her eyes and watched the countryside flash by at seventy miles an hour. A farmhouse, a town in the distance… the people who lived here had feelings, ideas, and opinions. How could she stand up for them in Washington? How could she possibly make decisions that would affect their lives? How could she accept the responsibility? Maybe she should give up. Go home to Minneapolis and putter in the garden. Spend afternoons reading novels about people whose lives were neatly contained and under control by the final page. In the evenings she could snuggle next to Edward on the couch and watch a Jimmy Stewart movie while eating Ritz crackers and squirt-on cheese. She could wake up in the morning, stretch, and ask the air, "What should I do today?" She could forget all about the presidency, all about the mustard seed pins, all about Haven —

A billboard loomed close. *Pass it on!* Julia stared at the

sign, ignoring the illustration of a soft drink.

Pass it on.

She had used the phrase in speeches. It was apt. It was right.

The sign was a sign.

She couldn't give up. Wasn't there some verse about passing it on? Julia reached into her bag and pulled out her Bible. Didn't David say such a thing to his son, Solomon, when they were planning to build the temple? Julia turned the pages of the Old Testament slowly, hoping the verses she'd previously highlighted would stand out. It had to be in 1 Chronicles somewhere...Julia's eyes darted to the middle of a page.

The words stood out as if larger than the rest: PASS IT ON. She backed up and read the verse that went with them. "Be careful to follow all the commands of the Lord your God, that you may possess this good land and *pass it on* as an inheritance to your descendants forever."

Julia sat back and smiled. God certainly had an answer for everything, an answer to every doubt and every thought. She returned to the page. A verse later, the words spoke to her again. "Serve Him with wholehearted devotion and with a willing mind, for the Lord searches every heart and understands every motive behind the thoughts. If you seek Him, you will find Him, but if you forsake Him, He will reject you forever. Be strong and do the work."

She began to laugh. Edward looked at her from across the aisle. "Secret jokes, missy?"

Julia leaned her head back and nodded. "The joke's on me. Just when I was thinking of giving up and giving in, God saw fit to show me the way."

"And how, pray tell, did He do that?" Edward leaned close. "I'd like to know for future reference."

Julia ran a hand over the smooth page of the Bible. How could such power come from something that appeared so powerless? "It boils down to shut up and do it."

"I could've told you that." Edward grinned smugly. "In fact, I think I *have* told you that."

"Once or twice." She closed the Bible and set it aside. "I've made a decision."

"Oh goody. Is this going to change our lives, save the nation, or bring about world peace?"

"Probably." Julia turned toward him. "I'm going to tell people about Haven."

Edward closed his eyes, then looked at her. "Oh, Julia. I don't know. You've talked about the mustard seed pin, you've talked about God. Don't you think that's enough?"

"No." Even as she said it, she knew she was right. "It's time. The feeling's been stirring in me for weeks, nagging quite insistently. I haven't completely fulfilled my promise made in Haven. We were supposed to pass it on, let people know what God has done."

"Are you sure the stirring's not just indigestion?" Edward gave her a hopeful smile. "When I think of all the mediocre food we've eaten in the last six months—"

"I saw a sign."

Edward leaned forward to look out her side of the bus. "A sign? And I missed it?" She swatted him back to his own place. "Not another tornado, I hope?"

"No, Edward. A sign. An actual sign. A billboard that said, 'pass it on.'"

"I hate to tell you this, Julia, but that's an ad campaign for a soft drink. It did not come from God. I guarantee it."

"God uses our circumstances to speak to us, Edward. The sign may not have been there especially for me, but I *did* see it at just the right time to spur me into action."

"At this moment, if I saw a sign that said, 'sleep it off' I'd certainly point it out to you."

"Cynic."

"Governor Carson?"

Julia turned to see Thad Kelley.

"Sorry to disturb you." Thad displayed his cell phone as if it were a prop on a commercial. "But I was just talking to headquarters and they said that Bradley's not letting up on this abortion issue. He's saying you broke a law and anyone who breaks a law of the United States has no right to be—"

She turned her face to the window. "I've already addressed the issue as much as I'm going to. It's closed."

"I agree."

Julia was shocked. Thad put a hand on the top of her chair, leaned toward her, and lowered his voice. "We've received new information that Bradley had an affair this June when he was campaigning in Pennsylvania. The woman contacted our office and says she has pictures, proof that Bradley was unfaithful." He opened his hands. "And as they say, 'unfaithful to wife, unfaithful to country.'"

"They say that, do they?" Julia fixed Thad with an even look.

Thad reddened. "Well...I say that. But it makes for good copy, don't you think?"

Julia rubbed her eyes. "No, I don't think."

He shook his head, clearly frustrated. "We can hit back. They've been hounding you mercilessly about the abortion and making fun of the pins and your God-talk. This would be a way to show the country what kind of character Bradley has." He looked at Edward and snickered. "Actually, I think he's fresh out."

Julia arched her back. She needed her own bed in her own bedroom in her own...Oh well. She was where she was supposed to be. That was enough. "It's true that character should win over charisma, faith over fallacy, but in order for me to have character I cannot act as a judge."

"But he had an affair! There have always been rumors—in fact there's talk of another woman in Georgia right now. But this time we have proof."

"*We* have proof?" Julia narrowed her eyes. "Is that what we've been spending our campaign funds on? Getting proof that my opponent has sinned? I don't think Mr. and Mrs. Public, sitting at their kitchen table after a dinner of meat loaf and Jell-O, would appreciate the twenty dollars they contributed being used for such espionage."

Thad looked to the floor, and Julia touched his hand. "Thaddeus. We Christians have a bad reputation for being judgmental. Since we are all too aware of the difference between good and evil, we are often quick to point it out in others. However, by doing so, we are falsely elevating ourselves as if we are superior. We are not superior. The more we get to know Christ, the smaller we become as our actions are brought up against his perfection. Every time I judge, I condemn myself."

Edward leaned into the conversation. "'Why do you look at the speck of sawdust in your brother's eye and pay no attention to the plank in your own eye?'"

"Governor Carson is not an adulteress." Thad looked at Edward, then toward the back of the bus to see if anyone had overheard.

"I should hope not." Edward's tone was gentle. "It's not apple for apple, Thad. The point is, it's not our place to point fingers. 'Do not judge, or you too will be judged.'"

Thad stuck the phone in his pocket. "So we can't use it."

"We *can* use it," Julia said. "But we won't. If God chooses for the world to know of Bradley's blunders, then so be it. But such news will not originate from this camp." She eyed him. "Is that understood?"

Thad shuffled away as if he'd been told he couldn't put a frog in the bully's desk.

Julia returned her chair to its reclining position. Edward leaned across the aisle and touched her hand. "It's hard being good, isn't it?"

Julia nodded and closed her eyes. "I would have loved to see Bradley squirm his way through that one."

"Another time, darling. Another place."

The Woodside was an inn whose pride showed in the capital "The." It was a regal resort from the beginning of the century with huge trees canopying the drive and ivy crawling up the front portico.

Julia looked out the window of their hotel room. A dozen protesters stood in the parking lot, shoving placards in the air.

"Leave God where he belongs – in church."

"No God in Government!"

"Presidency, not Deity."

Julia backtracked to the bed, sat on it, and fell backwards. Edward joined her. She turned onto her side and rested her head on her hand. "Why do they bother me so?"

"The protesters?"

She nodded. "I know they're entitled – free speech and all that – but when they take the time out of their day to stand in a parking lot waiting for me to see and hear them..."

"You wonder why they don't have anything better to do?" Edward shrugged. "Or do you want them to just go home and be quiet?"

"I want them to like me."

He laughed. "We move from a discussion of the implications and philosophy of free speech to 'I want them to like me?'"

Julia nodded.

"Vanity, thy name is Julia."

She pretended to pout. "Watch it or I'll start singing some country tune like, 'All My Exes Live in Texas.'"

"You don't have any exes."

"You can be the first. I'll buy you a one-way ticket."

"But then you'd lose the election. The people may not tolerate a president with exes."

"They'll make an exception – a mercy clause after I tell them all your dirty little secrets." Julia slipped a pillow from beneath the bedspread.

Edward did the same, keeping his eyes glued to his wife. "What happened to," he mimicked her voice, "'I want them to *like* me?'"

Julia raised her pillow, ready to attack. "I want to be liked by everyone, but not by an everyone like you." She let him have it across the face. He parried and hit her left side.

"Is that another country song?"

"It's *going* to be." Julia whammed the pillow into his stomach. "I'm composing it as we speak. I'm already into the second verse."

There was a knock on the door. The pillows halted in mid-swing. Edward took a breath and cleared his throat. "Yes?"

"Excuse me, but I have a message for Governor Carson. They said it was urgent."

Julia and Edward tidied their hair and straightened their clothes. Edward opened the door. A young woman smiled, her eyes huge. She glanced past Edward to see Julia. Julia waved. The girl waved back, then her eyes made note of the rumpled bed with the pillows strewn about.

"You have a message?" Edward tucked in the back of his shirt.

She reddened, then handed him a pink paper. "I wouldn't have..." she glanced at the bed, "bothered you if the message hadn't been urgent."

"I understand," Edward said, closing the door. "Thank you."

The girl halted the door's swing. "Is there anything else I can get you?"

"No."

Julia called from the room. "We could use some more pillows."

Edward closed the door and pointed at her. "You are an evil woman. After word gets out that Mr. and Mrs. Carson had a tumble in the hay within minutes of getting to their room, we will have protesters outside our window."

Julia snatched the message from him. "What are they going to protest?"

"They'll think of something."

Julia read the note and moved to the telephone.

"What's up?" Edward watched her carefully.

"It's a message from Kathleen Kraus."

"Your friend from Haven?"

She sat at the edge of the bed and dialed Kathy's number. "I wonder why she's in town." She looked up, remembering. "She lives here! I'd forgotten all about—"

"Hello?"

"Kathleen, this is Julia."

"We are so glad you're here!"

"We?"

"Natalie's here, and Del...and Walter's on his way."

"That's wonderful, but why is everyone gathering?"

"We don't know why. Not exactly. Natalie came with a friend, and Del came after Natalie *because* of her friend--who he doesn't like or trust one whit. You're here on your campaign. And Del called Walter."

"A little odd, but wonderful. I'd love to see all of you. Let's see...I have this rally tonight at seven, but afterward maybe we could get together and go over old times."

"There's more to it... it's Natalie's friend, Beau."

"The one Del doesn't like."

"Nobody likes him, Julia."

"That's too bad, but I'm not sure what I—"

"He's evil. Do you understand? Not just bad. Evil."

Julia fingered her mustard seed pin. "As in good versus evil?"

"I think it might come to that. I think that's why God has brought us together. To fight for Natalie. To win her away from an evil influence. Beau's telling her lies that could hurt her. I know he is."

"How do you propose we help her?"

"I have no idea. That's why we need you. You were our leader in Haven. You can tell us what to do."

"But I don't know this Beau. How can I possibly help?"

"I don't know. We have to get together. I know you're busy, I know you may not have time for people from your past but—"

"I have time for you." Julia looked at Edward, and he nodded. It was the right thing to do. "I'll make time."

THIRTY-ONE

"Be self-controlled and alert.
Your enemy the devil prowls around
like a roaring lion looking for someone to devour.
Resist him, standing firm in the faith,
because you know that your brothers throughout the world
are undergoing the same kind of sufferings."
1 PETER 5: 8-9

AFTER DRIVING AROUND town hunting for Beau's car, Del and Jack tried Natalie's and Beau's rooms again.

"They're still not here." Jack leaned against Natalie's door. "What's the use of driving all the way down here to save her if we can't even find her?"

Del tented his fingers on his forehead, trying to think. He had been so certain they were doing the right thing by going after Natalie...and when Kathy had known where she and Beau were staying, it had seemed like fate. Del and Jack would find her, declare themselves her white knights— "Unhand her, you villain!" —and take her safely back to Lincoln. Once in Lincoln, Del had no doubt that Natalie would be safe. Jack would make sure of that. They had it all planned out, but life wasn't listening to their plan. Del nudged Jack's foot. "Let's go find Mrs. Ransom. Maybe she's seen them."

Jack sank to the floor, using the door as a guide. "You go ahead. I'll camp out here. She's got to come back eventually."

Del shook his head and held out a hand to pull him up, but Jack didn't take it. "Listen Jack ol' boy, this is a tourist town with plenty of things to keep people occupied—all day, and well into the evening. Plus, Natalie has her meeting with the publisher sometime today, meaning she may not be back until nighttime." He dropped his hand. "I suppose you could wait, but as for me, I'd rather take the offensive and go after her."

Jack ran a finger along the rose pattern of the carpet. "We could hunt and hunt and still never find her. Be two steps behind. Constantly miss her."

"We could, but I feel in my gut that God wouldn't bring us this far if we weren't supposed to meet up. We're here for Natalie, and so we *will* find Natalie. But not by sitting around. There's a delicate balance at work here. We have to have faith as if everything depends on God, while we work hard as if everything depends on us."

There was a moment of silence. "You realize there is absolutely no way I can argue with that logic."

"True brilliance is absolute."

"It must be exhausting being right all the time."

Del sighed. "It *is* a burden."

Jack added his own sigh. "I believe this would be the perfect moment for a prayer, don't you? Something inspiring to send two heroes out to conquer evil and save mankind?"

"You got it." Del bowed his head. "Heavenly Father, we both feel you've brought us here for a reason. We think it's to save Natalie from the influence of an evil man. But we can't find her. Lead us. Guide us. Show us where she is, and then give us the wisdom and strength to do whatever is necessary to bring her safely home. We are your faithful heroes-in-waiting. Amen."

Jack held out his hand and Del pulled him up. "Ditto."

They went downstairs and found Mr. Ransom in the kitchen, washing out a paintbrush.

"Is your wife around?" Del asked.

"Should be back any minute. Went to get groceries. Can I help?"

"I was looking for Natalie Paster—"

"Boy, is she popular."

"Why do you say that?"

"Another man was just here asking after her."

"The man she was traveling with?"

"No, not him. Some other guy. Late forties. Business man type. Said his name was Walter."

"Walter *Prescott?*"

"Dunno. Just Walter."

Del turned to Jack. "Walter. I knew he'd come."

Jack nodded. "And Kathy said Governor Carson is coming tonight. You're all here."

Del gave a low whistle. "We're all here."

Jack put a hand to his mouth. "'For where two or three come together in my name, there am I with them.'"

"All together but Natalie."

Mr. Ransom let the brush run under the water. "Is the girl in trouble?"

"Why do you say that?"

"She left with her suitcase, snuck out the back way. Did more than sneak. Ran. Didn't want her boyfriend to know."

Jack handed him a towel. "He's not her boyfriend."

"No?" Mr. Ransom shrugged. "Boyfriend or no, she ran."

Del looked out the back window. "Did she get our message?"

"Dunno." He turned off the water. "Say, do you know when the boyfriend's coming back? I don't want to get stiffed for two rooms."

Del turned to leave. "Dunno."

Lenny Kraus sat in his mother's kitchen reading the morning paper. It was good to be a part of real life again. A part of normal. Sleeping in a bed, eating food that didn't come from a box or a dumpster. Reading about the world. If he could only figure out a way to see his kids regularly. Maybe even win Kathy back. But that was probably asking too much. He didn't blame Kathy for hating him, not with all he'd done.

Lenny caught a glimpse of something moving in the backyard. He got up from his chair and went to the window to get a better look. It was something near the shed.

It was a girl. A girl carrying a suit—

Suddenly Lenny saw Beau spring across the yard and pounce on her. Lenny ran to the door.

"Beau! What're you doing?" Beau shot him a look while he yanked the girl to her feet. Lenny frowned. The girl looked familiar. "Natalie?"

Natalie put a hand to a cut on her forehead. She blinked. "Lenny?"

Beau shoved Natalie forward. "Enough of the reunion. Get inside and shut up."

Lenny got out of the way as Beau shoved Natalie into the kitchen and slammed the door. Then in one slick movement, Beau pushed Natalie against the wall and positioned a hand around her neck. He held her at arm's length, raising his arm just enough to make her rise to her toes. "You thought you could get away? From me?" He took two deep breaths, his face red. Natalie squirmed and choked. Beau was going to kill her.

"Let her go!" Lenny took a step toward him.

Beau swept his other arm toward Lenny. Although no bodily contact was made, Lenny flew across the kitchen table, where he slid through the dishes onto the floor.

Seeing Lenny in a heap, Natalie began to whimper, her toes grappling to keep her balance. Beau lowered his arm so her feet found the floor. He moved his face close, his eyes locked onto hers. His eyes...how had she ever thought he had beautiful eyes? They were horrid. Opaque. Cold.

She closed her own eyes, trying to escape their power.

"No you don't! Look at me! Concentrate on *me!*" She opened her eyes. "We're going to leave here together, Tally. I have to find a place to keep you out of commission while I handle business at Julia's rally."

Julia's rally! He *was* after the others.

Beau looked toward the front of the house. "We're going to walk to my car as if we're two lovers. There will be no calls for help, no attempts to run." He pointed to Lenny, who lay dazed on the floor. "What I did to Lenny was a small shove. Don't make me use my power, Tally. You won't like it." He nuzzled his mouth against her ear. "Do you understand, my love?"

Natalie nodded. *Please, Lord. Help me get away ... please*

protect the others.

Beau turned to Lenny who cowered on the floor. "I've got a job for you."

Lenny didn't react.

"Do you hear me, you nothing of a man?"

Lenny rubbed the back of his head and nodded.

"That's better. I need you to be at The Woodside banquet room this evening for Julia Carson's rally. It starts at seven, but I want you there early. There's a service closet up near the stage with a light switch right outside the door. I'm going to cause a ruckus tonight. When you hear a lot of yelling I want you to hit the lights. Plunge the place into darkness."

"But how can I? Surely they've got tons of security around, checking every closet, every—"

"You're implying a few security officers are more powerful than I am?"

"No, no."

"Good. Just do it. Julia, the great leader of the Haven disciples, is going to suffer a setback tonight. I'm not going to let her tell the world about Haven. United they stand and divided they—"

Lenny stepped toward him. "You're not going to hurt her, are you?"

"And if I do?"

Lenny didn't have an answer. Natalie coughed under Beau's grip. She wanted to scream, to cry out, but she couldn't. Her entire being was focused on the pain and her need for air.

God…Father, please!

Suddenly Beau released her neck. She stumbled from the loss of his support and gasped for air. He put an arm around her shoulders and gave them a friendly squeeze. "Ready, dearest?"

◆◆◆

Beau drove with one arm draped across the back of Natalie's seat, its presence a reminder of the clamping power of his grip. He hummed as if they were on a Sunday drive. This was absurd. She was riding in the car with...

"Are you Satan?"

"You flatter me, Tally. I am but his loyal servant."

"A demon."

"At your service."

Natalie's heart started to pound. *Dear, Lord. I know there's a way you've given us to handle this, but I don't know what it is.* She wanted to rake her nails through her hair and scream at her own ignorance. *I'm sorry...I should...my mind can't...help me. Protect me!*

Suddenly, a wave of calm came over her and she heard a voice within herself. *'I am with you always.'* The still, small voice she'd heard others speak about, was speaking in her own heart.

Beau's voice broke in. "What are you grinning about?"

She opened her eyes and let her smile spread. Everything would be all right. God was with her. He would show her what to do. She took a cleansing breath. "Where are we going?"

Beau did a double-take, obviously unnerved by her calm. "To...to meet your destiny!"

"I know my destiny."

A moment's hesitation. "Not the destiny I have in mind. I'm done giving you a choice."

Natalie nearly laughed as his lies became clear. "I always have a choice. God's the One who gives it to me and you can't change that."

"I've invested a lot of time in you."

"Invested?"

"Nothing's free, Tally. Not love, not happiness, not your soul."

She felt a stitch in her throat as fear tried to regain entry, but God's promise rang clear. *'I am with you.'*

Beau leered at her. "I'm so glad you've chosen me. If you hadn't, I would have had to do something quite naughty to convince you."

"Naughty?"

"Maybe if one of your precious friends had paid the price... if something happened to Kathy or Del or —"

She felt a rush of anger. "You leave them alone!"

"Then be mine, dearest Tally. Be mine, heart, body, and soul."

"Never!"

Beau turned sharply onto a gravel drive. "Wrong answer."

Natalie had to brace herself against the dashboard as Beau raced up the road. "I *demand* to know where you're taking me."

Beau laughed. "You demand? I believe you are misinformed about the power structure here. *I'm* in charge. I'm in control. And I'm taking you to a safe place. A sanctuary. A *haven* of sorts." His smile was sickening. "You like havens, don't you?"

Natalie saw a sign flash by. "The Ozark Bird Sanctuary?"

"It's closed for renovations. No one will bother us here. No one will hear you scream."

She felt a shiver of fear. Doubt followed close behind, and her courage left her. "Beau...don't."

"Don't what?"

She tried the door. It was locked. Panic rushed in. "Beau, let me out! I'll go out to the highway and hitch a ride back to Lincoln, to Estes. Anywhere. I'll never mention a word about you to anyone."

"But I want you to mention me, Tally." Beau pulled into a parking lot. "I want the world to know that my kind are in control." He shut off the car and got out. He went to the passenger side and opened her door like a perfect gentleman. "After you, *mademoiselle*." He held out a hand.

She stared at it, trying to recapture the calm of God's presence. *Please! Help —*

"Take it!"

She took his hand.

✦✦✦

The entryway revealed a gift shop and a reception area with a fountain, turned off during the construction of an addition to their right. To the left was a three-story botanical garden built into the side of the hill, a glassed-in slice of forest. A waterfall spilled into a pond. Trails wound their way through trees, bushes, and flowering plants. Benches spotted the way. The chatter of the birds was irritating, the smell was damp and musty.

They walked up the path and Natalie tried to let the beauty around them fill her with hope. "It's like the garden of Eden."

"You're right." Beau filled his lungs, thumping his hands against his chest. "I feel right at home."

She hugged herself, forcing her voice to stay even. "I've never really believed in you—or Satan."

He cackled. "Well, then we must not exist, must we?" He shook his head. "You humans are so naive. You live in this goody-god world where you let yourself believe lies about a loving *Jesus* who forgives all sin. And all the while, legions of evil are conspiring and transpiring around you." He leveled her with a look, and when he spoke, it was as though his words echoed with countless voices. *"Legions."* He blinked, tilted his head, and returned to normal. "You are totally blind."

She stared at him, throat dry. *God... Lord... why didn't I see?* "I do see the evil in the world. I just never thought of it coming from—"

"Satan?"

She nodded. "I thought evil was just people gone astray."

He laughed again. *"Gone astray.* An innocent platitude for death and destruction."

"People have a choice. They can choose to do good or bad. God lets us choose."

"Ah." Beau raised a finger. "But only to a certain extent. Your freedom is an illusion. God doesn't give up. He keeps hounding you."

God doesn't give up. She wrapped that truth around her, warming in its comfort. "I like knowing that no matter how I mangle things God won't give up on me."

Beau flipped her opinion away. "You are so naive. Don't you think God has better things to do than concern Himself with you? His patience is not infinite. He's weary of you just as you're weary of yourself and your own failures. Trying and failing is too much work. Why make things so difficult?

"What's the alternative?"

He smiled broadly and picked up a stone. "At last, she asks the question."

"What question?"

"What's the alternative to God?" Beau held out his arms. "This moment and all the moments that come after it--that's the alternative to God. The past is done. The present is here to be enjoyed. And the future is ours for the taking."

Natalie tried to understand. "God promises us an eternal future. Eternal happiness."

"With what guarantee?"

"Christ—"

"*No!*" Beau heaved the stone into the waterfall. "Jesus was a weak, ineffectual man who's been gone for two thousand years."

"But He still lives—"

"Where?" Beau spat out the question, flinging his arms in the air. "Have you ever seen Him?"

"Not in the flesh. But I believe He's here, with me. He sent his Holy Spirit to live in each—"

Beau grabbed her hand and pulled it to his chest. "*I* am here! *I* am with you. *I* am flesh—and so much more. *I* can make you happy now. Who cares about tomorrow? Live for the moment. Live for what you can have *now!*"

Natalie yanked her hand free, her stomach turning. "But there's more to think about than this world, this moment."

"Who says?"

Natalie's head hurt. She was just an ordinary person. She wasn't supposed to have debates with demons. *Lord, give me the understanding, the words. Your words.* She felt a surge of strength. She nodded to herself and raised her chin. "God says."

"You're letting yourself be drawn from one lie to another. Because you believe in God you therefore believe in heaven and eternal life and Jesus and—"

"Yes." Yes. She did. She truly did. It felt good to be certain.

"But if I take one of those beliefs away, the rest crumble and you are forced to doubt. You *must* doubt."

As he said the word, Natalie felt it—felt the tug and cut of it, as real and as painful as anything she'd ever felt. *What if he's right? What proof do I have that God is real?*

No! She shook her head fiercely, trying to dispel the traitorous thoughts. But the battle waged on, and she was so weary...*I can't do this. I'm not smart enough.* She looked toward the entryway. She had to leave. Escape.

"Think about it, Tally. If you take away the idea of heaven, then what happens to eternal life? It has no place to go. If you take away God, then Jesus becomes an impotent man who couldn't stand up for Himself when it counted. If you take away eternal life, then you'd better start having fun now because now is all there is." He shook his head in disgust and clamped his hand around her chin. "If you don't start paying attention to me, I'll have to do something drastic to prove to you that I'm right." He paused and slowly ran a finger down her neck and chest, and made a sharp jab above her heart. "Don't make me hurt you."

She felt the intent of his pain as though it were real. *He means it.* Natalie took in a breath and stared at him, dread churning. She could only imagine his power. What was she supposed to do? Why wasn't God showing her the way out? Arguing with Beau was futile. He twisted her words, no matter how truthful they were. And who knew the truth anymore? Suddenly, she couldn't grasp it. It hung just beyond her reach. She was alone. No one knew where she was. Beau could do anything he wanted and no one would find her.

The panic exploded. *I have to leave!*

She bolted. Beau grabbed her arm and yanked her into his chest. "Where do you think you're going?"

She fought him, amazed at her own strength. "Let me *go!*
I don't need to listen to you. I don't need to be with you or
debate God, Jesus, or even what day it is. I've had enough!"

Beau spun her around to face him. *"You've* had enough?"

She whipped her arms upward, escaping his grip.
Stumbling backward, she felt the panic ease. Cognizant
thought returned. "You say I can be happy now. But I'm *not*
happy. Not here. Not with you. God offers free will. Do
you?"

He didn't answer.

"I want to leave." She forced herself to look him in the
eye. She raised her chin. "So I'm going." She turned and
walked toward the door.

Beau sprung. He grabbed her shoulders and hurled her
onto a bench. She fell on her wrist and felt a shooting pain.
Her chin hit wood.

"Stay!"

Natalie cowered, the physical pain secondary to her fear.

He stared down at her, his chest heaving, his eyes
blazing. His lips curled in a sneer. "You are not worth the
trouble! You are nothing but a weak, indecisive, annoying—"
He leaned over her, bracing his arms against the bench,
locking her in. "You are *revolting*. I have no idea why I was
supposed to waste my time on the likes of you."

Natalie made herself hold his stare. "Then let me go."

Beau pushed himself away and laughed. "Let you go? It
doesn't work that way, Tally. I'm here on a mission and until
that mission—"

"What mission?"

He pointed a finger at her. "To stop you and your kind
from passing on information about Haven. Information about
what God is up to. He must be stopped."

Natalie rubbed her chin and discovered blood on her
fingers. "He will never be stopped."

"That's where you're wrong. That's the lie He tells you."
Beau closed his eyes ever-so-slowly, then opened them. They
were lifeless. He smiled slightly, letting his gaze draw her in.
"There are other forces in the world. Forces that have more

power than your god. You're deceiving yourself when you act as if He really longs to know you, and you long to know Him."

"But I do—"

"You don't. You may think you do. But the only reason you want anything to do with God is so He'll make you feel good about yourself. So He'll answer your pitiful prayers. So He'll do what *you* want Him to do."

No, no! It wasn't true. "*You're* the one who always talks about feeling good, Beau. And now you say feeling good about ourselves is bad?"

"No, it's *not* bad!" He lowered his voice as if the birds would be bothered. "Feeling good *is* good. That's all there is. But God won't *let* you feel good. He always has conditions. He wants you to get to know Him, to love Him, to pray to Him. But does He give you any of those good feelings in return?"

"Yes—"

"Wrong! He makes you discover things about yourself that *He* doesn't like. He brings them into the open like a parent pointing out that your pants don't match your shirt. And once He makes you see all your vices, He doesn't push them into the background so you can go on with things, He makes you want to change. He's a dictator. He's got to have things His way."

"And you don't?"

Beau tilted his head and smiled. "Touché. Maybe you're not as stupid as I thought."

"I am not stupid." *Just desperately in need of God's wisdom.*

Beau's voice softened and he sat beside her. "Ah, but you are a stupid sinner. You haven't done one thing right your entire life. You're not a writer, you're not a lover, you're not a girlfriend, you're not even a mother. You are nothing. Admit it. Say it: I am a sinner."

Natalie felt tears threaten. "I know I am...I *am* a sinner. I've never been afraid to admit—"

"You are *always* afraid!"

Natalie shrank into the corner of the bench.

"You're afraid of your own thoughts, you're afraid of being tempted. You're afraid of doing the wrong thing, choosing the wrong thing. Why, you're even afraid of being afraid."

"I just want to be a better person."

Beau raised a fist to her face. "Blind *fool!* Do you think living a life full of fear is making you a better person?"

"No, but—"

"Your life is a waste." Beau shook his head and stood back. "No wonder God's given up on you."

"God hasn't—" She tried to remember the comforting words, "*I...I am—*"

"He has!" Beau waved an arm at their surroundings. "Look at where you are, Tally! While you've been abstaining from life, while you've been floundering after your spiritual pipe dreams, God's forgotten you. Is He here? Here in this sanctuary? I tell you, He is not! *I* am here. You are here. And the rest of the world is going on without us."

"God has plans for me."

"Ha! He *had* plans for you. It's been two years. How long do you think God is going to wait around for you to do something? *Time is up!* He's abandoned you. You are alone. I am the only one who's stood by you, who cares what happens to you."

That's not true, that's not true, that's...true. Natalie drew her knees to her chest. "Someone will come after me. Kathy, Walter...someone will miss me."

Beau knelt beside her and put his hands on her knees. "Nobody is coming. Your friends have deserted you. They are going on with their lives, all thoughts of you forgotten. And why shouldn't they? You rejected them. You chose me."

"I didn't choose you. I—"

He slapped her. Then he grabbed her upper arms and lifted her to her feet, suspending her off the ground. "You are mine!"

She started to whimper. She wanted to call out, to pray, but the power of his touch burned through all reason and left behind a blankness. Only one word found its way clear.

"No..."

"Yes!" Beau shook her. Her head lolled up and back. "You are mine. Do you feel it? Your old life is gone forever. You are an empty shell." He raised his face to the sky. "She is mine now! I claim her! Natalie is no more! Tally is mine!"

He let go. She collapsed.

THIRTY-TWO

"Neither death nor life, neither angels nor demons,
neither the present nor the future, nor any powers,
neither height nor depth, nor anything else in all creation,
will be able to separate us from the love of God
that is in Christ Jesus our Lord."
ROMANS 8: 38-39

JULIA FASTENED A string of pearls around her neck. She ran a fingernail along the edge of her lipstick.

"You look beautiful," Edward said. "As usual."

"Two brownie points for Mr. Carson."

"What does that make? Two thousand, three hundred, and twelve?"

"When you hit twenty-five hundred you get a free set of steak knives."

He gave her a kiss on the back of the neck. "I'll work on it."

Julia looked out the window at the parking lot. It was full. "Are the protesters still around?"

"As vociferous as ever." Edward grimaced. "Thad is keeping us apprised of the situation."

"Will they be allowed in the banquet hall?"

"*Allowed* is not the right word. We will attempt to keep them out, but I wouldn't count on it."

"Great." She put a hand to her stomach. "Maybe we should call it off. Say I'm sick or something."

"Or something?"

"I'm scared."

"Nervous, I understand. But scared? Since when? There are local police around and we have our own security people. Besides, you have to go on. All your friends from Haven are here."

"Natalie is still missing. Del and Walter have been looking for her all day."

"Then let's say a prayer for Natalie."

"And me too. I have the feeling I'm going to need all the

help I can get."

He studied her. "Julia. What's wrong?"

She shook her head. "Something's different this time. Ever since I decided to tell people about Haven, I've had nervous knots in my stomach."

"Nervous knots *can* signal the importance of your message."

"Or they can signal that I'm not supposed to share that message."

"Do you really believe that?"

Julia hesitated only a second. "No. These nerves are my own doing. I'm nervous because telling about Haven involves taking a risk. I might lose the election because of this. The media will have a field day questioning my sanity. I can see it now: `Carson Claims She was Invited by God.'"

"I might have trouble believing that one, too." Edward shrugged. "It's a solid example of 'you had to be there.'"

"Are you saying I shouldn't tell about Haven?" Julia studied his face. How she loved him, how she trusted him...

He ran a hand across her back. "I think you need to decide what's important in your Haven story. The fact *you* got an invitation from God? Or the fact that God has an invitation for all people to stand up and do His work." He took his much-used Bible from the table. "Maybe this will help. I found these verses while you were taking a shower." He patted the bed and they sat with the Bible spanning their laps.

Julia closed her eyes. "Read to me. I want to hear your voice say the words."

Edward cleared his throat. "From Ephesians. You remember that Paul was writing to the church at Ephesus from his jail cell in Rome and—"

Julia opened one eye. "The verses, dear one. Time is short."

"Yes, yes, of course. I found chapter six, verses thirteen and fifteen especially interesting. 'Therefore put on the full armor of God, so that when the day of evil comes, you may be able to stand your ground and after you have done everything, to stand.'"

Julia's eyes shot open. "That's the verse I read right before I made my acceptance speech at the convention!"

"Really?"

She nodded. "It made me think about taking a stand."

Edward put the earpiece of his glasses in his mouth. "Interesting..."

"What's the other verse?"

Edward put his glasses back on. "'Stand firm then...with your feet fitted with the readiness that comes from the gospel of peace.'" He closed the book. "Peace."

"I've always said you bring me so much peace."

"That's why the verse stuck out. Ben told me that too."

"But those verses...they're all about spiritual warfare, aren't they?"

"The armor of God."

Julia took his hand. It suddenly made sense. "*That's* why we're here. All the Haven people, brought together, Natalie in trouble, this Beau, who is evil..."

"It sure seems that way."

They sat silently, letting this truth sink in. Then Julia took a deep breath. "I expected something like this to happen. God didn't get our attention to let us wander about aimlessly, year after year. He had something in mind from the beginning."

"This?"

"For now anyway." She put a fist at her stomach. "I've had a feeling that something was up, that we were traveling a road that had a specific destination in mind."

"Heaven?"

"Eventually. Surely. But for now, something more earthly. More immediate."

"You think it all begins tonight?"

She stood and pulled him up. "I think it began before we were born. After all, God said, 'Before I formed you in the womb I knew you, before you were born I set you apart.'"

"Ah." Edward gave her a kiss on the forehead. "We're talking *ancient* history."

She thwacked his arm. "Speak for yourself."

He looked at his watch. "Actually, it's time for you to speak *for* me. For all of us. Are you ready?"

Julia put a hand on her chest, trying to calm its flutter. "It's like this was meant to be."

"Then let it *be*. Let it play out according to His plan."

"But what if I get it wrong?"

"Trust God to help you get it right."

"I do trust Him. It's me who could get it wrong."

The angelic mentors gathered.

"Julia needs our help," Louise said.

"As does Natalie," Anne said. "She is beaten."

"No," Fran said, "she is not beaten. Her eternal salvation is assured. She has not lost that. She cannot lose that. 'God has said, "Never will I leave you, never will I forsake you."' But Satan *has* made inroads as to her physical, mental and emotional well-being."

"I'm afraid the battle has not even begun." Louise shook her head.

"God is aware of the plight of our charges and the evil that is against them." John held out a hand. "He has told us, 'Do not be afraid or discouraged because of this vast army. For the battle is not yours, but God's.'"

Gabe nodded. "But He wants to hear their voices. He wants them to call out to Him. At their voice, He will be at their side. 'Then you will call, and the Lord will answer, you will cry for help, and He will say: Here am I.'"

"They are unaware of the stakes." Anne hugged herself. "My Kathy may suffer."

"They all might suffer." Fran turned to the new additions to their group. "It is good to have reinforcements. I would like to introduce all of you to Cosmas, La Salle, Jerome, and Christopher. Their charges will be involved in this evening's events."

"Your charge is Roy?" John studied Cosmas.

He nodded. "He has been a joy."

Christopher, the other mentor, looked away. "My Lenny is very troubled."

Jerome spoke up. "We will all help as we can. My Edward—each soul is special and precious to our Lord."

Christopher took his hand. "Pray for Lenny to open his heart. Pray for his soul."

"And pray for my Jack." La Salle joined the circle. "He is a man close to our Lord."

John spread his arms. "Pray for them all."

Lenny peeked out the door of the utility closet in the hotel ballroom. The room was busy with hotel employees making final preparations for Julia's rally. He closed the closet door. Using the wall to guide him, he slid to the floor. His eyes adjusted to the dark, the slit of light at the bottom of the door acting like an illuminated line dividing Lenny from the rest of the world.

Was it a line he could cross?

He was tired of doing Beau's dirty work. He was tired of being a prisoner of fear. Everything he did was because he was afraid. He was sitting in this stupid closet because he was afraid. Of Beau. Of living again.

It's not too late.

He cringed when he thought of Natalie. Poor Natalie, dragged away by Beau. Was she dead? Did she wish she were dead?

"I should have done something." Lenny clenched a fist. "I should have saved her."

The door opened, bumping into Lenny's feet. Beau slid in and shut the door, then turned on the light. Lenny squinted.

"What's this about saving her?" Beau glared down at him.

Lenny got to his feet. "Where's Natalie? Is she all right?"

Beau shoved Lenny against the wall, pinning him with a hand around his neck. "You tried to help her. You know

308

what I should do to you, Lenny?"

Lenny couldn't have answered if he'd wanted to. He struggled for a breath. Beau let him go, and he slumped against the wall. Beau flexed his hand.

"Since when are you Natalie's friend?"

Lenny tried to hide his fear and pain. "I didn't see her until you pounced on her. Honest." Lenny teased a dust bunny with his toe. "Where'd you take her? Is she all right?"

"Tally is safe and secure in an appropriate place—a haven." He laughed. "Do you see the irony of the symbolism? She's a prisoner in a haven. Just as all these simpletons are being held prisoner of Haven."

"Yeah, I get it."

Beau moved his hand toward Lenny's neck, and Lenny had the clear impression Beau would like nothing more than to crush his windpipe.

"You'd *better* get it, Lenny. And you'd better get how important this evening's rally is to me."

"Can you tell me why?"

"Because they're all here. I have a chance to stop them and put an end to their inane quest."

"Quest?"

"It's absurd, isn't it?" Beau snickered. "These nothing people believe they have a grand goal to attain for their God. They're running after air. Not one of them is special." Beau checked his watch. "A half hour to start time. I'll let Julia ramble a few minutes, and then the festivities will begin."

"What are you going to do?"

"Make Julia Carson self-destruct."

"How are you going to do that?"

Beau flipped off the light, plunging the closet into darkness. "You do your part, Lenny. I'll do mine."

✦✦✦

The ballroom was full. A woman at the piano offered innocuous tunes while the crowd waited for the main attraction. When Julia entered the room, the woman struck up a rousing rendition of "Stars and Stripes Forever." The audience rose in a standing ovation. Julia and Edward walked toward the podium, waving to the crowd. Her friends from Haven lined the front row. Julia took her place center-stage and waved the audience to silence. Those who had chairs sat. A large group stood in the back. Julia made note of their position. She expected any protests to come from that direction.

As she began her opening remarks, she noticed a man with long, dark hair stroll among those who were standing. He spoke a word here, a phrase there, leaving behind puzzled looks. His smooth movement among the stillness of the crowd continued to draw her eyes.

What is he doing?

Julia fumbled a sentence, her thought lost. She looked down, trying to recapture her idea. When she raised her eyes, she saw the man looking at her. He stood at the back of the room, capping the middle aisle, his hands clasped in front of him, his legs spread. He stared at her, a tight smile on his face.

She continued. "I'd like to speak with you today about something that happened to me two years ago, something that changed the course of my life." She waved a hand at her row of Haven friends. "Along with these special people, I visited a very unique place called Haven. The place isn't important, nor how each of us got there. But the essence of what we learned in Haven is something I feel compelled to share with you."

She glanced at Edward. He nodded his approval.

"Each of us are searching for something in our lives. From the moment we are born, we are seeking, hunting, looking. But for what? Do we seek happiness? Fulfillment? I think our search goes deeper. We long to know why we were put on this earth, at this time, in this place, among the people we find around us. Will we make a difference? Are we a part of a larger plan or are we merely individuals, each floating in our own minute sphere of influence?

"I believe there is an intricate plan where our lives

intertwine and complement each other. God has granted each of us unique gifts that He expects to be used for His good, for His will. You see, our country is like a symphony orchestra. Some of us play violin, some oboe, some percussion. Some of us set up the music stands. Some—"

Julia found her eyes drawn to those of the dark-haired man. He had not moved from his station. His smile had not changed. It still mocked her, challenged her.

"Some of us write the music, or sell it. Some repair the broken instruments. Some sit in the audience and applaud. So many people with so many gifts. All coming together for one common goal: to create something worthwhile, something of beau—"

The man pointed at her. Julia recoiled in pain as though shards of glass had darted from his finger, piercing her mind.

The audience fidgeted with uncertainty. Edward took a step toward her. With a surge of will, Julia forced her eyes away from the man and motioned Edward back. She took a moment to clear her thoughts. "Excuse me, let me continue. I was saying..."

The next words that sounded throughout the room sounded like Julia's voice, but they did not come from her.

"You don't need God, you are God."

The audience did a communal double-take. Julia tapped on the microphone. It didn't work. The Julia-voice continued. *"You don't need to change your ways or feel bad about what you've done wrong. You don't need to depend on God to save you."*

Edward rushed to her side. He put a hand over the mike. "Julia, what are you saying?"

"It's not me," she whispered as her counterfeit voice rang throughout the room.

"Forget about sin. It is something to be ignored as we become one with great cosmic unity—as we become our own gods."

The people nearest to the podium saw that Julia wasn't speaking, but the rest of the audience murmured with shock at her words.

"They don't know it's not me." Confusion warred with despair as she looked at Edward. *It's begun. The battle has begun.*

"Step away from the mike," he said. "Let them see you're not talking."

The moment she took a step to follow his instruction, she saw the dark-haired man raise his hands like a director cueing a stage entrance. The group of protesters came to life, talking, shouting, chanting.

"God is dead!"

"We want a president, not a preacher!"

"Man is in control!"

All eyes turned toward the protesters. The sudden attention fed their flame, making them spread from their position to the side aisles. The dozen protesters of the morning had grown to four times that number. They raised their fists and shouted, making the rest of the audience shrink into their seats.

Security sprang into action, but they couldn't quell the spread of the demonstrators. The yelling horde seeped through the human barricades like floodwaters around a pesky levy.

The teeming crowd sounded far away in her ears, like crowd noise at a distant stadium. Julia's gaze was locked to the man--and his was locked on her.

The audience noticed the intensity of Julia's gaze. They turned in their seats to see what had mesmerized their candidate. They saw a man with long, dark hair. A handsome man, who was looking back at her and smiling—

Kathy stood and pointed. "Beau!"

The lights went out.

◆◆◆

Screaming. Shouting. Clashing bodies. Toppled chairs. Bruises. Cuts. Chaos.

A spotlight slashed the darkness in two. It found its mark. Julia. She blinked at its intensity and raised a hand to shield her eyes.

"Say something, Julia," Edward coaxed. "Get things

under control."

The brilliance of the spotlight made it impossible for her to see the audience. But she could hear them. The protesters shouting against God and her candidacy. Others shouting against the shock of the darkness. And still others shouting because there was shouting.

Please help me, Lord. Help me to restore order. She pushed the microphone aside and called to them. "Calm—" She tried again. "Take your seats everyone. The lights will be back on soon." She hoped she was telling the truth.

As she spoke, Thaddeus came forward and whispered loudly, "Keep talking, Governor. I've tried the lights, but nothing happens. Same with the mike. This is all we've got."

The music of the piano cut through the noise. Julia turned toward the sound. The accompanist was seated at the instrument. She played a familiar introduction to an Irving Berlin number.

Julia smiled. Who could object to Irving Berlin? Who could object to...

"'God bless America...'" Julia sang. With all her heart and soul. "'Land that I love.'"

The decibel level of confusion lowered as people took a moment to figure out what was going on. A few brave voices joined in.

Julia squinted, looking down at her Haven friends. She saw Kathy take Roy's hand and pull him onto the stage. Del, Jack, and Walter followed, all singing the familiar song.

Slowly, the crowd righted their chairs and stood at attention. As more joined in, others followed, not wanting to be left out. The song ended and began again. And again, until the protesters were drowned out by the unison of the voices gaining strength. Sounding triumphant.

✦✦✦

Lenny peeked out from his hiding place. He ignored the chaos Beau had created—that he had helped Beau create. His eyes were drawn to the stage where the people from Haven stood, hands clasped, united against the confusion around them as a lone spotlight lit their solidarity.

It was as if a choice were being offered. Lenny could either choose to stay in the darkness or cross the threshold and enter the light.

A stirring started, deep inside him. Oh, how he yearned to leave the shadows behind. But what would happen when Beau saw him? Would Beau turn his evil eyes on Lenny's disobedience? Would Lenny disappear into the pit of those eyes?

Lenny let the strength of the singing voices feed him. Was the cowardice he felt any worse than what Beau might do to him?

The ideas that took root in Lenny's heart could not find words. The pleading of his soul could not break into his conscious mind. Yet the essence was there, alive, struggling, fighting to survive. With the determination of a spirit longing to be free, a single word wound its way to Lenny's lips. And the Spirit that was within him, grabbed hold of that word and presented it to the Lord with His endorsement and prayers.

"Please..."

At that moment, Lenny felt a strength he'd never imagined possible flow through his body. It was as though he was filled with light, with music and glorious, wonderful light. Something...no, someone, surrounded him, held him, enfolded him. And the words, "Welcome home, child," rang in his mind, in his heart, in his soul.

"God..."

The word came out of Lenny in a whispered breath, and he knew it was true. God was there. With him. Accepting him.

Tears streamed down his face and he stepped out, leaving the darkness behind. He moved to the stage, singing with the rest of the believers. Rejoicing. Praising the God who loved him. He took a place next to his wife.

Kathy gasped and tensed. Lenny smiled and held out a hand, wordlessly asking forgiveness. When Kathy met his eyes, her own widened. She returned a tentative smile. Then they looked toward the audience and sang.

"'God bless America, my home sweet home.'"

✦✦✦

The accompanist stopped playing. The crowd erupted in cheers and applause. The lights came on. The spotlight dimmed.

Julia took a deep breath, pushing away the last of her daze. With each note of the song, her head had cleared until she felt renewed and strong. Julia gave Edward a hug and answered his questioning look with a kiss on his cheek. She took over the microphone, tapped it a few times, and found it working. She crossed both hands on her chest and inhaled, breathing in the rejuvenating air as if a special, rare element fueled the atmosphere in this moment.

"Do you feel it?" Her whispered words soared over the room. "Do you feel what it's like to have God bless America?"

Heads nodded in unison. Shouts. Whoops. Applause. The protesters remained silent. Maybe they had felt it too.

"That's all I want." Julia struggled against the tears that choked her voice. "That's all I've been talking about all these months. I don't want *my* agenda, or the agenda of any man. I want what this country needs, what this country hungers for with all its heart. 'Blessed is the nation whose God is the Lord, the people He chose for His inheritance.' I want us to *let* God bless America!"

Julia stepped from the podium, letting the crowd continue their celebration.

✦✦✦

Thad and Edward stood to the side, taking it all in. The pianist sat at the piano, her face beaming as she unashamedly played her favorites, "America the Beautiful", "The Battle

Hymn of the Republic," and "This is My Country." The audience lingered, singing and swaying with their hands around each other's shoulders like revelers at a pub.

Thad shook his head in amazement. "Only Julia could turn a disaster like that into a triumph."

"Julia — with God's help. That spotlight sure saved us," Edward said. "And the lights coming back on, lighting the audience at the end. How did you do it?"

"I didn't do anything." Thad looked at him. "When I finally found the light switches and flipped them, nothing happened. I didn't try again."

"The timing was perfect. But that spotlight. That was the clincher." Edward pointed to the ceiling where the beam had originated. He took a few steps forward to get a better view. "Thad? Where's the spotlight?"

They looked upward. The usual lighting fixtures dotted the ceiling. But there was no spotlight. None.

"Where'd it come from?" Thad stared. "And who turned it on and off?"

Edward started to laugh and walked away.

✦✦✦

Beau fled outside, propelled by the need to be away from *It*. He'd seen *It* work before and the experience continued to disgust him. He'd seen the Holy Spirit fill the hearts of the audience, he'd heard their voices change from protests to words of affirmation. He'd witnessed them forget the traitorous words he'd spoken in Julia's voice and remember only God's message of encouragement. He'd felt the hatred and anger drain from the humans' souls as if a seam had been opened, letting out what was useful to him and letting in what was useful to God.

But the seams could be opened again — in his favor. Beau deplored the thought of starting over. It was so much work. Each time It won, his job was a little harder. Each time the stitches holding God's Spirit within were a little stronger, placed a little closer together.

Beau paced in the parking lot, his eyes flitting from the ground to the entrance of the resort. Forget the audience. Forget the inane, weak, inadequate protesters who were overcome like slaughtered lambs. They were nothing to him. And Lenny? Lenny was an expendable fool. But the rest of them...

Beau saw them come outside. The Haven disciples stood on the wide porch and talked. *Laughed.* Julia was with them, her candidacy secondary to her friendship. Her entourage stood a short distance away, watching. Watchful. The group acted as if the paltry victory inside really meant something in the whole scheme of life.

But it wasn't over. Beau still held the trump card: Natalie. He felt his hatred grow. He inhaled the emotion as if it were life-giving air. It strengthened him and made him bold.

He would show the lot of them his power. They would see how insignificant their faith was against him. And they would make their choice. They would denounce their God — or die.

It would be so easy. Especially now while they basked in their pathetic victory. Their defenses were down. They thought the entire world was theirs. How easily pleased they were. How piddly were their conquests.

How large would be their losses.

✦✦✦

The Haven disciples moved through the parking lot toward Walter's and Roy's cars. Julia felt elated to be part of the group again. And they'd won! Good had conquered evil. It hadn't been as hard as she'd expected.

"Come to my house," Kathy said over her shoulder. "We'll celebrate."

"Maybe Natalie is at your house." Del sounded hopeful. "Maybe—"

A man stepped in front of them.

Julia stopped, catching her breath. "It's him! It's the man I told you about!"

317

"Beau!"

The man from the rally was the same man everyone was afraid of?

Thaddeus came running, security on his heels. Julia held out a hand, holding them away — at least for the moment.

Jack rushed at Beau. "Where is she? Where's Natalie?"

Beau held out an arm. Jack's progress was halted as if a force field had been summoned.

Del pulled him back. "Stay away, Jack."

"Listen to him, weakling." Beau sneered at them. "The fool speaks the truth."

Roy stepped forward. "What have you done with Natalie?"

"She is safely —" Beau stopped and addressed his enlarged audience. With an exaggerated air of concern he said, "Perhaps *safely* isn't the correct word. Let's just say she is exactly where I want her."

"If you've hurt her —"

Walter and Del had to hold Jack back a second time.

Beau looked pained. "Are you implying she needs to be rescued? From me? Her *friend?*"

"You are not her friend." Kathy stepped forward. "She's only with you under duress."

"Exactly."

Beau's smile made Julia's skin crawl. Who was this man?

"I feed on duress." He shivered, an expression of foul pleasure on his face. "I must say that Tally's fear has been quite a feast. Perhaps not as satisfying as Gloria's," Julia saw Beau direct a smile at Del, and saw Del stiffen, "but then again, I'm not done with her yet."

Del lunged at him. Walter and Roy restrained him. Julia realized Thaddeus was still there with the security staff and turned to them.

"Thaddeus, it's all right. You can go back to the hotel."

He stared at her doubtfully. "I'm not going anywhere. You need help."

"This is Haven business. We can handle it."

"Are you sure?"

318

Julia nodded. "Yes. I'm sure." This didn't need to be a national incident.

Beau held out his hands as if calming an unruly class. "Now, now, *dear* disciples. Get control of yourselves. Let's see if we can work something out."

"Like what?" Del's anger seemed on the verge of exploding.

Beau took a step toward him, visibly sizing him up. "Your participation, *priest*, might make all of this worthwhile."

Del didn't flinch. "All of what worthwhile?"

Beau walked toward his car and opened the door, then turned to face them. "The battle for your souls."

Shock jolted Julia. He couldn't be serious!

Beau got in his car and started the engine. He called out his window. "Follow me and let the games begin."

Julia glanced at the others. Clearly no one knew what to do.

"He wants us to go after him," Del said.

Walter hesitated. "I don't think that's a good idea."

Jack clenched his hands. "But he's got Natalie!"

"We can't just stand here." Roy looked at Kathy, and Julia saw fear and anger on her friend's face.

"He's evil," Kathy said. "What match are we against him?"

Julia stepped between them, her arms outstretched. "It's why we're here. It's the battle God has called us to fight."

"But I don't *want* to fight." Walter waved any such thought away.

"I don't think we have a choice."

Roy stared at her. "What if he has a weapon?"

"He doesn't need one."

At the voice behind them, Julia and the others spun around. Lenny stepped out of the shadows.

Kathy turned toward her husband, and Julia wondered when and how Lenny had come back from the dead. It was obvious he'd changed... there was something different about him compared to the bitter man she'd met in Haven.

Kathy took a step toward her husband. "Lenny, what do you mean he doesn't need a weapon?"

"He's a demon."

Again Julia felt as though she'd been punched. Hard. And yet she'd known it. The minute his eyes had met hers, something deep within her had told her he worked for the dark side, but she hadn't wanted to believe it.

Lenny went on. "Beau doesn't need manmade weapons to hurt her—or us."

Jack took Lenny's arm. "Do you know this for a fact?"

"I know." Lenny's voice was grim.

Julia bowed her head. "Dear Lord, please be with us. Protect us."

Jack moved beside her. "Protect Natalie."

The friends bowed their heads and added their own silent prayers. Kathy was the first to say, "Amen." She took Roy's hand and pulled him toward his car. "God is with us. Now it's time to go."

She was right. It was time.

THIRTY-THREE

*"The Lord gives strength to his people,
the Lord blesses his people with peace."*
PSALM 29:11

NATALIE LAY ON the ground at the bird sanctuary, and stared at a beetle crawling through the pebbles on the path.

I can't sink much lower than this.

She closed her eyes, hoping that when she opened them, she would be awakened from this awful dream.

It didn't work.

Beau's crazed gloating echoed in her mind ... *You are mine...you are mine...*

The words were like razors, slicing through her heart and spirit, annihilating all the positive words she'd heard in her life. It wasn't true...it couldn't be true...why was it so much easier to believe the negative?

Natalie rolled onto her back and looked to the ceiling of the sanctuary. The glass dome seemed to disappear as she focused on the sky beyond. Gray clouds tinged with pink extended across the blue like wisps of cotton candy pulled from its cone.

A bird flew by outside. Another flew above her, but inside. One free. One not. Both existing. The bird trapped inside thought its life was good enough—which it was, as long as it didn't experience the true freedom of soaring close to God in His world, not merely surviving in a false world created by man--a world full of walls and limitations.

I've experienced true freedom.

Natalie smiled. The thought was enough to let hope enter.

She found herself repeating the twenty-third psalm— which amazed her. She hadn't realized she knew it by heart. "'The Lord is my shepherd, I shall not want. He maketh me lie down in green pastures, He leadeth me beside the still waters, He restoreth my soul.'"

He restoreth my soul!

Natalie raised her hands, wanting heavenly comfort. "'He guideth me in paths of righteousness for His name's sake. Yea, though I walk through the valley of the shadow of death, I will fear no evil, for Thou art with me, Thy rod and Thy staff, they comfort me.'"

They comfort me!

"'Thou preparest a table before me in the presence of my enemies. Thou anointest my head with oil, my cup runneth over. Surely goodness and mercy will follow me all the days of my life, and I will dwell in the house of the Lord forever.'"

Forever!

Natalie sat up, bowed her head, and let the tears come. Everything was all right. She remembered God's earlier words of comfort: "I am with you always."

She was not alone. She had never been alone. She'd been overwhelmed by Beau, she'd let herself become confused, and the confusion had made her doubt, and the doubt had made her lose her focus on the only One who could save her — the One who had already saved her on the cross.

Jesus, forgive me…

Her prayer was heard, and forgiveness was granted.

Her slate was wiped clean.

✦✦✦

Natalie sat on a bench and watched the sunset. The colors of the sky, the sounds of the birds and the falls, the smell of the damp air and plants were vivid and very real. This was not a dream or the plot line of a novel. This was earth and air and water and flesh and blood.

There it was again. That phrase: *flesh and blood.*

She touched her chin where her flesh was cut. The blood was dried. Beau had hurt her. Left her alone. But he would be back.

She took a deep breath and was surprised at its strength. She wouldn't need to face him alone. The Lord was with her.

Though the day was ending, Natalie felt it was a new beginning. All that had happened in the past week — in her past life — had been erased. It was as though the edges of her life, blurred by her own mistakes, had been drawn again by God and reinforced until they were bold and distinct.

With a start, Natalie realized she could leave.

She could walk out of the bird sanctuary, hitch a ride into town, and make her way back to Lincoln — or even to Estes Park. She would never have to see Beau again. Although he had power — more, certainly, than she did — he did not have ultimate power. That belonged to her God.

As did she.

Natalie glanced down the path leading to the exit. Just a few steps and she would be free.

Stay.

She held her breath a moment, unsure. Then she turned around to find the source of the whisper. But she was alone with the birds, the trees, and the waterfall.

Stay.

Natalie put a hand to her heart … the whisper was coming from within.

Finish it.

She nodded. It was not a fluke or a mistake that she was in this place, facing this challenge. She felt with an intense certainty that she had been brought here, just for this.

And for the first time in a very long time, she was not afraid.

"There he is!" Kathy pointed to Beau's black sports car, which was pulled to the side of the road.

"How accommodating of him to wait for us," Roy said from the driver's seat.

"Yeah, what a guy." Lenny shook his head. These people had no idea what they were dealing with.

Beau's car pulled out in front of them, and Jack leaned forward, his face filled with anger. "I should have grabbed Natalie when I had the chance. I should have fought with him."

Lenny put a hand on his shoulder. "It wouldn't have done any good. Beau's got power you'd never be able to beat."

Kathy turned toward him and looked over the seat. "So how are we going to save her if he's unbeatable?"

"There might be ways..."

"Such as?"

Lenny looked out the window, avoiding their eyes. "I know more about Beau than I ever wanted to know. I've been traveling with him for two years. I've been helping him."

"You've been helping a demon?" Kathy flashed an incredulous look.

"He was all I had." Lenny knew how it sounded.

"But what about us? We were here, mourning you. You put your family through the pain of grief when you could have prevented it? You chose Beau over us?"

Lenny wrapped his arms around himself. "The truth is, well...I'm sorry, Kath."

"Truth?" She had an odd expression on her face.

"I didn't have a whole lot of options." He risked a glance. "In Haven, God gave me a choice and I rejected Him. Then I did what was expected of me."

"I don't buy that." Roy glanced back at him. "You had choices. There are always choices."

"Such as going after another man's wife?" The minute the words left him, Lenny felt ashamed. He might be new inside, but his mouth was still the same. A full change was going to take time.

Jack raised a hand. "Enough. We have another battle to fight." He looked at Lenny. "Tell us how to beat him."

Lenny thought for a moment, wondering where to start. "There *were* times during the last two years when Beau would suddenly stop what he was doing and say it was time to move on. I couldn't see a reason for it, but he was always set on it. We'd have to get out. Right then. I'd ask him why but he'd just say things weren't right."

"Maybe they were too right. Maybe people caught on to him."

"Maybe they prayed," Roy said. "The Bible says, 'Though one may be overpowered, two can defend themselves. A cord of three strands is not quickly broken.'"

"Which means?" Lenny asked.

"Which means we can beat him if we band together. If we all pray."

Lenny shrugged. He didn't like that this new man in Kathy's life was right, but... "Beau couldn't tolerate praying. As soon as somebody started, he'd fidget around like he was being poked by knives or something. He'd carry on something awful. Sometimes, he'd try to drown the people out, screaming, having a fit, trying to get people to shut up."

Jack shifted in his seat. "So we need to win a spiritual war? A war of words?"

Lenny saw — and understood — his nervousness. "Could be."

Kathy grabbed onto the dashboard as Roy took a curve too fast. "I'm glad we have Del and Julia on our side. They'll be the ones with the words."

Roy looked at Lenny in the rearview mirror. "Maybe we all have the words."

Now Lenny was *really* confused. "That's news to me."

Kathy pointed. "Beau's turning! Turn right. Right!"

They turned onto a narrow gravel drive. Rocks spit from under the tires.

"Kathy, where's this go?" Roy leaned forward and peered through the windshield.

"I don't remember." Kathy pointed to a sign. "Oh, wait, it's the bird sanctuary. I haven't been up here in years."

Jack frowned. "What would Beau be doing at a bird sanctuary?"

Lenny knew his answer was incomplete, but it was full of truth. "Nothing good."

◆◆◆

There was a hush as the two cars shut off their engines. The dust from the gravel settled. When the headlights were

325

extinguished, the dark melded with the silence like a smothering shroud. The blackness of a large building loomed in front of them. Walter heard birds. He hated birds.

"What now?" When there was no answer, he turned to Del. The priest had his eyes closed. His lips moved in silent prayer. Oh, boy. This was going to be bad. He knew it. "Lord, help us."

Del opened one eye and smiled. "A condensed version, but it will do."

Edward squinted at the dark. "What's Beau doing?"

Walter peered into the darkness, but before he could answer, Julia said, "He's just standing there by his car."

Crossing his arms with a huff, Walter leaned back in the seat. "Well, this is fun. A standoff at the bird sanctuary. Sounds like a Perry Mason novel."

"Fortunately, we know who did it," Edward said. "It's just a matter of convincing the judge and jury."

"Think God will accept a jury of eight?" This was ridiculous. Walter couldn't believe he was here. Suddenly, Del opened his door. Walter reached over and pulled it shut. "What are you doing?"

"I'm going to save Natalie."

"What happened to our plan?"

"Since when do we have a plan?"

"That's what I thought you were doing when you were...you know."

"Praying?"

"Yeah."

"I'm afraid God kept His game plan to Himself."

Great. Just what Walter wanted to hear. "That's not good."

Del put his hand on the door handle. "Plan or no plan, somebody has to move. We have to do something."

"Such as?"

"I'm going to go up to Beau and ask him to give Natalie back."

"And when he spits in your face?"

"Or worse?" Julia's voice had a hitch in it.

"We can't just sit—"

Walter cut Del off. "Look!" He pointed to Beau who strode to the front door of the building and called back to them. "You coming or not?"

Not. Walter wondered if anyone else voted for staying in the car. Or sending a representative. Del would be good. Or Julia.

Car doors opened, and Walter's wishes evaporated. *I don't like this, God.*

Beau went inside. Walter huddled with the others for a conference.

Kathy hugged herself in spite of the heat. "We should have called the police."

"What good would that do? He's a demon." Del eyed the building. "Besides, God gathered us here. He wants us to win the battle with His help, not man's."

Walter snorted. "And we do that *how?*"

Del fixed him with a firm look. "We keep in mind who is God and who's not. Remember, Satan is not the opposite of God. He is merely a fallen angel. Only God is God."

"Oh, that's profound."

Julia stepped forward. "Actually, it is. It's all we need." She pulled a tiny New Testament from her pocket. "Before the rally this evening, Edward found some verses about spiritual warfare."

"Warfare?" Kathy took Roy's arm. "I just want to get Natalie back, I don't want to go to war with Beau."

Walter shook his head. "Me neither."

"But that's why we're here." Jack looked certain, then unsure. "Isn't it?"

Lenny waved his arms. "Hey, I'm not one of you guys, I'm just along for the ride."

"Are you?" Kathy put a hand to her lips as if she hadn't meant to say the words. "I mean…I thought you'd changed. Tonight, at the rally, you did seem different."

Lenny scuffed a foot on the ground and shoved his hands in his pockets. He shrugged. "I guess I am. At the rally I…I made a choice. I don't want to be with Beau anymore."

"That's a good start."

He nodded and laughed nervously. "I know it's a long time coming. It only took Beau tossing me across the room a few thousand times for me to wake up." He rubbed the back of his head as though it was sore. "I could've used a combat helmet dealing with him."

Julia held up a finger. "Helmet... that's in here too." She paged through the Bible until she found the page she wanted. She held the book toward the fading twilight. "'Take the helmet of salvation and the sword of the Spirit, which—'"

"Sword of the Spirit! That's the phrase that's been following me around lately." Del rushed beside her to see. "May I?" Julia gave him the book. He took a moment to read the verses. "These are the armor of God verses."

"Exactly," Edward said. "Read the whole passage, Del."

He nodded and began. "'Be strong in the Lord and in His mighty power. Put on the full armor of God so that you can take your stand against the devil's schemes. For our struggle is not against flesh and blood, but against the rulers, against the authorities, against the powers of this dark world and against the spiritual forces of evil in the heavenly realms. Therefore put on the full armor of God, so that when the day of evil comes, you may be able to stand your ground, and after you have done everything, to stand.'"

"That's my verse," Julia said. "It spurred me to talk about taking a stand."

"'Stand firm then, with the belt of truth buckled around your waist, with the breastplate of righteousness in place—'"

Kathy raised a hand. "The belt of truth! That's mine. Over and over I've heard that! It was Ryan's memory verse. He even put on a belt and played the part. Lately, people have been trying to get me to see the truth all over the place. With my paintings, my feelings for Lenny, my family, my—" She turned to Roy, her hand on her mouth. "And the breastplate of righteousness... that's yours, Roy."

Roy nodded and took her hand. "The word *righteous* was in the verse I was given in Haven. And since then, it seems to be *the* word in my life. The focus."

Walter was getting excited. This was cool. "Read on, Del. Read on."

"Let's see...'breastplate of righteousness in place... and with your feet fitted with the readiness that comes from the gospel of peace—'"

"That's my verse," Edward said. "I've come to think my job is to be ready and calm and bring peace to situations. Especially with Julia in the limelight like she is."

Julia slipped an arm in his. "He keeps me sane."

Walter was getting impatient. This was all wonderful, but what about him? He wanted to hear the words that had repeated themselves in *his* life. He wanted the confirmation that he was a part of this too. *Come on, Del, read about the shield... please.*

Del cleared his throat. "'In addition to all this, take up the shield of faith, with which you can extinguish all the flaming arrows of the evil one.'"

"Ha!" Walter clapped his hands. "That's my verse! Bette quoted that before we moved, and my dad quoted it before he died. Shield... faith..." His voice trailed off as his throat tightened with his memories of Pop. "Lately, my faith has been tested and I've had to shield it in nearly every area of my life."

Del put an arm around his shoulders. "And your faith has prevailed."

Walter nodded, unable to say any more. Del reopened the Bible to continue. "Now we come to Lenny's portion. And mine. 'Take the helmet of salvation and the sword of the Spirit, which is the word of God.' Then it says, 'And pray in the Spirit on all occasions with all kinds of prayers and requests. With this in mind, be alert and always keep on praying for all the saints.'" Del lowered the Bible.

Jack took a tentative step forward and lifted a hand. "I claim that part about praying. My mom used to tell me to pray in the Spirit and I've always felt compelled to pray for other people."

Del raised his right hand like he was taking an oath. "I can vouch for that. Jack has a heart for prayer."

They looked at each other, their expressions full of awe and understanding. Walter wondered if they all felt like he did, like they were eight parts of a whole. He felt stronger than he ever had in his life. To think that God had been speaking to him—and he had heard. He wished Bette were here. She would be so proud of him.

But with the knowledge came responsibility. It was time to do something. But what? Although Walter knew it was uncharacteristic of him to be the instigator, he felt the urge to get things going. He cleared his throat and tried to sound like he knew what he was doing. "We need to get back to the problem at hand, people. Natalie is in there with a demon. We've been given the guidelines to beat him. Now we need to apply them."

Del put a hand on Walter's back. "Now I've heard everything. Did God's Word actually make Walter Prescott brave?"

"Hey, don't knock it, I'm on a roll."

Del smiled. "Your *faith* is on roll. Go to it, friend." He turned to the others. "Walter is right. It's time."

There was a moment of silence. Then Julia stepped forward. "I am to stand my ground against his evil."

Kathy nodded. "I am to use truth against him." She looked at Roy.

"And me? Righteousness."

Edward moved next to his wife. "I am to be ready and keep the peace."

Walter took his turn. "I am to shield us with faith."

Lenny looked to Kathy. "What am I supposed to do with a helmet of salvation? This is all new to me..."

Kathy went to his side. "You've said no to evil, next you have to say yes to God. To Jesus."

"How do I do that?"

She touched his hand. "When we get out of here, we'll sit down and have a long talk. Okay?"

Lenny blushed. "Okay."

Del brandished an arm with an imaginary sword. "Hooray for Lenny! And I yield the sword of the Spirit, which is the Word of the Lord!"

They all laughed, but their nerves were evident. Del waved his arm to the last in their group. Without a word, Jack got down on his knees and bowed his head.

The rest of them did the same. And Walter knew with his entire being, that their prayers were heard.

They were finally ready.

+++

As they entered the lobby, Julia felt shivers travel up and down her spine. She had the impression that they were on the edge of a life-changing moment, but there was no certainty whether the moment would turn out good or bad. *Help us, Lord.* Her prayer drove the fear back and replaced it with the knowledge that God had prepared them well.

Roy shrugged. "'Onward Christian soldiers...'"

"Great," Walter said. "'Marching as to war?'"

With a cleansing breath, Julia opened the door leading into the actual sanctuary, and they all followed her inside. The chatter of the birds added to her unease — their squawks a bizarre counterpoint to the white noise of the waterfall. The damp air made it hard to breathe. Floodlights lit designated areas, but shadows reigned. The final, red glow of sunset shone through the glass roof, and Julia swallowed. Darkness would soon engulf the world. *Let your light shine, Lord. Don't let the darkness overcome us.*

Edward moved beside her and spoke softly. "The building was unlocked. Why didn't Natalie leave?"

Jack heard him. "If Beau has her tied up — " He scanned the pathways.

Walter followed Jack's gaze, then shook his head. "Where are they?"

"One way to find out." It was time for her to take a stand. Julia cupped her hands. "Natalie? Beau? Come out, come out, wherever you are." She moved to a clearing next to a pond. "Come on, Mr. Demon. We're tired of playing games. Give us Natalie, and you can go terrorize someone else."

331

"I'll give you this much, you are one gutsy lady."

Julia started, and looked up. Beau was at the top of the falls, twenty feet above them on the far side of the pond. Flashing a mocking smile in their direction, he dragged Natalie into view. She didn't seem to be bound—not with the way she fought against his grip.

"I'm fine!" Natalie's voice was surprisingly strong. "Don't let him—"

Beau slammed the back of his hand against her mouth. Julia let out a cry as Natalie fell backwards.

"That rotten—"

Julia held up her hand, stopping Walter's outburst. "Wait, look. Natalie's moving." She'd felt sure the blow would knock Natalie out. But Natalie had pushed herself up on her elbow and was shaking her head as though to clear it.

"Natalie!" Jack called, and Julia's heart broke at the anguish in his voice.

Beau laughed. "Go ahead and call her, you wimp. She's *mine* now. By her choice."

"That's a lie!" Kathy pointed at Beau. "The truth is, you hit her. *You* chose."

"Ooh, did the little woman take her courage pill today? Are you sure you didn't get it mixed up with your *stupid* pill?"

Julia bit her lip. Things were already getting out of hand. Emotions were taking over. They had to focus,

Julia turned to Jack and whispered, "Do your part, Jack. Pray." He nodded and got to his knees.

Without instruction, Walter stepped in front of him, shielding Jack from Beau's view. *Good Walter, good.*

She saw Del move toward the edge of the pond, drawing Beau's eyes. "Why did you bring Natalie here?" he asked. "Why choose this place for your battle?"

"Ah, Father Delatondo to the rescue. Always a day late and a dollar short, right, Father? With Mellie? With Gloria? You have dreadful timing, *priest.* You need a new watch—or a new profession."

Julia saw Del take a deep breath, as if he was fighting

back anger. *That's it, Del. Don't be reckless. We have to keep our heads. God's in control here, not Beau.*

Del raised his chin. "You made Gloria kill herself, didn't you?"

"It was my pleasure." Beau reached down, yanked Natalie to standing, and held her in an embrace. "But not before I'd partaken of a bit of her earthly glory." Beau kissed Natalie roughly, and Julia wanted to applaud when Natalie jerked away and spit in his face. Beau's hand drew back, and Julia tensed, expecting another brutal slap, but suddenly Beau jerked his head, looking down at them.

"You!" Beau hissed the word. "Get back where I can see you!"

Julia saw Roy inching away from the group. She gave him a warning glance, and he returned to his place beside Kathy. *Lord, keep us calm. We don't need any Lone Rangers here...be righteous, Roy, not reckless.*

Beau surveyed the garden below him, as though taking note of everyone's location. "Six against two. Such uneven odds. Should I be scared?"

Edward took Julia's hand. "Perhaps you should be. There is power in loyalty and love. You should try it sometime."

"Love is a joke, and loyalty is not my problem. I am extremely loyal—to *my* lord."

"Satan," Roy said.

"Of course, doctor. You would know him. He reveled in the death of each baby you killed."

"Leave him alone," Walter said.

Beau turned his attention to Walter, and Julia saw him flinch.

"Ah, the old man speaks."

Walter straightened abruptly. "I am not an old man. Don't call me that."

"You're much too old to have a baby daughter. Do you think Addy's going to be proud of her middle-aged dad? You'll be an embarrassment to her. She'll turn to her friends for comfort, and if I have my way, I'll make sure her friends are *my* friends."

333

"Shut up! Stop talking about my daughter. You can't hurt me with words. You can't hurt any of us. Our faith is strong."

Beau flipped a hand, dismissing him. "I can hurt you any way I want. I can reach Bette. Addy—even Pop. The cigars finally did him in, eh, Walter?"

This was getting them nowhere. What had Beau said...? *"Six against two..."* Yet there had been eight. Who was missing?

Julia tried to look casual as she made a head count. Six, plus Jack, who was on his knees praying, with Walter blocking Beau's view of him. But surely Beau could still see him. Unless—Julia saw Jack's lips moved in fervent prayer—*unless...* Had Jack's prayers made him invisible to Beau's sight?

Thank you, Lord!

But even so, that made seven, and there had been eight. Julia caught her breath. *Lenny.*

Please, Father, please... A wild hope surged and she looked back toward Beau. *Let Lenny be doing what I think he's doing.* Maybe if she kept Beau occupied..."Give us the girl, Beau."

Beau stared at her, and she felt cold slice through her when their eyes met. "You think just because you're running for president you have clout with me? I am not one of your impressionable zombies who listens with a vacant mind, soaking up your tripe about God and hope."

Julia forced a small smile. "Too bad. It might do you some good."

That hit home. She saw anger contort his features. "Come work with the winning side, Julia."

"I already am."

He cackled. "I didn't say *whining* side. I said winning side."

Roy gripped the back of a bench. "If you're winning, why did you have to kidnap a girl? That's an act of desperation."

"Don't talk to me about desperation, doctor. You lived off desperation. Girls came to you, desperate for help and what did you give them? You ripped the life from them. *You* take a life, doctor, *I* take a life...we're in the same business. Being an

abortionist is bad enough, but being a *righteous* abortionist..."
Beau shook his head. "My side is winning because of people
like you. You've been playing for our side your entire life,
you just won't admit it."

"You liar!" Roy ran to the edge of the pond, but Kathy
followed him, putting a restraining hand on his arm.

Del turned to his friends. "Listen to me! Roy is right. The
demon is a liar. Satan gets his power from lies. He wants
your fear. And fear breeds on half-truths and distortions."

"My, my." Beau adjusted the squirming Natalie under his
arm. "The good father thinks he's got me all figured out. I
don't tell lies, priest. I reveal the truth in all its naked glory."

"That's a lie."

"Is it? All of you have secret sins, sins you keep hidden
even from your God."

"God forgives our sins when we confess them," Edward
said.

Beau raised his arms in the air. "Forgives? Ah yes, the
great fallacy of Christianity: no matter what you do, God will
forgive you."

"He will." Kathy's voice was firm, assured, and she
slipped under Roy's arm.

Beau shook his head, and Julia frowned. Was he getting
nervous? It seemed that when they spoke truth about God,
Beau grew more agitated.

"You stupid creatures! Your god wants you to *think* He
forgives. That's how He keeps you under His control, by
teasing you with thoughts of forgiveness and eternal life. But
there still comes a time, doesn't there, when the game is over.
When the clock — runs — *out.*"

At the carefully emphasized words, Julia's heart caught in
her throat. She took a step toward the falls, but she couldn't
stop her greatest fear from happening before her eyes. With a
terrible, roaring laugh, Beau grabbed Natalie's arms and
shoved her toward the edge of the cliff. The girl screamed —
sending birds fluttering and screeching everywhere — and she
clutched at Beau, holding onto him for life.

"Natalie!" Julia could hardly breathe. *God, please, Father!*

She glanced at Jack, who was praying feverishly, his eyes locked on Natalie.

"Stay where you are unless you want Tally to do a swan dive."

Julia froze, as did those around her. She raised a calming hand. "Hold on, Beau. Let Natalie choose who she wants to be with. Certainly, if you're so sure of your appeal, you have enough confidence to let *her* make the choice?"

Beau raised a finger. "A very good idea, Madame President. Let's do just that." He pulled Natalie back, and she teetered beside him. "Tell them, Tally. Tell them you've chosen me."

✦✦✦

Natalie stared at Beau. Evil disguised as beauty. The deceiver hiding behind a mask.

She hated him. Despised him for using her, and reproached herself for ever enjoying his touch, longing for his attention.

"Tally!" Beau gave her an abrupt shake. "*Tell* them."

She opened her mouth, when a commotion drew her attention. Natalie looked over the edge toward the pond, and her heart jumped. Her friends had been joined by others. Hugs were being exchanged. Backs were slapped in celebration.

The guardian angels had arrived.

"Fran!"

At her joyful exclamation, Beau looked down, and his features convulsed. With a foul curse he dragged Natalie farther up the trail.

✦✦✦

Lenny watched the action from the safety of his hiding place. The group had doubled, each person hugging a newcomer. Where had they come from? He could see the door to the sanctuary and he hadn't noticed anyone come in. One minute Natalie was on the edge, the next, the clearing was full of people.

Lenny looked after Beau. Where had he taken the girl? He risked standing to get a better look. He heard a ruckus to his right and turned...

Beau was dragging Natalie up the trail toward a higher point above the falls. Blast! Lenny had been this close to jumping out and saving her, and now... He spread the branches of the bushes, intending to move to a new hiding place. He stopped himself. He sat back down.

You aren't responsible for Natalie. You don't have to be the one to save her. You've just been saved yourself. Let one of her precious friends take the risk. Sit back. Stay out of the way and you can leave in one piece and start over, grab yourself a second chance.

"She *is* your responsibility."

Lenny jerked at the voice, bumping his head on a branch. He saw a man with curly black hair and a five-o'clock shadow stooped at the entrance of his hiding spot. The man held out a stick of Juicy Fruit.

"Want a piece of gum?"

Lenny's heart clenched, but he reached out and took it warily. He did not unwrap it. The man slid to a seated position. "Natalie *is* your responsibility, Lenny."

"How do you know my—"

The man shook his head. "The name's Christopher. I've been wanting to meet you for the longest time. Until recently you've been inaccessible. But let me assure you, I've kept tabs. Actually, I've been aching to be of service, but there are rules about such things."

Lenny stared at him. What was this guy talking about? "I don't get it."

Christopher ran a hand across his mouth. "Obviously, my communication skills are lacking. I'm a little out of practice. Rusty, as it were." He took a deep breath. "I'm your mentor, Lenny, your guardian angel, just like the others down there." He waved toward the clearing by the pond.

Lenny wasn't sure what was harder to believe—that *he*

had an angel sitting beside him or that the assortment of people below were angels too. He opened his mouth, but words did not follow.

Christopher held up a hand. "I know it's hard to accept, especially since you've been traveling in other circles." He cocked his head upward, indicating Beau. "But God has seen the changes in you, Lenny. He's heard your prayers."

"I haven't prayed."

"Ah, but you have. And not just with the one *please* and *God* you spoke earlier — as eloquent as those prayers were. God has heard your every thought, He knows the longings of your heart. 'All my longings lie open before you, O Lord, my sighing is not hidden from you.' Even if you had never put it into words, He knows. He takes the time to know. Think of Him as a great teacher who does everything in His power to make sure you learn, understand, and get an "*A*". He wants you to succeed."

Lenny felt a lump in his throat the size of Arkansas. When he spoke, his voice was hoarse. "Then why have I failed?"

"Because you've chosen to fail."

His mouth fell open. "I have not."

"Now, now." Christopher rearranged his position against the uneven ground. "Back in Haven — and before that, when you were unfaithful to Kathy — you made choices that screamed failure."

Lenny almost gave a cocky excuse, blamed his actions on Kathy, his job, and his dad. But something stopped him. The words stuck in his throat. "I blew it."

"You see? *That's* the proof you've changed. A month ago you would never have admitted such a thing."

A strange lightness filled Lenny's heart. "You're right."

"Absolutely. That's why I'm finally able to be a part of your life. You've opened the door to God by opening your heart. 'You will understand what is right and just and fair — every good path. For wisdom will enter your heart, and knowledge will be pleasant to your soul.'"

"I did that?"

Christopher nodded. "Take the helmet of salvation. Save yourself—and the girl."

"Save Natalie?"

"When you first came into the sanctuary, you set yourself apart from the others. You took it upon yourself to find a way to save her. Why?"

Lenny shrugged. "My motives aren't what you think. At first I kept to the side because I didn't want to be a part of it."

"Your honesty is admirable."

"But when I realized Beau didn't know I was here...I started thinking I might be able to do something to help."

"You moved from selfishness to selflessness."

"I did?"

Christopher put a hand on Lenny's shoulder. "Allow yourself to be good, Lenny. You've chosen the evil path for so long, it's time you realize there are positive choices available. 'There is a time for everything, and a season for every activity under heaven.'"

"But I've done a lot of bad stuff." Lenny shook his head with the weight of it. "Certainly God can't forget all that." He looked up. "Can He?"

"He sent his Son, Jesus, to do just that. God said, 'I will put my law in their minds and write it on their hearts. I will be their God and they will be my people. For I will forgive their wickedness and will remember their sins no more.'"

Lenny couldn't believe what he was hearing. Of course he'd heard the stories about Jesus and God when he was a kid, but he'd never thought that much about it. Until the rally... in the closet. And now. "Wow."

Christopher laughed. "Yeah. Wow." He glanced at the path leading to Natalie. "Our time is up. The battle is about to begin."

"Battle?"

"Beau must be conquered."

Lenny swallowed. "Am I the one who's supposed to do *that?*"

Christopher got to his feet. "That's up to you, Lenny. You and Christ Jesus. Be assured, I will be with you. God will be with you because He loves you." He walked away.

Lenny bowed his head. And for the first time in his memory, he made a conscious decision to pray.

✦✦✦

Natalie screamed, and Del's heart jumped.

All eyes turned toward a higher ledge above the falls. Beau held Natalie fast, an arm around her waist. He stood triumphant, like a hunter and his trophy.

"Hail, Satan! Satan is victorious!"

Del stepped forward. "Bring her down—"

Julia put a hand on his arm. "Wait, Del. Not that. I think I was wrong in calling him out. I don't think that's what we're supposed to do."

Del looked puzzled. "But we read the verses...the armor of God..."

Julia was fingering her Bible. "But I think there's more. What is the *power* of God? What name has power over every other name? There's a verse..."

Del closed his eyes, ashamed that he'd had to be reminded. "In Philippians..."

Julia nodded and flipped the pages. She found it. "'Therefore God exalted Him to the highest place and gave Him the name that is above every name, that at the name of Jesus every knee should bow, in heaven and on earth and under the earth, and every tongue confess that Jesus Christ is Lord, to the glory of God the Father.'"

Beau yelled from his perch. "Stop that! Shut up!"

Del and Julia smiled at each other. As if with a common thought, they extended their arms and drew the others together. They joined hands and linked themselves and their mentors in a circle of prayer.

They bowed their heads in the presence of the Almighty and Del opened his heart to God's guidance. He felt their prayers rise like a spectrum of energy toward heaven, intertwining with like thoughts and hopes, growing stronger as the filaments of their pleas wove themselves into a potent rope of supplication and praise.

"*Jesus! Jesus!*" There was such power in His name!

Beau began to yell, and Del knew he was trying to drown them out, trying to divert their thoughts away from their pursuit of the Lord. Del struggled to concentrate.

Then another voice was heard, a wail that cut through the sanctuary, its pitch plummeting from high to low.

Del spun, looked up... and saw a form fall from the precipice.

THIRTY-FOUR

*"Do not worry about how you will defend yourselves
or what you will say, for the Holy Spirit will teach you
at that time what you should say."*
LUKE 12: 11-12

THE WATER FROM the pond splashed onto the disciples and
their mentors.

"Lenny!" Kathy ran into the pond, stumbling on the
muddy bottom. Roy ran after her, his extra height allowing
him to bridge the gap faster. The other men followed.

Lenny lay face-down in the water. Roy turned him over,
laying his head in Kathy's arms. Lenny coughed and
sputtered.

Beau's triumphant voice came to them from above.
"Serves you right, you traitor! How *dare* you try to save Tally!
She's mine! She doesn't need saving by the likes of—"

Walter extended an arm. "Quiet, demon!"

Beau withdrew to the shadows.

Kathy watched the pain contort Lenny's face. Sorrow
swept over her in waves. "Roy, *do* something!"

Roy's expert hands flew over Lenny's body, assessing his
injuries. A sudden stream of blood spilled from Lenny's
mouth.

"Roy!"

He shook his head. "He's got internal injuries, Kath. We
should get him to a hospital." His eyes met hers. "But I'm not
sure there's time."

Lenny opened his eyes. "Time. A time for everything..."
He winced with pain, then seemed to focus on someone else,
standing above him. Kathy looked up and saw a man she'd
never seen before. An immediately she knew it was an angel.

The angel took Lenny's hand and spoke, his voice
resonating, "There is 'a season for every activity under
heaven. A time to be born and a time to die, a time to search
and a time to give up, a time to tear and a time to mend, a

time to be silent and a time to speak, a time to love and a time to hate, a time for war and a time for peace.'"

Lenny managed a smile. "Christopher..."

Kathy stifled a sob. This wasn't happening. It couldn't be happening. But when Kathy looked into Lenny's eyes, she didn't see panic, but peace.

"It's my time?" he asked the angel.

Christopher nodded.

Kathy grabbed Lenny's hand. "No!"

Christopher knelt beside her in the water, and she felt him place a comforting hand on her shoulder. "He has been very brave, this child of God, Lenny Kraus. And God has heard his prayers."

"Prayers?" Kathy didn't understand.

Lenny's eyes glazed with pain as he looked at his wife. "I believe, Kath. I believe. What we were going to talk about? Jesus is my Savior too."

"He has confessed his sins to the Lord. He has acknowledged the Son. And the Lord has saved him."

"Saved him?" Kathy struggled to take it all in. Lenny had found Christ? He'd found life? But... "He's dying!"

Lenny coughed and flinched with a spasm of pain. He gripped Kathy's arms and pulled her face close. She reached to touch the face she'd once loved so dearly.

"I'm so sorry, Kath. I didn't know how to...but now I'm free. I'm finally free."

His eyes closed. His head fell gently to the side.

Kathy looked up at Roy, and he nodded. "He's gone. I'm sorry, Kath."

She was unable to speak, torn between grief and an emotion she couldn't even name. Lenny was free. Life had been painful for him in so many ways, but now, at last, her husband was free. And he belonged to God.

Bowing her head, Kathy gave in to her emotions and wept for all that could have been... and all that would be, one day, in eternity when she'd see him again.

Christopher raised his hands to heaven, lifting his face to its glory. As Kathy watched, his contours began to glow, and the hues of his clothes were washed with a brilliant light. He extended a hand to Lenny.

Kathy looked down at the body that had contained her husband. She glanced back to Christopher and started when he smiled as though his hand *had* been taken. Then he rose from the water and disappeared like fog giving in to the sun.

Suddenly, a white dove skimmed the pond and flew upwards, and Kathy knew — she *knew* — that the angel had taken the precious soul of Lenny to their Maker.

✦✦✦

They carried Lenny's body from the water. Anne came toward Kathy, took her hands, and looked into her eyes. "'Lift your eyes and look to the heavens: Who created all these? He who brings out the starry host one by one, and calls them each by name. Because of His great power and mighty strength, not one of them is missing. The Lord is the everlasting God, the Creator of the ends of the earth. He will not grow tired or weary, and His understanding no one can fathom. Those who hope in the Lord will renew their strength. They will soar on wings like eagles, they will run and not grow weary, they will walk and not be faint.'"

Kathy nodded and attempted a wistful smile. "Amen."

✦✦✦

Beau's voice bellowed from above. "Now, wasn't that sweet? You can have him. He was never any good to me, anyway. I have the lot of you. All nicely brought together for my convenience. Thanks, of course, to Tally." He yanked her close, and she stumbled into him. She felt her body giving out. His abuse was taking its toll, the constant pushes, slaps, and jabs were making it hard for her to think. She squeezed her eyes shut, trying to focus. God...she needed to focus on God.

She saw Del look up at them and for a moment wondered

what he was doing in Estes Park. She glanced around her. What trail was this? She didn't remember hiking here before.

She heard Del's voice. "Listen to me, demon! This is not a war of the flesh. This is a war of the spirit."

With a flash, Del's words zeroed in on Natalie's weary brain. Suddenly the verses from the diner sparked in her mind and she blinked at the memory. *'For our struggle is not against flesh and blood but against the spiritual forces of evil in the heavenly realms.'* She looked at Beau, saw that he was yelling at someone below, but suddenly couldn't hear the words. All she heard was the reading of Beau's card from the old woman. And as she heard the words, she spoke them aloud and with a strength she didn't know she had. "'Away from me, Satan! For it is written: 'Worship the Lord your God, and serve him only.'"

Beau spun to look at her in fury. And fear. *"No!"*

"That's it, Natalie!" Del yelled. "Order him away from you. In Jesus' name!"

Beau's eyes were ablaze with shock and alarm. She felt her heart begin to pound as a surge of adrenaline fed her body. In the moment it took to take a few breaths, her mind cleared and she knew that this was the answer she'd been waiting for.

Her strength returned and with a burst of energy she pushed away, brimming with this new power. *Thank you, Lord. Thank you!* She pointed at Beau and he tried to grab her hand, but she pulled it away, her reflexes restored.

"No." Her voice began small, but quickly gained strength. "No, no, no!" She reveled in the torrent of God's power that filled her. "Get away from me, demon! By the power of my Lord Jesus' name, get away!"

Beau's eyes widened, and he sucked in a breath. Then he turned from her and ran off the edge of the cliff. But rather than falling, he floated in the air, lowering himself to the ground. As he did so, he transformed before their eyes. Gone was the handsome man. Instead, coming to rest on air a foot above the pond, was a hideous, contorted creature. Scales covered his body and his features were black and void. He was a living gargoyle, its grotesque mouth curled in a sneer.

Natalie took this all in in but a moment. With God's help, she'd forced Beau away, but now he was confronting her friends! She ran down the trail, praying she wouldn't be too late.

✦✦✦

Del could hardly breathe. His heart pounded in his throat at the sight of the demon's horrid form. *He's trying to scare me...and he's succeeding.* He swallowed to moisten his bone-dry throat. "God did not create you this way, demon. You were an angel of heaven. Pure and glorious. This, " Del motioned toward Beau's appearance, "this caricature, is for our benefit, meant to scare us." Del forced himself to look away from the creature's eyes. "I won't be afraid of you."

The voice that spoke bore no resemblance to a human voice. It rasped and grated, as pervasive as the foul stench that surrounded him. "An empty boast, priest. You *are* afraid. I am what you've made me. And now we see eye to eye."

The friends and mentors all turned when Natalie joined them, and Del cringed at the sight of her injuries. Yet, though her body was bruised and bloodied, her eyes were sharp and blazing. She pointed at Beau. "Order him out! He is nothing! The name of Jesus holds all power over him!"

Understanding stuck Del. With Natalie's presence their armor was finally complete. But before he could say so, the creature's black eyes widened. He extended his arms, and with a sweeping motion waved them over the pond. The water surged and rushed at the shore as if a hurricane lifted and drove it. Del and the others raised their arms, ready to fend off the gale. But the water never reached them. It was turned back as though a wall protected them. They lowered their arms, staring at each other, unbelieving.

The backsplash drenched Beau. *"Damnation!* That's not fair!"

Del quickly got his bearings. "You? Speak of fair? You have just witnessed the power of our Lord! He hears our

346

prayers. He protects our souls!"

"I'll *show* you what I think of your souls!" The creature waved an arm toward the trees. Three huge ravens burst out of the branches and descended on Lenny's body, screaming in their quest to devour their prey. They landed on his remains, pecking at his skin. Fresh meat.

Revulsion filled Del, and he recoiled. He glanced at the others, and saw that they too were reacting to this assault, moving toward the horrific display, wanting to stop what was happening.

"No." He whispered it at first, then spoke more loudly. "No!"

As though to reinforce what he was saying, the mentors raised their voices. "Gloria, in excelsis deo! Gloria in excelsis deo..."

Del breathed a sigh of relief when first Jack, then Julia, then the others stopped, averted their eyes from the pond, and returned to their first line of defense: prayer.

Turning his attention back to his adversary, Del shrugged. "Devour the body as you will, creature. Our brother is not there. His body was temporary. Now he lives in the house of the Lord."

A flock of sparrows swooped down from the trees-- dozens of sparrows, joined in one mission. They dive-bombed the ravens, and Del found himself smiling as the ravens fled with a raucous cry.. The many against the mighty. "See how the sparrow, small and ineffectual alone, bands together to conquer the enemy? So you will be conquered."

"I will never be conquered!"

It was time to end it. The power of God's words surged through his soul. "Be gone, you demon. I *order* you away in the name of Jesus Christ, my Savior! Be gone from this place and leave us alone!"

"No-o-o-o-o-o!" Beau's flailing arms tried to fend off Del's words.

"Jesus commands it!"

Suddenly, the pond parted and a blackened hole in the

earth opened up. With a huge whooshing sound, Beau was sucked downward, his arms and legs drawn forward, folded in on himself, as he was drawn into the tightness of the cavity. His screams of agony echoed until they were extinguished when the ground closed in upon him. The water fell back into place, covering the hole to hell that had consumed him.

A sudden silence filled the sanctuary as if the Lord had stilled the moment with a wave of his hand. Del held his breath in awe and reverence.

Jack was the first to move. "Natalie!" He threw his arms around her. The friends broke out of their prayer chain and hugged each other.

"He disappeared!"

"We did it!"

"Glory to our Lord, *Jesus* did it!"

Kathy ran to Lenny's body. She fell to his side, her hands touching, probing. When she looked up, she was shaking her head in disbelief. "They're gone! The wounds are gone! It's as if the birds never touched him." Roy joined her.

Jack put a gentle hand on Natalie's bruised face. "Are you all right?"

The girl nodded, the tears of tension finding release. Fran had a special hug for her. "Praise the Lord. You are truly free."

Julia raised her hands. "We are all free. Praise the Lord!"

As the friends fell to their knees in thanksgiving, the sanctuary filled with a luminous light. The disciples raised their faces toward its brilliance and saw their mentors transformed into their angelic glory. Gone were their human imperfections and the restraints of their earthly bodies. Still evident were their gentle eyes and the caring empathy of their loving concern.

As the angels rose toward heaven, the believers raised their hands, lifting their faces as if to bask in the warmth of the sun.

And of the Son.

THIRTY-FIVE

"Therefore, since we are surrounded by such a great cloud of
witnesses, let us throw off everything that hinders
and the sin that so easily entangles,
and let us run with perseverance the race marked out for us."
HEBREWS 12: 1

A WEARY KATHY and Roy returned to Kathy's house. Ryan
and Lisa met them at the door. Roy paid the babysitter while
the kids hugged their mother.

"Mom, where have you been?" Ryan hugged her fiercely.
"The rally's been over forever. I saw it on TV. The lights went
out, then everybody sang. I saw you and Daddy holding
hands."

Rally? Julia's rally was ancient history. Since then they'd
suffered through a fight with the devil—and won. They'd
witnessed the wonder of God's power and had seen their
mentors in all their angelic grandeur. They had saved Natalie
and had been saved themselves.

And Lenny had been saved—and died.

Ryan took hold of Roy's arm. "You're cut." His young
voice was filled with concern.

Roy looked at his arm as though he wasn't sure it
belonged to him. He had a three-inch cut on the outside of
his left forearm.

"Wow." Ryan's eyes were huge. "Was there a fight?"

You could say that.

Lisa stared at Roy's arm. She stuck out a finger and
touched it, then looked up at his eyes.

"What's wrong, sweet cakes?"

Lisa grabbed Roy's hand, then her mother's, and pulled.
"Come downstairs."

"Not now, Lisa."

"But I want to show you. I saw—"

"In a minute." Kathy turned to Ryan. "Why was Lisa
downstairs this evening? She should have been resting."

Ryan shrugged. "She wanted to play with her dollhouse.

I went with her, Mom."

"Come on! I want to *show* you!" Lisa said again.

Kathy ran a hand over her eyes. *I can't do this. How can I tell them their father is dead — again?* She picked Lisa up and carried her to the couch. Kathy patted the space next to her and Ryan sat down.

"Something's wrong, isn't it?" Ryan's eyes were worried.

Kathy nodded. "It's Daddy."

Lisa sat still a moment. Then she nodded. "I know. *Daddy.* That's what I want to show — "

"Please, Lisa. Let me talk." It took Kathy a moment to get on track. "Your father is dead. Oh, dear..." She rubbed a hand across her eyebrows. "I didn't want to blurt it out like that."

"Did Daddy die at the rally?" Ryan said. "Did he cut Roy's arm?"

"No, no, sweetie." Kathy had no idea how to explain.

Roy moved to the couch next to Ryan. "Your Daddy was a hero. He tried to save Natalie's life. But he fell and died."

"Was God proud of him?" Ryan asked.

"Very, very proud." Kathy wiped away a tear.

"I'm glad Daddy did something really good. I knew he could."

They sat quietly. Then Lisa squirmed and said, "*Daddy*...come see! Come see in the basement!"

"Don't you understand, sweet cakes? Your daddy died."

Lisa shook her head adamantly and slid out of Kathy's lap. She faced her mother and Roy and stomped a foot. "Come with me! *Now!*"

Kathy and Roy exchanged a look. They followed Lisa toward the basement.

"Be careful of your stitches, honey," Roy warned at the top of the stairs.

Lisa led them down the steps carefully, but with great determination. She walked directly to Kathy's easel and pointed at the painting. It was the one Kathy had been working on after Sandra Perkins had refused to handle any more of her landscapes.

Roy studied it, then smiled at her. "I like it. You've talked about your paintings of children, but you've never shown me any. This is good."

"It's a daddy's arms holding a little girl," Lisa said.

Roy stooped and put an arm around her. "I can see that."

"But look!" Lisa pointed to a specific spot on the painting. To the daddy's left arm. There was a thin red line. A cut about three inches long on the outside of the forearm. Lisa pulled Roy's arm and turned it so everyone could see. "It's just like yours. You're the daddy in the picture."

Kathy stared at the painting, touching the red line. "I don't remember painting that. In fact, I *didn't*. Why would I paint a cut? I tell you, it wasn't there before, it wasn't—"

Roy took her hand. "But it's there now, and there's nothing you can do about it. Lisa said it. I'm the daddy in the picture. The question is, am I the husband of the woman who painted the picture?"

Kathy looked at her children. Their faces were hopeful. *Oh, Lord, I don't deserve this—*

Then she remembered, *Put on the belt of truth...* The truth was, she loved him. Kathy smiled and felt fresh tears. Then she wrapped her arms around Roy's neck and kissed him.

Ryan and Lisa clapped.

Natalie sat on a bench along the winding streets of Eureka Springs' shopping district. Jack sat beside her, sipping a malt. Tourists, out for a Saturday night stroll through the shops, passed by carrying ice cream cones and sacks of souvenirs. Natalie's bandages caused a few double-takes.

"I could stay here forever." Natalie sighed, dipping one of her French fries in Jack's malt. When he didn't object, she did it again, offering him a taste. He liked the combination enough to dip his own.

Natalie smiled at him. "This is the first time I've felt fully safe since I moved away from home." She took a cleansing breath. "I was so blind to be swept up in Beau's charm. He was so exciting...yet he scared me."

"We can thank God he didn't kill you."

Natalie nodded, looking at the sidewalk. "But death isn't the worst thing..."

"Being without God would be worse."

Natalie took his hand. "I am so amazed God never gives up on us. Lenny proved that. Beau made everything complicated and cloudy. Nothing was clear and certain. What he offered wasn't enough. But with Christ, everything will keep getting better and better—"

"And we've got heaven to look forward to."

"Exactly." She handed him the rest of the fries, full in every way. "So where do we go from here?"

"We go back to being a teacher and a writer."

"Two ordinary people." Her disappointment showed.

Jack frowned. "God never said that in order for our work to count we have to be famous or showy. Faith—like Haven—is a place in the heart more than a place on the map. Everyone is invited to spread the word."

"But if I were famous, I could reach a lot more people."

"Reach one, Natalie. One at a time. When you get to heaven and find that you touched one person on this earth, won't it be worth it? Just one person."

She considered this. "Maybe I already have."

"Who?"

"My daughter, Grace."

Jack's mouth fell open. "Your *daughter?*"

Natalie put a hand on his. "She's nearly two. I put her up for adoption when she was born."

Jack looked at his feet. "Where's the father?"

"Back in Estes. Sam wants to get married."

"*I* want to get married."

"*What?*"

He knelt on the sidewalk and took her hand. Tourists pointed and smiled. "Will you marry *me*, Natalie? I love you."

She almost laughed, then saw the sincerity in his eyes. "Jack, I...I love you too, but—"

He sat back in the bench. "You don't want to marry me."

"I don't want to marry anyone right now."

He sighed and looked over the bustle of the street. "Is it because I'm so plain?"

Natalie started, then looked at him. Oddly enough, Jack's looks had *not* entered her mind. She nudged her arm against his. "I think you are the most beautiful person I have ever known." She smiled when she realized she meant it. "I know I have a history of being attracted to handsome men, but where has that gotten me?"

Jack grinned. "That's gotten you sitting here, beside *me*."

She laughed. "Exactly. But I've had to go through so much..." She sighed, feeling it throughout her entire body. "I'm tired of dealing with crises. Can't I just coast along? Sail through life without having to deal with a constant barrage of waves trying to capsize me?"

Jack was quiet a moment. "I don't think so."

She gave a short laugh. "Thanks for the encouragement."

He held up a hand. "We think life's supposed to be easy once we believe in Jesus. But the struggles don't disappear. In fact, we may struggle more as we become aware of all we *could* be with Him beside us. The good thing is that problems don't affect us in the same way. There are still waves, but because of our faith and our trust in Him — because we know He's always there to help us — we cut through the waves instead of being tossed around by them. Or drowned by them."

She let the words sink in, let the truth of them fill her. "I've let myself be tossed, haven't I?"

"It's human nature. "

"But not God's nature." Natalie slid her arm through Jack's and watched as a firefly blinked at her. "Why don't I think about God more? Why do I only go to Him as a last resort?"

"Habit."

"There's got to be more to it than that."

"Not really." He tried to grab at a firefly, but missed it. "Finding God in everyday life takes effort. We have to train ourselves to think of Him. Like Pavlov's dogs reacting to a bell, every time we begin a new task or a new thought, we need to have an inner bell sound to remind us to check in with God."

"Will it ever just happen?"

"Sure." Jack crossed two of his fingers. "Eventually, as you and God get closer, you'll find you can't untangle yourself from Him if you tried. Your purpose will be His purpose."

"I can't think of anything more wonderful."

Jack got up from the bench and held out his hand. "Let's go home."

"Home?"

"Let's drive back to Lincoln tonight."

Natalie hesitated only a moment. Feeling a surge of energy, she jumped up and ran down the sidewalk. "Race ya!"

✦✦✦

Jack carried Natalie's suitcase up the front stairs to her apartment door. They'd made the drive back to Lincoln in record time. "It's been quite a trip."

"Not exactly the weekend I'd envisioned." She made a face as she pulled out her key.

She glanced across the hall at Beau's apartment. When Jack saw the direction of her gaze, he crossed to the door, and turned the knob.

"Jack! Don't go in!"

"Why not?" The door was unlocked. "It's open. He's gone. Finished. Defeated."

Natalie found herself drawn into the apartment. The room felt stale. Dead. She shivered. "Jack, let's go."

He circled the room, running a hand along the lushly upholstered couch. "Demons obviously don't shop at garage sales like I do."

Natalie peeked into the bedroom. "He certainly had good taste, but there's something about this place that always bothered me..." On impulse, she opened a dresser drawer.

She opened the others. Then the closet.

"What are you doing?"

She walked back to the kitchen and flung open the cupboard doors. Then, the refrigerator.

"They're empty." She turned to face Jack. "It's like he moved out before he left for Eureka Springs."

"Or never moved in."

"What?"

Jack looked across the room with new eyes. "There's nothing on the walls, not a magazine on the table. No dishes, clothes, not even a toothbrush."

"This whole thing was a front."

"Demons probably don't need clothes and food. It was all for show."

Natalie sank onto the couch, shaking her head. Then she looked up at Jack. "Did Beau move in here just to get close to me?" She didn't wait for an answer. "He moved in the day before I did, as though he knew..."

"And I moved in a few days later." His eyes flashed. He dropped on the cushion beside her, excited. "Remember when I said I was supposed to move in the weekend before, but a lot of strange things happened to stop me?"

"*He* stopped you?"

"Or his kind *tried* to stop me." Jack took her hand. "I truly believe God wanted me here to meet you. So even though I had to deal with some opposition to get here, I *did* get here."

"And we met."

"And we met."

Suddenly Natalie stood. "When I was moving to Lincoln I prayed for a soul mate. At first I thought that Beau was it...in fact, he used those exact words."

"He knew the words to use. He knew what you were looking for."

"And he tried to give it to me. But..."

"But what?"

She held out her hand. "You're my soul mate, Jack. You're my answer from God."

He stood and they embraced, celebrating the joyous

revelation.

"So I ask again, ya wanna get married?" He grinned at her, waggling his eyebrows.

She took his face in her hands and groaned. "You have a one-track mind!"

"Marry me and I promise to change tracks."

She wandered away from the couch. "Like I told you, I don't want to marry anyone right now." She turned to face him. "In fact, I'm going back to Colorado."

"Why?" He moved toward her.

She raised her hands to keep him where he was. "I need to grow up. I need to write my Haven book. And I need to get to know God a whole lot better."

"You can do all those things here. With me to help you."

She shook her head. "I have to work through the issues of my youth."

"Sam?"

She shrugged. "He's part of it." She looked out the window. "I need to go home. Start over. Again."

She noticed something sitting on the window sill. She picked it up, unbelieving. She turned toward Jack.

"What is it?"

Natalie put a hand to her mouth as tears fell. She held it for him to see.

It was her mustard seed pin.

Jack tossed his mail on the table. He didn't feel like going through bills, ads for vacations he couldn't afford, or offers for credit cards he didn't want.

A padded envelope caught his attention. He picked it up. No return address. It was very light. He opened it and pulled out a card.

On the card were two verses: "'So do not throw away your confidence, it will be richly rewarded. You need to persevere so that when you have done the will of God, you will receive what He has promised.' Hebrews 10: 35-36."

Jack felt something else in the envelope. He turned it over. A mustard seed pin dropped into his hand. He fell to his knees and praised God for his promises.

✦✦✦

Del turned into the church parking lot and shut off the engine of Beau's car. He rested his head on the steering wheel. He was exhausted. The long drive back and all that had happened in Eureka Springs — and before — had left him more drained than he'd ever been in his life.

Del looked up and saw Monsignor Vibrowsky stride out of the rectory.

"Great." Del climbed from the vehicle, bracing himself for the monsignor's verbal onslaught. He paused, almost stumbled, when he saw the monsignor smile and extend a welcoming hand.

"So glad you're back, Father. We were beginning to worry about you."

"You were?"

"Indeed. We saw you on television with Julia Carson. At the rally. We saw the chaos and then heard the revival of the masses as they sang 'God Bless America.'"

"Revival of the masses?"

Monsignor Vibrowsky put his arm around Del's shoulders and walked him toward the rectory. "Some people are calling it overkill. I mean, it was a bit maudlin singing that song and banding together like that, but the dissenters generally come from Senator Bradley's camp. The majority of the public ate it up. Patriotism reigns triumphant!" He shook his head. "To think you were a part of it."

If you only knew what happened after the rally...

They reached the building, and Monsignor ushered Del to his office. "I'm sure you'd like to rest, Father, but the phone *has* been ringing off the hook."

"Why?"

"Parishioners who saw you on television. You're a celebrity. People want to talk to you."

As Del picked up the stack of messages, he eyed the monsignor. "I thought you didn't want me drawing attention to myself. I got the idea you resented my presence at St. Stephens."

The monsignor put a hand on Del's. He lowered his eyes. "I'm truly sorry, Father. I am guilty of envy, and jealousy, and bitterness."

Del stopped the confession. "It's all right, Monsignor. I do tend to overwhelm."

The two men shared their first sincere smile.

Monsignor Vibrowsky held out his hand. "Truce?"

They shook on it.

Del took out the keys to Beau's car and gave them a jangle.

"What are those?" the monsignor asked.

"These belong to a car that now belongs to St. Stephens. It's a terribly long story, but I was thinking a charity auction would be appropriate."

Monsignor looked out the window at the car. *"That's* ours?"

"It is now. Proof that in the end, good has more horsepower than evil."

After a two-hour nap, Del returned to his desk and began to sort through his messages. The church receptionist appeared in his doorway. "There's a woman here to see you, Father. She says you don't know her, but you have a mutual friend." She looked at her note. "The friend is Natalie Pasternak?"

"Show her in."

A thirtyish woman came in the room, bringing with her an enormous amount of energy. She held out her hand. "Hayley Spotsman, Father. Natalie works for me at—"

"Hayley's Antiques." He shook her hand. "Nice to meet you." He offered her a seat. "What can I do for you?"

"I just got off the phone with Natalie, and she told me she's moving back to Colorado. Goodness sakes, we'll miss her. She's a nice girl with a lot of potential."

"I can't argue that one."

Hayley looked at her lap. "I guess I'm here because of another one of Natalie's character traits." She took a deep breath, drawing courage. "Her faith. Natalie told me about Haven. I'd seen her mustard seed pin and was curious...I'm afraid I'm a lapsed Catholic."

"A little regression can be remedied with a little confession."

"That confession might take a while." She eyed him. "It's been a *long* time."

Del laughed. "God—and I—are very patient."

"I figure it's the first step," she said, sighing.

"To what?"

"To getting on with my life. After what happened to Gloria...her death made me think about things. I've got a good business, but a business can't keep you warm at night, can it, Father?" She blushed. "I want to get my priorities straight. God, family, job—`course I'll need to *start* a family before I can prioritize it, but that's another problem. You don't happen to know any nice Catholic men, do you, Father? Mature family men, who want to—"

Del looked toward the doorway. "Stevie! Good to see you."

Stevie Wellington stepped into Del's office, holding Tasha on his hip. "Sorry to bother you, Father, but I had a question about the memorial fund for Gloria?"

Hayley stood. "Stevie. How are things going?"

Stevie eyes showed a slow recognition. "Hayley...pain moves slowly, but it does move."

Hayley held her arms out to Tasha, who readily filled them. "If you ever need a babysitter, I'd be happy to take this little one for about twenty years."

"It's clear you like kids. And they like you." Stevie seemed to forget his business with Del. He moved into the hall and Hayley followed him, letting Tasha play with her necklace.

"I love kids. Especially cute little girls with curly, blond

359

hair and pretty blue eyes."

Del sat in his chair and listened to their voices filter down the hall. He put his hands behind his head and grinned at the ceiling. He had his own confession to make: life was very, very good.

◆◆◆

Walter burst through the front door of his new house. "I'm home!" He rolled his suitcase inside, then listened. There was no answer.

"Bette?" He moved from room to room, searching for his wife and daughter. As each proved empty, he began to panic. Had something happened to them while he was gone?

As he passed through the kitchen, he caught a glimpse of movement in the backyard. He paused at the window to look on the scene.

Bette sat in an old swing that hung from a branch of a huge elm. Her elbows were linked around the ropes but her hands cradled Addy's head. The infant faced her mother, snuggled on her lap. Bette was smiling at her, talking with her, her voice weaving through the open window.

"*Wheel*, little pumpkin. Isn't this fun? Mommy will take you on this swing every day. And when you're big enough, I'll show you how to hold on and then I'll push you so high you can kick at the clouds."

Walter put a hand to his chest. "I'm going to have to get used to this melting business. Every time I see them I turn to mush."

He opened the back door. Bette saw him and started to get up. He motioned for her to stay put. "It's a nice thing to come home to—mother and daughter on a swing."

"We planned it this way." Bette accepted his kiss. "We've been out here for hours, just waiting for you to walk in that door." She studied his face. "How did it go? I saw Julia's rally on television."

"I'll tell you about it later. Right now, I'm just so glad to be—" He stopped, then pointed to her blouse. "I'm glad you

360

decided to wear Pop's mustard seed pin. I told you he wouldn't mind."

Her face glowed with a smile. "It's not Pop's. It's mine. Come see." Bette stood and carried Addy toward the house. Walter followed her into the kitchen. She put Addy into her infant seat and retrieved a padded envelope from the counter. She removed a note and handed it to him. "This came for me yesterday."

Walter read the note: "My heart is not proud, O Lord, my eyes are not haughty, I do not concern myself with great matters or things too wonderful for me. But I have stilled and quieted my soul, like a weaned child with its mother, like a weaned child is my soul within me."

He looked up at her. "What does it mean?"

"It means that the mustard seed pin is mine. I earned it. My place is here. The great and glorious work I can do for the Lord is to bring up Addy to be a child of God. I don't have to worry after 'great matters or things too wonderful for me.' Our child is a great matter, and her existence has quieted my soul. She is the proof of my faith."

Walter gave her a kiss. "We're a two-mustard-seed family."

Bette polished her pin with a finger. "Don't you wonder where they're coming from? I mean, I'm thrilled, but don't you wonder?"

Walter took a seat next to Addy so he could study her. "I don't wonder anymore. I *know*."

"Are you sure they're from God?"

Walter kissed his child's tiny hand. "One-hundred-percent positive."

✦✦✦

That evening Bette took Walter to the evening services of the neighborhood church.

When she first said they were going, he moaned. "But I'm tired, Bette. I'll go next week."

"No, Walter. We have much to be thankful for. And we

are going to church to prove it." She grinned conspiratorially.

"There's something you're not telling me."

"You bet there is."

Walter went to church. They sat in a pew, listened to the organ's prelude, and stood for the opening hymn. The purple robes of the choir were in sharp contrast to the white painted woodwork of the chancel. The congregation joined the choir in the processional.

"A mighty fortress is our God. A bulwark never failing."

Walter was amazed at how many people were in the choir. They just kept coming...

"Our Helper He amid the flood of mortal ills prevailing. The Prince of Darkness grim, we tremble not for him, his rage we can endure..." When the entire choir reached the front choir loft, Walter felt his heart fill as their voices turned toward the congregation. They were good. Clear and resonant. Brimming with God's—

Bette must have been watching Walter's face, because when his jaw dropped she leaned toward him.

"That's right, Walter. Emma Emerson, our friendly family realtor, is singing in the choir. She told me she started going to church because of you. Because of *you*, Walter."

"Me?"

"You."

Walter stood taller in the pew. He'd made a difference in someone's life—even someone as unlikely as Emma Emerson. He sang the last stanza with extra exuberance.

"God's truth abideth still, His kingdom is forever."

INAUGURATION DAY

Julia placed her hand on the Carson family Bible. She held up her right hand and repeated the words:

"I, Julia Genevieve Carson, do solemnly swear that I will faithfully execute the office of president of the United States, and will to the best of my ability, preserve, protect, and defend the Constitution of the United States, so help me God."

Edward leaned over and kissed her. "My wife," he whispered. "My president."

The audience roared their approval. Julia moved to the microphone. She looked out across the crowd and felt the looming presence of the Capital behind her. The green Mall was covered with people, lining Pennsylvania Avenue to the White House, their American flags waving.

Julia felt a tug in her throat. She had worked so hard. She still couldn't quite believe she had won. Yet God had wanted her to become president, and so she was. The responsibility was staggering, the challenge exciting. Above all, she was humbled by the knowledge that without God she wouldn't be standing here.

She had worked hard on her speech, praying she'd find the right words to express what was in her heart. A cold January breeze made her cheeks sting. The sun broke through the clouds.

Thank You, Lord. Be with me now...and always. She cleared her throat and began.

"Today is day one. Day One of the Renewal of America. It must begin this day, this hour, this minute. The time has come. The time is now. Every one of us hates change and yet every one of us begs for it." She smiled. "Such is the human animal. Scared, yet courageous. Idle, yet ambitious." How much *she* had changed.

"Words. So easily said and so quickly forgotten. But we must not forget. We are reaching a point where it can no longer be just talk. Our words must be realized and produce action. If we as a people are to improve, if we are to rid ourselves of the problems that plague us, we must band together under a set of moral rules based on the truth."

She tapped a finger against her cheek and pretended to ponder. "Now, let's see...how many of these rules should there be? A hundred? Twenty? Ten?" Her eyes lit up. "Now there's a good number. Ten. Let's put into effect ten rules. But...no one likes the word *rule*. There has to be a better word. A more powerful word...directive? Instruction? Commandment? That's it! Let's call them the ten commandments!"

She made a face to the audience, asking their forgiveness for her ploy. "Isn't it wonderful that no committee, no task force, no petition has to be instigated in order for us to come up with these guidelines for ethical, moral, common-sense behavior? We've had them at our fingertips for 3500 years. Imagine that. These rules have endured for 3500 years. That must have significance. The founding fathers of this country saw that. They recognized the importance of these rules—and the Maker of these rules—and they built this nation on that bedrock. Have we changed so much that we can do better? I think not."

Julia smiled and leaned on the podium as she had done so many times before. "I want to challenge each and every one of you to believe. Right now. Today. Believe in this country. Believe in yourselves and your family. And believe in God. Not believing won't make God go away. We are here, our family is here, our country is herechauf, and our God is here. We must believe or die in our apathy. 'He who stands firm to the end will be saved.'

"Our quest for renewal is an honorable one. We will not be judged on our failures as much as we will be judged on our ignorance and our indifference. We must try. We must stand up. We must raise our voices, speaking the truth."

She glanced back at Edward, offering him a smile. "It is time. So, now, in this moment, let us go forth in Day One of the Renewal of America. A renewal of our country and a renewal of our hearts. Have faith in our God, in ourselves, in each other, and in our country.

"'Your faith has saved you, go in peace.'"

✦✦✦

Ben Cranois clapped with the others as President Carson finished her speech. He stood with the rest in a standing ovation. He listened to the cheers around him, and felt his soul grow cold.

He did not believe in anyone or anything but himself.

"It's not over."

It was a vow. To himself. To Julia. To God. "The battle has just begun."

THE END

"But thanks be to God!
He gives us the victory through our Lord Jesus Christ.
Therefore, my dear brothers, stand firm. Let nothing move you.
Always give yourselves fully to the work of the Lord,
because you know that your labor in the Lord is not in vain."
1 CORINTHIANS 15: 57-58

Dear Reader:

They say, "Write what you know". That's a tough one, for if we limit ourselves to that, then what's our imagination for? Besides, my life is quite ordinary.

Yet ordinary is in the eye of the beholder. For as I wrote *The Invitation* and *The Quest*, extraordinary things started happening that I would not have noticed before God was front and center in my life. I would have passed over them as mere coincidence.

Mysterious things do happen. We can accept them, or ignore them. That is our choice. I have chosen to accept these events and even look forward to them.

A variation on the experience Walter had with the "Trust Jesus" graffiti happened to me. And Del's pennies? I found dimes. And who hasn't held the Bible on its spine like Walter, hoping it would open to just the right verse?

But the most amazing thing that happened while writing *The Quest*, came about because of my new knowledge regarding evil. I'd never considered evil much—which is a good thing in that we shouldn't dwell on it. But ignorance in spiritual matters is not bliss. In researching this book, I began to recognize evil's presence and influence in the world. And as I did so, I got its attention.

The event happened while I was copying the chapters of *The Quest* from the word processing program I used to save in the program my original publisher used. Once I got the hang of the repetitive process, I mindlessly hit the right buttons. I copied Chapter 32. Chapter 33. Chapter 34... Suddenly, Chapter 34 would not copy. I tried again. And again. It made no sense. Why wouldn't this one chapter copy after all the others had done so without a hitch? I tried Chapter 35. It copied. Why not 34?

Then I realized what was in Chapter 34. It was the climax of the book where evil is defeated. I got a chill. Satan wouldn't like that chapter very much. It would be to his advantage to interfere, to oppose its transfer. This was a very disconcerting revelation. What should I do? Me, Nancy Moser, ordinary person? Things like this didn't happen to people like me.

In my research for *The Quest*, I'd discovered that we *all* have the power over evil—through the name of Jesus Christ. So, feeling a bit foolish sitting in my office in Kansas, I said the words Jesus instructed us to say. "Satan, leave me alone. Leave this computer and the files alone. Get out, in the name of Jesus Christ, my Savior!"

I took a moment to calm my breathing and even laughed a bit nervously at what I'd just done. I took a deep breath and tried to copy the file. It still wouldn't copy. Then I realized I'd only done part of the process: I'd ordered evil out, but I had not invited God in. So I prayed.

The file copied.

I don't tell you this story to make you afraid. Fear is Satan's business, not God's. We have nothing to fear. But be aware—and be triumphant. Satan is already a defeated foe. God is supreme. God is love.

"There is no fear in love. But perfect love drives out fear, because fear has to do with punishment. The one who fears is not made perfect in love. We love because he first loved us." (I John 4:18-19).

That is our quest.

Nancy Moser

VERSES in *THE QUEST*

CHAPTER	TOPIC	VERSE
Chapter 1:	Mustard seed	Matthew 13:31-32
	Faith	Matthew 17: 20
	Teach	Exodus 4: 12
Chapter 2:	Giving	Proverbs 11: 25
	God's armor	Ephesians 6: 13
	Hope	Psalm 71: 14
	Suffering	Romans 5: 3
Chapter 3:	Guidance	Isaiah 48: 17
	Faith	Ephesians 6: 16
	Hope	Psalm 119: 114
	Abraham	Genesis 12: 1
	Faith	Hebrews 11: 8
Chapter 4:	Motives	Proverbs 16: 2
	Sinners	1 Timothy 1: 15
	Humility	Proverbs 11: 2
Chapter 5:	Work	1 Corinthians 15: 58
	Truth	Ephesians 6: 14
	Testing	Psalm 66: 10
	Work	John 4: 35
Chapter 6:	Flattery	Romans 16: 18
	Temptation	Matthew 26: 41
Chapter 7:	Consequences	Proverbs 6: 27-28
	Trust	Psalm 118: 8
	Angels	Hebrews 1: 14
	Compassion	Psalm 116: 5
Chapter 8:	Submission	Job 22: 21
	Faith	Ephesians 6: 16
	Free will	Genesis 2: 16
Chapter 9:	Calling	2 Peter 1: 10
Chapter 10:	Good works	Philippians 2: 13
Chapter 11:	Love	Psalm 103:17-18
	Perseverance	James 5: 11
	God's attention	Psalm 34: 15
	Comfort	Psalm 121: 5-8
	Blessings	Psalm 112: 2
	Love	1 Chronicles 16: 34
	Wisdom	Proverbs 2: 12
Chapter 12:	Endurance	2 Timothy 2: 3

	Justice	Psalm 9: 8
	Righteousness	Psalm 22: 30-31
	Righteousness	Ephesians 6: 14
Chapter 13:	Friendship	Proverbs 12: 26
	Weakness	2 Corinthians 12:9
	Time	2 Peter 3: 8
Chapter 14:	Listening	Malachi 3: 16
Chapter 15:	Motives	1 Corinthians 4: 5
	Light	Psalm 36: 9
Chapter 16:	Protection	Psalm 97: 10
Chapter 17:	Work	2 Corinthians 2: 14
	Faith	Matthew 17: 20
	Nations	Psalm 9: 20
Chapter 18:	Acceptance	Ecclesiastes 7: 14
	Protection	Psalm 121: 7-8
Chapter 19:	Temptation	Matthew 6: 13
	Speaking	Colossians 4: 6
	Constancy	Ecclesiastes 1: 9
	Help	John 21: 17
	Purity	Romans 13: 12-14
	Death	Psalm 23: 4
	Darkness	Job 15: 22
	Holy Spirit	Ephesians 6: 17
	Word of God	Hebrews 4: 12
	Good vs. evil	Matthew 12: 35
	Trials	James 1: 2-6
Chapter 20:	Heritage	Acts 17: 28
Chapter 21:	Comfort	Isaiah 46: 4
	Faith	Ephesians 6: 17
	Honor	Psalm 112: 5, 9
Chapter 22:	Evil	Isaiah 66: 4
	Prayer	Ephesians 6: 18
	Beauty	Isaiah 53: 2
	Gentleness	Philippians 4: 5
Chapter 23:	Responsibility	Luke 11: 50-51
	Rewards	Proverbs 14: 14
	Faith	James 2: 26
Chapter 24:	Knowledge	Mark 4: 15
	Troubles	Psalm 46: 1
	Healing	Psalm 147: 3-4
	Choices	Jeremiah 6: 16
Chapter 25:	Protection	2 Thessalonians 3:2-3

	Deception	Luke 21: 8
	Worship	Psalm 103: 20-21
Chapter 26:	Sin	Romans 7: 22-23
	Evangelism	Matthew 28: 19
Chapter 27:	Purpose	Psalm 33: 11
	Faith	James 2: 14, 17
Chapter 28:	Protection	Psalm 40: 11-12
Chapter 29:	Omnipresence	Psalm 139: 7-10
	Strength	Ephesians 6: 10
	Satan	Matthew 4: 10
Chapter 30:	Trust	Psalm 56: 4-5
	Obedience	1 Chronicles 28:8-10
	Judging	Matthew 7: 3
	Judging	Matthew 7: 1
Chapter 31:	Resist enemy	1 Peter 5: 8-9
	Community	Matthew 18: 20
Chapter 32:	Love of God	Romans 8: 38-39
	Destiny	Jeremiah 1: 5
	Assurance	Hebrews 13: 5
	Fear	2 Chronicles 20: 15
	Comfort	Isaiah 58: 9
	Blessing	Psalm 33: 12
Chapter 33:	Strength	Psalm 29: 11
	Encouragement	Psalm 23: 1-6 *
	Strength	Ecclesiastes 4: 12
	Longing	Psalm 38: 9
	Wisdom	Proverbs 2: 9-10
	Time	Ecclesiastes 3: 1
	Forgiveness	Jeremiah 31: 33-34
	Jesus' name	Philippians 2: 9-11
Chapter 34:	Defense	Luke 12: 11-12
	Timing	Ecclesiastes 3: 1-8
	Omnipotence	Isaiah 40:26, 28,31
Chapter 35:	Perseverance	Hebrews 12: 1
	Perseverance	Hebrews 10:35-36
	Motherhood	Psalm 131: 1-2
	Strength	Matthew 24: 13
	Faith	Luke 7: 50
	Victory	I Corinthians 15: 57-58

* King James Version

Discussion Questions
for *The Quest*

1. Kathy and her paintings, Natalie and her writing...instead of doing the hard task that was the right task they worked on what was easy and fast. What 'hard and right' task do you have in your life, and how are you tackling it?

2. In *The Quest*, the people experience signs that help them know God's will. Have you ever experienced a sign that led you to make a decision? Did you attribute it to God? Should you attribute it to God?

3. Julia is a candidate who speaks freely of her faith. Do you think a real-life candidate could or should speak with such conviction and passion? If they did, would you vote for them? If they did, do you think they could win their election?

4. Gloria's death is tragic (and as the writer I questioned whether to include it) yet it shows the danger of straying into the dark places that exist in this world, and the danger of not being in touch with God in the process. Have you ever experienced such dark places? How did God lead you into the light?

5. Natalie is blind to Beau's true character, only seeing what she wants to see. Have you ever been involved with a person who drew you in beyond reason? How did you get away from them?

6. In Chapter 17, do you think Julia's campaign should have supplied mustard seed pins for those who asked?

7. In Chapter 18, Bette talks to Walter about women's intuition. She says it is God's gift to females. Do you think that is true? Why or why not?

8. In Chapter 18, Walter has a wonderful visit with his father, and his father says he's proud of him. That night, his father dies. Have you ever experienced a

meaningful visit with a relative or friend, that turned out to be the "last" visit? What made it meaningful?

9. In Chapter 25 the angels gather to discuss and pray for their charges. They worship God and do as He tells them to do. This is obviously a work of fiction, but do you believe that angels take on human form to do God's will? Do you believe demons take on human form?

10. Beau tries to confuse people, making them question their faith and their choices. Have you ever gone through a time of such confusion? Could Satan have been trying to move you away from God?

11. Lenny has spent years on the dark side. But God didn't give up on him, and reached out for him yet again. Who do you know who's come back from a very dark place?

12. "A strand of three is not quickly broken." There is strength in banding together. Name a time you and a few others banded together to overcome an obstacle or affect change.

13. God's Word and the name of Jesus conquered evil. What verses are the verses that have power in your life?

14. Do you agree with Natalie's decision to go home to Colorado? Or should she have stayed with Jack in Lincoln?

ABOUT THE AUTHOR

NANCY MOSER is the best-selling author of twenty-seven novels, including Christy Award winner, *Time Lottery;* Christy finalist *Washington's Lady;* ten historical novels, and the contemporary novels *Solemnly Swear, The Good Nearby, John 3:16, Weave of the World,* and the Sister Circle series. Nancy has been married for forty years—to the same man. She and her husband have three grown children, six grandchildren, and live in the Midwest. She's been blessed with a varied life. She's earned a degree in architecture; run a business with her husband; traveled extensively in Europe; and has performed in various theatres, symphonies, and choirs. She knits voraciously, kills all her houseplants, and can wire an electrical fixture without getting shocked. She is a fan of anything antique—humans included.

Website: www.nancymoser.com

Blogs: Author blog: www.authornancymoser.blogspot.com, History blog: www.footnotesfromhistory.blogspot.com/

Pinterest: www.pinterest.com/nancymoser1

Facebook and Twitter:
www.facebook.com/nancymoser.author, and
www.twitter.com/MoserNancy

Goodreads:
www.goodreads.com/author/show/117288.Nancy_Moser

EXCERPT FROM BOOK 3:
THE TEMPTATION

THE WHITE HOUSE drew Ben Cranois across the street like a
sorceress luring a victim close with graceful, mesmerizing
hands.

Ben shook his head, wanting to stay back, keep his
distance. He had not planned to come here on his day off.
He'd tried to resist. *This does me no good. This makes things
worse. I hate her. And I hate Him.*

President Julia Carson. And God. Two enemies that made
Ben's mind rebel, his heart battle, and his gut threaten
mutiny. Two enemies who wanted to claim his soul. But they
wouldn't. They couldn't. Ben wouldn't let them. He'd erected
a door between their influence and his soul that he kept shut,
locked, and guarded. Nothing got in and nothing got out.
Not them...and not the *other*...

Ben stepped onto the sidewalk. The White House
grounds were dead. The leafless trees reached to a gray sky,
creating a stark backdrop to Ben's black mood. He raised his
shoulders and dug his hands deeper into his pockets. He
kept himself separate from the line of tourists waiting for the
tour, from Julia's gullible fan club, braving the cold to enter
this palace of Pollyannas. This castle of Christianity. He let
out a soft snicker. Even the windows of the White House
should be rose-colored. Hope, faith and love...Julia was
destroying the country with such mindless—, Ben did a
double take. A figure stood at a window. He grabbed hold of
the wrought iron fence and stared between the posts. Was
that her? Was that the president?

His hand began to wave. *Hey, Julia! It's me, Ben! Remember
me?*

With a violent jerk Ben's hand retreated to its grip on the
fence. The knuckles whitened as the energy that lived inside
took control. His body tightened, bracing against the inner
rush. He had not been able to identify the cause of this new

intensity — this *other* power —, but he found it fascinating. And just a bit dangerous...

It was an urging. A push from the inside out. A feeling that something important might happen at any minute. And he liked it. If his gut wrenched a bit too hard sometimes, so what? It was a small price to pay for living on the edge of expectancy.

Ben closed his eyes and tried to take a deep breath, but the presence was heavy...demanding. He stopped resisting — resistance only made the urgency tighten its grip until it got its way. It was best to surrender willingly; sooner rather than later. He had known he would get punished for coming here, for giving into his desire to be close to —

Move on, you weak fool! Get away from the sickening hypocrisy of this place. You have work to do. You must show the world the truth.

Ben nodded, then opened his eyes, letting the command settle into his pores. He released his grip on the fence, relieved that he'd been given the strength to leave, while at the same time, reluctant to go. He shrugged his overcoat into place. He walked away.

He had work to do. Important work. He was on a mission.

CPSIA information can be obtained
at www.ICGtesting.com
Printed in the USA
LVOW12s1749270716

498005LV00001B/162/P